# Daughter's Search

Thaddeus Nowak

www.ThaddeusNowak.com

Published by Mountain Pass Publishing, LLC.

ISBN: 978-0-9863946-0-7

First Printing: March 2015


Set in Adobe Garamond Pro
Cover art Copyright © 2015 by Mallory Rock
Maps by Thaddeus Nowak

Map of Calis, Midland, and Cothel.

Map of Kynto, Salzen, Uvar, Calis and Midland.

# Acknowledgements

I would like to thank the many people who have helped make this work possible. My wife Sherri, my best friend Chad, my brother Joe and his wife Samantha, my other brothers Dave and Dan and their wives Jenni and Linda, and my parents. I would also like to thank my editor Judy Reveal and my friends Priya S. and David J. as well as the others who have inspired and offered advice. Any errors left in the work are entirely mine.

# Chapter 1

Stephenie leaned forward onto Argat's withers and reached out to pat the chestnut's strong neck. The gelding's ears twitched back to her as he walked lazily down the road. She caught his right eye and grinned at him before she sat up, pushed her heels into the stirrups, and with a squeeze of her outside leg, easily pushed him into a canter. Ignoring the brief calls of those behind her, Stephenie urged Argat faster as they veered from the road and through a gap in the fieldstone wall to their right. The tall hay, still green and growing, pulled at Argat's legs, slowing his pace. Wanting more speed, Stephenie maneuvered him onto a deer path, freeing him from the entanglement of the blowing grasses. Energized by the wind in her face, she gave Argat his head as she squeezed him again, pushing him into a faster gallop. The gelding responded with enthusiasm. Like her, he had grown bored from the weeks of slow travel and he eagerly ate up the ground under his hooves. The shouts of a farmer standing in the field off to their right caused her to slow Argat's pace and turn back toward the road. The brief run through the field only left her wanting more; the exercise had not drained off the restless energy from either of them.

She waved an apology over her shoulder to the farmer and continued back to the fieldstone wall at a canter. Squaring Argat to the wall, she slowed him slightly to avoid coming up short, and then rode his smooth leap over the three feet of stone. They landed with a slight stumble on the rutted road, but he recovered easily as Stephenie leaned back and resisted with her seat. She brought him to a halt after making a tight circle. "Yeah," she said, patting his neck again, "someone always takes away our fun." She looked back toward the others and waited as they maintained their slow walk down the road.

Eventually Henton brought the others to her. "Getting a little full of yourselves, are you?"

She grinned at her broad-shouldered friend.

"What?" He asked.

"You are in need of a haircut." Henton's coarse brown hair hung well over his ears and touched his shirt in the back. He wore a threadbare shirt with multiple unrepaired tears and more stains than original color. When she had first met the twenty-eight-year-old, the marine sergeant had just been transferred off the ship he had served on and would never have allowed his state to fall into such disrepair. Pushing back her own long red strands that had come loose of her ponytail, she continued the abuse. "You look like you've been dragged through the mud and that saddle is so scuffed and dirty you'd wonder if it had ever been polished." She glanced at Henton's gelding, "At least Furball is brushed," she conceded, referring to the name he gave his horse once he realized how much hair they shed in the spring.

"Funny, Your Highness, I must be looking in a mirror."

Stephenie's grin widened; her body itched and knew she needed to bathe. "The Uthen's just a few miles to the north," she hinted, "the water's probably cold, but I'm up for a swim if you are."

Douglas cleared his throat. The one-time corporal shook his reasonably-groomed head. "I thought you and Islet wanted to get home as quickly as possible now that we've crossed the bridge. Otherwise, I would have insisted we stop in one of those fancy inns along the road last night so we could all be presentable today."

"You just wanted some of the beef you smelled roasting," Stephenie responded. Douglas' clothing was in better shape than anyone else's in the party and his successful fastidiousness remained a mystery to all of them. "You hardly look to have done any work these last couple of months. Have you been on holiday?"

Douglas made the effort to find a spot of dirt to pick off his shirt. "Why do you think I have you along?"

"I could cut your hair, Henton," Ryia said from where she sat behind Douglas on the horse they were sharing. Her windblown hair was a tangle of knots and a strong counter point to Douglas' cleanliness. The sixteen-year-old had come a long way from when Stephenie had first met her. Endless weeks of traveling with her and Henton tended to harden anyone to long days and lots of work.

"No. Thank you for the offer, but for the last time, I saw what you did to Douglas and it took nearly a month for his hair to grow back out. I'll wait until we get into Antar."

Stephenie glanced at Islet near the back of the group. Her older sister sat on their fourth horse, a flea-bitten grey nearly a hand shorter than Henton's gelding. Islet's torn shirt and breaches were stained beyond anything one of her maids would ever wear.

Islet appeared lost in thought for a moment, and then met Stephenie's eyes. "We have been astride these beasts since before winter ended," her regal tone and expression incongruent with her appearance. "We are entitled to desire warm and comforting accommodations. Anything less than a rose scented bath and a meal of pheasant and duck is less than acceptable." Stephenie snorted as a smile broke across Islet's face. "What? Isn't that what people expect me to say?"

Henton shook his head, "Only if you want me to tell you that some of us have been riding since well before winter, froze our rears in the mountains, and then worked on ice covered docks unloading ships, all before you decided to grace us with your presence."

"Well," Islet said, her tone growing wistful, "I finally grew tired of the vastness of my chambers and thought traipsing across countless countries was a much more enjoyable use of my time."

Stephenie smiled at the banter. Islet's first response to Henton had been outrage at him daring to 'take the liberty to speak to her without leave to do so.' After months of travel, Stephenie no longer cringed at the prospect of spending time with her sister. *Of course, she's also now my only sister.*

"That farmer's coming this way," Douglas remarked, his apparent attention still turned down the road and not into the field. "We should get moving before he wants the damages taken out of your hide."

Stephenie did not need Douglas' warning. She felt the man's approach in the periphery of her mind. Unless she worked to block out the world around her, she simply felt the ripples in the energy fields caused by movement or the thoughts from living beings. *Of course, I can't make sense of most of what comes out of people's heads,* she admitted. *It's one thing to see the energy waves; it's something else to understand them.* Just like a foreign language, she could not easily read the farmer's thoughts from this distance. However, the tone of his emotion stood out clearly.

"Josh will not be happy if you anger some farmers by getting caught riding through their fields," Islet added.

Although Stephenie kept her outward expression neutral, Stephenie suspected Ryia could sense the irritation building within her. While Islet was a year and a half older, Islet had never truly acted as an older sister. Her attempts at playing one now seemed ridiculous; Stephenie knew herself, knew her capabilities, and accepted her responsibilities. *I crossed half a dozen countries and rescued Islet from the Senzar and have nearly gotten everyone home and none of us have died.* Keeping her tone casual, she responded calmly, "I didn't do much harm, but I'll compensate the man."

She pulled a couple of coins from her nearly empty pouch and held them up high enough for the farmer to see she had something in her hand. Nudging Argat over to the fieldstone wall, she opened her mind to the energy that existed all around them: in the air, the ground, in Argat, and even within herself. Her eyes lost focus for a moment, allowing her mind's eye to see the energy potentials in everything. Just like a river, the energy flowed from areas of higher potential to areas of lower potential. It always tried to balance the differences and follow the path of least resistance. However, Stephenie could craft fields with her mind, forcing the energy to move in ways she desired.

A smile threatened her irritation as memories of Kas first trying to teach her magic filled her thoughts. He taught her the truth of what she was and that she should not consider herself evil for having magic. The early days of their relationship had been difficult, but it had been a long time since she had felt exasperation with her skills from him. Now, when they were together, pride filled his expression.

Pushing aside the past, she released the coins and immediately built a field around them, diminishing the pull of the force Kas called gravity on the beaten bits of metal. No longer strongly attracted to the ground and the stone wall, the coins slowly floated down, settling gently in place instead of bouncing off the rocks and into the tall grasses.

She turned Argat away from the wall and the farmer who was still too far away to have observed Stephenie's display. Silently, she reminded herself again to practice discretion. Her use of magic had grown far more casual in the last few months, and while she could reveal her identity to avoid the threat of being burned as a witch, she did not want to do so.

Not bothering to wait for the farmer, she squeezed Argat's sides and pushed him into a trot. She slipped through the others who were still stopped around her and she resumed her place at the front of their line. Antar was only a handful of miles away and she looked forward to surprising her brother, Joshua, with her successful rescue of Islet from the Senzar. Now that their mother was dead, she knew the three of them would be able to heal their emotional wounds and be an actual family again.

Stephenie had barely gone a mile when she sensed a muted presence coming quickly in their direction. She opened her senses further and confirmed it was Kas who rushed toward them. Reaching out further, a multitude of tiny energy threads leaped from her mind and spread through the environment. Through these threads, she felt the blowing of the wind, the grinding of the tree limbs against each other, and the movement of the mice, rabbits, deer, birds, and other wildlife around them. She sat like a spider in the middle of a giant web, waiting for a thread to relay the subtle information of a threat, yet she sensed nothing alarming. While she waited for Kas, she kept her mind active, but maintaining such a wide search drew energy through her and that extra energy burned slightly as it coursed through her body. When Kas grew close enough, she dropped her fields and focused on her friend. *What is it?* She asked him mentally.

She knew the others had slowed behind her, though only Ryia would have been able to sense Kas as he closed upon them. No one else would have seen him, for Kas was not expending energy to generate any luminescence. His body having died nearly a thousand years ago, Kas was now nothing more than a cloud of energy and particles far too small to see. The ghost survived by willing his energy fields to remain together, preserving his memories and essence. Only when he wanted to, did he luminesce a visible form that others could see.

*A dozen men on horses are moving this way,* he responded in Dalish, the language of his people, which he had continued teaching her. *They are dressed in Joshua's colors.* Reaching her side, he hovered on her left. *I have concerns with their approach. This road is small and infrequently traveled. They are moving with enough purpose that I suspect they are somehow aware of your presence.*

"How could they know where we are?" She asked aloud, signaling Henton and Douglas with a quick hand gesture that indicated company was coming. Immediately, Douglas fell back, taking up a protective position behind Islet, while Stephenie continued slowly forward, enlarging the distance between her and Henton. If an attack came, she intended to take the initial encounter.

"I am unable to provide reason or method behind their presence," Kas' voice came to her from out of nowhere. The ghost lacked any physical means to make sounds, but he had learned to generate his own gravitational fields to vibrate the air in a manner that Stephenie assumed resembled his voice.

Stephenie continued to move slowly down the road as she watched the riders finally crest the nearest of the rolling hills. She narrowed her eyes, but could not make out more than their general colors, which confirmed Kas' report that they were Joshua's soldiers.

She slowed Argat to a halt in the middle of the road while Kas moved away, placing himself at the edge of her ability to clearly sense him. If any of the approaching soldiers were holy warriors or priests, she did not want Kas' presence detected by someone else with magic.

At a hundred yards, the bulk of the riders slowed to a stop, allowing the leading two to pull ahead. As these two grew closer, Stephenie recognized the image of a black wolf on the armor of the leader. "Sir Walter?" She wondered aloud. When the lead man was within forty yards, she recognized the Knight's tightly cropped red hair and bearded jaw. The other man with him slowed and fell behind

Walter. When they both stopped, Sir Walter was a dozen paces ahead of the second man.

Stephenie avoided touching either of their minds with her powers. While she generally had trouble reading thoughts at a distance, with determined focus, she sometimes found it possible to pick up surface thoughts. However, when it came to soldiers, or people who were mentally disciplined, most of the time even those remained muted. With physical contact, much more could be done to force oneself into another person's mind, but that carried the risk that the other person, even without magic, could take over her mind.

The Knight bowed his head to her, "Your Highness, I am glad we were able to find you. I have been asked to help speed your safe journey home."

Stephenie's jaw tightened. Sir Walter had kept his expression extremely neutral. The tone fit his character, but under it, she heard a trace of anxiety in his voice. "It seems a rather significant effort to send a dozen men several miles into the countryside in the hope to find me and hurry me along. What is the purpose of that and how did you even know where to look?"

"Ma'am," he said bowing his head again. "Your presence was reported by a couple of soldiers who recognized you. Using a pigeon, they sent word of your crossing the bridge at Ivar. I—"

Stephenie felt a sudden spike of emotion from him as he obviously noticed Islet urging her horse closer to join the conversation. Stephenie felt Henton hasten to catch up to her sister.

"Your Majesty," Sir Walter said, bowing his head even lower than he had for Stephenie. "I am without words. The report made no mention of you and those of us who knew Stephenie's purpose had no idea she had been successful in your rescue." He dismounted and stepped closer before dropping to one knee. "You may not remember me, but I am Sir Walter. I had just joined His Majesty's service a month before you left for your wedding. That was nearly six years ago."

Islet nodded her head. "I remember you were a friend of Joshua's before you joined his service, though we were never formally introduced." Islet looked around as the other soldiers, still a long distance away, appeared ready to dismount. "Please, stay on your horses," she called out to them.

Stephenie cleared her throat. "Sir Walter, why are you here? There should be no reason my group could not quietly pass through Antar to the castle. We've heard of no unrest."

The red-haired soldier rose gracefully to his feet. "Your Highness, your brother, His Majesty, received word of your approach and wanted to have me ensure your safe arrival, even without any known threats."

*Can't he simply trust me to do something on my own?* Stephenie tried to keep her tone neutral and the pain from her voice. "We would draw far less attention in our worn travel attire than we would escorted by the King's personal guards."

"Ma'am, if I may approach?" Stephenie nodded her head and Sir Walter closed to her side. "Ma'am, if I may speak freely."

"Walter, you know me," she said quietly as Islet moved her horse even closer. The nearest of Sir Walter's soldiers turned his head and attention away from them. Henton, Douglas, and Ryia were less respecting of the assumed privacy, but Stephenie did not care. "Please, just spit out what you want to say."

The Knight nodded his head, but the tension had not left his eyes. "Ma'am, His Majesty was quite angry that the first report of your return came from a pair of soldiers guarding a bridge."

"We've kept a low profile so we could move across country without drawing too much attention. Messages can get lost and read by people you don't want to have read them. The first place I thought I might be able to trust a messenger was in Berylam, but we heard Baron Turning is here in Antar, so we didn't bother even going to that city."

Sir Walter nodded his head. "I am in agreement, Ma'am. However, your brother is still displeased with this situation. He has been worried for months about your condition." He glanced to Islet, who watched silently, then turned back to Stephenie. "If I may offer a suggestion." Stephenie nodded her assent while she focused on keeping her fingers from clenching. "If you will take your time once we reach Antar Castle, I will promptly inform His Majesty of your success. I believe that may put His Majesty into a favorable state regarding yourself." He quickly added, "Nothing too long, such as grooming your horse, but long enough that I will have a chance to make my report before you are introduced to the court. I suspect the session will still be in progress when we arrive."

Stephenie forced herself to pause before responding; her vision of a warm welcome dying in her mind. She contemplated simply ignoring Joshua and turning around to head elsewhere.

Islet took the opportunity to speak, "Is Joshua so angry he would make a scene?"

Sir Walter turned his head toward Islet. "His Majesty has allowed his anger at Her Highness to build and he may speak without considering the consequences." Walter shifted his gaze between them several times. "It was merely a suggestion."

Slowly, Stephenie opened her hands and relaxed her shoulders. She could tell the Knight obviously hoped to find at least one of them rational. "Sir Walter, we are ladies and will not be rushed to any meeting."

He bowed his head again to Stephenie, this time as low as he had bowed to Islet. "Thank you, Ma'am. There are many people in Antar at the moment and I would be most pleased for them to see a joyous reunion."

Stephenie nodded her head and Sir Walter quickly returned to his horse. As he mounted, Islet leaned closer to Stephenie, "Has Josh become a problem?"

Stephenie tried to push away the memories of her last few days with her brother before she left to rescue Islet. While they both wanted to rescue Islet after she spent a year in Senzar captivity, Joshua had significantly different views on how Stephenie should have done it. Some of the arguments still hurt. "I don't know." She bit her lower lip. "I wouldn't call him erratic, but he's still quick to jump to conclusions. He's as stubborn as he ever was and before I left, too easy to anger."

"Those are not good qualities to have in a king."

Stephenie did not respond. She loved her brother and knowing that people were actively working around his behavior frightened her. It meant that an even greater number of people had taken notice if those closest to him were working to protect him from himself.

*    *    *    *    *

Stephenie stared at the back of Sir Walter's head as they rode toward Antar. The Knight and three other soldiers were leading her and Islet. The remainder of the soldiers rode directly behind Henton, Douglas, and Ryia. *We might as well be prisoners,* she told Kas, *being led to face the wrath of our King.*

*He is not my King and I do not believe Douglas considers him his liege any longer either.*

Stephenie did not respond. Kas' mistrust of Joshua started shortly after their initial meeting in the Rim Mountains. Douglas' she had seen grow over time.

As they came over a rise, Stephenie's attention turned to her left. The city of Antar lay before them, spread widely across the valley and up to the edge of the cliffs that overlooked the Sea of Tet. In the distance, she watched as the cranes that hung over the edge of the land worked to draw up the supplies and goods too heavy to carry up the switchbacks carved into the rocky cliff.

Although she could not see the tops of their masts, she knew there would be ships in the protected harbor. Beyond the harbor, whitecaps dotted the waters of Tet, stirred up by the strong wind blowing from the southeast. The salt air smelled familiar and somehow right; it was definitely different from the odor of the Endless Sea off the western shores. Perhaps that had been due to the winter winds, but for Stephenie, Tet's smell offered comfort.

Stephenie knew Kas' history and she looked upon the largest city in Cothel with fresh eyes. The wattle and daub buildings that covered the valley were a recent reincarnation of a city that had been around for at least fifteen-hundred-years. But like the newness of these buildings, the people now living in Antar had no realization just how rich of a history lived under their feet. Instead, they focused on their current needs and desires and for the few that understood the pull of the past, most only acknowledged the last four-hundred and thirty-six years, which marked the length of Cothel's calendar.

As they rode into the outskirts of the city, Stephenie's focus turned south toward Antar Castle. The large complex, still several miles away, rested upon even higher bluffs that overlooked both the city and the harbor. Stephenie's tower, near the middle of the complex, rose more than fifty-feet above the height of even the massive gatehouse that protected two pair of huge doors and portcullises.

She knew people said the castle lorded over the city, but having grown up on, and within, its walls, she felt the old stone as much more of a benefactor, protecting the city and the port. Although not always a happy place, it had been home until her mother tried to keep her captive with the intent of cutting out her heart and sacrificing her.

Stephenie turned her head sharply; her focus pulled involuntarily by the emotions of the people who watched them ride past. She wanted to scream a righteous curse at her brother, telling him that five travel-worn people escorted by soldiers made people curious. The further they went, the more people slowed their pace and turned to look, as if a wagon wreck had just occurred.

Suddenly she sensed a spike in the emotional tone and a voice called out, "The Prophet! The Princess has returned!" And like a fire catching in a dry field, the energy and voices around them surged. She pulled her focus back as her senses became overwhelmed.

She continued to stare at the castle rising in the distance, hoping to avoid meeting anyone's eyes. She swallowed down the loss of being simply herself: just an eighteen-year-old traveling with family and friends. Half a year had passed since she truly played the role of prophet and she wished she could simply turn around and walk away from the responsibility. *Too many expectations and lies go along with that title and at some point, disappointment and ruin are inevitable.*

Ahead of her and Islet, Sir Walter picked up the pace, the tension in his movement showing his desire to avoid being caught by the crowd of people. Stephenie was thankful the Knight had more sense than her brother did.

"I've told you to dye your hair," Henton whispered after he moved up to protect her immediate right. Douglas and Ryia also moved forward protecting Islet's left with their physical presence.

"Quiet," she responded, not willing to have that discussion again. She always blamed Kas for her refusal to change her appearance, but internally she knew her own pride and vanity played as much a role as anything else.

With the increased speed, they outpaced the spreading rumor of her return and made quick progress toward the southern edge of the city. Once they passed the last of the buildings, all that lay between them and the castle was the winding road that meandered a mile though fields made rough by scattered stones.

*Why, Kas? Josh should not fear me. I'd never hurt him.*

*Those not ruling tend to desire what they do not have,* Kas responded, *and those ruling assume everyone else wants their power. Too often, even in my time, only a few who achieve the goal of rule ever truly realize the responsibility and burden. Fewer still ever become a good ruler.*

She nodded her head. *Those who desire to rule usually do not do so for the benefit of others.* A smile found its way to her face as she felt Kas' sense of pleasure in sharing her company. The fact that he considered her intelligent and cunning, even though lacking in experience, pushed away much of the anger she felt.

As the gatehouse drew closer, Sir Walter pulled ahead of the group. He paused when confronted by the guards and after what appeared to be a brief conversation, rode into the twenty-foot wide passage that led to the bailey of the castle. When the rest of the group reached the first set of open doors and the raised portcullis, the soldiers who were standing on either side of the opening dropped to one knee and bowed their heads in their direction. Most of these men would never recognize Islet. Her sister had married the King of Ipith shortly after her fourteenth birthday. However, many of Joshua's current soldiers were men Stephenie had freed from the Senzar and they easily recognized her. The fact that those men still lived caused many of them to become followers of Catheri. *At least once the High Priest of Felis had declared me cleansed of Elrin's evil,* Stephenie thought.

Their group did not pause as Sir Walter had. Instead, they continued into the gatehouse tunnel, under the murder holes, past the arrow loops, and through the second set of doors and portcullis. On the other side, they emerged into the bailey and the complex that had evolved over the centuries.

Directly ahead of her stood a remnant of the old castle's outer wall, that small section of stone now supported the back wall of the auxiliary stables. Beyond that wall was the large Square Keep that had been constructed by her ancestors more than a century prior when they expanded and refurbished much of the castle. The four stories of light-colored stone that formed the keep was an eyesore in Stephenie's mind. The sharp lines and severe nature cast a cold eeriness to the building.

Just ahead and to her left, sat a more pleasant part of the castle. The old barracks, Stephenie's seven story tall tower, and the old Great Hall formed from grey stones that time could not crumble. The buildings, adorned with gentle curves, subtle patterns, and weathered carvings added interest and character. *Those have life in their bones*, she thought to Kas. *They are buildings of beauty.*

*You will not find me in disagreement.*

Stephenie turned her attention back toward the soldiers who led them toward the main stables built against the outer curtain wall on their right. Servants crossed their path, moving with purpose and energy, possibly desiring to remain out of her notice. As they approached the main stables, several people came forth to collect their mounts.

"Argat is not to be ridden by anyone," Stephenie said to the young man that stood waiting for her to give him the reins. Slipping out of the saddle with the grace of an accomplished rider, she turned back to the man who was half a head taller than she. "I mean it, Argat is my horse," she repeated, slightly fearful of the difficulty she was having in handing over the reins as a wave of possessiveness returned to her.

"Of course, Ma'am," the man said, bowing with a slight tremble in his limbs. "I will take the best care of him."

Stephenie sensed his fear rising beyond the normal fear everyone held of her. Forcing herself to remain calm, she spoke more gently. "Thank you, both Argat and I will appreciate that." Slowly, she handed over the reins. "Be a good boy and don't cause trouble," she said to the chestnut as she unbuckled a small saddlebag. Stepping forward again, she patted his neck and then pushed away his nose as he hunted for a treat.

"Your Highness," one of the soldiers who had escorted them said with a bow of his own. Stephenie would prefer they refrained from all the pomp. Henton and the others never really bowed or scraped; they simply treated her as a friend and she loved them for that. "When you are ready, we will escort Her Majesty and yourself to the Great Hall. It is confirmed His Majesty is still holding court."

Stephenie looked to the east and past the servant and guest quarters. She looked beyond the kitchens and the Square Keep to the new Great Hall and sighed.

With the increase in court size, the castle had run out of room and so the construction of that building move to the outside of the curtain wall. The tiled roof stood above the height of the walls and the new outer walls of the hall had been reinforced to provide protection. The building was ugly and she did not want to greet her brother there with a crowd of strangers watching.

"Steph," Islet said, coming over to her side. "We are ready if you are."

Stephenie had turned her focus toward Ryia and did not notice the slight raise of the soldier's eyebrows. The months of travel with her in charge removed Stephenie's appreciation for the differences in rank between her and her sister. "Of course, please lead on. I just need a word with Henton, Ryia, and Douglas as we walk."

The soldier bowed his head and started walking slowly across the cobbled ground. Stephenie held back as Henton came beside her. Wordlessly, she handed him the small saddlebag, which he slid his hand into to remove a couple of small books that he placed inside his shirt.

Stephenie nodded to a group of men who bowed as their paths crossed. She recognized colors from three noble families in their number. Several of the tunics had a patch of white with an image of an embroidered black hand sewn into it.

"It seems Will has recruited even more followers for you," Douglas said quietly after they were out of earshot. "Definitely a lot more than when we left."

She ignored the tightening of her stomach. Once Will, one of her former protectors originally under Henton's command, had seen her consumed by fire in the Rim Mountains, nothing had stopped him from talking about the 'Claw of Catheri' burned into her left breast. A mark that Kas left when he tried to freeze her heart and only coincidentally had any resemblance to the long-dead god's sigil.

*It turned into a means to save your life,* Kas remarked to her unvocalized thoughts. *Who would have realized the implications of where this has led?*

She did not reply to Kas, instead she leaned closer to Ryia. "It's likely we will all get introduced at court."

"What does that mean?" The girl asked.

"It means we are going to get paraded in front of a lot of nobles who will be judging us. Most of the attention will be on Islet and myself, so don't let it bother you. Just stand straight and look proud."

"The three of us are not fit to be presented at court," Henton said quietly.

"And you think I am any cleaner or better dressed?"

"I was referring to us being commoners," Henton replied.

Douglas scoffed, "You're a knight; you've been presented before."

Stephenie glared at Douglas, but waited to respond as five servants spilled out of the kitchens and quickly turned left to avoid them. The aroma of roasting meat and baking bread made her stomach growl with a momentary distraction. She put the thought of food from her mind and continued, "Douglas, I'd declare you a knight if I could, but everyone here knows who you are and it is not in my power. However, Ryia," she said looking at her protégé, "I want you introduced as a Lady. It will give you more status."

Ryia shook her head vigorously. "No. They'd cut my hands off," she said in Pandar, the trade tongue. "Someone would find out and people don't like commoners pretending to be something they are not. Don't call me a Lady."

Stephenie bit back the normal scolding she would give Ryia for not using Cothish and the honest fear in the girl's eyes made her hesitate a moment. "I'm only trying to help you," Stephenie whispered. "No one is going to know who you are and they will accept my word for it."

Ryia shook her head. "I don't want to lose my hands."

"We don't do that here. And no one would risk doing that to you when you are under my protection."

"Steph," Henton said as they closed upon the steps leading into the Great Hall. "It's probably for the best. It would make Ryia too uncomfortable."

"Well, she can't get out of being declared a priest of Catheri," Stephenie said as she started up the steps. She could already feel the large number of people in the building. It resurfaced a sense of dread she had lived with for as long as she could remember: the fear of being burned for being a witch.

"Obviously," Henton responded, his right hand on Ryia's shoulder.

# Chapter 2

Stephenie waited with the others in the ornamental foyer. Before them stood the carved doors leading into the actual Great Hall. She sensed the multitudes of privileged people inside the large room. She also felt the scores of less fortunate servants and retainers not permitted into audience with the King. Those people waited for their Lords in the smaller antechambers and rooms of the building. The braver of them peeked through doorways or invented errands that suddenly needed performing in order to catch a glimpse of her and her companions.

The emotional energy in the building churned around them on the realization the Prophet waited upon the King. It made Stephenie's head throb. *What's Josh thinking? We're not fit for an audience. If we don't knock someone out from our odor, I'll be amazed.* She quietly tried to smooth the worst of the wrinkles in her dirty shirt as she waited for Kas' response. He remained close, enveloping her in an attempt to hide his presence from anyone who might be able to sense him. While prudence would have dictated he remained away, she did not like continually excluding him from everything and if she had to admit it, she enjoyed the closeness.

Eventually, she forced herself to stop adjusting her clothing. *Josh got what he asked for.*

*Your appearance will likely give ample warning to any with a limited constitution for strong smells.* Stephenie silently agreed with Kas.

Just a step ahead of her, Islet nodded to the trio of footman guarding the Great Hall and then two of the finely dressed men pulled open the large doors. As the doors moved, the splendor of the Great Hall revealed itself to them. Paintings, tapestries, and finely decorated carvings accented the strong wooden timbers and thick stone construction of the room. Most of the decor Stephenie had never seen before. Almost everything was a replacement, as her mother had emptied the castle of valuables when she fled to Kynto.

Her brother, King Joshua, sat at the far end of the hall. Beside him, in a slightly less lavish throne, sat Queen Rebecca, the High Priestess of Felis. Perched above the level of the rest of the hall, their chairs stood upon a dais carpeted in deep red.

Stephenie took special note of the tapestries hanging behind the monarchs; the intricately woven cloth merged the Marn crest with a leaping mountain lion, the symbol of Rebecca's family. For a moment, her breath caught in her chest and she had to fight the moisture building in her eyes. She knew she should not have expected to see her father's crest, but on some level, she still had not completely let go of him.

*I am here for you,* Kas' thought whispered through her mind.

The mass of people sitting in upholstered chairs on either side of the long carpeted aisle turned at the opening of the doors. She observed more with her mind than with her eyes the third footman slipping inside the hall. To most of the richly dressed persons, he would be nearly invisible. Even when his deep voice rang out, carrying through the voluminous hall, drowning and silencing any quiet murmurs from the guests, these people would never notice another servant performing his job.

"Her Majesty, Queen Islet of Ipith and Princess of Cothel." The man took a breath as Islet walked forward and the crowd gasped. The low rumble of murmurs returned, filling the hall as Islet continued forward with her head held high. The state of her clothing would never go unnoticed, but to Stephenie, Islet seemed even more regal because of the torn and stained garments.

"Prophet of Catheri, Defeater of the Senzar, and Protector of Cothel, Her Highness, Princess Stephenie of Cothel," the footman continued. Stephenie pushed back her shoulders and lifted her chin as high as Islet. She followed a couple of steps behind her sister and though everyone sat stunned at her sister's presence, their undivided attention still turned to her.

Stephenie never cared for balls or large ceremonies. The fancy dresses, styled hair, and false sincerity did not appeal to her. She preferred her battles won with swords and daggers. However, she knew this room contained conflicts as vicious and deadly as any campaign lamented and immortalized by bards and heralds. The difference lie in that these people scarcely ever lifted their own hands to the task; instead they manipulated others to do their bidding.

Instinct kept her mind active for any hint of threats, and while most of those in the room had long ago learned to school their emotions, the younger people or those old enough to no longer care, let their feelings come to the surface. The resulting emotions swirled about her, ranging from total support and gratitude to loathing and, most strongly and commonly, fear. A fear so deep and primal, that people would wake in the middle of the night, dreading the idea that she might select them as a victim. While many of the soldiers she had saved felt some amount of gratitude, those who did not directly join the battle against the Senzar assumed her power was a potential threat.

"Sir Henton, personal guard for Her Highness. Corporal Douglas, personal guard for Her Highness." She knew Douglas would bristle at the mentioning of his rank. He had been released from duty and had sworn himself to her in what some might say was a nearly treasonous abandonment of his King. "Priestess Ryia of Catheri."

Stephenie felt her friends walking slowly behind her, their own discomfort spilling out of them. Even Henton's normally quiet mind leaked some emotion. This homecoming did not live up to her expectations.

She turned her attention forward as Joshua left his throne and hastened his approach to Islet. He grabbed her up in his arms and squeezed her in a manner most unfitting the reserved and calculating ruler he portrayed a moment earlier. Islet hesitated only a moment before returning what should have been more private affection.

"Dear sister, I am so relieved to find you safe and sound," he said, his voice carrying through the nearly silent hall. "Your journey must have been arduous," he added, examining her masculine clothing. "What has our sister dressed you in?"

"Josh," Islet said, stepping back, though his hands remained on her shoulders. "The journey was better than it might have otherwise been. Stephenie and the others took very good care of me." She smiled and glanced at the people to her left. "In fact, I find the clothing quite comfortable, compared to a boned corset laced so tight I can't breathe."

Stephenie noticed his brows narrow ever so slightly, but then he released Islet and turned to Stephenie. She waited for her own embrace, but Joshua hesitated to approach. Feeling the stares of the crowd upon her and knowing they were wondering if she considered herself equal to the two monarchs before her, she chose to curtsy. As she lifted her eyes, she felt his anger at her grow. Pride hardened her jaw and straightened her spine. *What does he want from me?* She asked Kas.

Instead of addressing her, Joshua turned toward the nobles, shifting his gaze to both sides of the aisle. "It should be obvious, but now that they have returned, I am able to tell you just what Princess Stephenie has been doing." Stephenie could not help but bristle at his emphasis on 'Princess.' "As I stated time and time again, there was no nefarious purpose. No plot. She is not dead and she did not abandon Cothel as some people have been reported to whisper behind closed doors."

The acid in Joshua's voice burned her ears. Though he tried hard to smile and look friendly, she could see the stiffness in his movement. The crowd remained hushed and quiet, emotions racing in all directions. Outwardly, Stephenie noted only smiles and nodding heads, but the small number of those not schooled at hiding their emotions radiated a sense of irritation strong enough that Stephenie could feel it over their fear of her.

"I refused to give details on her travels because she needed to work in secret to free my dear sister from the clutches of the Senzar. It was these Senzar, still clinging to the western coast that held Islet. I would not risk word getting back to the heathens about what we planned." He took a deep breath, hesitating slightly. Then as if he changed his mind, he continued more honestly, "So, please, everyone, welcome home my dear sister, the Queen of Ipith!"

Cheers and applause erupted throughout the nobles, drowning out any sense of anger in the emotional energy around them. Everyone stood and Stephenie, having spent most of her life outside of mass public scrutiny, felt the discomfort of all the eyes still upon her. For while Islet might have been placed forefront in Joshua's statements, everyone truly watched her. Worse, she knew Joshua observed the same thing.

Joshua raised his arms and waved down the noise in an effort to silence the crowd and get them to return to their chairs. As the noise settled, but not completely ended, he turned to Stephenie, "What have you to report, dear Sister? You have been gone long on your journey. Nearly six and a half months by my count."

She forced herself to remain calm despite her brother's acidic tone. Only through Kas' reassurance did she keep tears from her eyes. *If he thinks a public forum will protect him, it won't. Just wait until we are alone.*

Pausing to reconsider her response for the third time, she pulled back her mental awareness of the people around her. The emotional feedback distracted her thoughts. Eventually, she spoke with a measured voice, "As you know, we had to travel all the way to Ulet." She avoided looking at the nobles around them. "That involved crossing several countries, not to mention a mountain range in the middle of winter. And once there, extracting Islet from a heavily fortified castle took time and planning. After that, we had to return here without being caught or drawing attention to ourselves. The distance is rather far. Many hundreds of miles one way."

"I helped you plan this mission; I seemed to recall a more southerly route that we agreed would not take so long."

"Josh," Islet interrupted, "you know me. When have I ever enjoyed traveling, let alone riding for days and days on a horse? Did you expect Stephenie to have me ride forty miles in a day? Or me to do so even if she demanded it?"

Joshua's mouth opened at Islet's raised eyebrows. He stammered a moment and then shook his head. "No. Please accept my apologies. I am too used to estimating travel based upon that of a company of fast cavalry or what Stephenie can manage when driving her men. I should have made allowances for your needs. As a Queen, no one would expect that you would ride that hard. It would put many men down with sores, let alone a Lady."

Stephenie's eyes narrowed; while she did not want to dress and be restricted as a Lady might, she was still a woman. Joshua did not seem to notice her bristling. "And I can see plainly that you have traveled roughly." He bowed his head to Islet as Queen Rebecca approached quietly behind him.

"Greetings, Queen Islet," Rebecca said, her voice soft, but carried easily through the room. Both of them bowed their heads to each other.

"Islet, Steph, let me introduce my wife, Queen Rebecca. We were married on the first of the year."

"Queen Rebecca," Islet said, "it is a pleasure to meet you."

"Actually, we were introduced once before. It was just after your fourteenth birthday."

Islet nodded her head, "You will have to forgive me, but I cannot recall the introduction, it was too many years ago."

"And you were rather busy with your impending wedding I am certain," Rebecca offered.

Stephenie watched as Rebecca smiled; it was warm and inviting and it gave Stephenie hope that she would be easier to work with than her brother.

"I was," Islet said, returning the smile.

"Let me offer my condolences on the passing of your husband."

Islet nodded her head. "I spent more than a year locked in a small cell. I have come to terms with his murder. Stephenie has done much to avenge his death."

"And, we'll get you back on your throne," Joshua offered.

Islet shook her head. "No, Brother, I do not think to do that. My husband was killed and I produced no heirs for him. As I understand it, his entire line has been executed and the Senzar on the coast have put some of my husband's enemies on the throne to act as puppets. I have no legitimate claim I can or will make. I do not want to see more war and blood over this. I am content."

Joshua nodded his head, but Stephenie could see his disapproval of Islet's statement of concession. Growing up as the oldest, and the only boy among girls, his rulership of Cothel was never questioned. That certainty shaped him.

Stephenie, growing up the youngest, and suffering under the belief she was a cursed witch, never had expectations of ruling anything. Surviving each day without someone discovering her secret and demanding her death constituted her goal for life.

Islet she knew to be somewhere in between, the third girl to survive past infancy, their mother raised her to marry into a powerful house and with her marriage to a king, she had outshone both her older sisters. And yet, Islet remained more cautious and less outspoken than either Kara or Regina had been.

Sensing the conversation finished, Joshua stepped back and returned to the raised dais. He lifted his hands over his head as he looked at the nobles and gentry. "To celebrate the return of my dear sister, we will have a feast tonight! Tell the kitchens to start preparing and have this hall readied with tables. I have not felt so joyous since my wedding day." He looked around as the nobles nodded their heads and murmurs of approval filled the hall. "For now, I will adjourn court so that I may spend some time with my sisters." Everyone stood and bowed to Joshua. Lowering his voice some, he met Stephenie's eyes, "Come, let us go back to the Square Keep."


Even if Stephenie had not been sensitive to Joshua's mood, his ever increasing pace and subtle violence of movement would have told her enough. By the time they reached the third floor of the Square Keep, she and Islet nearly had to jog to keep up with their brother's longer legs.

The slamming open of the door to his personal study provided the final provocation. "All right, damn it, what is the problem?" Stephenie demanded.

Joshua spun around, his jaw set, "We had agreed upon a plan and you blatantly disobeyed my orders!"

"A field commander has to make adjustments based upon the current state of events."

Queen Rebecca followed Islet into the room, closing the door behind them, though Stephenie remained barely aware of their presence. Her focus remained on Kas, who positioned himself between Joshua and her. Whether Kas thought to protect her or Joshua, she did not know.

"You never planned to do as we agreed! You were supposed to go on a southern route. You were not supposed to go any further north than to visit Baron Turning and then head south."

"What difference does it make?" She swore; her hands clenched into claws. The heat of the energy coursing through her body radiating outward. Kas' shifting presence offered her a warning.

"In the days before you left, I had sent people ahead of you to make sure you were safe. They saw no sign of you after you left Berylam. Then a report came in that you were nearly killed by Senzar warlocks when you went chasing after priests that were executing witches. What in Felis' name do you think you were doing?"

Stephenie's mouth dropped. "You are mad that I went to investigate some Senzar murdering citizens of Cothel? Really? My mission involved facing down a castle full of Senzar and you are mad that I took on a couple of warlocks who were killing people in our country?" Stephenie shook her head. "Josh, your priorities are screwed up."

"Stephenie, Josh," Rebecca said, placing her hand on Stephenie's shoulder. "Perhaps we could take a moment and hear what happened from Stephenie. It sounds like she has put some thought into what she did."

"We already know what happened," Joshua snapped. "She went rogue and executed the ruler of a foreign land and has put Cothel at risk of reprisal." He turned toward Stephenie, but spoke to Rebecca, "My priorities are screwed up? She's a danger to every citizen of Cothel! How can she be trusted when she starts murdering monarchs?!"

Stephenie pulled her shoulder free of Rebecca's grasp. She could sense Kas trying to speak with her, but she kept him out of her thoughts so she could concentrate. "You ordered Mother's execution, Josh. We both agreed she should die. She was a traitor. She's the reason father is dead and you were captured by the Senzar. She's responsible for thousands of soldiers dying. She sent people to capture me so she could cut my heart out and eat it. She sent people to kill Will. She killed Regina and she tried to kill Islet. The bitch needed to die. I will not apologize for that. However, it was not something appropriate to talk about in front of all the nobles. But if you want another reason it took so long to get home, it's because I went north and cut mother's head from her shoulders. Happy?"

"I'm not referring to her, though we heard rumors a month and a half ago that she had been executed. What is beyond me is why you then went and killed Uncle? That is what I want to know! He was the King of Kynto and now Midland and Calis are demanding answers. He was a bastard, but for you to execute him is inexcusable."

Stephenie straightened. "Why would you accuse me of that? I didn't kill Uncle. I never went near him. I've never even met him. Mother was in Rativyr. Which is a long way south and west of Wyntac."

Islet stepped forward. "Josh, I was with her the whole time. I had initially been against killing Mother, but once we confronted her, it was obvious she was sick. She would continue to hurt others." Islet swallowed, "But once that was done, we started for home. It took time to avoid the soldiers who pursued us, but we left Kynto as soon as we could."

Rebecca moved to the other side of the desk to stand next to her husband. "We had discussed this, Josh," she said, "and you even penned it in your responses to Calis and Midland, while we have heard no one yet take credit for the assassination of King Willard, his country is filled with the mercenaries he had hired to keep control. His funds were limited after what Stephenie stole back for your coffers. We know he had started to lose control. It was only a matter of time before one of his hired swords took over. Which, if the other rumors are correct, it is one of his generals who has declared himself King. Likely, that man is responsible."

Joshua nodded his head to his wife. "Perhaps you are correct. Steph, if you say you didn't kill Uncle, I will believe you."

"I said I didn't."

Joshua's shoulders lost their edge and he looked much older than his twenty-five years. He slowly looked backward for his chair and took his seat. He motioned for everyone else to sit. Once Rebecca pulled over a chair that appeared to be there for her use, Islet and Stephenie sat in the two that were in front of his large desk.

"What actually occurred over the last six months?" He asked. "We are missing many details."

"It is a long story, but not much interesting to tell," Stephenie said, her own energy gone and leaving her drained; she loved her brother and hated to argue with him. "Most of it is boring. As I mentioned, on the way out to free Islet, we discovered some Senzar warlocks killing people who could end up being our next generation of priests." The lie hurt her to tell, but Joshua did not know the truth that fundamentally no difference existed between priests and those the priests burned as witches and warlocks.

Joshua nodded his head. "William, and Rebecca," he inclined his head toward his wife, "have managed to add several new priests to their ranks based on what you found on the other side of the Uthen Mountains. We had never expected to see the gods choosing older people to join the ranks of the empowered."

*Kas, why are some people so convinced of the lies?*

*You cannot dismiss centuries of people repeating those lies over and over again. Additionally, you have not wanted to risk trying to explain the truth to Joshua. And based on Rebecca's belief that he would take it very badly, it is probably wise to avoid that argument.*

Stephenie mentally nodded her agreement to Kas. Of the five of them in the room, Joshua was the only one who had not been told the truth of what their gods were. "Well, we face powerful enemies who bring great power against us. The gods know we cannot wait for children to grow old enough to fight."

"That is what we understood Catheri pronounced through you. I can say that William has done wonders with those that Catheri has embraced into her ranks of empowered. I had my doubts, but in truth, he was a good choice as High Priest of Catheri."

Stephenie's eyebrows narrowed; Joshua's sudden approval of her friend confused her. At the time she left Antar, her making Will the High Priest of Catheri remained a contentious argument. She even feared Joshua might have tried to have Will removed. At the very least, she expected Will would garner no support from her brother.

Putting the change out of her head, she continued, "Well, as you seem to know, we found the Senzar executing those with the potential to become the next generation of priests." *Yet another lie I have to repeat.* She knew the Senzar, pretending to be priests of various gods, were driving people who actually had powers west in the hopes of recruiting them. The people they executed had no power. "When I heard about the increase in witch burnings, I had to go further north and find out the truth behind it. I am glad many of the people who might have otherwise been accused of witchcraft came to Antar to be tested."

Joshua nodded. "Looking at it from that perspective, the decision was probably a wise one. But, crossing the mountain range in winter? You should have turned back south and taken the boat."

Stephenie shook her head. "Josh, don't pursue this discussion."

"Yes," Islet injected. "Stop attacking Steph, she risked her life to rescue me. While I might not have liked every decision she made on our journey home at the time she made it, every decision turned out to be the right decision."

Joshua turned his attention to Islet, "I don't recall you ever sticking up for Stephenie when we were growing up. You generally sided with Mother and Regina."

Stephenie was about to correct Joshua, Islet had stood up for her against their mother once and it had gone very badly for Islet. However, Islet caught her eye and Stephenie held her tongue.

"Josh, I had given up hope of ever seeing anyone who cared for me and was simply waiting to die in my cell. Steph defeated the leader of the Senzar as well as a large group of his followers. She freed me and got me home safely. I can say from witnessing Steph first hand that she is a great leader and a cunning warrior. She deserves praise, not censure. I do not understand why you attacked her so publicly today."

Joshua nodded his head, but Stephenie sensed his fear of her rising. She had no desire for his throne, or any other one, but deep down, he, as most people did, expected she would desire to replace him. After a moment, he turned to her. "Steph, I am sorry. I should not have been so harsh. But things have not gone well lately. The nobles have speculated for too long as to what you were doing, why you missed the wedding, and why no one would say anything about you." He glanced between Islet and Stephenie, "Arnold Turning kept swearing you were doing the work of the gods. He's one of the most ardent defenders of your honor, but as weeks have turned to months, and with no word from you, people began to speculate. Especially after word came that Uncle was executed so soon after the rumors of Mother's death."

Joshua's jaw tightened as he looked down at a rolled up scrap of paper on his desk. Suddenly he snatched it from where it sat, holding it aloft for Stephenie to see. "Then I hear from some common foot soldier that you were spotted riding leisurely toward Antar. I've heard nothing from you, no letter, no status, no report of any kind. I have to hear from a guard at the bridge over the Uthen River!"

Stephenie took a deep breath, not liking the sudden change to rage she felt from Joshua. "It was only myself, Kas, Henton, Douglas, and Ryia to protect Islet. Who should I trust with a letter to you conveying the results of our travels or even that I was on my way home. We were on the back roads to avoid notice, which meant there were no towns with any messengers suitable to carry such a letter. There was no reliable way to get word to you. I was not going to risk someone trying to harm Islet or my friends."

Joshua seemed ready to protest her explanation, but then nodded his head and the anger subsided. "Perhaps you are correct." He put the paper down and leaned forward. "I have worried myself sick with fear that you had died. Not knowing your fate for months and months. You were the last of my family."

"Well, I've brought Islet back, so there are three of us now."

Joshua's eyes narrowed as he appeared to recall what had been said earlier. "Did you say that Mother killed Regina?"

Stephenie nodded her head. "Her vileness goes even further than that. When we were in Vinerxan trying to rescue Islet, Henton and Douglas encountered a man who was working for Mother. The man wanted to get Islet's hand cut off and shipped back to Mother so she could send it to me and demand I come to her or she'd send us the rest of Islet cut up into pieces."

"The one with the birthmark?" Joshua asked as Islet raised her hand with the dark splotch of skin.

"Well, through Henton, Douglas, and Kas, we learned Mother was in Rativyr and so we went to confront her after we freed Islet. I was not going to let her send more people to kidnap those close to me so they could be used against us."

Islet interrupted, "When we confronted her, she had a necklace around her throat. I saw it well, because Mother grabbed me by the neck and threatened to kill me."

"You let Islet get taken by Mother?!"

Islet raised her hand. "I insisted on confronting her. Stephenie ensured I was protected the whole time. But this necklace had Regina's fingers strung on it. She had sacrificed our sister in the hopes it would protect her from Steph's powers."

Joshua shuddered. "The woman was damaged. The two of you did right in executing her."

Islet nodded her head. "She was not right in the head."

Joshua turned to his wife, "Her sins drew Elrin's attention and caused Stephenie to suffer under the curse my mother should have born. Elrin's evil makes people do vile things. I am only glad that Catheri chose Stephenie and cleansed her in holy fire. When Catheri used Steph to bring down the mountain peak on the Senzar invaders, freeing thousands of us and routing their forces, I knew it was a sign that things were changing. I had a vision the future would be better."

"Josh," Stephenie said, not wanting to listen to him go on about Catheri or exulting her deeds, *or making up memories of things that never occurred.* She knew he was looking foolish to everyone in the room, only he did not realize it. "Do you mind if we go clean up? None of us have had a real bath in a very long time and bathing in streams and lakes is not quite the same."

Joshua quickly nodded his head, as if just realizing the state of their clothing. "Of course, please. I should have allowed you to refresh yourselves before seeing you, but I had missed you too much." He stood, "Islet, you'll stay here in the keep, yes? We will have your old rooms readied for you."

"It would be my pleasure."

"And Steph, your tower is as much yours as it ever was."

Stephenie stood up, feeling the soreness in her limbs. The pain did not come from physical exertion, but having held all the energy she drew into her body. Holding on to the power slowly burned her from the inside. She could not remember the last time she felt this level of soreness. "Thank you, Josh. A bath and a nap in my own bed sounds wonderful."

"Steph," Rebecca said from beside Joshua, "I will have dresses sent to you and Islet."

Stephenie nodded. "Thank you."

"Also have someone send clothing for Henton and Douglas," Joshua added. "As well as that new priest of yours. They are all invited to the feast as well. I'd like to thank them all personally."

Rebecca nodded her head as Stephenie took her leave of them. Islet remained behind at Joshua's subtle cue. A normal person would not have noticed, but even with her back turned, the motion of Joshua's hand stood out in her mind. However, Stephenie did not care; Islet had stood up for her and that warmed her heart.

# Chapter 3

Henton led Douglas and Ryia up the stairs of Stephenie's tower. He carried both his and Stephenie's gear over his shoulders and in his arms. Those who removed the items from their horses simply left everything inside the door of her Great Hall. The stairs, just like the hall, suffered from a layer of dust and an accumulation of cobwebs. It confirmed few people, if any, had recently passed through this part of the castle.

Handing the lamp to Douglas, Henton pulled a key to the second floor door from his pouch. It had taken some time, but they discovered Will had left the key in the care of the Seneschal when Will moved into more lavish rooms in the Square Keep. That move had occurred shortly after they had departed.

Henton pushed open the door, revealing a large space that had served as a storage room before they took up residence. The fifty-foot wide room held a vast emptiness that none of them had filled. Having come from very limited space on board ship, none of them had acquired much in the way of personal possessions.

Aside from the original wall blocking the stairs, only a couple of hastily constructed dividing walls sectioned off a small space for a washroom and tub. That left the rest of the open floor for three beds and chests that sat against the northern wall. The brazier they installed for warmth still stood next to a window to let out the smoke. A small table rested against the opposite wall; its four chairs scattered about the edges of the room.

Keeping his opinion silent, Henton noted the half-burnt coals Will had not cleaned from the brazier as well as Will's unmade bed. A chunk of bread lay near the large central support post. Evidence of animal's teeth carved into the rock hard remnants spoke of the neglect. *Where is the discipline?*

"Wow," Ryia said, pushing past Douglas with her armload of gear. "This room is amazing. Look at the size of those beams!"

Henton glanced overhead. The floor of the room above them rested on tree trunks that spanned the width of the tower to the central post. "According to Stephenie, the trees that went into the construction of the tower were felled as many as four hundred years ago, perhaps more. You won't find anything that big around here anymore."

Ryia set her equipment on what had been Douglas' bed and continued to move about the room, checking out the open area and then moved into the washroom as though she needed to evaluate the property before deciding if it was fit to rent. "Hey, what's this big copper thing next to the window?"

Henton slid his backpack off his shoulder and placed it softly on the trunk in front of his bed. "It's a cistern. They added it for us. Rainwater from the roof is directed down a pipe and flows into it so we don't have to lug buckets of water up here to bathe."

"Let's hope it hasn't leaked or overflowed," Douglas said as he moved Ryia's belongings to what had been Will's bed.

Henton hoped those sheets were not filthy, *but still likely cleaner than some of the places we've slept.*

"A bath without lugging water? You rich people."

Henton smiled. He had watched with genuine interest when they had installed the cistern. As long as nothing broke, he knew any overflow went out another pipe and continued down the side of the tower. The men who installed it insisted they wanted it to work without requiring people to constantly watch it. The work fascinated Henton and it gave him ideas for other things he wanted to try, *once I'm no longer chasing Stephenie across half a dozen countries.*

Henton lifted his gaze from the floor when he heard the splashing of water. After the sounds continued for a while, he went to check on Ryia, fearing she might flood the room below them. Fortunately, either the large iron bucket had already been under the tap or she had decided to place it on the hook. Reaching past her, Henton quickly turned off the flow of rushing water before the bucket filled. "What are you planning?"

"I assume the brazier in here is to heat the water. There's another hook above it. If I'm going to a feast, I want to look at least as good as the servants."

Henton grinned as the sixteen-year-old slip of a girl grabbed the thick handle and strained her arms and legs to lift what was already a heavy bucket and was now full of water. He felt a slight chill fill the air as she finally managed to heft the burden. With water sloshing onto her front and the floor, she wobbled over to the hook. In a feat that would rival his own strength, she lifted the handle to the height of her chin and placed it over the brazier. Having learned the truth about magic, its allure continued to appeal more and more to him. *Only, I wasn't born with the ability.*

She smiled at him as she picked up an armload of wood and dropped it into the brazier. After stacking the wood to make it burn more effectively, she put her hands against the rough scraps and concentrated. Having heard Stephenie teaching Ryia, Henton knew the fundamentals of her efforts: when you direct energy into something, the ever-so-tiny parts get excited and rub against each other. The more energy Ryia pushed into the wood, the faster the particles moved and the hotter it became. With enough heat, fire would spring into existence by itself.

Since Ryia started most of their campfires, he was not surprised when the wood suddenly erupted in flames. Reaching over Ryia's head, he pushed open the narrow window to allow the smoke a way out of the room.

"This will feel so good," she said, gazing happily at the large metal tub.

"It will take a while before you can heat enough water to fill the tub. Most of the time, we just ladle the warm water over our heads."

Ryia shrugged. "We'll see. I'm not Steph; I can't fill the tub and simply look at it for a couple seconds and make the water hot. It'd burn out my brains if I tried to push that much energy." She looked up at him with the flirty smile that she wielded quite effectively on most men. "But, as long as the water's not cold, what touches my skin will warm up and feel nice."

"Yeah, and what are Douglas and I supposed to do? A cold bath?" During the time they spent in the frozen mountains, he had wished desperately that his body would automatically regulate its temperature as effectively as Ryia's and Stephenie's did.

She slipped around him and out into the main room. Henton followed her. "The two of you've been going on about how I need to learn to be a real soldier and accept bathing in a creek; I'll let you deal with the cold water as a man should." Having pulled what would still be dirty clothing from her pack, she went back into the washroom and closed the door.

Douglas smiled as he pulled clothing from his trunk and started to pull off his shirt. They both knew that Ryia could get as sassy as any sailor. The three months of traveling together since Ryia joined them in Vinerxan left the girl with a bit of an attitude. Though Henton knew much of her confidence had been earned. He had drilled her in blades and hand-to-hand combat while Stephenie had taught her magic. *We've probably been harder on her than any man I've ever trained.* He opened the trunk at the foot of his bed and pulled out fresh clothing he had left there. He was thankful that she had responded well to their drills. *She has to be better than everyone else. People will assume she's the weak target and try to eliminate her first.*

"Someone's coming," Ryia called softly from behind the washroom door.

Henton, still dressed and wearing his sword belt, glanced at Douglas who had just pulled a dagger and hid it behind his back. From the sounds in the bathing chamber, he assumed Ryia was quickly dressing.

Frowning, he turned back to the door and stood casually. While it was unusual for someone to come into Stephenie's tower, he was not overly inclined to think the intruder would be an immediate threat. A few moments later, a knock preceded the handle turning to allow the door to slowly creak open.

"Sarge?" Will asked as his head appeared in the opening. Seeing Henton, Will's smile brightened and he stepped into the room, his fine cut of clothing moving loosely with each step. "I heard you were back. Sorry I wasn't here when you made your grand entrance, but it took them a while to get word to me that you had been seen."

Despite the voluminous clothing, Henton noted Will did not appear quite as spry as he had when they left six months ago. His cheeks were also fuller and a momentary pulling of his shirt by his belt indicated Will had grown a bit of a belly. Henton did not want to think poorly of his friend, but his automatic assessment of potential foes told Henton that Will had lost some of his edge.

Henton covered his momentary assessment easily, "Wasn't much to see, His Majesty paraded us into the Great Hall and down past a bunch of nobles. They stared and after a short bit of back and forth between Steph, Islet, and our King, Josh dismissed court and a feast was called for this evening."

Will let out a half chuckle. "Yeah, Josh has been irritated with the lot of you. No word for months. Though I must say, we were definitely aware you had gone north from Berylam." He smiled and shrugged in his innocent way that always put Henton's nerves on edge. "We've had several people who might have been burned as witches brought to Antar. Fortunately, I've added most of them to Catheri's ranks. A few have gone over to Felis, but that's causing Rebecca a bit of a problem, since Steph left without teaching either her or Sara enough to be effective in using magic. And so Rebecca is still trying to figure out how to train a witch to pretend to be a priest without—" Will stopped talking when the door to the washroom opened.

Henton glanced back at Ryia, dressed once again in her dirty pants and blouse. Her left hand was on her sword and her right was behind her back. Her movements were cautious as her eyes quickly took in the situation.

"Sarge," Will started, accusation and worry in his voice, "you should have stopped me. I didn't know you had company."

"Ryia," Henton said holding out an open hand in Will's direction. "This is Will, Steph's High Priest of Catheri."

Ryia nodded her head, but said nothing. Very much like a cat, she would wait and watch before approaching anyone new. However, once trust was established, her familiarity could border on the inappropriate.

"Will, this is Ryia, Steph's newest recruit and priestess."

Will's eyebrows rose and he stepped forward; his hand held out toward her. "A pleasure to meet you." His grin grew wider when Ryia transferred the dagger from her right hand to her left so she could shake his hand. "Not the trusting sort are you?"

She shook her head, never removing her eyes from him.

"He's one of the good guys," Henton offered.

Henton watched her meet his eyes before returning her attention to Will. "I've heard all the stories Douglas told," she said in Pandar.

"Keep to Cothish," Henton reminded Ryia automatically.

Will grinned. "In my defense, Douglas lies." He moved his hand through his nicely trimmed hair. "I'm really a nice guy."

Douglas shook his head and went back to pulling things from his trunk. Over his shoulder he said, "Don't try to woo Ryia, Will. The four of us will protect her."

"Hey," Will said, turning his attention to Douglas, both hands raised. "I'm guessing you and Henton have been training her, so I'm not going to take any chances there."

"As has Steph," Ryia added with a grin.

Will smiled back at her. "And definitely not where Steph is involved. Plus, I'm a married man. I'm not looking to woo any other women at this point."

"What?" Henton blurted out before he could stop himself. "Sara?"

Will turned back to him. "Yup, about a month after you left."

"Was it by choice?" Douglas asked, his attention back on Will.

"Yes," the hurt in Will's voice sounded genuine to Henton, but he knew how well Will could play any role he wanted. His ability to switch parts in the blink of an eye amazed anyone who witnessed it. "Sara didn't become pregnant for another month after that."

Henton chuckled. "Wow, you've been busy."

"Are you sure she's the one pregnant and not you?" Douglas asked.

Will turned quickly. "I got left behind," he said with his hands on his hips. "Being High Priest is not easy work. I'm dealing with more every day than the two of you likely dealt with in any given month on the road. I'm not able to go running across the country to keep in shape. I'm stuck behind a desk, so yeah, I've put on a little weight, but I'm working from dawn to dusk every day."

"Hey," Douglas said, raising his hands in surrender. "I'm not saying you haven't been working hard, I'm just giving you crap for getting fat, married, and becoming a father. The last I'm sure you probably already are, but the first two, those surprised me."

"I'm not anyone's dad. Not that I'm aware of."

"Is Sara coming up to join us as well?" Henton asked, wanting to change the subject to something hopefully less hostile.

Will shook his head. "Not until she hears the all clear from me. She could tell Steph wasn't too keen on her the last time they were together and now with us married...she figured she'd draw less attention to herself if she stayed away."

"A little bit of advice," Henton said, coming closer to the man he had practically raised in the marines, "you'll draw more attention to Sara by hiding her away than having her here in plain sight. And Steph's issue with Sara was more due to what the Senzar mage had done to her, than with Sara."

"Steph okay? No lasting issues?"

Henton nodded his head. "She's doing well, a little more protective than she had been, but...," he said, wanting to steer the subject again. While Will's personal life was interesting, he needed to get a concise report on their current situation in the kingdom. "Between us, it seems there are others who feel His Majesty is getting a little erratic. Sir Walter practically asked us to tiptoe around Josh. Is there a problem we need to be aware of? If other people are trying to filter things for Josh, then even more people are seeing issues."

Will shook his head. "No. Actually, Josh has been doing a great job and the people are generally happy with him. I think this is likely just about him being angry with the lot of you, and honestly, I can't blame him. Your activities have caused trouble. Her mother was one thing, but taking out the last of the royal family in Kynto is a bit too much revenge. It's made a political mess."

"What are you talking about?"

Will gave him a questioning glance. "You're the ones that killed that bastard, good old King Willard."

Henton shook his head. "Not us."

Will raised his eyebrows. "You sure? When we...how much can I say?" He asked, glancing once toward Ryia.

"She's aware of everything," Henton said.

"Even the old guy?" Will demanded.

"I know about Kas," Ryia responded. "I'm in on all the secrets."

Will turned toward her. "Not all the secrets, I am sure. Steph doesn't share all her secrets with anyone. I've been there from the beginning, or near enough, and she won't tell me half the things she tells Henton. I'm her bloody High Priest, and still, she leaves out important details." Will glanced back to Henton, "Heck, I'm sure there are things even you don't know."

"Things even Kas doesn't know," Douglas offered. "But I don't see a problem with that. Not everyone needs to know every thought in someone else's head."

"Very true," Stephenie said, coming in through the open door.

Henton watched as Ryia grinned at Stephenie. The girl had known she was coming; it was a simple fact of being a mage. Ryia had an awareness of people and movement that someone without power would never feel. His initial thought was to chastise the girl for not giving him a sign, but he knew that despite how much of a mentor he was when it came to combat, Ryia followed Stephenie first and foremost. For a brief moment, he felt a little sadness about that, but put it from his mind as he turned fully to Stephenie. "How are you doing," he asked, knowing from the tension in her face that her discussion with her brother had gone about as well as he suspected it would go.

"They think we killed my Uncle. The man was a tyrant and deserved to die, but I hate that they automatically thought we were responsible." She sighed, "I'm sure stealing back all the gold they took from us didn't help him, but we didn't directly kill him." She shook her head and scratched at her scalp. "One of the abused nobles or one of his merc generals was likely responsible."

"Will was just telling us there's a lot of political mess," Henton said.

"Only repeating what's been said," Will commented with raised hands. "And personally, it eliminates Kynto as a threat to Cothel, so not all bad."

Stephenie shook her head at Will. "It makes their neighbors nervous. There will be power struggles in Kynto. A country that messed up will have bloodshed and that could spill over into other nations." Stephenie pulled a chair away from the wall and sat down. "How are things going with you?"

"He's married," Douglas said from across the room. "And has a kid on the way."

Stephenie raised her eyebrows. "Really, that was fast."

"Sara is a good woman. A Lady in fact," Will demanded.

"I never said she wasn't," Stephenie retorted.

Henton cleared his throat. There were still too many details that needed to be discussed before delving into everyone's personal life, but before he could speak, Stephenie did.

"Josh seems to think you've been doing a good job as High Priest. What changed?"

Will smiled and grabbed a chair of his own from the wall and pulled it into the middle of the room to sit across from Stephenie. "You know me. I simply brought him around to seeing me as indispensable. Heck, we both had a bit of mutual complaining to do about you lot. I think that helped him see I wasn't just some useless bit of baggage." Will glanced around to meet everyone's eyes. "I told him what he needed to hear me say and with Rebecca on my side... she's helped with a number of administrative things." He leaned back, trying to appear relaxed, "We're making great progress and have sixteen empowered priests now, with the addition of Ryia," he added, nodding his head in her direction. "However, we need some more training. Rebecca and Sara both."

"Yes, I know. The good thing is, I have practiced a bit with Ryia and she's come a long way in the last couple of months." Stephenie glanced to her left, which Henton assumed to be where Kas was hovering. She continued slowly, "There are a couple of people approaching the tower from the Great Hall." A moment later she nodded her head. "Looks like people bringing a couple of arm loads of clothing.

Henton lifted a set of folded clothing he had pulled from his trunk. "I have what I wore to get knighted. I assume that should be sufficient?"

Will frowned. "It's a bit frumpy, if you want to know the truth. But with the time you have available, it will be the best you'll get."

Will crossed his leg and slouched down further in the chair. "You really need to let me do some shopping for you and Douglas. I've got a tailor on retainer and he's making most of the new tunics for Catheri's priests. He made this," Will said, using his hands to highlight the bulk of material he was wearing.

Henton had no intention of dressing like Will and he knew Douglas would not waste his money on such displays. "I thank you for the offer, but I think I will find a more traditional tailor...should I have to start attending more formal functions. Otherwise, I'd rather people think of me as a simple guard."

With the sounds of feet moving up the wide stone stairs of the lower tower, everyone turned and looked out the open doorway. When a servant carrying an armload of dresses passed the door, she had to take a step back after she realized where everyone was located.

"Your Highness," she said, trying to curtsy with her burden. The man behind her gave a clumsy bow. The woman kept her gaze on the floor as she spoke. "I was instructed to bring you a number of dresses and gowns that Her Majesty and others have provided for your use. May I enter?"

Stephenie rose from her chair. "Yes, please, come in."

The woman looked up as she made her way into the room and Henton could see the slight tremble in her limbs. She obviously noted the mixed crowd of men with Stephenie and Ryia and did a poor job of containing her surprise and disapproval. Her glance at Will, who had remained seated, told volumes. Even though the woman was young, the cultural acceptance that Ladies had to always be sequestered away from men was very strong.

"Ma'am, where do you want me to display these garments for you?"

"Well, the tub is on this floor and I need to bathe before dressing," Stephenie said, the ever slightest hint of a growl in her voice. Henton doubted the woman would have heard what he could so easily detect as the change in Stephenie's tone.

The woman nodded her head and took further note of the lack of dividing rooms outside the small bathing chamber.

Henton stepped away from his bed. "Here, place the garments on the bed and we can sort out the details. Ryia will be able to assist Her

Highness with dressing while the rest of us check the supplies in the cellars."

The woman nodded her head again and quickly complied. Whether she believed him or not, the statement offered her enough absolution of responsibility that she felt safe in leaving the women in a room filled with men.

The man with her set down the fine pants and shirts next to the dresses. He then set down a large cotton bag and removed one of a number of smaller pouches. Opening the pouch to demonstrate they contained shoes, he set the one pair on the bed and left the others in the larger bag.

"Thank you," Henton said, escorting the two servants to the door and shutting it behind them.

"I already started filling the tub," Ryia said once they were gone. "I was about to take a bath when Will interrupted. It would be the first time I'd get to use a tub and I really want the first bath."

"I don't know about that," Stephenie said with a grin. "You want me to bathe after someone who skipped at least half the streams and ponds we had a chance to get washed up in? I doubt the water will be fit to touch after you're done."

"Rank and privilege," Will said from where he slouched. "As your High Priest, we'll need to go over some basic teachings. I suspect Steph has neglected most of them, if she even knows what I teach. But, if nothing else, it is important to understand rank and privilege. Which in this case, Steph has."

Henton could see Ryia tense. Not as used to Will's sometimes-caustic humor, Ryia obviously took his statement seriously. However, the more he watched Will, the more Henton wondered if his former corporal had been serious in that statement.

Stephenie did not bother glancing in Will's direction, but kept her focus on the girl. "In front of Henton," Ryia said suddenly. "Under William's chair," she said a moment later. Henton watched as the girl's brow narrowed. "Just in front of the door?"

Familiar with the challenges Stephenie would create, Henton guessed she had tested Ryia's ability to sense places where Stephenie had concentrated energy. When Stephenie nodded, he turned back to his bed and the clothing stacked on it. It would be a while before he would see the tub.

"All right, you bathe first, but only because you noticed the third field."

Henton watched the smile spread across Ryia's face as she went to the trunk in front of what had been Will's bed and tossed her pack inside. She was on her way to the bed with the dresses when Stephenie cleared her throat.

"Ryia, you can't stay here."

"What? Why would you say that?"

Stephenie stepped closer. "People would talk if you stayed here with two men. I'm trying to look out for you. To protect your reputation. You had to sense what those two who brought the clothing were radiating. The disapproval was nauseating." Stephenie crossed the room and put her hand on the girl's shoulder. "I'd like to have you in the tower, but I'm a bit particular about my room and I don't want people on the floor above or below me." She pursed her lips and looked off into the distance.

"You could stay in the temple complex," Will offered. "We have several people there already and as a priestess of Catheri, it would almost be expected."

Ryia cursed in what Henton assumed was her native tongue, and then she resumed her complaints, this time in Pandar. "What was the bloody point in bringing me here if you just want to toss me away? I'd rather never have come!"

"Ryia," Stephenie said, squeezing the girl's shoulder to keep her in place. "I am not throwing you away. I just want to make sure you have a chance to move about society without people shunning you. If you ever want to make a good match, you can't have people thinking the worst of you."

"I don't care what people say," Ryia protested. "I don't want a husband. No one would want me anyway. I'm already spoiled goods. So what does it matter that people think I give myself to Henton and Douglas every night?"

Stephenie squeezed harder, drawing Ryia's attention to her face. "You are not spoiled goods. There is nothing wrong with you and don't let anyone tell you differently." Stephenie released Ryia's shoulder and shook her head. "It's not for me to decide. Your staying here affects Henton and Douglas as well."

Douglas responded immediately, "Let her stay. I don't have a problem if she doesn't."

Henton watched as everyone turned toward him. Ryia's expression was nearly one of pleading. Stephenie's held a trace of sympathy, but there was no judgment. Personally, he agreed with Stephenie, the girl would not benefit from living in a room with two men. If she ever changed her mind about finding a husband, it would ruin her chance at finding anyone respectable. *However, her being a witch would also impact that.*

He held his jaw firm. Aside from the impact to Ryia's future, he also valued his own privacy. While living with a group of men in barracks or on a ship was one thing, he would not be able to be as relaxed with his behavior in mixed company.

"Please, Henton, I don't want to live with strangers. Plus, we've slept in the same tent for months. How is this different?"

Knowing he would regret it, he slowly nodded his head. Although he wanted to be the hard sergeant he had been in the marines, he was no longer that man. Stephenie had changed him for better or worse. Plus, he liked the girl and even though it was likely the wrong decision, he did not want to see her angry with him over something such as this. "You can stay, but I think we will need to get some additional walls put up in here. I think we are important enough that we can all get private rooms created on this floor. There's plenty of space."

Stephenie smiled at him and then nodded her head. "I'll find some money to get the work done."

Will rose and patted Stephenie's shoulder. "I've got workers I trust. I'll have them here first thing in the morning. Being High Priest of the King's second favorite god is a good position to be in."

# Chapter 4

Stephenie entered the Great Hall beside Islet; Henton, Ryia, and Douglas trailed just behind them. The calling of their names by the footman disappeared into the background and she hardly even knew it occurred. She felt Ryia's and Douglas' tension and wished they would settle their fears. *All eyes are on me, not you,* she thought silently. The room was already filled with nobles and ranking gentry, no one wanted to miss the entrance of the 'honored guests' and despite trying to arrive early, it appeared Islet, and Stephenie and her entourage, were practically the last to enter the hall.

For a fleeting moment she desperately missed Kas' presence. However, while they took the risk on their arrival, too many people in this room would likely be able to sense him and overtime that would lead to questions. *He would have laughed at that hat,* she thought as she walked past a woman whose head cover must have weighed at least ten pounds.

The five of them passed along the outside of three long rows of tables that stretched the length of the room. As they moved toward the head table, she continued to smile and nod to the people that rose and bowed to Islet and herself.

She automatically pushed away the heat that radiated from the large fireplaces that lined the walls and blazed with fires on this warm evening. The richly decorated tables were covered with silver candle stands and gilded plates that spoke of power and influence. An army of servants stood ready every few feet along the walls with tailored uniforms and pitchers of wine. Ryia's outfit, while beautiful by normal standards, actually looked a little worn in comparison to the servants. *Oh Kas, I understand the need to prove he has wealth, is capable, and is in control, but this lavish show is a waste of money.*

Two well-dressed stewards approached Stephenie and Islet. When they were within ten-feet, they stopped and bowed deeply. "Your Majesty. Your Highness, please allow me to escort you the rest of the way to the high table. Relan will kindly escort your companions to their seats."

Stephenie nodded to the steward who had spoken and she caught Henton's eye with a glance. She knew he would keep the others safe in this room filled with potential threats, even if this battlefield remained unfamiliar to all of them.

Glancing toward the far end of the hall, she noted Joshua and Rebecca sitting at the center of the long table. This time the table did not rest on the dais, but just in front of it. The high table crossed the three long rows of tables and those sitting close would be both blessed and cursed with the proximity to their King.

The steward escorted Islet to Joshua's right and then delivered Stephenie to an empty seat between Rebecca and Will, with Sara on Will's left. Stephenie approved of the placement; Islet had Duke Yaslin Forest on her right and the evening would have grown very long if Stephenie had to maintain conversation with that man. Although he had supported her father, she held no respect for the Duke.

Baron Arnold Turning sat at the far left end of the high table. He smiled at her with a twinkle in his eye. While not much older than her brother, the man ran his barony well and his people seemed to like him. However, she worried those in court might consider his expression too jovial most of the time and therefore abuse his honesty. Following the Baron's quick glance down the long table in front of his position, Stephenie noted his daughter several seats from him. Isabel's head craned around a tall man Stephenie did not recognize. With the girl's hand on the man's arm, Stephenie guessed he was the suitor Isabel had intended to marry.

Trying to ignore the room full of emotions as well as the stares, she carefully took her seat. Pulling her freshly washed hair to the side, she managed to keep the loose strands from catching on the back of the tall chair. She noted the tension in the room and reluctantly admitted Henton and Kas had been correct, *a sword strapped to my waist would not have gone over well.*

As she sat, Joshua stood, causing a scurrying of commotion in the hall as everyone scrambled to his or her feet. She thought at least one person let slip a curse near the far end of the hall, presumably as a drink spilled on the white tablecloth.

"Sisters," Joshua said, leaning around Rebecca to take her hand for a moment; his other already held Islet's. Stephenie smiled at him. Had the war never occurred and had they been alone, she would have teased him for all the layers of embroidered fabric and furs that hung from his shoulders. Their father, at least to her knowledge, had never dressed in anything as flamboyant as Joshua's current outfit. She noted the gold and jewel encrusted crowns on both his and Rebecca's head. She realized they resembled the epitome of what tradition said a king and queen must look like. *Foolish, would be my description.*

Islet caught her eye and the smile of reassurance from her older sister warmed her heart. Islet had chosen a simple dress, though the calmness about her almost made her more regal than Joshua. *Of course, that could be due to the fact that she is a disposed queen and no longer has the concerns of a ruling monarch.*

Joshua released their hands and looked about the room. "Please sit," he said and when everyone had, he continued. "Ladies. Lords. Honored guests," his strong voice carrying through the hall. "We are here tonight to honor my sisters. It has been many long years since Islet graced Antar and Cothel with her presence. As Queen of Ipith, her responsibilities were great and she was honored by her new people for her deeds and her love of their King.

"She, with her husband, King Fraden Greene, was the first to oppose those heathen Senzar. Those evil, Elrin-worshiping demons. Those beasts that landed their first ships in Esland and killed our dear sister Kara. Islet and her husband bought the rest of us enough time to mobilize and bring the wrath of the gods to those demon worshipers. Unfortunately, as reward for her love of her sister, the Senzar attacked Ipith in secret and a team of demons destroyed the royal family, killing her husband and then taking Islet hostage to use as leverage against Cothel and my late father. However, their plan failed. Though we suffered a great many losses and treachery from within," he almost snarled the last, "Catheri, the goddess who brings the cold hand of justice, returned to the world to destroy these demons and bring a mountain peak down on their heads."

Stephenie glanced from her brother to the numerous people who filled the hall. While half the faces watched him, the others still looked at her. Keeping her countenance as expressionless as possible, Stephenie returned her focus to her brother.

"And through Catheri's influence, we drove those heathens back to the west by destroying their leadership." Joshua paused a moment and looked around the room. "Then, when I had resolved myself to having just one sister left to me, Catheri showed us her graces once again. And through her insight, we learned of Islet's fate and my dear sister, Stephenie, put herself in danger once more, crossing uncounted lands to rescue my other dear sister." Joshua turned toward Islet and held out his hands to her, bringing her to her feet. "So, tonight, we are here to honor, Islet, Queen of Ipith, Princess of Cothel, and my dear sister."

Stephenie sat quietly as the hall erupted in applause. *If Josh uses the term 'dear sister' once more, I will throw my wine at him.* She knew part of her irritation stemmed from Joshua's promotion of Catheri, but he had also never downplayed her role quite so much. She really did not want the attention, but to give all the credit to an imaginary god, further dampened her mood for the festivities of the evening.

"You look wonderful," Rebecca said quietly to Stephenie as Joshua and Islet resumed their seats. "You have a real grace and beauty about you. I wish my hair would fall as nicely as yours."

Stephenie smiled at Rebecca and tightened her controls on her emotions. She did not know if Rebecca's comment was provoked by something Rebecca felt from her or just the fact that Rebecca also knew the truth that the gods were not what everyone believed them to be and therefore held some empathy for her. "Thank you," Stephenie said, as she lifted a section of her red hair so she could look at it. She allowed the wavy hair to slip through her fingers and fall back over her shoulder. *That is another secret,* she silently remarked, knowing she inherited it from the man who raped her mother. A man her mother claimed to be Elrin, the demon god himself. A man that was not the King. *But the King was my father,* she swore silently. *He raised me and loved me, even knowing what I was.*

Stephenie inhaled and slowly released her breath. His loss left an emptiness in her, but she had known the truth of her lineage long enough that it did not raise her panic anymore. She believed that only Kas, Islet, Henton, Douglas, and Ryia knew this secret, *but if I could figure it out, what about others?*

"You okay," Will asked from her left, drawing her attention and a forced smile.

"Always," she lied easily. "Hello Sara," Stephenie said, looking around Will. "Congratulations on all accounts."

Lady Sara bowed her head to Stephenie. "Thank you, Your Highness."

Stephenie could feel Sara's discomfort. The woman was four-years older than herself, and although the priestess should have learned to contain her emotions, Stephenie knew she terrified the woman. *Not the least of which because she had just crawled out of Will's bed before we were introduced.* Stephenie pushed down the memories of the odor of the woman on Will. She had never desired Will in that fashion, but even after all the months that had passed, she still felt possessive of her friend.

Forcing herself to feel pleased for Will, she smiled at Sara. "If you are up to it, tomorrow we can resume our training."

Sara smiled and nodded her head. "Of course, Prophet."

Stephenie turned her attention back to the main hall. She knew Sara learned the truth about the gods by reading Will's mind while the two of them engaged in a physical relationship. A relationship that had somehow triggered the strong possessive response that Stephenie still did not understand or want. *I won't chastise her now, but she also knows not to call me that.* Stephenie hoped the comment was Sara trying to play to what people would expect a priestess of Catheri should do and not as a means to antagonize her, but it was hard to tell.

Picking up a crystal glass, Stephenie drank deeply and allowed the dry wine to slide down her throat. She repressed a shudder caused from the shock of the alcohol hitting her system. The moment she set the glass down, a servant stepped forward and refilled what she had consumed.

Another servant came up on her other side and placed a bowl of stew in front of Rebecca. A moment later, a porcelain bowl of the rich stew slid before her. *Food. That is something I can deal with.* She picked up the silver spoon from the table and started to eat.

She finished half the bowl before she even realized how much she had eaten. Slowing her pace, she set the spoon on the edge of the bowl and straightened her back. People were still watching her, some more covertly than others, but she was on display and had to behave as expected.

Before she could pick up the spoon again, the bowl was removed and a silver plate covered with various meats and a glazed bird appeared in its place. The food smelled delicious and she could tell it was all very juicy and well cooked. A glance into the hall showed similar, if not quite as richly prepared, plates and bowls were making their way to and from the tables.

"Your Majesty," said a man sitting at the center row of tables. He sat only two seats away from the high table and his voice drew everyone's attention. Stephenie recognized the older man, but did not remember his name. "If I may inquire, my son, Nalin," the man nodded his head to indicate a man in his early twenties two seats further away, "is interested in when you planned to announce your next tourney. We were rebuilding one of Felis' temples in our holdings during your last one and could not attend."

"Baron Vitav, a tourney would be a great idea." Joshua smiled at the man. "My father always had one late in the summer and with Islet's return, I cannot think of a better reason to have one."

The Baron smiled and glanced at Stephenie. "Would Her Highness, Princess Stephenie, also participate? I have heard her sword work is legendary."

Stephenie grinned. Her sword work had suffered since her father had left for the war, now few remained who were willing to practice with her. *Not since everyone learned what I am.*

"I am afraid not," Joshua said. "As Prophet of Catheri, she would have an unfair advantage over everyone else. However, I might be inclined to pick up a sword and join the fun," he added with a grin.

"Not to win the prize, but just for entertainment. I'm fairly handy with a blade myself and taught Steph most of what she knows."

Stephenie's lips tightened despite her effort to remain expressionless. She had long ago exceeded Joshua's teaching and before the war, the weapons masters would teach her privately.

"Of course, Your Majesty. Tales of your prowess are without rival. I think you won your father's tourney three years in a row, right before you turned nineteen. Beat a number of proud knights at their own game."

Stephenie watched the grin spread even further on Joshua's face. "Indeed. I had to stop competing to give others a chance."

*More exaggerations.* Stephenie remembered Joshua's rather heated argument with their father, even though she had only been fourteen at the time. It had been a lesson her father had tried to instill in her: *appearance is often more important than substance when leading others—but never compromise substance.* The real reason Joshua had to stop was due to rumors that his winning had more to do with people throwing the competition to gain favor than from his skill. True or not, Joshua's tourney days ended.

Looking back to her food, Stephenie picked at the meat, eating the select bits, but she avoided overfilling herself. Based on the pace of the feast, she needed to save room for several more courses. The wine, she drank slowly; however, because her glass always remained full, she could not remember if this counted as the start of the third glass or not. By the end of the fourth course of food—seasoned with too much salt—she suspected she had consumed the better part of a bottle of the dry wine. Leaning back, she called over a servant and requested a glass of water. When the servant looked up, Stephenie suddenly realized a man stood in front of the high table.

Cursing the fog in her head, it took her a moment to sense the man's repressed agitation. Now regretting leaving her weapons in her room, she fumbled for the knife beside her plate before lifting her gaze to meet the man's right eye; his left was lost to a wound that scared his face. Her mind cleared as energy ran through her body; she noted the man's clothing was cut from quality cloth, but it did not hang correctly from his frame, as if he had shrunk five inches since the tailor had sewn it together.

She opened her mind further, examining the fields that surrounded the man, looking for any higher concentrations of potential energy that would indicate a metal weapon hidden on his person. The silver buttons of his overcoat stood out in her mind's eye, as did the buckle that cinched tight the excess fabric around her waist. However, she sensed no weapon, even when using her powers to look through his body to the fields behind him.

"Your Highness," the man said, a repressed curse buried in his tone. He bowed stiffly, not ever completely removing his eye from hers. "I am Roalen, son of Martin," he said almost as a shout, his Kyntian heritage strong in both his face and his consonants. "Your treachery and murder of King Willard has cost me my wife and son!"

He spit at her, but her instincts stopped the wet glob in midair. It hung there a moment before she pushed it back to the other side of the table and let it fall to the floor. Joshua's shouts for the guards rang through the hall. Stephenie raised her hand and through her presence, countermanded his order simply by standing.

The entire room fell silent and the man before her trembled. She stood silent for a moment as the energy coursing through her body cleared away the last effects of the alcohol. The tension in the room rose with every beat of her heart. The guard that had come halfway down the long aisle hesitated, caught between fear of failing his King's order and that of what she could do.

Stephenie turned her attention back to the scared man before her. "I am sorry for your loss," she said softly, although her voice carried through the hall. "However, I did not kill Willard. I did not even know he was dead until earlier today." She glanced about the room and back to the man before her. "My Uncle was a bastard. He treated his people with contempt. I have seen it first hand and knew the truth of it through the numerous stories my father told me over the years. However, while I disagreed with Willard's methods, I cannot, and could not, justify taking personal action against him for what he was doing in his own country."

"You—You killed your mother," Roalen said, his voice initially breaking, but grew stronger. "You were seen there. Why should I believe you did not kill her brother as well?"

Stephenie stood straighter and looked passed Roalen to the crowd that watched her. Even the young people in the room had grown silent. Turning her attention back to her accuser, she continued without expression. "The woman who birthed me, my sisters, and my brother, was a traitor to Cothel and her life was declared forfeit. My Uncle, while he likely played a part in her treachery, did not take personal action that I know of. I will not reiterate my Mother's crimes beyond the death of my father, thousands of citizens of my country, and the capture and imprisonment of my brother. Yes, I took her life because even in exile, she continued to harass my family and friends, threatening their lives and the safety of Cothel." The volume of her voice had grown and now reverberated through the hall. "She deserved a thousand deaths to pay for what she did. Instead, I simply took her head in what I would call a great act of restraint on my part. I will not allow harm to come to my friends or family. Ever." The word hung in the air for several moments.

She glanced around the room again, some of the people showed shock, others grim satisfaction, possibly from the fact that someone dared to stand up to her. Taking a breath to settle the heat she felt from all the energy burning within her, she gradually sensed the rage fuming from Joshua. At whom he felt the anger, she could not say. To the man, she continued. "You are misguided, Roalen. Although, I can see why people might have thought it was my hand that killed Willard, it was not. Since I have no desire to see you lashed for your insult, leave this castle and the city of Antar and do not return."

The guards finally decided to move forward and quickly reached Roalen's side. They looked between her and Joshua. She hoped her brother would not override her commandment. She lacked the strength to fight with him yet again and so she simply sat down. When the guards did not throw the man to the ground, she suspected Joshua chose not to show any infighting. Instead, she watched as they escorted him away.

*Kas, I really wish you were here,* she thought.

Servants rushed the next course to a hushed crowd as though no disturbance had occurred. The food looked succulent, but Stephenie only picked at it before the plate was removed. Those in the room now tried very hard not to look at her. The general discomfort left the hall muted and distant.

"Your Highness," someone said from behind her and Stephenie immediately reached out with her mind to find Baron Arnold Turning, his daughter Isabel, and the tall man Isabel sat with standing behind her. Stephenie turned and rose from her seat, the smile on the girl's face finding its way to Stephenie's lips as well. "Isabel, you are looking beautiful. You appear to have grown in the last six months."

The three of them bowed and curtsied to her. "You are quite generous, Your Highness," Arnold said. "It is you who are radiant. Your hair is beautiful. It is hard to believe you ever fit into Isabel's dress last year."

Stephenie smiled, but did not want to recall the pain she endured during that period.

Isabel took advantage of the silence. "May I present my husband, Camris?"

Stephenie looked at the nervous man, who once again bowed to her. "Your Highness, it is my pleasure to meet you."

"He took my name and so based on your great grandfather's decree, we have secured a line for our barony."

"Indeed they have," Joshua said, injecting himself into the conversation from where he sat. "They were married just a month ago here in Felis' temple and have been enjoying themselves at court."

Stephenie glanced to her brother and smiled with relief to see his mood held no hostility at her for the outburst, *at least for the moment.* Turning back to the couple, she said, "I am very happy for you both. Camris, you look like a strong man and a good match for Isabel." Stephenie waited, wanting to hear Kas complain that he was two heads too tall for the still rather short Isabel, but the comment would have to wait until later.

Lowering her voice to just a whisper, Stephenie leaned closer to the man who stood more than a head taller than herself and her brother. "Just remember, Isabel is a good friend of mine and I will check in with her to make sure she is always happy. Not that I think you would treat her wrong, but always treat her right."

"Of course, Ma'am," Camris barely choked out.

Stephenie clasped his hand and nodded her head. "I truly wish you both the very best. If you should ever need anything, let me know."

"Thank you, Ma'am," Arnold said with a smile. "You will always have my sword at your call. You freed me so that I could come home to my daughter and for that, you have my life."

"All this grim talk," Joshua said, and then raised his voice. "We need more wine and less talk of the war and executions. Islet has returned home! Where are the minstrels?" He demanded. "We need music to improve the mood!"

Stephenie accepted a kiss on the hand from Arnold. The Baron, observing people coming down the aisles between the tables, ushered his daughter and son-in-law away so that Stephenie could turn around to face the next group of petitioners.

"You are popular tonight," Will said just loud enough for her to hear.

"Prophet, may we provide you with a tribute?"

Stephenie nodded her head and motioned for the group of kneeling people to rise and approach. She knew the prospect for the rest of the night did not look any better than the first half had.

# Chapter 5

The next morning Stephenie descended the steps of her tower well before the sun reached the horizon. She continued past the second floor and spiraled down past the ground floor, finally stopping at the lowest cellar, which stretched out under her Great Hall. Passages and tunnels existed below the second cellar; ancient paths that led to the long forgotten city of Arkani where Kas had lived. However, very few knew anything about the lost city. Kas had already checked to ensure those passages remained secured and undisturbed even before Stephenie had joined the others in the tower the previous day.

Stephenie reached out and touched the cold stone of the wall in front of her. She had played many games with Joshua in these old cellars, exploring the more recent secret passages that led between the castle buildings. She swallowed down the building tears and centered her thoughts. "The past is but a fond memory, dream instead of the future," she spoke in a voice that carried through the pitch-black passage and the rooms beyond. Without even a hint of light, even her eyes that could see in near-darkness, could see nothing. Ignoring her sight, she concentrated instead on the energy potentials all around her. The passage and numerous rooms that branched off to the sides came alive in her mind's eye. The stone was cold, limiting some of its energy, but it held far more potential than the stale air that slowly drifted over the cedar flooring. She pursed her lips and blew so she could watch her warm breath cause chaos down the hall as energy currents swirled and spread out, slowly equalizing with the surrounding air and stone.

"Do you think they will be punctual?" Kas asked as he gradually luminesced, bringing a pale blue-green glow to the hall.

Stephenie shrugged. She knew Kas felt the more substantial energy currents, but he would not have felt the slight changes from her breath. Stepping forward, she continued to the third room on the left. "After last night, I'm not sure I care. I was far happier on the road worrying about running out of money while sleeping in a tent that leaked rain on my head."

Kas moved past Stephenie, drifting further into the room. A vague outline of his feet appeared as he stepped on the raised flooring only to disappear when he lifted them. Stephenie grinned inwardly and suspected he did that more on purpose than otherwise.

"Do you think we've really damaged the prospects for finding powerful mages in this part of the world?" She asked, rekindling one of their long running debates. "The priests have been killing anyone who they found with significant ability for hundreds of years. What if only the Senzar and those beyond the Rim Mountains have significant skill?" She rolled her shoulders as she followed Kas across the floor. "We've killed a number of Senzar that had a lot of power and age, but we've not seen anyone born around Tet with that strength. Ryia..." She let her voice trail off; they both knew the girl's limitations.

"I assume you mean aside from your illustrious self, correct?"

She frowned at him. "You know what I mean."

Kas nodded his head as he turned to face her. "You are assuming your sire, this red-haired man with dead eyes, is not a native of your lands."

"It would make sense that he's not." She gathered her hair and pulled it tight before letting it fall loose again. She remembered Joshua always liking her hair long and flowing, but now their relationship felt cold and distant. "I killed people claiming to be sixth and seventh generation. But generations of what? Generations from whom? Orlan said that those two we killed were not related."

"At least as far as Orlan knew," Kas snapped. "The man may not have been a mage, but the danger he presented remained significant."

Kas moved closer, not bothering to move his legs. "You are indeed special. I have mentioned this to you before. To me you are an enigma. The speed of your learning; your ability to observe what for myself is theoretical in nature. These aspects are highly unexpected. Those traits would garner you an honored and coveted seat in the class of any master of my time." He raised a finger, "However, all of that pales to insignificance in the face of your capacity to draw energy through your body. You have performed feats that would have burned out the minds of every mage I have ever read of or of whom I have heard stories."

"Which means I need to find my sire. I have to figure this out. Magic is hereditary. Just like my red hair. As you've said before, my capacity means my sire had to be very powerful."

Kas shrugged, his shoulders becoming fully opaque. With a glance around, he blinked out of sight and a moment later sat cross-legged on the floor. "If you recall, my repeated statements have been warnings to tread this path of yours carefully. The man raped your mother and frightened her so badly that she obsessed over her assumed curse to the point that she killed her favorite daughter."

"Regina was a bitch, just like mother." Stephenie sighed and joined Kas on the floor. "But she didn't deserve to be sacrificed." She turned her face to Kas and met his eyes. "We need to recreate a body for you. I've learned a lot, but I can't transform matter from one thing into another. Not yet. And none of the books we have access to give us any hint at the secret. So we have to find the most powerful person we know of, which right now appears to be the bastard who raped my mother and told her not to kill me."

"However, Stephenie, what reason did he hold for doing so?" Kas shook his head. "I would rather remain as I am; frustrated in my lack of being able to touch you, than have you succumb to a man such as that."

She hated to agree with Kas. Those very concerns had been running through her head ever since she got the first inkling that finding her father might be possible. Her mother's failed attempt to shock her into inaction had instead given her the first set of clues to finding his identity. *A red-haired man who claimed to be a messenger from the north with a trade agreement.* "I just hope my father's logs from nineteen years ago were not destroyed."

Stephenie watched Kas and easily picked up his distress over her continued desire to pursue this avenue. Of everyone she knew, she could read his emotions the easiest. She suspected that ability was a result of the mental bonds they shared as their only real form of intimacy.

*Not to change the subject,* Kas said, *but aside from your search for the red-haired man, do not forget your promise to help destroy your people's use of the augmentation devices. My people died in that fight, now your people call them holy symbols and worship the death of beings in another world.*

*They are not my people,* Stephenie shot back. *Not all of them, at least. And most do not know the truth, so it is a stretch so say they worship the death of these beings. They are unwitting killers.*

*They are bleeding the life from the beings by consuming energy through the devices and the traps. There are some, like Rebecca, who know the truth.*

Stephenie understood Kas' anger. She wanted to say she had not forgotten her promise, but she knew she had not actively worked on trying to destroy the devices in months. The one device in her possession she left behind when they went to rescue Islet. The devices defend themselves aggressively and she had suffered more than one injury in her attempts, which meant the road was not the place to work on them. *Kas, I promise, I will continue to try and stop the deaths. I've just not been able to make any progress and, perhaps if I can figure out how to make a body for you, so that we can be together physically, the same knowledge would help in destroying a holy symbol.*

Kas nodded his head. *I know. And I should not pressure you so. Even without working on the devices, you are working to change the views and beliefs of people very set in their ways. If we stop the use, perhaps that is almost as good.* He looked toward the stairs beyond the stone walls of the room. *I think the others are coming,* he said as his form faded from visual sight, leaving Stephenie in total darkness once again. *I will go and rouse Ryia from her extended slumber.*

Stephenie said nothing as Kas floated up through the stone ceiling above them. She knew he did not want her to search out her sire and she wished there was another way. However, she could not see how they would figure out how to recreate a body for Kas or destroy the traps that fed the augmentation devices he despised without help. The ability to transform matter from one substance to another was something only a few people of Kas' time had mastered and those that had, appeared to guard the secret closely. When she freed Islet from the Senzar, she found some hints that perhaps some of the Senzar had significant skill and knowledge. However, she was not about to approach the enemy of her lands for that kind of help.

"I know you are down here," came Rebecca's voice from the hallway.

Stephenie closed her eyes and relaxed her mind and body. The reprimand hidden in Rebecca's tone was probably justified, and though she owed it to them to conduct this training, she really did not want to.

"Did she just disappear?" Came the more timid voice of Lady Sara.

Keeping her breathing slow, Stephenie continued to suppress her mental activity. She could tell the two women had come to the door of the room and even knew from the waves of energy radiating from their position that Rebecca held an oil lamp, but this knowledge remained passive. In hiding herself, she had to draw in all her active energy threads.

With a twitch of a grin, Stephenie sucked the energy from the flame, casting everyone into darkness. The involuntary shriek from Sara drew Stephenie from sitting on the floor into the air. In the dark, she bent the gravity around her and she flew halfway across the room before Rebecca found her voice.

"Stephenie, we are not your enemy!"

Touching down gently so that her boots made no sound on the aged wood, Stephenie watched the energy move around them. Rebecca drew power into herself much faster than Sara did, but the flow remained minimal in comparison to the Senzar or herself. "Since you were wise enough not to bring the augmentation devices, relight your lamp and come into the room."

It took a while, but after Rebecca lifted the lamp to the height of her face, a flame jumped to life inside the lamp. Stephenie knew the field Rebecca created lacked focus. Rebecca had heated the whole interior of the lamp and even raised the temperature of the copper housing. However, Stephenie could not chastise her. When she left to rescue Islet, she had only conducted a couple of limited sessions with the High Priest. *I just can't figure out what bothers me about her,* Stephenie admitted to herself.

"You are being a bit off-putting this morning," Rebecca said, her tone having grown even harsher than earlier. "Demanding last night that we attend you at first light and then you practically attacking us when we arrive on time."

Stephenie came closer and dropped to the floor to sit cross-legged a dozen feet in front of them. It pained her, but she nodded her head. "Sorry. I'm not quite in a good mood. I've been yelled at, accused of murder, accused of abandoning Cothel, spit at, and generally treated like it's my fault everyone kept coming over to me last night instead of Islet." Stephenie shook her head. "I've not even been home for a whole day yet. So, what fun will today bring?"

Rebecca sat down and Sara followed more slowly. "So you want to feel sorry for yourself and take it out on us?" Rebecca asked.

Stephenie bit her lower lip. "Okay. Yes, you are right. I am honestly sorry for being rude this morning. I should not take it out on you. You have obviously protected Will while I was gone. Thank you for getting Josh to lighten up on him."

Rebecca chuckled. "I hardly deserve credit there. Will did that on his own. I was actually defending you against the two of them most of the time."

Stephenie stared at the floor for a moment; she knew Will was good at ingratiating himself with just about anyone. Half the time she never really knew what he truly believed as his opinion could change with the breeze. "Thank you. I probably don't deserve the defending."

"You did bring your sister back and it was just the four of you that went...Sorry, but in case Will has not already told you, Sara is aware of Kas."

Stephenie shrugged. "That was not a secret I expected to remain hidden from Sara."

"Your...Steph...." Sara started, and then continued after a moment, "I really never intended to learn your secrets from Will. It's just hard to keep things separated when...."

"Don't worry about it." Stephenie hated getting apologies from people even more than giving them. "Let's work on magic. What have you worked out for yourselves?"

Rebecca cleared her throat. "Unfortunately, not much. I've not been able to switch any of my priests over to using their powers. Too many of the existing ones would suspect something was wrong. Our holy symbols behave in a very specific fashion. They respond to us and the teaching of their use was a burden shared by many. If I suddenly said we had no more parts to construct replacement symbols and we now had to use something else, I would lose the faith of Felis' followers."

"By using those augmentation devices, you are directly responsible for the slow death of a creature in another world."

"I know," Rebecca said, the hard tone of a queen and a high priest coming through clearly in her voice. "But it would do no good for me to be accused of being your puppet and for people to start wondering if you were ever cleansed of Elrin's evil. You want to go back to being threatened with a burning?"

Stephenie's own voice grew hard. "I am not saying throw caution to the wind, but we have to find a way to transition people."

"I've started by not burning people," Rebecca retorted. "And Will is able to take many of the new people on and bring them up with the stone holy symbols he's made. It works because of the legend he started about Catheri coming back through the bones of the world. Thanks in great part to your legendary destruction of a mountain peak."

"I'm sorry I'm late," Ryia said from the doorway, a lamp in her hand.

Sara spoke up, ignoring Ryia, "Will and I have had success in getting people to believe in Catheri's different approach to recruiting new priests. I just don't know a lot about using my natural abilities, so they are getting discouraged in not being able to do much with their skills."

"Ryia, please join us." Stephenie waited until Ryia crossed the room and stood next to her. Ryia quickly curtsied to Rebecca and then Sara. "Ryia is from Epish. She was with me when I rescued Islet and I've spent several months teaching her on our journey here. If she speaks in Pandar again, you have my permission to smack her. She's learning Cothish by being allowed to speak only it."

Ryia swore under her breath in what Stephenie had come to understand was Epish.

"Ryia, this is Queen Rebecca and Lady Sara."

"I met them last night."

Stephenie nodded her head. "However, while we are learning to use magic, there are no queens, ladies, princesses, or prophets. Just students and teachers." Stephenie watched as everyone's head nodded. "Good." Turning her attention back to Rebecca, she indicated the lamp next to the high Priest with her head. "Your focus was quite broad when you rekindled the lamp. You need to narrow your field and it will be easier for you to get the flame to take." Rebecca nodded her head without comment. "For now, I want to start with an exercise I have been using with Ryia." Stephenie generated a field that concentrated a pool of energy in the air right in front of Rebecca. It blazed in her mind's eye like a white-hot brand. "Tell me where the best source of energy is in the room."

She felt Ryia fidget beside her. To Ryia, this would be easy. Stephenie had graduated Ryia to a level of potential energy only twice that of the surrounding area. Her attempts to get the girl to notice anything less had so far failed and Kas suspected they had reached Ryia's level of sensitivity. However, Stephenie was not going to give up just yet.

"I don't know," Rebecca finally said. "The floor? You said stone has more...density."

Stephenie kept her eyes from rolling with a bit of effort. Trying to make it more obvious, she pulsed the energy field. A moment later Sara raised her voice to that of a squeak. "In front of us?"

"Yes. In front of Rebecca to be precise." Stephenie dropped the field. "Before I left the last time, I told you that you have the ability to draw energy into your body by forming an area of lower potential inside yourself. Just like water running downhill, you can channel sources of power from a higher potential to a lower potential by generating the proper fields."

"Which sounds great in theory," Rebecca said, "but how do we do it in practice?"

"May I?" Ryia asked.

Stephenie nodded her head to the sixteen-year old.

"When Steph first start teaching me—"

"Started teaching," Stephenie corrected automatically.

"All I knew was stupid spells and focuses and true stupid chants."

"Truly."

Ryia mumbled another curse not quite under her breath. "These limit our power. They make us weak. Steph," Ryia said with a nod of her head, "talked about fields. But I can't see them. Not like her."

"We cannot see them either," Rebecca said, moving to make herself a little more comfortable. "Can you really see the fields you keep talking about?"

Stephenie let her sight lose focus for a moment and concentrated on what her mind could sense. It was not so much a wash of color, but simply an understanding of the world. "Yes. I wish I could show you, but I don't know why I can see these and most others cannot."

"You're The Prophet," Ryia joked.

Stephenie hit the back of her head with a burst of gravity that would have been the equivalent of a light slap. Her attack had been so fast that Ryia's natural defenses did not have time to respond. Improving both her and Ryia's speed at forming fields remained a priority. The truly powerful mages she had faced were many times faster and more accurate than she was. Only by luck or simply overwhelming them had she survived. *And as Kas tells me, that luck won't last forever.*

Ryia's smirk remained on her face, despite rubbing the back of her head with her hand. "Anyway. What I do is...." She turned to Stephenie, "What's the word I want?"

"Pretend."

"I pretend I am blind. If you can't see with eyes, then you hear with ears. I listen for the energy. Hear the movement. The stirring. It's not really with ears, but it is similar. Can't see directly; find by looking for what it does to the world around it."

Sara pursed her lips. "I don't know...."

"We do it in the dark." Ryia picked up her lamp and glanced at the flame. Stephenie noted the narrow field she created to block the flow of energy into the flame. A moment later, the lamp went out. Then Ryia turned her attention to the lamp beside Rebecca. Stephenie sensed Ryia's difficulty in narrowing and controlling her field at the distance. The amount of effort to control anything increased dramatically as the distance increased. Just like gravity, the further away the object, the weaker the pull. Eventually, Ryia's field narrowed and the draw increased enough to break the flame's ability to sustain its existence.

"Now listen for the movement for...pulsing of the energy as Steph makes the field."

Stephenie created a field in the floor just in front of Ryia. She pulled energy from the surrounding stone and forced it into a concentrated sphere that was as bright as the first one she created.

"In front of Ryia," Rebecca said after a moment. "I could almost feel it move."

Stephenie nodded her head. Though it was dark, she knew Ryia would at least be able to sense the physical movement. Without a word she continued providing the demonstration and allowed Ryia to continue teaching.

They worked into the late morning before Stephenie rose to her feet and excused herself, leaving Ryia to continue working with Rebecca and Sara in the dark room. She answered the questions about where she was going with a simple: "I've got some things to attend to."

On her way out of the cellars, she directed a pulse of energy toward her room. It had become her way to signal Kas she was looking for him. While others who were sensitive to magic would easily feel it, most people would be unaware anything had occurred.

*You summoned me?* Kas inquired a moment later as he floated down the stairs.

*I am heading over to the Square Keep and wondered if you wanted to join me.*

*Is your teaching done for the day?*

*Mine is, but Ryia's will continue.* She smiled in Kas' direction as they headed into her Great Hall. *Thank you for the suggestion I groom Ryia into being their teacher. I really don't have the proper reference to teach someone from scratch.*

Kas shrugged mentally, *You have learned your skills from mimicking the effects of others. The others are unable to apply those techniques because they are unable to observe.*

*And if you hadn't helped in teaching Ryia, we wouldn't even have that.*

Stephenie led Kas across the yard from her Great Hall to the Square Keep. When her father had lived in the keep, Stephenie spent much of her time there. However, once he had left for the war and her mother had full control of the castle, she only entered when required to do so. At one point, she had believed her mother had spells cast upon the stone walls to keep her out. *That was before I knew anything about magic, but the building still feels wrong to me.* Suppressing the shudder that built under her skin, she easily climbed the steps to the pair of arched doors that protected the outer entrance.

"Your Highness," said a group of guards who bowed to her once she reached the top of the steps. "How may we serve you?"

"I would like the see the Seneschal," Stephenie said, thinking of the old man who had served both her father and grandfather. Renild had been a good man, but once Stephenie had learned he had lied to her and blocked the communication between her father and brother and herself, she lost any desire to ever speak with him again.

"Of course, Ma'am", the taller of the guards said as he knocked on a smaller door set into the larger doors. "Her Highness is here to see the Seneschal." With that pronouncement, the guard stepped aside and opened the door for her.

Stephenie grinned as she stepped into a small chamber that provided the guards protection from the elements. A dozen feet away was another set of double doors. The normal sized door set into this pair was already open with a smiling guard welcoming her to enter the castle. *An improvement since Mother's time,* she said to Kas.

Inside the keep, the entrance hall rose two stories over her head. On both the left and right hand walls were large stone staircases that led to the second floor and a balcony that permitted the residents to greet guests from a high vantage point. New works of art decorated the walls, replacing the tapestries and paintings she had seen growing up. *Oh, Kas, you should have seen the history that had hung from the walls before my mother robbed this place.*

*Stephenie, I have seen the actual history.*

*Yeah, but you missed about a thousand years locked in your city.*

Stephenie did not go up to the second floor; instead, she headed straight back and into a passage that opened into the wall below the balcony. She glanced to the door at the far end and then looked away. That door led down into the dungeons. When she was younger, she had often wanted to explore that part of the castle. However, neither her father nor her brother had given her leave to do so. The weeks that she spent hiding among the Senzar in her attempt to free Islet had given her far too much familiarity with dungeons. She had even learned her own capability of helping to torture someone to achieve her goals.

*Orlan insisted you heal him while they tortured him,* Kas reminded her, too easily knowing where her thoughts had drifted. *It was his choice. He utilized you in an effort to gain his own freedom as much as you used him to buy sufficient time to affect Islet's release.*

Stephenie did not respond to Kas' comment. His statement held truth and she understood it, but until those events, she had never considered herself capable of that kind of act.

She put Orlan out of her mind and continued halfway down the hall until she reached the clerks' office. Knocking on the door, she waited until a voice on the other side gave her permission to enter.

Before Stephenie opened the door, she already knew there were three people in the room that was twice as long as it was wide. With the door open, she saw five desks scattered among the numerous cabinets, shelves, and stacks of paper. Despite the number of documents, the office looked as neat as she ever remembered it being.

The closest man looked up from his writing and then scrambled to his feet. "Your Highness," he said with a bow, resulting in the others, who had paid even less attention to the door, jumping to their own feet. "How can we serve you?"

"I would like to see the Seneschal."

"Seneschal Cedric is in his office, please go in."

Stephenie nodded her head to the older man, whose thin hair had turned white. She reached out with her mind and confirmed just one man occupied the room to her right. In doing so, she also confirmed the secret passage running along the back wall did not hold any listeners. She knew Duke Burdger had opened many of the passages Stephenie had inadvertently revealed when her mother caught her spying on a treasonous conversation. Nodding to the clerks, she walked to the back of the room and the door to the Seneschal's office. She knocked before entering.

This smaller office was about half the size of the outer room. As it had been when Renild had been Seneschal, the room contained about as much paperwork as the outer room. The far wall contained another door, leading to a storeroom that should hold even more documents, which had another door leading to a fourth room the size of the first. Stephenie knew the keep could be a maddening warren of rooms and passages for someone not familiar with the layout.

"Your Highness," the young Cedric had said, rising from his wooden desk. "It is a pleasure to see you."

Stephenie smiled at the man who was just a handful of years older than she was. She had not checked, but Cedric might have been the youngest man appointed to the position in the history of her family's line. Of all the clerks and stewards who had survived the war, he had worked twice as hard as any of the others. "Congratulations. I did not have anything to do with your appointment, but I would have said it was deserved if they asked."

"Thank you, Ma'am. If you had not heard, Renild died before the start of the year."

Stephenie shook her head no. Burdger had deposed him during the brief period the Duke had taken over the country. However, Stephenie had never pursued any information on the old seneschal's fate after that. "Cedric, I need to find some information. However, the nature of the information is rather sensitive."

"Of course, Ma'am. What are you looking for?"

"Well, as you know, my mother was a traitor. She influenced a number of people and I was hoping to review records of people who visited my mother and father. I don't know that there is any cause to suspect anyone of anything, but as Defender of Cothel," she hated the title, "I have a duty to protect the country from potential threats."

"I see. And if it gets out that you are looking for threats, it will make people nervous."

"Exactly."

Cedric nodded his head. "Well, your grandfather had started keeping meticulous records. So much so, even the two storerooms behind me cannot hold everything. However, your mother wanted very little kept after your father rode out to fight the Senzar. I am afraid you will find she covered her tracks well."

Stephenie nodded her head. What she really wanted was records from about nineteen years ago, but she knew Cedric was quite capable of drawing conclusions from fragments of information. If she asked to find any visitors from the north who were red-haired and showed up about nine months before she was born, it would not be long before the Seneschal suspected the truth. With everyone else in her family having dark brown hair, she was already a little surprised no one had made any comments.

*Well, my dear, if people do suspect you are not the King's offspring, do you think they would discuss such a matter openly and in sufficient proximity to yourself that you would have a chance to hear their speculation?*

*I would expect you to be skulking about to hear it for me,* she said to Kas. To Cedric, she continued, "That is fine. I doubt her betrayal started only after my father's departure. I will simply work my way back from the start of the war looking for patterns."

Cedric nodded his head. Picking up one of the three oil lamps providing light for this interior room, he escorted her into the back room. Shelves and cabinets lined the walls, including the space over the door into the last storage room. Cedric placed the lamp on a small table that sat in the middle of the organized chaos.

"We have many ledgers on these shelves here. They will record the date, who arrived, perhaps a description, if the person was not well known, as well as the nature of their visit." He pulled a wood-bound tome from the shelf and opened it on the table. "This is from about three months before your father left. Your mother requested the ones after this and we were unable to locate them after she departed."

Stephenie looked at the off-white paper and the neat handwriting that covered the page. She noted several other columns in the log, some of which had a code of letters and numbers. "What are these?"

"If there was correspondence or papers that are related to the visit, this is an indication of the location where it is stored." He shrugged. "Unfortunately, before Renild took over, the prior Seneschal decided to rearrange many of our documents. All the older ledger items from your grandfather's early days are worthless. We would have to read through all the archives." He smiled, "But that would be before your mother came to Cothel. So hopefully that will not hinder your search."

Stephenie nodded and sat in the spindly chair sitting next to the table. "May I borrow this lamp and browse through the logs?"

"Of course, Ma'am. Would you like some paper and ink to take notes?"

Stephenie smiled up at the young man. She had remembered him as somewhat awkward, but he had come into himself and carried an air of confidence that made her want to like him. "You have anticipated me well."

He bowed his head, "It is my pleasure. Let me fetch the supplies and leave you to the task."


It was early evening before Stephenie finally gave into real hunger and left Cedric's offices at the insistence of a footman who informed her that her brother and sister expected her in the dining room on the second floor. She assumed the guards at the front door had informed others she had gone to visit with the Seneschal and so her brother had been able to locate her.

Much earlier in the day, she had asked Kas to inform Henton of her activities so he would not worry. However, her friends had either respected her desire to focus on her task or detested visiting the keep enough that they never called on her.

"What were you doing all day in the Seneschal's office?" Joshua asked from the head of the table.

Stephenie turned her head and looked passed Islet, who sat between her and her brother. Ignoring his tone, she decided not to use the cover story she had told Cedric. "I was looking to see if I could find some of the families that had done portraits of our family. Mother had stolen or destroyed most of what we had. I wanted to have a new one painted of Islet now that she is back."

Joshua frowned. "We have artists on retainer who did a series of portraits for Rebecca. I can have them do some of Islet. And yourself," he added.

Stephenie nodded her head, not liking Joshua injecting himself into her activities. "Well, I just remember one that was done of Grandma Kara. There was just something about the brush strokes that I loved. I was hoping to find that family. Perhaps they are still painters and have passed on the technique."

Joshua shook his head. "You've got better things to do with your time. William needs you to make an appearance at Catheri's temple tomorrow. He was looking for you earlier, but you seemed to abandon Rebecca's and Sara's training in a pointless search of a painter." He picked up a drumstick and took a bite of the juicy meat. "You need to get your priorities straight."

Stephenie noticed a questioning look from Islet, but she said nothing. A moment later, Islet turned to Joshua. "I would like a painting similar to the one we had for Grandma Kara. Our sister was named for her and she was the first of our family to fall to the Senzar. I think it would honor her to have it done in that technique."

Joshua did not roll his eyes, but Stephenie could tell he thought the idea a waste of time. "Fine, I'll have one of the clerks look for the family." He pointed the half-eaten chicken leg at Stephenie, "But in the morning, after you eat here with us, you will take a carriage to the temple and support William. You are Catheri's prophet."

# Chapter 6

Stephenie looked out the window of the carriage as they rode through Antar. Henton and Ryia sat across from her; Kas and Douglas remained behind in the castle. Douglas because he did not want to visit the temple and Kas because of the potential for the people in the temple with magic to sense him.

Both Henton and Ryia had avoided trying to draw her into conversation, for which she was thankful. She understood the need to promote Catheri, but the lies continued to weigh heavily on her and she would rather be searching for her sire. *My life is riddled with deception,* she complained silently. *I just want to find a place where I can be happy with Kas and my friends.*

"Are we there?" Ryia asked, drawing Stephenie's attention back to the city outside the carriage. They had stopped in the middle of a crowded street located many blocks from the temple. The anger, fear, and agitation of the gathered masses hit her the moment she opened her mind. Fearing the safety of the others, she reached forward and unlatched the door despite Henton's sudden protest for her own safety.

"I won't just sit here," she said, leaping from the carriage. Without conscious thought, she used a slight burst of energy to ease her landing. Dressed as The Prophet of Catheri and Defender of Cothel, she appeared more soldier than princess. She wore a fine pair of leggings and a silk shirt, both held in place by a polished sword belt and a well-used blade she had borrowed from Will.

Around her, the mob of people blocking the street stepped back from the carriage, though their recognition of who stood in their midst took a moment to spread. As it did, the crowd quickly parted, revealing nearly a dozen of the city guards managing to keep things civil.

The members of Joshua's personal guard that noticed her emerge from the carriage started calling for her to return to her seat. She shook her head as she moved into the center of the gathering. Silence spread through the crowd, leaving the street in an unnatural state of quiet.

She ignored the bows and curtsies, but slowed enough to allow Henton and Ryia to trail in her wake. When she reached what appeared to be a lieutenant of the Guard, she paused and waited for him to finish his bow to her. Three citizens stood behind him, all were in obvious distress and still weeping, though now silently.

"Your Highness," the lieutenant stammered.

"Please, tell me what is going on here." Stephenie extended her senses further. The smell of blood hung barely discernible in the air and she could feel the disciplined minds of several soldiers in the tailor's shop on her right.

"The murderers, Ma'am. They struck again."

"Again?"

"Yes. Though we are dealing with it."

Stephenie turned toward the building.

"Ma'am, you don't want to go in there. It is not a sight for a Lady."

Stephenie shook her head and continued forward; she felt no need to justify her actions and while she did not like the visage of death, she would not run from it. However, when she entered the darkened room, the coppery smell of blood and sickly-sweet pungency of death filled her nose and mouth. Her sight, compensated by her magic, adjusted immediately to the change in illumination and she turned her face away. The reminder of what the Butcher had repeatedly done to Orlan filled her head. Unfortunately, the Butcher's deeds paled in comparison.

Taking a breath, she forced herself to continue into the room and look at the devastation. The shell of a body lay in the center of the floor. A wide smearing of blood radiated out in a deliberate attempt to spread the horror. A severed head sat on the empty chest cavity; the eyes pulled out and dangling down the front of the face. The person's entrails lay about the room in what had the appearance of a sacrifice instead of a simple murder.

Two other soldiers stood in the room, each of them showing a nervous twitch in their movements. When they realized who had entered, the first one started to kneel, but stopped when he remembered what covered the floor.

"Please, you are fine," Stephenie said, waving away their attempt to show respect. Behind her she heard Henton tell Ryia to stay outside. The tone of his repeated order left no doubt as to his seriousness.

Stephenie moved a little further into the room, carefully trying not to step in the congealed blood. Much of it had dried, but the deeper pools remained moist. "Who could have done this?"

The lieutenant had followed Henton. "Ma'am, we have called for the Captain. He will be here soon. You should allow us to handle this. It is not a place fit for a Lady."

Stephenie turned toward the man. "It not a place fit for anyone. Who did this?" She demanded.

The lieutenant stepped back one pace. "Ma'am, my apologies, but we do not know who is doing this. All we know is they left another letter."

Henton took the bloodied letter and handed it to her. She opened it carefully and quickly read the page. Her jaw tightened as she continued reading and by the time she finished, she could feel the burning of a large reserve of energy in her body.

Henton glanced at her; it was not a demand for information, but simply a request for anything she might feel safe to provide in front of the others.

"They claim to be from Kynto and this was done in retaliation for my killing of King Willard."

"You didn't kill Willard," Henton responded automatically, which Stephenie knew would be for the benefit of the others around them.

"We did not," she agreed. "However, whoever did this is using it as an excuse. This is their 'gift' to commemorate our return to Antar."

She saw no point in hiding the information; it would spread even without her repeating it.

The lieutenant cleared his throat. "This is not much different than the others, so I would not take it personally."

"The others?"

"The murders have been going on for weeks. This is the tenth one."

Stephenie turned away from the soldier; she could not trust herself to avoid swearing. Forcing her fists to unclench, she looked at the letter again, rereading it twice more. The sick ranting of the writer left her pacing toward the back of the room.

"Ma'am, we think the man was killed upstairs and dragged down here."

Stephenie turned to the new speaker, who was the man that had almost knelt in the blood. "Show me."

The soldier took her to the stairs located against the back wall. Her enhanced eyesight noted the drops of blood on the floor and on the steps. Several footprints of smeared blood accompanied the drops. Judging on how dry it looked, she suspected the prints were not from these soldiers.

Carefully moving up the creaking stairs, she followed the soldier down a hall and into a bedroom. More devastation filled this room. Stephenie suspected a struggle with multiple people based on how many things were knocked over and scatted about. Three more bodies lay on the floor. Specks of red dotted most surfaces. However, none of these three women, one older, and two under ten, were dismembered.

"These Kyntian bastards need to die," the lieutenant demanded. "We've had people looking about the city questioning anyone who is from Kynto."

Stephenie did not feel like reminding the soldier that her mother originated from Kynto. Instead, she glanced at the letter still in her hand. It was written in Kyntian, but something about the way the letters were drawn and the choice of certain characters over others made her think the letter was written by someone who was well educated, but for whom Kyntian was not their primary language.

Henton watched her from the doorway. His reluctance to enter obvious in his posture. Stephenie walked over and handed him the letter. "This is the tenth one," she said softly.

"So they indicated. Steph, you okay?"

She wanted to take a deep breath, but the stench of blood hung in the air. Considering Henton's question, she slowly released some of the energy that had started to burn uncomfortably within her. As she let the raw power trickle back into the environment, she glanced at the overturned chamber pot and crossed the room again. Bending down she picked up the copper bowl. It appeared squished into a partial oval. Standing, she took a closer look at several other objects strewn about the room and then knelt to examine the wooden floor in more detail.

"What is it?" Henton asked, finally joining her.

"The floor boards are compressed here," she whispered. "And across several boards. Almost like something very heavy, but without sharp edges, struck the floor." Looking up, she nodded her head toward a number of the objects thrown about the room. "The things moved from this side of the floor and were knocked over there."

Aware of the soldiers watching and listening, including the lieutenant who stood in the doorway, she decided not to share her appraisal just yet. With a shake of her head, she stood. "I don't know."

"The Captain will be here soon. If you want to wait outside...." The lieutenant said slowly. It was more of a plea than anything else. Having seen enough, Stephenie indicated the lieutenant should lead and then followed him downstairs and out of the building.

Outside, the sun helped to melt away the discomfort of seeing the devastation. Searching for Ryia, she saw the girl's pale face and wide eyes. Stephenie held her tongue, the sight inside held enough punishment for disobeying Henton.

Joshua's guards stood beside Ryia with faces as pale as hers. "Ma'am, we need to get the carriage out of the road and get you to the temple." The soldier nodded his head toward the lieutenant beside her. "These men can handle things. They know what they are doing."

Stephenie looked at the nearly silent crowd; their expectation thick in the air. Turning to address them, she partially amplified her voice, "I don't have an answer for you at the moment, but you have

my word, I will do everything in my power to end these murders."
With a look to Joshua's guards, she saw Henton hand back the letter
as they walked toward the carriage. The crowd, knowing the carriage's
occupant, parted quickly and they were soon on their way.

"Okay, what is it you noticed?" Henton asked quietly.

Stephenie glanced out the window and then turned back to
Henton. "How come no one thought to mention these murders, or
more accurately, sacrifices, which are supposedly done because of us?"

He shrugged. "I don't have an answer."

Stephenie forced her fingers wide and she pushed the palms of her
hands into her thighs. Rolling her head to ease the tension in her
neck, she met Henton's eyes. The concern showing in those brown
eyes was not fear she would overreact, but sympathy for what she was
feeling.

"It was a mage or mages that did that," she said. "And I don't
think they were from Kynto."

Henton nodded his head.

"It was obviously a gravitational attack in the bedroom. The slight
crushing of the floor and bending of the chamber pot. And the letter
just felt wrong somehow. I can't say why for certain, but something
about it doesn't feel right. I could be wrong, but...."

"What are you going to do?" He asked.

"Well, once we're done at the temple, Josh can hear my demands
instead of me listening to his."


When the carriage stopped again, they had reached the walled
complex that held the temple of Catheri. Stephenie still did not know
if Will had developed the idea to make her Catheri's prophet on his
own or if that had been a culmination of things he had heard. She
had been unconscious for a few days after she destroyed the mountain
peak in the Greys, which unfortunately revealed to the world her
witchcraft. And even after she regained consciousness, many more
days passed with her heavily isolated. Therefore, her observations of
the events were incomplete, *and Will never tells the complete truth.*

She glanced at Henton; he knew the truth behind what happened
in the Grey Mountains and understood her. He did not look at her

and consider her divine. The peak, which had already been partially collapsed long before her, had likely exploded because she had tapped into the artifacts the Senzar had been searching for in the ruins buried in the mountain. The mark of Catheri burned into her breast was nothing more than a remnant of Kas' handprint, left when he tried to kill her by freezing her heart. Kas' attack had come before Kas had regained awareness of the world around him. It happened when Stephenie had first disturbed the mindless trance he had fallen into from the countless years of being trapped in the underground city of Arkani. The accidental resemblance to the old god's sigil was coincidental. *There is nothing special about me.*

Henton smiled at her, offering his friendship and loyalty and it almost quelled the nagging thought still in the back of her mind. *How did I manage to survive?* Not even Kas had an understanding of why all the energy she had drawn through her at various times did not burn out her mind.

"Steph," Will said as he opened the carriage door, drawing back her attention. "Welcome to the grand Temple of Catheri!"

Stephenie stepped out of the carriage, already aware of the mass of people who had gathered behind Will. Everyone wore white tunics with a black hand print over their left breast. *The Claw of Justice,* Stephenie thought to herself, *Kas' claw.* "Thank you for inviting me. This is the first time I really have had an opportunity to visit." She looked past Will and the four dozen people to see a number of whitewashed wattle and daub buildings surrounding the cobblestone square. A large stone statue of a woman, surrounded by flowers, stood in the middle of the square. Stephenie glanced at the face and after confirming it did not bare her likeness, she smiled.

"There is a temporary temple building, which will later become an indoor training facility. We also have the main temple under construction. The stone work is coming along, but it will be a few years before it is truly complete."

Stephenie could see the piles of stone and the ramps for the workers to carry up the blocks. "It looks very well done. Is the fence around the whole complex?" She asked, noting the gate the carriage had passed through.

"Yes, we initially had too many people roaming in and out of our buildings." He raised his left arm to direct Stephenie away from the carriage. "However, the main gates are open pretty much the whole day and we let people come and go as they like." Stephenie followed beside Will, with Henton and Ryia directly behind them. "Let me take you on a tour. Then if you would like, we can call a gathering and allow you to address everyone in the temple."

Stephenie nodded her head. She appreciated the work that Will had put into the complex and all of the old buildings looked to be in good repair. It gave an impression that pride existed in those responsible.

Inside the temple building, older pews covered the floor, but the walls were bright. Another stone statue stood ten feet high in an alcove on the far end. Unlike the metal statues in the holy shrines dedicated to the other gods, this statue did not distribute energy to augmentation devices. To differentiate Catheri's supposed return, Will declared the goddess had come back through the very bones of the world. She knew it fit well with her toppling a mountain peak. *Again, did he plan that from the start?*

The tour of the library and classrooms impressed Stephenie. The sight of so many books on the shelves warmed her. The fact he had acquired so much in such a short time offered another testament to Will's determination.

When they reached the dormitories for the students, Stephenie stopped the tour. Waves of distress radiated from people she sensed down one of the corridors. "What is going on?" Will's shoulder twitched slightly. Stephenie stepped forward, looking up slightly to meet Will's gaze and preventing his attempt to profess confusion.

"Steph," he said, stepping back twice and glancing down the hall. "We've got it under control. The people down that wing are simply being purified." He held out his hands and raised his eyebrows. "Really, they'll be fine in a couple of days."

"Will?" She growled, then softened her tone, sensing confusion from the outsiders who accompanied them. She swallowed the rage building in her and spoke calmly, though any of the people who were sensitive to moods would likely feel her anger. "Sorry, I need to rest.

We encountered a disturbing sight on the way here. Where are your offices, Will?"

Will glanced once more down the corridor and then nodded his head. "I am sorry your ride here was distressful. Definitely, follow me." With hastened steps, he led her out of the dormitory, away from the followers of Catheri, and across the complex to a two-story building.

Stephenie fought to hold her tongue until they had closed the door to Will's offices. The offices were located on the first floor of the freestanding building that he also used as his residence on the premise. Sensing no outsiders close enough to hear them, she grabbed his arm, preventing his retreat to the other side of his modest desk. Squeezing to the point he cringed, she spoke just above a whisper. "What do you mean being cleansed?"

"Steph," Will said, partially collapsing under her grasp. "We had to come up with a way to get Elrin out of the people who come to us." He leaned against his desk. "Please, you're hurting me."

She sensed Henton and Ryia shifting in place behind her. "You are hurting them," she said, nodding her head toward the dormitories. After a moment, she released his arm with a shove. "What are you doing to them? I felt the pain from forty feet away!"

Will rubbed his right arm. "Can we talk about this instead of you accusing me of crimes?" When no one said anything, he turned his back on Stephenie and moved to his chair. "What is it you want from me?"

"An explanation!" Stephenie said, slamming her fist on his desk.

"Don't yell at me!" He demanded and then shook his head. "You wanted us to find a way; that is what we have done. Half these people think they might be infected with evil from Elrin, some will even admit they knew they had a demon in them. The common people on the street don't fully trust us yet." He glanced at his arm as he continued to rub it. "We tried the old tap-the-guy-on-the-forehead-and-you're-cured approach, but the first person we did that to didn't believe us. Rebecca has the same problem; she had two warlocks come to her. How was she supposed to integrate people who knew they were warlocks with the priests that had been trained to burn them? We did the only thing we could think of short of burning them. Unlike you, they wouldn't survive a burning."

"I burn just like anyone else."

"Not when you start the fire yourself. I've seen you." Will pulled open a drawer and removed a journal. He flipped it open and leafed through several pages before turning it around to show Stephenie. "We came up with this. It makes their lives miserable for a couple of days. Things come out both ends, but when it is done, they feel they have been purged of all evil."

Stephenie scanned the list of items on the page, and based on what she learned while pretending to join the Senzar, she knew the recipe was toxic. "You are poisoning them!"

"It doesn't kill. It just makes them sick."

Stephenie looked back to the list. "The things on here can kill. This is not a joke, Will. You can't give them these things."

Will stood up. "You were not here. We risked being exposed as heathens and warlocks and all of us burned. We tried a very mild dose initially, but guess what? The people were not sure it worked. They wanted more. They want to suffer. They are conditioned by hundreds of years of priests telling them they are evil to believe they need something very strong to clean them out." He slammed the book shut. "That's what we've done. We've given them what they expect and it is saving their lives and allowing them the chance to perhaps change the world. So don't stand there and judge me because they want to suffer for a few days."

Stephenie leaned over the desk. "You risk killing them with that list of ingredients. How does killing them with poison differ from killing them with fire?"

"No one has died."

Stephenie straightened her back. "And you better make sure it stays that way. I don't want to hear about someone dying because we poisoned them."

"We keep an eye on them and if needed, Sara will heal them to make sure they stay alive." He shrugged and tossed his hands into the air. "I've got nothing else as a solution. You can't have everything happy and pretty. The world doesn't work like that."

Stephenie allowed herself a moment to calm down. She knew Will did not want to hurt people and she even understood his position, *but it is still wrong!* "Will, I am disappointed. I told you from the beginning, I didn't want any of this Catheri nonsense. I know you saved my life with it and I appreciate that you are saving the lives of other people, but I really don't like poisoning people."

Will bit his lower lip. "I understand. I probably should have warned you about that."

"You should have." Stephenie sat down and Henton and Ryia followed suit. "Now, why don't you tell us about something else that everyone has neglected to tell me?"

Will raised an eyebrow as he resumed his seat. "...do you mean the murders?"

"Sacrifice is a better description. My carriage got caught up in a crowd that had gathered to see the carnage."

"I've never seen worse," Ryia mumbled in Pandar, but Stephenie didn't bother to correct her.

"It's been going on for about six weeks. There were nine events...I guess ten now. Whoever is doing it has the city guards lost. They happen in random places across the city. It appears that someone, or some group, from Kynto is doing it. Blaming Josh and you for all the troubles there." Will looked down at his desk and then back to Stephenie and Henton. "They kill whole families. No one has seen anything. A few people have reported hearing noises, but the city is full of noises and arguments that no one really bothers to check."

"What's being done?"

"Well, the guards have been investigating anyone with any ties to Kynto, but so far, even with at least fifty arrests, the killings have not stopped. There are more patrols at night, but everyone is frightened. People try to avoid being out alone, but there was one family with five grown men killed three weeks ago...so how many people do you need to be safe?"

"I think it is a mage or mages doing it."

Will raised his eyebrows. "That won't go over well; we'd have a lot more demands for witch burnings. There is already grumbling that neither Catheri nor Felis has burned any witches lately."

"And neither of you better start."

"We won't. We're trying to save people, not kill them. Sometimes they need to suffer a little to feel like we did something. No one believes medicine is working unless it tastes bad and makes you feel worse for a while."

Stephenie wished she had a brilliant idea, but she did not have a different option for him. "I'm sorry about the arm," she said, realizing Will would have considered as many options as possible before choosing this one. He nodded his head and smiled at her. Changing the subject, she continued, "I should get back to the castle and find out what Josh is doing about these murders."

"Ah," Will said and then hesitated. "We promised that you would speak to everyone and there are a lot of people who want to meet you. Including some people from one of those villages where you killed the Senzar." He glanced to Henton and back to Stephenie. "Plus, Josh is not going to want you involved. He will think you are trying to interfere."

"Will, people are dying. If I can do something about it, you're damn right I am going to interfere."

"Yeah, I get that, but where your brother is concerned, the two of you are going to...well, I don't want to see the two of you arguing."

"Is Josh a problem? Is he a danger to Cothel?"

Will shook his head vigorously. "No, not at all. He's actually well liked by most people and really has been fair in dealing with everyone, including the nobles. He...he just has issues around you. I think he is lost with how to treat you. You don't fall into something he knows how to deal with."

Stephenie knew Joshua's problem was that he wanted to be in control and he had no control over her. What hurt the most was that he feared her, even though she would never hurt him. *Something else I have no answer for.* She was not about to lock herself up in a small room and learn needlework. "Okay, let's get this over with. Call the gathering so I can meet everyone and answer their questions."

# Chapter 7

By the time Stephenie returned to the castle, she felt more disappointment than anger. "Josh, you should have told me what was going on. People are getting sacrificed and the blame is being attributed to me!"

Joshua leaned back in his chair. Rebecca, sitting in her chair next to Joshua, said nothing, perhaps trying to remain a silent peacekeeper. Finally, he spoke, "Steph, I told you that your actions were causing trouble for us."

"But I didn't kill Willard!"

"I know that now, but at the time we didn't know for certain. And you were already overreacting to everything else." He shook his head. "Look, it is a matter for the city guards. And it is not like I have been ignoring the problem, I've added soldiers to the Guard to help track these people down, but they are random in their attacks." Joshua lifted a stack of papers, some of which had blood on them. "They are scattered across the city. It's too big for us to cover everything and these bastards know it."

The 'overreacting' comment reheated her blood and firmed her decision not to tell Joshua about the use of magic. No one needed the king demanding witch-hunts. However, she had already told Rebecca about it. "You should consider adding some of Felis' holy warriors to the hunt as well."

"Don't tell me how to run my country." He glared at her. "Do you think I am stupid? We've already done that. But there are not enough to patrol the whole city either. We are doing what we can."

Stephenie nodded her head and did her best to look contrite. "Could I have Henton look over a map of where the attacks occurred?"

"Why?"

"He might be able to offer some insight."

"I've got the best men in the city working on it."

Stephenie nodded her head. "Yes, but adding one more won't hurt and he's an experienced sailor. He's had to think about things differently than others. Anticipating how ships will move and making sure he is in the right spot at the right time."

"Josh," Rebecca said, placing a hand on his arm. "It won't hurt to have another person examine the problem."

"Fine, have it your way." Joshua pulled a map of the city out from under the pile of papers and slammed it on his desk. Visible marks on the map covered the whole city, indicating a trail of death. "Take the maps and letters. But have them brought back tonight and do not damage or lose anything. This is evidence."

"Thank you. I will make sure nothing happens to them."


"You did what?" Henton demanded as he looked at the pile of papers Stephenie had literally placed at his feet on the floor of his room.

"I asked Josh to let you look over these. He would have objected to me looking at them, but you were a sailor and had to think about things differently."

"Spatially and multi-dimensionally," Kas offered from where he sat, fully opaque and on the floor next to Stephenie.

"Multi-what?" Henton shook his head. "I was a marine, not a sailor. I waited until we got close to the other ship and jumped from one to the other. I was not the captain, nor the navigator, nor the helmsman." He stood over her with his arms crossed. "Steph, really."

She looked up at him. "But I've seen you fight. I've seen you out-think opponents all the time."

Douglas chuckled. "She got you pegged, Sarge."

"Shut up."

"Please. I wouldn't ask if I didn't think you could help."

Henton crouched down and glanced at the map. "Why is it you think we need to do everyone else's jobs?"

"I get bored at night?" She offered with a raised eyebrow.

Henton let slip one of Kas' favorite curses.

"What does that mean," Ryia asked as she knelt next to him, which caused Stephenie and Kas to laugh.

He did not precisely know the meaning, but if the word meant what he suspected, there was no way he intended explaining it to Ryia. He shook his head. "Let's focus. If we are going to do it, we should look at the order of the attacks."

"According to my brother, they are random."

Henton stared at the map for a little while. Each location was numbered, including the tenth one they had come across earlier in the day. "There are a lot of them, but really, for a city this large, it is not that many locations to really get a feel for a pattern."

"I'd say the next one will be over here," Ryia said, pointing to the area near the docks.

"Why do you think over there?" He asked, curious as to her reasoning.

"Nothing close to it yet."

Henton pursed his lips as he went back to studying the streets. Antar's boroughs meant little to him. Growing up in a northern city before spending years at sea, his time in Antar started just before his association with Stephenie. *And there has been little chance to wander about in her service,* he thought. He knew some traditional areas such as the area closer to the docks where poorer people tended to live. Their travels to the temples of Catheri and Felis gave him some exposure to those routes and he had a general idea of where the really wealthy lived. However, the map did not describe living conditions in the city. "What's this area like? Who lives there?"

Stephenie glanced to where he pointed. "It tends to be where mid-level merchants and skilled tradesmen live."

Glancing once more to Ryia's suggestions of near the docks, Henton responded to her as he continued to study the map. "I doubt these people want to hit every area on the map. They appear to want to shock and disturb people. They want to make a statement. Many people will dismiss attacks on the poor. However, attacks on the middle and upper classes will get noticed. They'd likely avoid nobles and people with lots of money because those people have better security. So, their target would be the tradesmen and reasonably wealthy merchants. It would do the most damage to public opinion."

Stephenie nodded her head. "Make the largest group of people in the city terrified to even stay inside at night and you generate a lot of unrest."

"And as long as you did it quietly enough, you'd be able to get away without getting caught," Henton added.

"Which," Stephenie said, "is why I want to figure out where they are likely to strike next."

Henton sighed. He could not count the number of variables that should be considered and the city looked huge with it drawn out on a map.

"What about finding where they are hiding?" Douglas asked from over Henton's shoulder.

Stephenie nodded her head, "That would be nice, but they could be anywhere. Cover up with a clean tunic or put the bloody ones in a sack and you could walk across the whole city without anyone suspecting you."

Henton picked up a document that listed the dates of each attack. He glanced back to the map, looking at the third and fourth attack. "The fourth set of bodies, a woman and a small boy, were found on the other side of town the day after the third attack. The fourth was close to the area of the second attack." Henton tapped the mark on the map for the third attack. "They are likely in this borough."

"Why?" Ryia asked.

He met the girl's brown eyes. "The first couple of attacks are going to be very frightening. There will be a lot of searching around them and everyone nearby will be questioned. The first one is up in the northeast; the second is more to the center of the city, just a bit north." He tapped the fourth mark. "This one is center, only a little south, but still close to the second one. The third one is southwest in the city." He looked between Stephenie and Douglas. "By the third attack, people would start assuming whoever is doing this is not doing it near where they are hiding, so perhaps a little less attention will be applied to the neighbors and people living in the area." Sitting back, he relieved the pressure on his ankles. "The fourth attack was the very next day; all the others had been three to seven days apart. That means people would get redirected away from the third attack quickly to investigate the fourth one, further reducing the chance of being found." He tossed the paper with the dates on top the map. "I would say they are held up near the location of the third attack, not that knowing that does us a lot of good. We can't search everything at once and likely they have not left evidence out in the open. Anything that was there would be destroyed as soon as word got out a new search was going on."

Stephenie picked up the paper with the dates and set it aside. "Any thoughts on the next spot to focus?"

Henton looked back at the map. "If I was going to do something like this, I would have people either in or watching the guards. That way I might get an idea of where they will be concentrated and then choose something else if there was overlap."

"You make it sound impossible," Douglas said, finding his own spot to sit on the floor.

"The city is huge," Henton countered. "They say it's the biggest in Cothel."

Stephenie continued to stare at the map. "How many people would you have involved?"

Henton leaned forward. "I'm not someone who would do something like this...ever."

"I know that. But if you were, how many?"

"I'd guess there are between four and ten, less if they have magic at their disposal. There might be a couple more not active in the killing. These murders are brutal. You're not going to find that many people willing to do the actual deed and be able to keep it quiet."

"I won't be sleeping tonight," Ryia said, looking at the map, but without focus.

"That's because I told you to stay out and you didn't," Henton snapped.

"Her nightmares will be punishment enough," Stephenie said. "A guess?"

Henton shook his head. "The borough I asked about before; the one with the merchants is what my gut tells me."

Stephenie nodded her head. "Okay, we can focus there."

Kas blinked into a standing position. "I am certainly aware there is little point in my asking the question, but what do you have in mind?"

"You and me, old friend." She started gathering the documents. "We can get up on the rooftops and simply wait. Keep an eye out for trouble and while the victims might not get a chance to make a lot of noise, there has got to be a lot of fear. Perhaps we can sense it and then get there before it is too late."

Henton stood up and moved beside Kas. "That is way too much of an area for you to be able to sense."

She looked up at them. "Assuming Kas is willing, I was going to ask him to continue to move about the area. He can do it a lot faster than I. I'd be in a central location and come when he called." With the papers in hand, she stood up. "We are the best people for this and if there are Senzar mages trying to destabilize the city, Cothel, and my brother, then we have to do something. The city guards would get slaughtered facing them."

Douglas got up and walked to his bed. "Josh won't like you getting involved. He's not very clear headed when it comes to you."

"I would agree," Henton added. He assumed Kas made a similar mental comment based on the look Stephenie gave the ghost.

"I realize my brother has issues. I don't plan to tell him." She turned back to Henton. "I need to get some new clothes, the dark things I have are really worn out. Plus I'd like to pick up a different sword and a long dagger. I miss the ones you guys gave me." She hesitated a moment, "How long do you think we have before they attack again?"

Henton wanted to throw his hands in the air. He had no way to judge and did not want to give her wrong information, but he also knew she would not hold any errors against him. "If your return to Antar is a factor, they might do something sooner rather than later. The other events were usually several days apart. I still think the one exception was an attempt to redirect suspicion. But if they want to make a statement about you...."

Stephenie nodded. "Okay. Kas, if you are willing, I'd like to start watching tonight. Just in case. I've got serviceable things for now."

She looked around once more at everyone else. "One other thing, I'd like to avoid telling Josh where we suspect they will attack. Instead, I'd like to offer our second best guess. If they do have people passing them information, than that might help drive them to your guess. If not and they go after our second best guess, then Josh will hopefully have people ready. We'd also be able to cover more of the city that way."

Henton forced himself to nod his head. "And if his soldiers don't see you, Josh might not realize your personal involvement."

She smiled at him. "There is also that."

# Chapter 8

After returning the documents to her brother and providing a guess for the next attack to occur in the northeast of the city, she went back to her tower and gathered what equipment she had available. It included a darker shirt and pants as well as the long rapier she had borrowed from Will. She preferred her blades a touch lighter, but the weapon had a quality edge. For an off-hand weapon, she favored simple ones with a blade about one and a half feet long. This night, she simply included a dagger.

A flash of rage filled her for a moment as she remembered the twisted remains of the blades her four men had given her. The possessive anger over their destruction at the hands of those mages in Vinerxan had not truly left her. *I won't let it control me*, she swore, not liking the danger she posed to others if she let the possessiveness take over.

Overcoming her inner demon, she ate an early meal, and then caught a few hours of sleep before Henton woke her after full dark. Despite his protests, she had no intention of bringing him with her. "Just remain ready in case something happens. If I need you, I'll send Kas."

"While we simply rot with worry in our beds?"

"Henton," she said, putting a hand on his arm. "I know I am not making it easy on you, but I intend to keep out of sight and wait. If they are Senzar, I'd rather they didn't sense a group of us. Plus, I'll need you to cover for me in case Josh or someone else comes looking for me."

She waited for him to nod his head. His posture showed how deeply he struggled with letting her go and she wished for a way to convince him that she would be safe. It worried her that his emotional state had grown easier for her to sense. The man who has always kept his mind quiet had either lost his edge or she had become better at reading minds.

*More likely, you have become more sensitive to him specifically. He is by far your closest friend,* Kas whispered to her mind.

*Aside from you, Kas.*

"Assuming you don't get yourself killed," Henton said, unaware of her conversation with Kas, "you'll have to keep Josh from hanging the rest of us. How are you getting out unnoticed? If I was in charge, the soldiers would be instructed to watch the skies as well as the ground."

Knowing she had his tentative approval, she slung a small leather pack containing food and a water skin over her shoulder. "I'll go over the seaside wall and then fly north just above the water. There should be minimal chance someone would notice that." She moved through her door and started down the stairs of her tower with Henton in tow. "I'll make my way into the city from the harbor."

"Steph, you know I really don't think this is a good idea."

"That's because it's not. But who else is going to do it?" She smiled to reassure him. She felt Douglas and Ryia waiting in her Great Hall. "If tomorrow we have not stopped them, we can see if there is a way you can help, but until then, I am already running late."

With a final reassurance to all of them that she would return, she walked through her Great Hall into the old kitchens at the far end. From there, she moved through a series of small passages to reach the old Square Tower, which barely stood higher than the Great Hall's roof. With crumbling mortar and wooden beams weakened by age, no one used the Square Tower. Everyone, including Stephenie, considered it unsafe.

To avoid the creaking of the tired floors, she pulled energy into herself and generated a field that changed gravity's attraction to her body. Lifting easily into the air, she altered the field to pull her forward and up the narrow stairs that spiraled up the southeast corner of the tower. When she reached the top, she carefully opened the door and gazed out across the dark night. A salty breeze came in from

Tet, but the moist air felt comfortable without the heat of the day. Only a couple of soldiers stood watch on the walls and towers on the seaside of the castle. The threat from ships was minimal due to the high cliffs and choppy sea beyond the protection of the harbor. She knew the other sides of the castle contained a higher number of more attentive guards.

*Ready Kas?*

*As always. Just remember, your death is unlikely to result in you becoming a ghost, so you will have to avoid any unexpected demise if you do not desire me to be alone.*

Grinning at his normal warning, Stephenie pulled in more energy and launched herself forward over the edge of the tower and then allowed herself to drop. She adjusted her motion just below the height of the next building's roof and flew along its side to avoid making a silhouette of herself from the lamps scattered about the castle's bailey. Racing toward the outer wall, she tucked her legs and lifted her elevation just enough to clear the crenelations. Once over the wall, she changed her field, amplifying her density and accelerating down the rocky cliff toward the water. The maneuver caused her stomach to lurch in a strangely pleasurable way.

Kas, easily keeping pace, trailed just behind her as she leveled out barely three-feet above the water. An occasional spray, flung into the air by the crashing waves, dampened her face and clothing. Thrilled with the pleasure of flight, she almost drifted out to sea so that she could lengthen the time of her adventure. However, the prospect of more people being butchered in their homes kept her on task.

Slowing as she reached the docks, she dropped herself even closer to the water. Kept calm by a seawall that protected the harbor, the gentle rising and falling of the waves did not threaten to make her wet.

Avoiding ships with active watches, she glided between a pair of merchant vessels that each had only had a single man on deck. When she reached the boardwalk, she rose to meet its height and stepped out, her legs moving the moment she touched wood. Anyone who might see her now would assume she came off a ship and with the dark night, her masculine clothing, and her hair in a tight braid, most people would assume she was a man.

The docks, which sat fifty-feet below the height of the city, lacked any significant establishments. To reach the city, the sailors and passengers had to climb the switchbacks cut into the rocky cliff. Those wealthy and lazy enough often hired carts to convey them into the city; the cranes were only used for merchandise.

Unlike most of the other people making the climb, Stephenie reached the city without feeling winded or taxed. Her magic continually repaired her muscles and provided strength, giving her an advantage she knew had helped her outclass the soldiers she had trained with before the war.

She moved through a scattering of young men that made a show of trying to decide which tavern they wanted to visit to cover how winded they were. After passing them, she headed west across the wide Cliff Road and then down a narrow cobblestone street lined with various shops and taverns. She ignored the handful of late night shoppers and suspected the area around the warehouses to the north would have less traffic, but moving through those streets would actually draw more attention.

A year earlier, a trip alone into the city would have filled her with excited fear. The possibility she might get robbed, murdered, or even worse, were threats she knew most woman feared, or at least consciously considered. Even now, with her powers, a youthful bad experience in the city when she had slipped away from her bodyguards still haunted her thoughts.

*You are easily more than a match for any common miscreants,* Kas murmured.

*But most people are not,* she responded as they moved purposefully down the street. *I know I can't protect everyone, but that doesn't mean I don't want to.*

*If it is indeed Senzar mages doing this, you may have to accept there will be casualties if an all-out battle ensues*

Stephenie nodded her head as they continued west toward the borough Henton had identified. She knew any battle between mages in the middle of the city would be bad. However, some decisions had no perfect choices, just differing degrees of consequences.

\*     \*     \*     \*     \*

Henton looked up from the weapons he had laid out on his bed. Ryia had suddenly moved to her feet and glanced at the floor in the direction of the Great Hall. After a moment, she calmed.

"Islet is on the stairs," she said.

Henton crossed the room and opened their door just as Islet passed in front of it. "Good evening. I didn't mean to startle you," he added as she recovered from her surprise.

"Good evening. I take it Stephenie is in here, since you knew I was passing."

Henton shook his head, "Ryia." He glanced into the dimly lit stairwell and did not see anyone else.

"I left the Ladies Josh assigned to take care of my needs in the Great Hall. They were happy to avoid the tower. It seems there is a rumor that Stephenie has placed spells on it to keep intruders out."

Henton smiled as he stepped back to make room for Islet. "Those rumors started before we left to get you. And while there is no truth to them, if it keeps people out of my things, then I won't correct anyone." Seeing Islet hesitate to enter, he said, "Steph is not available at the moment. We're sitting around fretting if you want to know the truth. You can join us."

Islet nodded her head and came into the room, which now suffered from the beginnings of construction of three separate bedrooms around the outer wall. She smiled at Douglas and Ryia as Henton closed the door behind her. "I had hoped to be able to give Steph some news to cheer her up." When Henton questioned her with a raised eyebrow, she continued. "Josh had blocked her from searching the archives, and while she hid her disappointment well, I could tell it bothered her. Fortunately, I managed to convince him to let her back in."

Henton faltered ever so slightly in his step, but recovered quickly enough that he doubted anyone noticed. Grabbing a pair of chairs from the wall, he set the better one down for Islet. The months of traveling together had removed the expectations of rank, but he waited until Islet sat before he lowered himself into the second chair. "I'm afraid she's out of the castle at the moment." He expected Islet's silent reaction and he trusted her with the knowledge. "She's afraid the attacks are from a group of Senzar mages who are trying to destabilize Josh."

Islet rubbed her brow and then pinched her nose as she looked to the floor. It took several moments before she looked up to meet his eyes. "So she went off on her own in the middle of the night." Sighing, Islet shook her head. "It doesn't surprise me, but if Josh finds out, he'll lose his mind."

"He's getting to be a problem," Douglas mumbled from where he stood next to his bed.

Henton wished he could get Douglas to be more careful with what he said against the King. When they were in Vinerxan, Douglas had verged on treason. While Douglas did not consider Joshua his King anymore, that would not change Joshua's thoughts on the subject. And although Douglas knew not to say anything outside of their group, someone might one day overhear him. *Then the trouble will come if Steph is not around to protect us,* Henton mused.

Islet looked to Douglas. "I admit I was surprised to find Josh so argumentative with Steph. They had been so close growing up, I simply expected him to sweep her up in his arms when we returned as he had done me." She turned to Henton. "I know that when we were younger, between Josh and me, I was by far the crueler one to Steph. I wouldn't stand up to Regina and Mother. I...I was not the best of sisters." She swallowed. "Now it seems things are reversed, and I will defend her where Josh does not."

Douglas kept his voice low, but not low enough. "I mentioned it before, Steph would make a better ruler."

"Douglas," Henton growled. He was glad to see regret on Douglas' face before the former corporal turned away.

"Actually," Islet offered, her voice a little too positive, "Josh doesn't appear to be doing bad. I sat in court today and he really seemed to treat everyone fairly and I would say that everyone appeared to respect him. It wasn't until someone mentioned Steph that he lost his composure." She shrugged. "And it was only for a moment. He recovered fairly well, though I would say people are aware there is something wrong between them."

"Like him getting angry we didn't follow his route to Vinerxan. What were his plans for us?" Douglas demanded of Henton. "What did we avoid by Steph disobeying him? That is what I fear."

"Enough," Henton snapped, "if you don't watch yourself, you'll end up dangling from a rope."

Henton felt Islet's hand on his arm. "I don't think he intended any harm to come to any of you. And Henton is right, Douglas, statements like that will get you in trouble. Get your anger and frustration out of your system, but make sure you do so quickly and privately. If you let them fester, they will get you into serious trouble."

Henton nodded his head, his heart racing in his desire to change the subject. "But for tonight, we just need to cover for Stephenie. We don't need her in more trouble with Josh."

Islet nodded her head. "I will not betray her activities. When she gets back, we can let her know I can get her back into the archives."

Henton swallowed. "Islet, I know you want to look out for her, but is this wise? You can guess what she was up to."

"What?" Ryia asked from where she sat on Douglas' bed.

"She's searching," Islet said. Then seeing Ryia's silent demand for more, she added, "for her sire."

Henton forced himself to breath before he voiced his protest. "Her father was the King—"

"Which," Islet interrupted, "is not the question."

Henton adjusted his approach, sensing the stubborn streak both sisters shared rising in Islet. "My point is, only six of us know about this man, which according to your mother, raped her. If Steph starts digging, she risks other people discovering the truth." Henton continued to return Islet's gaze, even after it had become uncomfortable.

"I realize that." She finally said, forcing her shoulders down and lifting her head higher. "When I was captured by the Senzar and tossed into a cell, I was furious. I was trapped. I hated everyone, while at the same time, desperate to see anyone I knew. I could trust no one and felt so utterly alone." She glanced to the others and then back to Henton. "Even after you rescued me, it took me a while to not hate you for taking so long, while at the same time, fearing you might leave me.

"Like you, I am fully aware of what she is doing," Islet said. "But I will support her in what she wants to do. For on our way back here, I realized something. While I was feeling righteous in my anger at the world, it occurred to me that Stephenie had been locked in a figurative cell most of her life. She had grown up not being able to truly trust anyone and was always surrounded by people who could at any moment have her killed. I decided then, if she was able to put the seventeen years before she met you behind her, than I should be able to get over one year in a cell."

"Islet—"

"If she wants to seek out her sire to find a way to rebuild a body for Kas, I will help her."

"Kas fears what this man might do. We don't even know for sure if what your mother said is true. But I also don't have a reason to assume it is not. The man has got to be very powerful and a very damaged person to do what he did."

Islet nodded her head. "Probably. And while I will give her my opinion on actually seeking him out, I won't make the decision for her by hiding the truth."

Henton lowered his gaze. His stomach churned with conflict and after a moment, he spoke. "You are right. I just don't want harm to come to her and she's obsessed over this." He lifted his eyes. "I fear what she will do, but I also don't want to be her jailer. I'll tell her your news if I see her before you do."

Islet reached over and put her hand back on Henton's arm. "I don't blame you for how you feel."

"But I do blame myself for what I was suggesting."

Ryia sat forward and spoke in Pandar, "So, how are you getting Steph back into the archives and how is she going to find her father? You really think her mother would have written something like that down in a diary?"

"Cothish," Islet corrected. "And no, not a diary, but logs. Steph told Josh that she was looking for the family of a painter who had painted a portrait of my grandmother Kara. It was done in a distinctive way. I can't say I was really partial to it, but Steph said to honor our sister Kara, she wanted to have a portrait of me done by that family." She glanced at Henton. "It was a weak excuse. However, it would give her lots of time in the archives and Josh seemed to buy it. The trouble was he said he would have someone else search for information on the painting." She turned back to Ryia and Douglas. "Today, I suggested to Josh that he allow me and Steph to search the archives together so we could rebuild the relationship we should have had when we were younger. And it would keep the two of us out of his hair."

Douglas snorted softly. "That would be the reason he agreed."

"Work out your anger, Douglas," Islet said. "However, you are likely correct."

"But how will that help?" Ryia demanded. "Your mother wrote in a log 'today I was raped by this charming man'?"

Islet cleared her throat. "Not likely. I can't be certain, but it may be that no one knew it happened. It would not be something I would want to share if it had happened to me. However, my grandfather kept immaculate records of everything, including anyone who had any business with him. He said he wanted future generations to be able to learn from the past.

"My father continued the tradition and I even convinced my husband to start doing it in Ipith." She looked away for a moment, "Though those records are now likely destroyed or worse, used by the Senzar." Looking up, she continued. "If it was a messenger from the north, there would likely be a record. There might even have been a description of the man. There would certainly have been notes about where he was from and what his business was. That may provide enough clues."

"Assuming they were not lies." Henton shook his head, "A man who rapes the queen of a country is not likely to leave a trail that others could follow back to him."

"A man that rapes a queen, and is potentially more powerful than Steph, is a man dangerous enough not to care," Douglas countered.

# Chapter 9

Stephenie managed to get back inside the castle just as the sky was brightening from black into a dark blue. She stumbled through the old kitchens as she rubbed her dry eyes. Kas tried to reach out to her mind, but she shook her head. "It hurts too much. I kept my senses wide open all night and other than finding a multitude of people with various problems, I was worthless sitting on that roof."

Kas spoke aloud as they moved into her Great Hall, "I should have checked upon your condition more frequently. You are again bleeding from your nose and it is telling that you have not even tried to wipe your face clean this time."

Stephenie automatically rubbed the blood from her upper lip onto her shirtsleeve. She had overextended herself in the middle of the morning, but had not wanted to allow the murderers a chance to get away with their crimes. The trouble was, and she knew Kas wanted to point it out, but for some reason he had not yet done so, that even if she had found them, she was now in no shape to deal with them. "Just don't."

"I will get you into bed and make sure Henton and the others let you sleep. They can say you are not feeling well, which will be the truth."

Stephenie stopped walking long enough to look over at Kas. His opaque form did not show disapproval, just concern. "Thank you."

As she started to climb the steps of her tower, the pounding in her head grew worse and she stopped to avoid losing the food she had eaten in the early hours of the morning. Her senses were so dulled that she did not realize Henton stood above her until she attempted to continue upward.

A moment later, he stood beside her. "Are you hurt? Damn," he added after he saw her face. "You've overdone it."

"Just a bit," she said, smearing the fresh blood across her face. "I don't do mental surveillance very well. Nothing too bad, but my head is killing me."

He reached down and swept her into his arms. She let out a moan of pleasure at no longer having to expend the effort to remain standing. "Did you find those responsible?"

"No," Kas said, becoming fully opaque again next to Henton. "If they deigned to do something, they were not observed by either Stephenie or I."

"Let me get you to your bed."

"You okay, Steph?" Ryia asked from the doorway a few steps above Henton.

"She'll be fine," Henton said as he turned and carried her up to her room. "Kas, can you remove the bar from the door?"

Kas disappeared as Stephenie slipped into sleep.


Stephenie gradually gained awareness. It took her a while to realize she was actually in her bed. She had yet to open her eyes, but sensing the energy potentials around her, she could tell which window the sun shone through and knew midday had arrived.

Her head still hurt, but it no longer throbbed. "There is that," she said aloud. She rolled onto her side, not yet ready to get out of the soft bed. However, there were people nearing her door and she realized it had been their approach that had woken her. Tossing off the covers, she moved to a sitting position as Henton slowly turned the door handle.

"I'm up," she said. Forcing herself to her feet, she watched as Henton pushed open the door and entered, followed by Will, Douglas, and Ryia. Kas had slipped into the room at the same time.

"You are looking better," Henton said.

*I need to practice mental surveillance,* she thought to Kas in answer to his unspoken comment. "Thank you for letting me sleep," she said to the others. Still feeling tired, she sat down on the bed as the others migrated to the table and chairs. "What is it?" She asked, sensing their general mood.

"Well," Will said, turning sideways in the chair to face Stephenie. "As I told the others, Henton's guess had been wrong. The attack came in the far west of the city. Two men chopped up in a back alley. Based on the way it was done, they think it is the same murderers."

"Damn it." She got to her feet and crossed the room to Henton.

"There were only ten prior events," he said, "I didn't have much to make a guess from."

She shook her head. "It's nothing against you. It might have been a case of opportunity. News of our return spread fast and perhaps they found one of their intended targets unavailable to them last night. Those that died might have just been convenient."

"Ugh," Douglas said. "You say that like you think they planned a dinner, but at the last minute had to find someone else to go to drinks with."

"From what I saw," Henton said, "this was done very methodically. There is no passion in it, just brutal business."

"And it is the business of fear," Will added. "These people are monsters."

Stephenie felt her headache getting worse. *I can't do what I did last night Kas. I really wouldn't have had anything left to fight them.*

*You have never been good at deciphering patterns from mental energy. Perhaps you just need to sit ready and wait for me to find something.*

"Steph?" Will asked.

Looking around, it was obvious he had said something to her that she missed. "Sorry, I was talking to Kas." Determined to keep her train of thought, she turned to Henton. "Do you think it will change where they will strike next?"

Henton shrugged. "I can't say for certain. I don't think this one additional event changed their behavior."

Will cleared his throat. "I came by, not to tell you about the attack or to discuss things I am sure your brother would disapprove of you being involved with, but to let you know that someone has come by the temple the last couple of days asking for you. I would have mentioned it yesterday, but I did not know of it until this morning."

"Who?" Stephenie asked, moving back to her bed so she could sit down.

"I don't know. They have so far refused to come into the complex. The guards at the gate were asked if you were at the temple and when this woman was told no, she said she would come back later. Apparently, this person, or others like her, may have come to the temple a few times before you returned. They had asked if anyone knew when to expect you. This woman was a foreigner. Spoke Pandar with an odd accent."

Stephenie glanced at Henton, but he shrugged.

"Any other useful information?"

Will shook his head. "The guards will get some more training. They couldn't remember for certain what she was wearing, hair color, or anything else." Will looked to Henton. "Do you have some time to drill soldiers?"

"No."

Will turned to Ryia. "I heard you did a good job teaching Sara and Rebecca, can I have you teach some of the others at the temple? They all believe in Catheri, so you'd need to put everything in terms of the Catheri's teachings. Justice and honor and the like."

Stephenie felt a pang of hurt that Will had not asked her. She knew immediately the emotion was out of place. She had done her best to avoid teaching his wife and without the frame of reference these recruits would have, Ryia made a far better choice. *But I still don't like it.*

Ryia raised an eyebrow, "Does it pay?"

Will chuckled. "We can see."

"Steph almost ran out of money on way back, so she's not been paying us."

"Ran out of money?" Will shook his head. "You should ask Joshua for a regular allowance."

"These attacks," Kas said, keeping her from responding to Will's comment, "do you believe they might have a connection with this woman who is seeking you out?"

She shrugged. "I don't know, but it could be some of the people from Vinerxan. I told them to come."

"You told that Captain Nerida and her band of bastards to come," Douglas said. "And probably told them more than you should have. Do you really want them here?"

Stephenie pushed herself to her feet; technically she had not told Nerida to come, but had offered that to the others in the hopes they would abandon the Captain. "Let me get changed and I'll go over to the temple. If Nerida is here, I'll deal with her. These sick attacks are actually her style." Feeling her stomach grumble, she turned and looked to Douglas, "Can you and Ryia run over to the kitchens and bring me back some food. I'm a bit starved." They nodded their heads. "Thank you."

As they stood up to leave, Henton spoke. "Islet came by last night. She wanted to let you know that she convinced Joshua to allow you and her to look through the archives for the family that did your grandmother's portrait."

*I would never have thought Islet would do that for me,* she told Kas. *I hope she doesn't really want to find that painter's family.*

"If you want my opinion," Henton continued as he and the others headed toward the door, "sometimes it is not worth digging through the past. Redoing the portrait might not bring you what you want."

Stephenie caught Henton's eye. While she could not read his thoughts, it was obvious he knew and disapproved of her real goal. *You behind that, Kas?*

*Stephenie, you know my thoughts on searching for your father. The man is not someone with whom I would want you to associate. We will all support you in your search, if you decide to pursue this. Just refrain from asking us to celebrate such a decision with a dance and music.*

She had heard the argument too many times from Kas and did not respond. Kas needed her to reconstruct a body for him and that meant learning transformative magic. Her sire, no matter how much of a bastard he might be, currently offered her the best possibility to learn that skill.

Stephenie looked at the five faces before her, but they were concentrating on Ryia. The girl had explained some of the fundamentals of magic in terms Stephenie could now repeat, but had never experienced.

These five were the most advanced students Sara had been teaching. Watching the energy, Stephenie noticed a young man from western Cothel generating a strong gravitational field. It lacked focus, but from a position of raw power, it held twice the strength of anything Ryia ever generated. However, Ryia had come a long way in the last few months. Although she could muster less raw power than most, she had learned control and subtlety. In a fight, that could easily be the difference between surviving or dying.

Stephenie waited for Kas to remind her that she lacked the subtle control she insisted Ryia learn, but her friend had remained in the castle. Glancing out a window, she watched two horses tied to a post groom each other while she continued to listen to Ryia explain the fine art of moving objects. *The waste of money on glass panes,* came unbidden to her thoughts.

"Prophet," a voice came from across the room.

Stephenie turned her focus to a young man Will used to run errands. "Yes?"

Everat crossed the room before stopping in front of her to bow. "Prophet, there is a woman who has asked for the pleasure and grace of an audience with you. I am told this is the one you were expecting."

Stephenie looked at the blonde man, his skinny frame thinner than her own. His eyes were still turned to the floor, as if he lacked the worthiness to even see her. "Where is she waiting?"

"Please follow me."

Stephenie rose to her feet and waved Ryia to remain. If Captain Nerida had come, she would keep Ryia from becoming a target. Though Stephenie considered it unlikely the Captain would risk confronting Stephenie directly. *Not after what I did to her.*

As Stephenie followed the young man into the back of the main temple, she recognized the presence waiting for her in a small office. "Jerylin," Stephenie said the moment she saw the woman's freckled face. She hastened across the room and hugged the woman who was about her own age. "Are you well?" Stephenie asked in Pandar, knowing Jerylin would not know Cothish.

Jerylin smiled and bowed. "Prophet, I am well."

"I was unsure if anyone would come all the way to Cothel, but I am glad you did."

"I want to offer our most sincere apologies for how we treated you," Jerylin said, honesty in her voice and manner. "We had no idea of who you really were until Nerida's team came back describing what you had done and what you had said."

Stephenie smiled but said nothing. She knew many factors played into her treatment, fear of Captain Nerida being a primary cause. However, Stephenie always believed in treating people fairly, even if they had little wealth and power. "Please sit," she finally said, taking a chair for herself and waiting for Jerylin to sit before continuing. "I went to Vinerxan to rescue my sister. You did what you had to do to survive. I took none of it personally."

Jerylin smiled with obvious relief. "I came on behalf of several others. We heard your offer to come to you and after learning more about who you really are, we decided to find you in the hope the offer is still open."

"Of course!" Stephenie allowed herself to relax. "I said I would take any of you in."

"We've been here for a couple of weeks. We did not want to risk being declared witches and warlocks without you to vouch for us. We want to be purified and cleansed of Elrin. You can do that for us, yes? We don't want to suffer under the demon god's curse any longer. We realize the Senzar were leading us on with their empty promises, but you are truly cleansing people, yes?"

Stephenie nodded her head slowly; the color and vibrance of the world seemed to vanish, leaving the room smelling old and musty to her. *Even when I tell people the truth, they insist on believing only what they want to believe. Perhaps Will is right,* she thought, still hoping people would not be so stubborn.

No longer overjoyed to see a person who had offered Stephenie a bit of kindness when she needed it, Stephenie changed the subject. "Is Captain Nerida with you?"

"Oh, no! We wanted nothing more to do with her." Jerylin's face wrinkled with worry. "We would never insult you by bringing her here. And I am not sure she even lives. There were twelve of us who left as soon as we could."

"What happened once I left with Ryia and my sister?" Stephenie asked.

"There was chaos for a while. Farfelee and some of the other Senzar tried to keep order after Lord Favian died. They were planning to leave because they feared trouble would be coming. But a woman arrived before they thought anyone would. She wasn't tall, but her skin was perfect, though darker than yours. Her beautiful golden-blond hair flowed down her back. Her eyes...her eyes were a deep green, like...Lord Favian...."

"What happened, Jerylin?" Stephenie did not like the distant look that came over Jerylin's face.

"The woman...she scared all the Senzar. Apparently, Favian had sent word to bring her shortly after you arrived. He wanted her to deal with you. She didn't ask us questions, she simply ripped what she wanted from our heads." Jerylin closed her eyes to fight back the tears that ran down her face. "You could feel the power coming from her." Jerylin's breath caught in her throat for a moment. "The first chance we got, we ran away. With nowhere to go, we decided to find you and ask for your help."

Stephenie swallowed, fearing the people causing trouble in Antar might have even more power than she thought. "What else can you tell me about this woman? Did she follow you as well?"

Jerylin shook her head. "She traveled with three men and a woman. They were not so much guards as they were servants, but they were also powerful Senzar. One of them struck down Farfelee with ease." Jerylin bowed her head. "I know you seemed to like the old healer."

Stephenie forced her fists to open, knowing from Jerylin's expression that Farfelee was now dead. "What else."

"The woman never told us her name, but we heard one of the Senzar say she was called Yreka. They called her something else as well, but I never heard the word before. I think she was related to Favian, though I am not sure how."

*Damn.* Stephenie's mind raced through possibilities, but none of them were pleasant. This Yreka terrified Jerylin; she could feel that easily. *And if the woman's older than Favian, perhaps she is an earlier generation. If so, I'm in a lot of trouble.* To Jerylin, she smiled and tried to project confidence, "You are most welcome here. As are the others, aside from Nerida and Isa."

"We did not bring them...and you can cleanse us of Elrin?"

"Catheri's High Priest can do so."

"Did Ryia come all the way with you? Is she here? I want to offer my apologies to how she was treated as well."

Stephenie nodded her head and then stood up. *Offer all you want, she's not likely to forgive you. And if you want the lie, then that's what you'll get.* "She did. Once you are cleansed, I will have her teach you how to embrace the power of the goddess."

# Chapter 10

Stephenie handed Jerylin, who returned with Elvira, Nilia, and nine others from Vinerxan, over to Will so they could be 'cleansed of evil.' She did not consider all of them completely honorable, but making allowances for growing up under the brutal threat of being burned alive, she had no strong objections to any of them becoming priests. As she expected, Ryia held a less positive outlook.

"Uran is a complete ass. He kept trying to get me to fail at things and get kicked out of Vinerxan."

"He wasn't as bad as Isa," Stephenie countered.

Ryia kicked the chair beside her, sending it tumbling to the floor. "Why should I teach any of them anything?!"

"One, because we need to have as many skilled people on our side as possible. Two, and probably more important to you, you can prove to them how wrong they were in dismissing you. You can outperform them and rub their faces in it."

Ryia shook her head. "I know I am weak. If I teach them everything I know, they'll soon be more powerful than me and will be able to push me around again."

Stephenie put her hand on Ryia's arm despite the girl using Pandar. "Don't let the fear of others achieving more than you drive you to try to hold them back. I know it can be hard to feel left behind, but just because they may one day be able to do more, doesn't mean you are any less. And perhaps, they may be there to help you in the future if the need should arise."

"But they were cruel to me. They...they never saw anything good in me. They didn't want me around."

Stephenie felt for Ryia, but she had to push. "I really need your help. You are actually better at teaching this than I am, so that makes you better than even me in that regard. And," she added raising a finger, "I can't do everything. If I keep up the work at night, I'll have to keep sleeping into the late morning."

Ryia nodded her head. "I know. But, you can't make me like them."

"That I am not asking you to do. Just make sure they learn how to be effective. I fear we will need their support sooner than anyone thinks."


Once Ryia and the people from Vinerxan were settled, Stephenie left Ryia at the temple to continue teaching those who had already been cleansed. With Henton in tow, she informed Sara she intended to walk back to the castle, and then the two of them slipped out a side door of the compound. The carriage would return Ryia, as well as Will and Sara, to the castle for dinner.

"What?" Stephenie asked, seeing Henton's smile.

"You look much more relaxed out here than you did in there," he said as they moved down a side street to get out of sight of the temple.

"I'm having a hard time settling into a fixed routine of someone else's choosing," she responded. "Especially after we've been on our own for months." She turned into a small market area and quickly purchased a couple of apples from a woman who looked uncertain of whom her customer was. Switching to the Old Tongue, which few outside the clergy and nobles knew, she opened up to Henton. "Do you really object that much to my searching the archives?"

She had caught Henton with his teeth in the apple. He quickly chewed and swallowed before replying. "What we know says the man should have his entrails removed. I fear what he might do to you if you find him." He raised his hand, keeping her from responding. "But I understand your desire for our friend. To be so close, yet so far from the one you love...it is hard. So I will support you, but we need to be careful."

Stephenie nodded her head. She knew how Henton felt about her, and while she loved him, she desired Kas. "Thank you." They continued down the narrow street for nearly half a block before Stephenie spoke again. "Have you checked into your holdings?"

"I never wanted that estate," Henton said. "Your brother wouldn't listen."

Stephenie shrugged. "It's part of the traditional gift when they make someone a knight. I don't think you can sell it, Josh simply gave you use of the land and any profits. It's a fair distance from Antar, so if you wanted to retire and live quietly, you could."

Henton chuckled. "Go there to become old and fat?" He shook his head. "I used to say I'd most likely end up on the end of some pirate's sword. Maybe drowned in a storm. However, now I think it more likely I'll be ripped apart by some Senzar."

Stephenie stopped walking. "Don't say such things. It won't happen as long as I am around. You understand that?" She bristled a little more when he laughed again. "I'm serious. You don't get to die on me. None of you do."

"Well, I'll do my best."

She sighed as she resumed walking. Lowering her voice, she continued in the Old Tongue. "One of the people from Vinerxan said we left just before this other Senzar arrived; a blond woman with dark skin and green eyes. A woman that struck fear into all the Senzar there." She looked up at his face. "I worry this woman might easily best me. I...I don't want you to get caught up in her wrath. I killed Favian, not you. If she's out for revenge, she should take it out on me."

"Do you think it is this woman that is killing these people?"

She shrugged; that fear had been running through her since Jerylin told her of the woman. "I'm not sure. Someone that powerful wouldn't need to resort to these tactics. From what Jerylin said, I'd expect she'd be more direct. But she had four people that arrived with her. Perhaps they are responsible."

"Or it could be someone else as well," Henton offered. "Look, we'll plan for the worst. I'll ready up some more poisons and when they surface again, we'll find a way to be there."

She wanted to tell him not to bother because she was not going to allow him to risk his life, but she knew it would be pointless. Her stomach growled at the smell of roasting pork. She reached for her pouch, but drew her hand away, knowing how little she had in the way of funds.

"It's on me," Henton said. "One of the stewards came by early this morning. Seems they wanted to resolve the issue of our back pay." He grinned at her. "It turns out being your personal guard pays a heck of a lot better than being a sergeant. Douglas will probably be complaining a lot less now."

"That's great! I was going to speak to Josh about it, but we've been yelling about other things instead."

"Well, since you paid us out of your funds on the journey, we probably owe you a bit back."

Stephenie shook her head. "Keep it. I'd probably incinerate it again at some point if I was carrying it."

After a very filling meal, they journeyed back to the castle without drawing any unwanted attention. Stephenie immediately sought out Islet and managed to escape into the archives. They shared a few stories as they read through the logs, but in truth, many of the gaps in their lives had been discussed in the months traveling together.

When they answered the summons for dinner, Stephenie feared Joshua would comment about Henton's guess regarding the location of the attack, but she was pleasantly surprised when Joshua remained quiet on the subject. Instead the conversation turned to the tourney he planned in honor of Islet's return.

Once dinner concluded, Stephenie returned to her room and immediately fell asleep. Before the third turn of the glass after the sun set, Kas woke her so they could patrol the city. This time, Stephenie refrained from actively searching with her mind and allowed Kas to look for the murderers. The night yielded no new leads for them and she managed to crawl back into her bed as the morning sun came over the horizon.

By the time she woke, Henton and Ryia had left for the temple of Catheri. Douglas remained behind to supervise the construction of the rooms on his floor and Islet had resumed the search of the archives. Relieved that no sacrifices were reported, Stephenie joined Islet in pouring through the dusty logs.

The next two days continued in a similar fashion, with Stephenie spending most of the night sitting on rooftops hoping that Kas would discover the monsters that could perpetrate such vicious crimes against innocent people. Each day that passed with no new victims worked to increase Stephenie's anxiety.

"Steph, you can't do everything," Islet said, flipping to the next page in the ledger before her.

"I'm not. You're helping. Ryia's helping. Henton's helping. Even Douglas, in his own way, is helping."

"What is he doing?"

Stephenie had to shrug. Will's workers were not done, but they were making progress and really did not need the supervision. "He's more than earned a holiday. Everyone has."

Islet frowned. "You look drawn and tired. Even marching whole days never made you look this bad."

Stephenie tossed a half-eaten roll at Islet. "Thanks for pointing that out." Stephenie rubbed her temples. They had found more than two dozen men who had come from the north and visited their father during the range of time when Stephenie could have been conceived. Another dozen they had already eliminated by looking at earlier logs. However, the inclusion of a description of the person visiting lacked consistency by those recording the logs. Which meant Islet and Stephenie had to reduce the list by looking for any people who made multiple visits, presuming the man who raped their mother only visited that one time.

"This scribe had terrible handwriting," Islet remarked. "I have no idea what half of the things on this page even say."

Stephenie was about to agree when she skimmed over a notation in the log before her. "Islet, what do you make of this. King Lartin of Calis sent a letter to our father. There is a cross reference...."

Stephenie reached into the pile of logs and pulled a journal from the stack. Flipping to the middle of the book, she scanned the page until she found the entry referenced in the other log. Checking the paper where they were recording their notes, she nodded her head. "This is suspect number four. The Lord Gunnarr Ralok, who brought a trade proposal from...Ista—have you found where that is?"

Islet shook her head. "Not yet. I've looked at several maps, but never heard of that country. The man's name is strange."

"Well, the note in the log speaks of a letter from King Lartin. It indicates the letter talks about a red-haired man baring a trade agreement. And it gives a reference to the first log entry. Lartin's letter is from around eight months before I was born."

"Does it give any more details?"

Stephenie shook her head as she stood. "But, it does give a reference to where the letter would be stored." Taking the book with her, she went back into Cedric's office to find the Seneschal working at his desk. "Cedric, can you tell me where to find this letter?"

He rose to his feet as Stephenie set the book on his desk. "Of course, Ma'am. Let me see what you have here." After studying the notation, he dipped a pen in ink and wrote down the reference on a small scrap of paper. "If we have it, it will be in the far room." Stepping around Stephenie, he led her back through the room where she had been working with Islet and into the room beyond that.

Shelves with bound stacks of paper filled the entirety of the room from the floor to the ceiling. The wealth of information in the room still inspired awe within her, even considering the numerous times she had pulled logs from the shelves.

"This notation marks it as private correspondence. Which means it is on the shelves near the back wall." Cedric pulled a logbook with a blue spine from the corner of one shelf. Flipping it open, he scanned down the pages until he found the desired reference. "On the third shelf, the book number eighty-three."

Stephenie followed his directions and pulled the tome from the shelf. The heavy, leather-bound book creaked as she opened it. The book held many pockets, each formed by folding parchment over and binding it to the spine.

"You'll want section six," Cedric said.

Stephenie flipped the pages and pulled a handful of letters from the sixth pouch. Cedric took the book from her hands so that she could flip through the letters. She felt her heart racing and wondered if Cedric would hear it.

The first three letters held no importance to her search, but the fourth one had the seal of Calis on the folded page. Carefully opening the old paper, she quickly scanned the page. When she reached the bottom, she handed the other letters to Cedric. "Thank you, I think this may have something of interest."

"Ma'am," Cedric said, his body reflecting apprehension.

"Yes?"

"I hate to make the request, but as keeper of these archives, will you be returning the letter to this book?"

Stephenie nodded her head. "Yes. I just need to study it a bit more, and then I will put it back."

"Thank you. I feared we might lose part of the archive. We managed to keep Burdger from destroying it, so...."

Stephenie patted Cedric's arm. "I fully understand. Thank you for your help."

"Ma'am," he said again, this time excusing himself and retreating from the room, leaving Stephenie with the lamp.

Taking the light and the letter, she returned to the outer room with Islet and sat down. "This is odd."

"What did you find?"

"I don't remember much of Calis' history, but the letter is a warning to...father," she said, her hesitation at using the word growing with each page they turned. "It seems King Lartin encountered a man wearing all the regalia of Ista, a very distant trading partner. The man had come to him promising a new trade agreement. Lartin says:

> *This man, who claimed to be Lord Gunnarr Ralok, towered over others and carried himself as king above kings. His red hair and haunting gaze unnerved me, though I did not throw him out because the little trade we do get from Ista is valuable.*

*I will not say what affront he made, but he was
gone by the next morning. None saw him leave and we
do not know his intentions. However, should a man
fitting this description appear within your court, I
would recommend the removal of his head without
pause or time for question.*

*Take heed at once and fear him, for he can be none
other than a warlock of the vilest nature.*

"That letter arrived after this Gunnarr had come and gone from
Antar," Islet said, leaning over the page to read the words as well.

"How are we related to Lartin?" Stephenie asked.

"His grandfather was our great grandfather on Mother's side. And
his grandfather's sister, who married into Esland, was Grandma Kara's
mother."

"How do you keep all that straight?"

Islet laughed. "Do you know how many hours I had to spend
memorizing these relationships? When I went to Ipith, I had to
memorize another army of relations. They breed like rabbits there,
everyone had at least six kids and half married their cousins. You
really had it lucky being able to run around and learn to fight."

Stephenie smiled. "I won't deny that." She sat down in the chair.
"There is a note down here that says the letter was responded to, but
no copy was kept for the archive." Turning back to Islet, she
continued, "I don't think I can ask Cedric to dig for anything specific
about this man. This letter gives away a lot of clues about me."

"I would say Father made the connection to this man after you
were born. It would explain how he knew."

Stephenie nodded her head and then folded the letter and slid it
into the middle of the stack of notes she and Islet had written.
Although she had promised Cedric she would return the letter, the
contents were too damning to risk his later curiosity. Sitting back, she
sighed. "There is not much to go by, a country and a name."

"I'm sorry. We can keep looking...."

Stephenie considered it, but suspected the archives contained little
more of value. If a letter did exist describing more of what happened
with the man, she felt it unlikely her father would have allowed it in

the archive. "I'll research more about the country. I think we're done here."

Islet rubbed her right eye with the back of her hand. "Thank you. I'm really tired of looking and to be honest, I don't want to sit for a portrait, at least not like the one of Grandma Kara."

"Sorry about that," Stephenie said as she gathered up the logs and started putting them back on the shelves. "I really had not thought of a good excuse for Josh and that was the first thing that came to mind. Cedric, I told him I was looking for other traitors. Hopefully, he'll think the letter is tied to that."

Islet handed her the last log they had examined and picked up the lamps. "Let's get some food. I can hunt around in the library for you regarding Ista. That will give you time to do the other things you need to do, including sleep."

Stephenie gave her sister a hug, as she did not trust her voice to keep from breaking.

# Chapter 11

Two more days passed with Stephenie helping at the temple instead of searching the archives. So far Islet had only determined Ista lay to the north. Cothel had no history of dealings with the country so far away and asking too many questions would draw suspicion. Stephenie would not give up on the search, but she had time. *A trail nineteen years old would not suddenly disappear any further over a few more days or weeks.*

Tired from spending the day helping Ryia conduct her classes, Stephenie allowed her eyes to close out the night sky. Wedged as she was into the corner of a thatched roof and a chimney, she would not slip from her perch even if she fell asleep. *And perhaps I will doze a bit,* she thought, allowing herself to relax and ignore all the complaints of the day, including Ryia's frustration and protests with the prospect of having to teach those who had tormented her in Vinerxan.

*I think I have found them!* Kas' voice sounded in Stephenie's head. His voice was weak due to distance, though quickly growing in strength as he rushed toward her. Suddenly fully awake, Stephenie launched herself into the air and used her magic to fly in his direction. The ghost reversed his travel as Stephenie increased her speed.

*Three in the last one,* Kas said.

With the risk of being overheard by those with magic, Stephenie did not respond. A few moments later, Kas slowed as he rose higher into the air above a long row of two story buildings that shared walls between them. Stephenie reached out with her mind and felt a sharp spike of terror coming from the end building. Getting closer, she sensed five people in the corner room. Of them, most prominently, a man and a woman expressed severe panic. The mental presence of the three others was muted, but they suddenly changed their movement at her approach.

Already diving headfirst toward the second story window at the end of the row houses, she barely got her blades from their scabbards as her leading buffer of energy smashed through the shutters. Her eyes instinctively closed as she flew through the debris of the mica-paned window that had existed behind the wooden shutters. With her downward angle, she hit the floor and immediately adjusted her gravity field, allowing her to roll to her feet.

The man closest the window swung a blade at her, but she easily deflected the blow with the sword in her dominate right hand. Thrusting with the long dagger in her off-hand, she aimed for the man's chest. Her blade hit resistance as the man responded instinctively with innate magic to protect his body. Pushing power into her attack, she increased the gravitational attraction between the dagger and the man's spine. Her field easily overwhelmed the man's and the blade sunk deep into his body.

Behind her, she felt Kas drop through the ceiling just as energy left the augmentation device the second man carried. Energy filled the air around her quickly raising the temperature. With barely any awareness, she compensated by drawing the excess energy into herself.

Pulling her long dagger from the man she stabbed, she used her magic to push the injured man away from her. The strength of her force slammed him into the wall.

The third person, a woman with long brown hair, threw two balls in her direction just as Kas buried his hand deep into the second man's head. Stephenie felt the man fighting Kas' effort to freeze his brain, but the balls flying at her took precedence. Instinctively sensing they were lightweight and hollow, Stephenie defected their flight away from her. However, the woman used her augmentation device to generate a field that ruptured the balls, filling the room with a cloud of red-brown dust that exploded in all directions.

"For Mertor!" The woman cried as she tried to turn her face away.

Stephenie flung a gravitational pulse toward the cloud, blowing it away from her, but a vortex swirled behind her force, spinning some of the fine particles back at her. She felt the dust burn as it hit her skin and eyes.

"Get down!" She tried to tell the couple that sat naked and bound on the floor. The effort burned her throat as some of the fine powder flew into her nose and mouth.

"Stephenie, keep it off you!" She heard Kas say aloud as she started to cough. Her initial surprise at his audible voice diminished as she found it difficult to breath.

The dust that landed on her tongue tasted of bitter metal. She spit it out between the coughs that were getting more insistent and served to draw more dust into her lungs. Her eyes watered and burned. Wiping them with the back of her hand only increased the pain.

"It is poison, get out of here," Kas insisted in Dalish, becoming visible in front of her.

The couple on the floor struggled against their bonds as they began to thrash and roll. The panic they felt overwhelmed Stephenie's own building terror. The memory of her suffocating the girl in Wyntac into unconsciousness came back to her.

Stephenie barely noticed the woman who threw the balls convulsing against the wall. Blood covered her front, running from her mouth as her screams quickly turned to a gurgle. The blast of air Stephenie used to protect herself had pushed the bulk of the dust back into the priestess' face. A red sheen engulfed the woman's whole body.

Stephenie continued to try to clear her lungs, but it felt like lifting an immense weight on her chest. She called out mentally to Kas, *Help Me!*

"Concentrate on healing yourself!" He responded.

Her head throbbed. Pain laced her chest. Her sight dimmed to a dark red as the burning of her eyes increased. There was no air left in her lungs to invoke a cough. She drew in energy as fast as she could. Her awareness of everything but the pain faded. As energy filled her, her frustration grew. Her body did not understand what was causing the damage; it simply wanted more energy.

Fighting the convulsions she distantly knew her body suffered, her lungs erupted with a far different burning. A moment later, her head flew back and her mouth opened to unleash a large gout of raw energy and blue flames. The burning of her lips and face instinctively caused her to draw more energy, and as she had done before, she expelled the raw power and flames from her upper body.

However, this time her eyes were open, and for once, she saw the energy leaping from her body. It swirled and pulsed with a life of its own, filling the air with waves of beautiful patterns. Her eyes had changed and flames flew from them, magnifying the room around her. She watched as a brilliant iridescence covered her exposed skin. The incredible beauty of it fascinated and frightened her. Her body had partially transformed to handle the power, *but, what did I become and will I change back?*

The surreal nature of the question stood out in her mind. But as the pain of the poison faded, and the pain of the energy grew more intense, she once again recognized the need to breathe drumming insistently in her head. As she cut the flow of energy, the flames coming from her lungs and covering her upper body instantly vanished. Gasping for air, she inhaled deeply. The fluid from her lungs was now burned away and the taste of burning wood filled her chest. However, that was highly welcome compared to not breathing at all.

Still sitting on the floor, her senses gradually came back to her. She felt Kas hovering just outside of the front of the building. The ceiling above her crackled with fire; the floor around her now a blackened scar. She shivered as a comparatively cold breeze hit her bare skin.

She remained on the floor and reached out to draw away the energy from the flames that covered the ceiling, killing the fire's ability to sustain itself. The effort hurt her taxed body, but it also warmed her.

"Are you well?" Kas asked. Coming back into the room, he luminesced into a visible form as he passed through the wall. "I lacked any choice except to retreat from your energy draw. I feared it would have killed me if I had chosen to remain."

Stephenie looked up at her friend. Her eyes watered, but this time from the joy of seeing him. Unable to bring herself to speak, she reached out mentally. *I am so tired.*

Kas nodded his head and then moved about the room, coming to rest next to one of the destroyed balls. *On a positive note, I believe your flames have cleared the air of the poison. However, I would recommend not moving, there is still dust covering most surfaces.*

"Great," she managed to force out of her irritated throat. To her ears, her voice sounded like old Ronaik, a famous bard whose gravelly voice had been tempered by years of smoking. She hoped the flames that shot from her lungs and mouth had not ruined her voice forever.

She closed her eyes, but kept herself from lying down. Everyone else who had been in the room was dead. The memory of the terror of those suffering from the poison was now buried under her own panic. Reaching out further, she sensed no one downstairs and no one in the adjoining home. Swallowing the spit in her mouth, she wished there was something in the room to drink, but the red tinge that covered everything kept her in place.

*You will no doubt experience trouble returning to the castle with no shirt. Fortunately, your pants only appear to be singed, so you will not be entirely indecent. I may have to agree with Will on this account, it would appear you enjoy showing off your body.*

She looked down at herself. She could still see some residue of the poison on her pants, so she tried to keep her arms elevated. However, her limbs ached with fatigue and she lacked the energy to respond to Kas' jests.

"I'll need help," she forced herself to speak, her voice already improving. "Go...bring Henton."

Kas came closer and his form blinked into a kneeling position in front of her. *There could be more of these cowards,* he said more seriously. *I should remain to protect you.*

"Bring me one of the augmentation devices," she told him. "I need to confirm what god they worship."

After a moment, Kas complied, taking the one that had been around the neck of the man she had stabbed in the chest. He placed the round holy symbol of Mertor on the floor in front of her.

Her lip curled slightly; priests of this god tended to be assassins and Elard Burdger had hired some previously to try to kill Joshua. *Kas, please go back and get Henton. I'll need his help to get back to the castle and the sooner you have him coming to help, the sooner you can come back and watch me. I think the noise that we made would have driven off anyone else. In fact, I'd guess the city guard will be coming soon.*

Kas nodded his head with reluctance. *I do not like leaving you alone. I will not be gone long.*

"I'll be here waiting," she said, forcing a smile to her lips, though Kas had already left, flying faster than she could. She glanced down at the augmentation device. *So, not Senzar then?* She frowned. A part of her had hoped it would be that Yreka Jerylin had mentioned, even if that woman posed a serious threat. While that conflict remained unresolved, it would weigh on her mind. *However bad this poison was, that woman will be worse still.*

She looked around the room, feeling a little more life come back into her body. "Is it bad that this keeps getting easier?" She whispered to herself, not wanting to stress her throat, but still hoping to hear her voice return to normal. The first time she had expended energy like that, it had left her unconscious for days.

Downstairs, she sensed someone come in through the outside door. Reaching out despite the pain, she sensed a timid person. A moment later, she heard a faint voice calling out for someone, but it was too low for her to make out.

She forced herself to her feet and left the holy symbol on the floor. Still unsteady, she walked to the door and opened it with her magic. Stepping over the dead woman, she went into the hall. "Please stay down stairs," she managed to say loud enough to be heard. Breathing a little easier now that she was out of the room with the poison, she felt more strength come back to her body.

Covering her breasts with her arms, she made her way to the stairs and carefully descended to the first floor. An older man stood in the front doorway, which was opened to the outside.

"Who are you? Where are Ole and Marget?"

Stephenie nodded her head to the grey-haired man, her legs trembling slightly. "I came here to try and protect them."

"Gods, another attack?"

Stephenie nodded her head and inclined it toward the outside. The man stepped back and allowed her to exit the building. She noticed a few others had gathered as well. Feeling dizzy from the effort, she sat down on the wooden steps that led up to the door. "I am sorry, but I was not in time to save Ole and Marget. However, I was able to stop three of the people responsible."

A murmur went through the crowd. "Who is it?" Someone asked another in the crowd. "It looks like her," someone else said and the level of commotion increased.

The old man standing next to her stepped down from the stairs and carefully examined her face. Then he dropped to his knees. "Your Highness."

Stephenie groaned inwardly, but kept her face neutral. "Please, there is no need for that," she said as others started to kneel as well.

"Ma'am, it is a rag, but please take my shirt."

Stephenie watched as the old man pulled the worn shirt over his head and handed it out to her, his eyes averted. "Thank you. What is your name?" She asked as she took the shirt from the man. She knew it would be a dress on her, but putting on a shirt that was not contaminated with poison would help her feel less vulnerable.

"Unhil, Ma'am."

"Thank you, Unhil." When she lifted her arms to pull it over her head, more gasps came from the crowd. Obviously, some people must not have been certain of her identity, but the solid black claw mark on her left breast offered confirmation. With her head clear of the shirt, she noticed several people quickly trying to look away. Despite the jests from her friends, she actually had grown used to other people seeing her naked body and even if she had not, she was too exhausted to care.

"Prophet, are the criminals dead?"

Stephenie resumed her seat on the steps. "Please forgive me for sitting, but the people who perpetrated this attack tried to use poison to kill me. I'll be fine, but it wasn't pleasant. And worse, there is poison all over the room upstairs."

"Who were they? Why they do this to innocent people?"

Stephenie turned to the woman wearing a faded dress. "I don't know yet. But I intend to find out."

The conversation stopped as soldiers appeared further down the street; they moved quickly in her direction. Some of the peasants left the area, while newcomers gathered to see what caused the commotion. Stephenie waited until the soldiers were in the middle of the crowd before addressing them. "Sergeant," she said as the man stopped in front of her. "I am Princess Stephenie. The building is currently secure, but unsafe. If you would have someone send for some holy warriors, I would greatly appreciate it." The tone of her voice, despite the gravelly quality, allowed no challenge.

Kas returned not long after the soldiers arrived. Upon Stephenie's request, he returned to the bedroom to examine the scene more closely. Henton, Douglas, and Ryia arrived nearly half a turn of the glass after Kas. "You don't look too bad, but you seem to have undressed yourself," Henton said, slipping easily from his horse.

"My shirt was covered in poison. My pants still are and my legs are starting to burn from it. Did you—" she smiled as he raised a bundle of clothing he pulled from his saddlebag. "Thank you." She turned toward the man who had lent her his shirt and waved him closer. "Henton, would you give Unhil some money. He graciously gave me his shirt and I am afraid it has been contaminated. It will need to be burned and I don't want him to go without for his kindness."

"Of course, Your Highness." Henton turned to the older man, pulled several coins from his pouch, and placed them in the man's hand.

"It is not necessary, Your Highness," the man said, before turning to Henton to return the money. "My Lord, I was pleased to help her."

Henton merely patted the top of the man's hands, keeping the coins in place. "You looked after her for me; it is my pleasure to buy you some new clothing."

Stephenie moved up the short set of stairs and into the house. "The lower floor should be safe. Since you are here, I really want to change."

Henton, Douglas, and Ryia followed her inside. Forgoing modesty, she quickly slid off her boots, unbuckled her belt, and removed her pants. Ryia used magic to light a lamp sitting on a table, illuminating her splotchy red legs as Douglas turned his face away.

"Does that hurt?" Ryia asked, coming closer.

Stephenie held her tongue as she pulled off Unhil's rough shirt. Taking a moment to examine the rash on her legs, she lifted her head to look at Henton, who quickly lifted his own eyes. "Can you see if they have any water in the kitchen and perhaps some soap?"

Kas appeared in a very faint form next to Ryia. "In my investigation, it would appear that the poison is carried by mold spores. I do not know if the mold is still viable, but it is possible it could spread."

Ryia looked at him. "In Cothish," she demanded.

Kas frowned at the girl. "Fungus...dust," he said, searching for the words. Turning back to Stephenie, he continued mentally, switching back to Dalish. *I am uncertain how they fabricated the balls, but they appear to have been hollow, made from several layers of paper and a thin outer coating of clay. I believe they feed the mold a toxic soup of poisons and let the mold spread though the inside of the sphere. When they ruptured the balls, the tiny spores filled the air, carrying the toxin with them. If you go near it again, keep a wet cloth over your face to avoid breathing the dust.*

Henton returned with a bowl of water, a rag, and some soap. Dunking the rag in the water, she lathered the soap on the rag and started scrubbing her legs.

"It looks like Sara, Will, and several others have arrived," Douglas said, his attention focused out the window and away from Stephenie's naked body.

Stephenie opened her tired mind and confirmed Douglas' appraisal. Grabbing the bowl from Henton, she walked into the kitchen to give herself a small amount of privacy. "Keep them from going upstairs. I don't know how safe it is."

*I will be near, but not too near,* Kas said as he left to avoid the holy warriors.

*I love you,* she thought back to him.

\*   \*   \*   \*   \*

She finished scrubbing her legs as quickly as she could. Another squad of soldiers had arrived, as well as a number of holy warriors of Felis. The tone of the men who had come to secure the scene grated on her nerves.

"I understand Her Highness is cleaning herself up, but if she is washing away blood to hide a crime, we cannot have that."

Henton's voice came to her, his icy response to the holy warrior losing none of its venom. "You want to go upstairs, by all means do so. I've already warned you what you'll find."

"Don't take an insolent tone with me. You tell me Her Highness just happened upon these murderers and managed to kill them single-handedly. How does that look to those of us who have been scouring the city for weeks?" The man demanded.

Stephenie slid on the pants Henton had brought her. The cloth rubbed against her irritated legs, causing a burning pain. She bit her lip in frustration with the poison as she tied her pants tight. With bare feet, she emerged from the kitchen.

More than a dozen people stood in the front room. Henton, Douglas, and Ryia formed a wall blocking everyone's access to her. Stepping around them, she spoke, her voice momentarily relapsing into a gravelly quality. "Should I explain to my brother your strong desire to see me without pants?" The holy warrior swallowed. "What of Queen Rebecca, your High Priest? You think she would appreciate that?" She asked before the man could respond. "I really don't care that you might look incompetent because I found them and you didn't. My concern was to stop the killings."

"And how do we know you killed those responsible and not just some random people." The holy warrior said in a feeble attempt to maintain some authority.

"Go upstairs, but I warn you to cover your faces with wet cloth. There is a red-brown dust covering almost everything up there. It is a poison and it kills quickly. It left me with this lovely voice. I burned most of it out of the air and off my upper body, but my legs are still raw from where it made its way through my pants."

The holy warrior before her motioned the men on his left to go up the stairs. "And you were the only survivor?"

"There are three dead followers of Mertor up there, plus their intended victims, naked and bound on the floor."

The holy warrior stood straighter. "Followers of that foul god were hired by Elard Burdger. They killed our late High Priest and tried to poison His Majesty when His Majesty held the castle from Burdger's forces."

Stephenie nodded her head. She had managed to save her brother and Rebecca before she killed Elard. *But that had been a different type of poison,* she acknowledged to herself. "I think we should minimize the number of people who know we found these priests here. I suspect there are others in the area and we don't want them to flee." The holy warrior nodded his head and went up the stairs. "If you find any small balls," she called to his back, "do not rupture them, that's what the poison was in."

Stephenie turned as Sara came over to her. The woman kept her discomfort under control, but Stephenie still felt it. Exhausted, Stephenie moved to the closest chair and sat down.

"Lord Ingles is a holy warrior of the fifth order, just shy of a master priest."

Stephenie coughed, hoping to clear the irritation still in her throat. "I don't take kindly to the accusations."

Sara nodded her head. "How are your legs?"

Stephenie shrugged. "Something in the poison has been resisting my ability to heal it."

"You should have gone total flame," Will said quietly from behind Sara. "If your upper body wasn't affected, it must have been due—"

Stephenie glared at Will; certain aspects of her life she did not share openly and there were too many ears in the room for her to discuss the transformation of her flesh. "My legs are getting more irritated with time, but I don't think I am in danger." Sara tilted her head. "What?" Stephenie asked, noting Sara's hesitation.

"Even after washing there still might be poison on your skin, slowly leaching its way into your body," Sara said. She lowered her voice, "We worked with many poisons to try and bring down witches. Something that acted slowly and is hard to remove would allow us to take someone prisoner and keep them under control so we could burn them later."

Stephenie bit her lip, this time not from the irritation of her legs. "If I need to take care of my legs, I will, but I won't do it here where I would need to walk home naked."

From the upstairs, she heard someone curse and then heard the movement of feet coming back to the stairs. Three holy warriors helped another one down the stairs. The injured man uttering a string of curses as he held one hand from his body and his other over his eye. The veins in his neck showed the tension in his body.

"Prophet," called Lord Ingles, "Calvin got poison in his eye. Can you heal him? Our efforts are not working."

Stephenie got to her feet and allowed them to put the struggling man in the chair. "I've not been able to heal myself fully. I burned the toxin off me. I can't do that for him."

"We saw the damage in the room. Calvin got some poison on his hand and then rubbed his eye."

"Let me try," Sara said, kneeling beside the man who was now being restrained by the three other men. She glared at the contempt in Lord Ingles' expression. "I may have only been a holy warrior of the third order before I left, but I am a competent healer."

The man looked away and then back to Calvin who continued to writhe in pain. Sara took that as permission and placed her hands on the man's leg.

"Careful," Will said, standing at her shoulder, keeping himself between her and the contaminated hand.

Stephenie watched as Sara drew energy into herself. The flow only trickled into her body, but Stephenie liked the fact she did not use her old holy symbol of Felis. She was happy that Ryia's instruction seemed to give Sara that ability to transition what healing she knew with the augmentation devices into skills using her own powers. Had Sara relied on her old augmentation device from Felis, she would have risked these men discovering it and that would have been trouble.

Despite Sara's efforts, the holy warrior named Calvin continued to struggle, prompting Will to lend a hand in restraining him. However, Sara remained calm, keeping her hands on his leg. Slowly, the man's struggles lost their violence. After much time, his resistance diminished into a trembling of his body.

Sara took a deep breath, moved to her feet, and took a step back. Will moved instantly to her side, helping her keep her feet. "I am fine," she said. "I've never felt a poison like that. It is designed to kill those with...those of us who have the blessing of the gods."

"Have you cured him?" Demanded Lord Ingles as Calvin continued to relax.

"I have eased his pain and the effect of the poison, but I am not sure of the damage done to his eye."

Stephenie raised her eyebrows. "I used holy fire to fight the effects." She hated the claim, but it would keep the men from asking too many questions.

"We found another two balls. They looked to be made of clay. We gathered their holy symbols and a few things in a basket, though I don't know if it will be safe." He watched Stephenie for a few moments. "The basket we took from a different room and it is on the floor above the stairs."

Stephenie glanced out the front door and then back to the others. "We take the basket and then burn the flat."

Lord Ingles raised a hand. "That could spread across the city. I don't know...."

"I will take responsibility, but the poison was carried by mold and I can't take the chance the mold will spread. Get the others in the area out of their homes and keep them back. Have the fire brigade standing ready, but I should be able to keep the fire under control."

"Steph," Henton started, but she shook her head.

"I am sore, but not beaten." She saw the concern in his eyes as well as the question she had asked herself earlier. "I fear we can't make the poison safe. Even a little on a hand rubbed in an eye did that. We incinerate the room and burn it all to ash."

Lord Ingles nodded his head and two of the other holy warriors quickly left through the front door. To another man, he said, "Retrieve the basket, but treat everything very carefully."

"The clothes I had on will be burned as well. I'd suggest you do the same with anything your men are wearing." Lord Ingles nodded as he ushered more of his men into action. Stephenie took a different seat and waited for the others to clear the area and ready the fire brigade. She doubted Joshua would approve of her decision, *at least not initially,* she thought. However, the poison proved to be incredibly dangerous and she could feel the effects still wearing on her.

Once word finally came that everyone in the surrounding buildings had cleared the area, she returned to the second floor and stood outside the room containing the devastation. "I am sorry I could not save you," she said to the deceased couple, not remembering their names. Without further ceremony, she started to draw energy from the surrounding environment. Instead of funneling it all through her already taxed body, she drew upon a small amount of power to construct fields that channeled the energy into the room. Like digging irrigation ditches, once a path of limited resistance existed, the power flowed easily into the wooden building. A moment later, it ignited in flames, but Stephenie held the fields, channeling in more energy until flames roared from the floor to the ceiling. Feeling the intense heat cooking her flesh, she turned and quickly raced down the stair. A strong wind was already blowing her hair as the intense fire pulled in air through the open front door.

Outside, she emerged into the crowd of people staring up at the flames that now leapt from the windows and had started burning through sections of the roof. "Lord Ingles, have your men add to the fire on this side. I want the whole thing burned to the ground, but try not to impact the adjoining buildings."

The Holy Warrior gathered his men and did as she demanded. Stephenie watched from afar, using her mind's eye to see the energy potentials in the fire. After the flames grew more intense, she turned to Henton, "Make sure to keep everyone away from me, including yourself. I have a feeling things will get very hot."

Quietly, he directed those around her to move away as the end of the row houses quickly became engulfed in flames. *Kas, I hope I am up to this,* she said to herself, knowing he was too far away to hear her. Looking into the dark sky, she could make out the plume of smoke from the heat signature rising into the sky. "At least it was at the end of the block," she said aloud, hoping that would minimize the damage.

*     *     *     *     *

It took less time than she expected, but the end of the building collapsed, bringing down the roof and the second floor into a pile of flaming timbers. The collapse sent flames and glowing embers higher into the air.

"We need to put this out!" Someone shouted aloud, but not quite directed at her.

She held out her hands, signaling everyone to remain back. *I hope that is enough burning.* She could see the next adjoining flat already suffering from the flames. Working slowly, she formed fields, linking the burning building to the cobblestone street twenty-feet from her. Closing her eyes, she watched the energy of the flames slowly move into the street. The debris on and around the stones smoldered and quickly blackened as smoke rose from the cracks. However, the flames shooting into the sky generated energy faster than she drew it off.

Digging deep within herself, she increased the flow through her body, forming stronger fields. The distance to the building and the scope of the fire made the process harder. It took far more concentration and effort than she expected. Her head throbbed with each rapid beat of her heart. She felt the pressure building in her and ready to burst through her skull. *Move, damn you! Energy, move!*

Growling from the pain. She poured more power into her fields, stretching them further to make a wider channel. A moment later, a wave of energy moved away from the burning building, causing the flames to sputter. *I just need to get you below self-sustainability,* she thought, hoping Kas would be proud of her use of the term.

The stones in front of her went from black to red and then in the blink of an eye glowed white-hot. The crowd gasped as the flames fell, dropping visibly in height and intensity. *Just a bit more,* she swore as she dropped to one knee. Drawing from the energy deep in the ground, she pushed everything she had into her fields. Once the fire lacked the potential to sustain itself, the removal of energy became much easier and the flames on the building died instantly. Had there been any moisture in the air, frost would have covered the remains of the building.

The street in front of her emanated waves of heat that overwhelmed her and many of those in the crowd. Turning away from the molten stone, she stumbled to her feet and moved into

Henton's arms. He half-carried, half-led her further from the glowing pool that had been the street. She felt hollow and ready to lie down.

"You okay?"

She took a deep breath and nodded her head. Using him to remain standing, she surveyed the situation. The people that filled the streets stared silently at her. She could sense none of them; her mind was completely numb. Leaning against him, she nodded her head to the people. Looking back to the building, she noted the wall to the next home had holes burned through it and a section of the roof had fallen. "I will ensure compensation is paid for the damage," she said. Her words carried only a short distance, but they still had conviction.

"Let's get you back to the castle," Henton said as the people around her continued to stare in awe.

# Chapter 12

"Let me help you," Henton said, taking Stephenie's arm and leading her across the floor to the small room Will's men had created for him. "Let me take a look at your legs."

Stephenie nodded her head. She had fallen asleep again in the carriage on her return to the castle. Her head still throbbed and at the moment, she would let Henton do whatever he wanted if he would let her sleep. Climbing onto his bed, she laid back and put her head on his pillow. She pulled Ryia's robe closed around her waist and closed her eyes.

"They are still quite red and even a bit swollen. I hope the bath helped clean off whatever residue was left."

"What is going on here?"

Henton turned quickly and bowed to Joshua. "Your Majesty, I—"

"Get out!"

Stephenie pushed herself up and moved to her feet, her robe barely remaining closed. "Henton was checking my legs," she demanded. "I've been exposed to poison."

"You're naked and you were allowing a man to claw his way over you!"

Stephenie closed her eyes and clenched her fists. Joshua knew Henton had done far more caring for her when they rescued Joshua in the Grey Mountains. Losing the fight against the tears leaking from her eyes, she opened them again and stepped closer to her brother. "What has happened between us? Why are you always yelling at me? I've only been trying to help and nothing I do meets with your approval."

Joshua's cheek twitched. "What in the world caused you to sneak off into the city? I was handling the situation."

"Josh, I thought we might be dealing with Senzar. I feared what would happen if your people actually did find them. I knew Kas and I could help."

"And even though you've been here for but a few days, you go out and solve this damn problem I've been fighting for weeks. How does that look?"

Stephenie stared at her brother; unable to find words to respond to the question.

"I'll tell you how it looks. It spurs more talk from people about how you are always saving the country...or me...." The muscles in his face twitched. "Treasonous comments about how it might be better to have you on the throne instead of myself."

Stephenie hoped no one had heard Douglas' complaints. He had never voiced them around her, but she knew of his growing dislike of her brother. "Josh, I've told you this many times before. I don't want the throne and would not accept it if someone offered it. I would never," she emphasized, "ever, hurt you. You are my brother and I have always loved you."

"So you say, but that won't stop others from thinking to assassinate me on your behalf. It doesn't stop the talk." He shook his head at her. "It undermines my position."

Stephenie bit her lip. Even mentally numb to the world around her, she knew the fear in his mind ran deep. She would never enter his thoughts; now more to avoid what she might discover than from respect. Finally she spoke, her voice almost breaking, "What do you want from me? You expect me to stay locked up in the tower and ignore everything around me? I had hoped one day things would go back to the way they were before."

"They can never go back, Stephenie. You are changed. You...you disobey all the time. You act as if I am not your King. A normal woman would have settled down by now. You'd have kids to raise and a house to run. Instead, you—"

"Stop." She raised her hand as tears continued to flow. "I am not property and never will be. I wasn't raised to expect to be that, so don't try to wrap that collar around my neck now." She pulled the robe tight and moved around her brother, starting for the door.

"Where are you going?" His voice boomed through the tower.

"I am going to my room. I am exhausted, my head hurts, my legs are raw, and I want to put an end to this conversation before anything else is said. We can continue it in the morning after I've rested."

"How dare—"

"Wait," Rebecca said from where she stood next to the door. "Josh, in all fairness to Stephenie, she did uncover a plot by priests of Mertor. Don't let the heat of tonight's events overshadow a larger issue."

"She burned down a building! She could have destroyed the city if the fire got out of control."

Stephenie held Rebecca's gaze for a moment as Rebecca moved closer. "I will not stand here and be yelled at," she told Joshua's wife.

"Josh," Rebecca continued, looking past Stephenie to her husband. "Stephenie maintained control of the situation. Right now we need to find out more of what happened and try to puzzle out why. From what I heard from Lord Ingles, there were only three of them stopped tonight and there could be others in the city."

Stephenie turned back around to face her brother; she pushed past her anger, wanting to make sure her observations were known. "The accusation that this is because of Kynto seems off. The letters were not written by a Kyntian native and those murderers tonight were not Kyntian. They looked like people from Cothel."

Rebecca nodded her head. "The priests of Mertor are paid assassins. They often recruit local people to act as their agents so they can hide more effectively in the area. I thought we had removed all of the ones Burdger hired to kill us." Rebecca pulled over a chair from the wall for Joshua. "Please, let us sit and discuss this."

Joshua slowly sat and glared at Stephenie. She forced herself not to turn her back and slam the door in his face. *To think he threatened me with being married off,* she told Kas in Dalish to prevent Rebecca understanding what she said if she could overhear it.

"Please, Stephenie," Rebecca said, pleading as much with her eyes as her voice. "I fear there may be more of them in the city."

Forcing her hands to unclench, Stephenie nodded her head. "Henton and I estimated at most ten people. The thought being that those actually sick enough to slaughter people in this fashion are normally few in number."

"It was reported to us that you kept the holy symbols. Can you provide one to me?" Rebecca asked.

*They are soaking in strong spirits,* Kas told her silently. *I am uncertain as to how effective the alcohol will be to remove the poison.*

"The symbols are soaking to kill the mold spores."

Joshua's lip curled. "If that ghost is here, make him show himself. He's always around you and I will not have someone standing behind me and not be aware of it."

Stephenie watched as Kas slowly materialized next to her. "Have some respect for Kas. Without his help, we all would be dead several times over."

Rebecca spoke first, cutting off Joshua's response. "Can you let me see one of them? I want to see if I can locate their shrine."

Stephenie narrowed her eyes. "What do you mean? How can you do that?" She ignored Joshua's questioning stare; he had at least held his protest about Kas.

Rebecca nodded her head, turning partially to face her husband. "Stephenie is Catheri's prophet and gets her powers directly from her god. Others of us must use the holy symbols to receive our powers. Therefore, Stephenie would not be aware of this." Rebecca turned to meet her eyes. "When commanded, each holy symbol will give the holder a fairly good idea of where, and how far away, each shrine is located. For Felis, the shrines are large and fairly fixed, though we have some smaller ones that are portable and are used on ships and when armies march. Each symbol is connected to a number of shrines, so as a person moves about the country, they can get power from any of them."

Stephenie nodded her head. Kas had told her before how these 'shrines' worked as relays, funneling power from the trap that extended into another world to the augmentation devices. The whole notion that the power came from various gods was invented at some point after Kas' death, before that, they were just another way for those with magic to have access to more of it.

Rebecca continued, "Well, the priests of Mertor do not have any large shrines. They chose to do things differently, acting primarily as assassins; they take small shrines from place to place. Their holy symbols are linked to a single shrine, or perhaps just a couple."

*It would make sense that certain people have created slight variations in the trap and relay mechanics,* Kas told her, unwilling to speak to Joshua directly. *If they always intended to deploy their soldiers into hostile territories, they risk less impact if a relay is captured.*

Rebecca did not seem aware of Kas' comments. "It is a long shot, because while the basic functions of each holy symbol are generally the same, requesting the symbol to tell us where the shrine is located requires forming the proper images in our minds. We captured other symbols of Mertor before and were not able to command them. But I want to at least try with these."

Joshua put his hand on Rebecca's arm. "You are the High Priest of Felis, will not Felis be angry with you if you try to use Mertor's powers? That god is foul and a haven to cowards."

Rebecca smiled at him. "I do not intend to draw upon Mertor's powers, only to ask the holy symbol to point me toward the shrine. If there are others in the city, they may be close to it."

"I will get one," Kas said slowly in Cothish before dropping through the floor and heading toward the lower cellars.

In the silence that followed, Joshua finally wrestled with a comment Stephenie had watched him mull over in his head. "You need to learn these things if you do not want to lose your following. Catheri needs a strong prophet, not someone who—"

"Josh," Rebecca interrupted, "Steph is not like the rest of us. She has a direct link to Catheri and Catheri is doing things differently."

"I know that," Joshua shot back as Kas finally entered the room followed by Henton, who carried one of Mertor's holy symbols wrapped in a rag.

"I will take that," Rebecca said as she rose to her feet, prompting Joshua to rise as well.

Stephenie watched Henton hand over the cold piece of metal. Like the other augmentation devices Stephenie had observed, she could sense a small draw of energy by the medallion. It always pulled some energy from its surroundings; however, its real power came from what Kas called an entangled link to a relay, which in turn received the power through another entangled link to a trap, which extended into another world to extract energy from a creature that was being effectively bled to death. Stephenie still could not sense or block this entangled link. *And until I can do that, I can't destroy those damn things,* she thought.

Stephenie looked up as Rebecca shook her head. She was exhausted and had almost missed it, but a field around the augmentation device drew her attention. "What did you do, Rebecca?" *Kas, did you see that?*

*I am not sure what I am meant to have seen. What was it you are wondering about?*

*A symbol above the device,* Stephenie replied.

"I merely asked it to point me toward the shrine," Rebecca said. "In the Old Tongue of course."

Stephenie got to her feet, pushing her robe closed as she did. "Do it again." She watched the metal closely, losing visual focus to concentrate on the fields around the device. For a moment, she saw it again, a faint field with a very specific pattern. It lasted only a moment before fading away.

Looking over her shoulder to Henton, she motioned him closer with her head. "Can you get me some paper and ink?"

"What did you see," Rebecca asked.

He nodded his head and went into Ryia's room, coming back with a small journal, a quill, and a closed ink reservoir. Taking the quill from Henton, she flipped open the book to a blank page while Henton uncorked the reservoir "I'll draw it. Ask the device again."

Rebecca complied and Stephenie quickly committed what she saw to memory. Then, before she forgot any of the details, she quickly reproduced the symbol on the paper. "Does this mean anything to anyone?" She asked, with mental emphasis to Kas.

*It could be a name,* Kas responded, as Rebecca shook her head no. *There appears to be some Denarian influence in the style of the form, but I am uncertain.*

"That is interesting," Rebecca said. "When I request Felis to tell me the locations of the shrines, I make the request, and then form a symbol in my mind. Those who don't know the symbol will not get a response. Let me try imagining that symbol instead of the one I use."

*That is brilliant, Kas! They built in a way to keep people from being able to access higher functions. Unless you are powerful enough, or someone shows you how, you can only do basic things.*

*It would be consistent with the idea of ensuring only those with power could use the devices, thereby maintaining their superiority. Not all magical devices were created that way, but these were.*

Stephenie watched the field form again and then fade away. Rebecca shook her head.

"Did you draw it correctly?" Joshua asked, breaking his silent appraisal of the events.

"If you think I drew it incorrectly, here's the quill," Stephenie said.

"Don't take attitude with me." Joshua responded.

Stephenie held her tongue. She felt energy coursing through her and had to release it. It burned immediately because of how much she had used earlier in the evening, but her instinctual response frightened her. *I could have hurt him just now.*

"Josh," Rebecca said, trying once again to mediate, "it is likely something different with this device that is the problem."

"Or Felis is taking issue with you even trying this."

Stephenie glanced toward Kas. *These were all created in the same fashion, right?*

*Generally. Different factions created different traps, but the fundamental concept behind them was the same. They all originally learned the skill from a single person or group of people.*

Stephenie's head pounded from her exhaustion, but she turned back to Rebecca. "Let me watch you ask Felis where the shrines are located."

Joshua frowned, but Rebecca nodded her head. A moment later, Rebecca pulled her holy symbol of Felis from under her shirt and held it in her hands. The raised image of the soldier-farmer proudly showing on the symbol. Stephenie's eyes widened as an energy field formed a faint character and then faded away.

"I can sense the direction of five shrines," Rebecca said. "The closest, and strongest, is behind me in the main temple."

Stephenie turned back to the journal and drew the symbol she saw. This one had an even stronger appearance of Denarian heritage.

"That is very close to what I visualize," Rebecca said as she watched Stephenie finish drawing the character. "It is amazing that you could detect that."

"Are you reading Rebecca's mind?" Joshua demanded.

"No," Stephenie shot back, not even looking in his direction.

Rebecca took the quill from Stephenie and added a small mark in the corner, raising Stephenie's eyebrows. She noted Henton shift slightly at seeing the mark. Stephenie did not even notice Rebecca tweaking other parts of the image.

*It is the accent,* Kas said. *At this point, I should not be surprised.*

"Stephenie must have been just too tired to get the image right," Joshua said. "Perhaps we should wait until she has rested from this night's activities."

Stephenie took Mertor's holy symbol from Rebecca. "You said that I need to ask where the shrines are in the Old Tongue."

"Yes. Dori fulv qipha talxa mi," Rebecca said in the Old Tongue.

*Talxa does not mean shrine.* Kas' irritation came through clearly in his mental voice. *It means link. And it is likely pronounced: doric fulv qipha talxac mi.*

Stephenie used Kas' version of the request. The augmentation device responded immediately. She felt a twinge of intelligence held inside the small bit of metal and she saw the symbol created through the energy field form above the raised surface of the device. Immediately, Stephenie responded by visualizing the same symbol, only with the accent she had learned to be associated with a secret group of powerful people—people who had tried multiple times to kill her.

The device's response staggered Stephenie, causing her to stumble. She felt an immediate connection, as if another mind had opened itself up to her. However, this mind lacked human thought and emotion. It had a fixed purpose and left her feeling pulled forward, as if the world now leaned in one direction. The sensation lasted but a moment and then left her feeling empty and still a bit dizzy.

"What did you do?" Rebecca asked.

Stephenie shuddered, trying to shake off the effects. "The shrine is that way," she said after a moment, pointing in the direction of the pull.

"How?" Rebecca asked.

After another moment, Stephenie took back the quill and added the accent to the image she had drawn earlier. "It is a question and response. The device asked a question, and the response requires you to add this mark."

"It is always the same word?" Henton questioned Rebecca. "Every...holy symbol of one god uses the same word?"

"For Felis, yes," Rebecca said and then glanced around the room. "This cannot leave these walls." After clearing her throat, she continued. "All of Felis' holy symbols are made from parts that were left to us. We basically assemble them. We have several small pieces of what we understand are bits of each shrine. We put them inside the form, depending on where the priest will operate, and then close the symbol. After we follow a prescribed set of instructions, the symbol fuses together and is blessed with Felis' power. Until that, they are just pieces of metal."

"Rebecca," Joshua demanded, "you should not talk about secrets that only the High Priest and Master Priests should know."

*Parts left over from the original creators,* Kas said in Dalish. *If you find them, you could prevent any new devices being created. We could end the death and suffering my people died trying to stop.*

*Kas, we can discuss that later.*

"Josh, they need to understand and I trust them. More so than some of the Master Priests that have been recently appointed," Rebecca added after a pause.

Joshua's scowl did not leave his face, but his topic of conversation changed. "Then if we know where the shrine is, we can attack those damn priests of Mertor and end this. We should move on them now."

Henton cleared his throat. "Your Majesty, if I might offer a suggestion?"

"What is it?" Joshua demanded.

"These are people who are operating through the night. They may not all be back to their base of operation yet. They may even be trying to ascertain what happened to those that died this evening. Which means, if we attack too soon, they might not be there, but they would learn we found them."

Joshua shook his head, "But if we wait, they might get scared and run."

Henton nodded and shrugged, "It is a balancing act. But, I would suggest waiting until midday. They will be tired and while they might be worried, if it was me, I would wait to change locations until this evening. If they are used to working in the dark, they may want to avoid the light of day as well as try to get some rest, assuming they believe themselves somewhat safe in their current location. We might spread the word there were no survivors and we are uncertain of who they were."

Rebecca spoke before Joshua could. "We also need time to gather holy warriors and soldiers. We don't want them to escape. Additionally, we need a better indication of where they are. We have a direction and Stephenie may have an idea of the distance, but we should get readings from different locations to be certain."

"Triangulate their position," Henton offered.

"Steph," Rebecca said, drawing back her attention. "You look completely exhausted. I can have one of my people take the symbol and go into Antar to narrow down the location."

Stephenie shook her head. "Henton, I think I can teach Ryia to do it. Can you take her and Douglas and find this house without letting anyone know what you are doing?"

Henton nodded his head. "I think so."

Rebecca smiled. "That would actually work better than bringing in another person to our secret. Not all of Felis' priests know how to search for a shrine. It was a fairly guarded secret. And once you show Ryia, you get some rest. You need time to recover."

Stephenie sat back down in her chair, far too tired to argue. "Just don't go after them without me. That poison kills quickly and is hard to fight." Stephenie watched Rebecca put her hand on Joshua's arm to prevent his protest. *Yes, she at least understands.*

# Chapter 13

"Do you think Steph will let me come with her tomorrow?" Ryia asked as they walked down the dark street.

Henton rubbed his tired eyes before responding. "It will be today, not tomorrow. It's only a couple turns of the glass before sunrise."

"But will she have me with her?" Ryia asked again.

Henton pulled her to a stop. "Which direction?" He asked, knowing he wanted to be back at the castle before dawn if he could manage it. While he had not abused his body the way Stephenie had, he would be functioning on less sleep than she would be. *I just want something of a nap before I have to answer more of Queen Rebecca's demands.* While Stephenie had taught Ryia how to use the augmentation device, Rebecca had discussed possible assault plans with him. His protest at not being qualified for that type of planning had been rejected. *'This will be close quarter combat, which you would be familiar with when fighting ship to ship'* he mentally mimicked in the queen's voice. *They expect too much of me.*

"It's still in that direction," Ryia said, her arm raised slightly more west than it had been on their last sighting. He did not need to look at the small section of map he carried to know they were very close to having triangulated the location. *But should we risk getting closer?* He wondered. He had argued earlier that they should take the final sightings just before the attack, only narrow in the block during the night. By waiting until people filled the streets, it would provide additional cover against the priests detecting them. *Damn it, I hate second-guessing myself.* Deciding to stick with his initial thought, Henton resumed their southerly route back toward the castle.

"Well?" Ryia asked again, more quietly this time. "If you suggest it, I'm sure she would agree. She listens to you."

Henton snorted despite himself. "She hears what I say, but she will do what she wants to do. She already told you that your job is to protect Douglas and me today."

"But we're only to look for stragglers or people who might escape. We won't see any action."

Henton could not see her face, but he could hear the frown. "Not having to fight would make me a very happy man. You should know better than to think battles are glorious by now."

"It's not that. I just want to prove myself. Everyone says I'm ready, but then they tell me to stay out of the fight."

Henton put his arm around Ryia's shoulder and drew her closer. "Steph didn't tell you to protect us because she thought you were not capable, but because she trusts you. She does not want us to face magic without a chance to fight back."

"More a commentary on how little we can do," Douglas remarked from just behind them. "And a punishment for us."

Henton allowed Ryia to squirm free and punched Douglas in the shoulder. Forgoing the stifling of a yawn, he continued on as the others hurried to catch up to him. The conversation appeared to have ended, which satisfied him. If they hurried, he would be able to climb into bed just as the sun broke the horizon. It would not be a long sleep he knew, but right now, it was the only thing on his mind.


Will roused Henton, Douglas, and Ryia around mid-morning. They quickly readied themselves and headed into a conference with Rebecca and a group of holy warriors. They allowed Stephenie to continue to rest, though Henton knew how she would want him to respond on her behalf.

Rebecca cleared her throat. "Based on the threat, His Majesty has given authority of this situation over to me as High Priest," Rebecca said to the dozen people standing before her. "Lord Ingles, as we have discussed, you will lead your team into the building, once the final identification of the location is made." She turned toward a shorter man with a much rounder stature. "Lord Burnis, your men will act as a second wave. Should Ingles' men succumb to these priests of Mertor, you will need to offer support. If things go well for Ingles, you will need to have your men watch for anyone that might escape toward the north.

"The rest of you will take your teams to the already designated locations around the block we have identified. We want no one to escape, but be wary, these assassins and murderers do not hesitate to use poisons that debilitate and kill quickly. Have wet cloth ready to put over your mouths and noses. Lord Ingles had a man who just got some of this dust on his hand and rubbed an eye. The man almost died from that small contact."

"Your Excellency," Henton said, raising his hand. "Her Highness intends to narrow in on the specific building just before the attack. She intends to be part of the initial wave into the building. She also wanted to stress the point that these people may have other weapons or poisons we have not encountered before. We'll have to be careful for the unexpected."

Rebecca nodded her head. "Indeed. These poison balls are unlike anything we have ever seen. If these followers of Mertor do something you don't expect, react to it as though it is a deadly attack."

Henton watched her look around for additional questions or comments. When none arose, she nodded her head. "May Felis protect all of you. Go get prepared. We will finish the move into the city before the glass turns again."

Henton remained with Ryia, Douglas, and Will as the holy warriors slowly departed the room. He caught a few glances from those leaving that could only be seen as resentful. These men had dedicated years of their lives to move up in rank, yet here a simple marine sergeant had garnered more access to their High Priest than they had. Having once been a strong follower of Felis, seeing the petty nature of these men saddened him.

"Do you plan for me to take part?" Will asked, breaking Henton's line of thought.

"No. You're a High Priest. If something were to happen to you, that would generate far too many problems."

"Plus, you're too fat to run," Douglas remarked just loud enough for Henton to hear.

Henton did not respond to Douglas, as Rebecca had already closed on their small gathering. "Ma'am."

Rebecca nodded her head in response. "Are you certain Stephenie will be up to this? You expressed some concerns about how she fought the effects of the poison and how drained that left her."

"I'll check on her now. At worst, Ryia will identify the specific building and we'll leave Steph here. However, she was in much better condition last night than I expected."

Rebecca nodded her head. "Then let's get moving. I don't want these foul people gaining a chance to escape."

Stephenie wiped her face with her hand and squinted at the building bathed in bright sunlight. The two-story waddle and daub building had every appearance of being abandoned. Thick shutters covered every window, despite the warmth of the noonday sun. No shingle hung above the door offering services and the exterior had received little care for a long time.

Three readings from different locations had confirmed for her the certainty of the relay, though she did not know if anyone resided inside the building. As of yet, she and Kas had remained far enough away to prevent anyone inside from being able to sense them. *If they are inside, hopefully they don't have watchers positioned to see everyone gathering down the crossroads and side streets.*

Stephenie glanced behind herself; Lord Ingles and his men remained a block away and she had worked to keep her distance from them as well as the building. With Kas enveloping her, the distance reduced their chance of sensing him. Holy warriors tended to have more natural skill than those who were made priests, and so the risk was greater. Ironically, without the augmentation devices, both groups tended to be less powerful than those considered to be witches and warlocks. The tests the priests developed years ago ended up weeding out anyone with significant ability, leaving only those with so little potential that they did not realize they could perform magic.

*Unless they are hypocrites,* Kas thought to Stephenie, *they will be limited by their ignorance and their reliance on the devices they carry.*

She shrugged mentally. *We know a couple who know the truth, one of which realized what she was before she joined Felis' ranks. There could be others. These followers of Mertor could even be some.*

She sensed Kas give her a mental bow of his head. *You are growing wise.*

She did not respond to the compliment with words, but still let him feel her appreciation.

*Are you well enough to do this?*

*My head is throbbing, but yeah, I can do this. Plus, I'm not going to let these murderers get away.* Unfolding the wet cloth in her hand, she readied the tightly woven silk; she had no intention of allowing another ball of poison dust to spread through the air.

*Your singing voice might never be the same, but you could always make a living as a fire-eater,* Kas said, drawing a smile to her face.

She glanced at the tall holy warrior down the cross street and nodded her head. Without further delay, she moved forward quickly, her boots sounding a fast staccato against the cobbled street. Distantly, she felt Ingles and his holy warriors start their advance.

Closing on the two-story building, she opened herself up further so she could sense what she had been too far away to feel. Her speed brought the people inside into quick focus. On the second floor, she detected several people congregated in one area while those on the first floor were spread out. However, as her picture of the situation cleared, the people inside suddenly started to move.

Drawing in energy, Stephenie wrapped a gravity field around herself. Pushing upward, she stopped running as her feet left the ground. Increasing her speed, she flew at the center window on the second floor and lashed out with a focused blast, striking the shutters and window frame behind it. Balled up, she followed the debris as it exploded into the building.

She landed in a room filled with the largest single concentration of people on the second floor. The four people, apparently just roused from sleep, stood above the mats they had rested upon.

Sensing a dagger flying in her direction, Stephenie knocked it aside with a thought. As the dagger bounced off the wall to her left, a wave of force struck her side. Her tired mind had not recognized it in time, but her instincts compensated, drawing off the energy before it could do more than shove her a foot to the left.

Releasing the energy inside her, Stephenie unleashed her own attacks against the four people in the room. The two on her right flew backwards into the wall behind them, one of them with such force that he broke through the wall, flying into the adjoining room. The other two, one in front of her and one to her left, also flew backwards, but they managed to use the power of their devices to deflect most of Stephenie's attack.

Switching her focus, Stephenie reacted to another dagger flying in her direction, this one she hit with such energy that the blade rebounded back into the woman that had thrown it. The woman cried out in pain as the heavy blade embedded itself in her chest.

Knowing Kas moved against the man who hit the wall on her right, she turned to the fourth man as he uttered a string of words that she did not recognize. Instantly noting an energy channel forming between the man and herself, she searched for the faint control threads the man used to form the channel. The moment she found it, she bridged the larger channel to the control thread, which led back to the man's head. When he released the surge of energy, lightning sprang across the room between them. However, it followed the path of least resistance and looped back into the man, killing him instantly.

The woman with the dagger in her chest threw a clay ball into the air. Stephenie tossed her wet cloth at the ball, and using her powers, wrapped the material around the sphere. The woman still tried to rupture the container, but Stephenie created a counter field that disrupted the woman's attack.

Kas ended the woman's life by plunging his hand into her forehead, drawing a terror-filled scream from her. However, she lacked the skill and power to drive him off and a few moments later, her screams died as her brain froze. It was the same attack he used on the man on her right.

The man Stephenie threw through the wall had regained his feet. Wanting to leave some of the people alive for questioning, Stephenie reached out with her magic and forced her way through the man's limited defenses. Knowing the augmentation device would resist any attempts to use magic against it in a hostile manner; she latched a field around the chain of his holy symbol and then pulled. The metal chain broke behind his neck and she drew both ends toward her. The man, not yet steady on his feet, panicked as his source of power left his chest. His feeble attempts to catch his holy symbol with his hands caused him to stumble and fall forward.

Stephenie caught the cold medallion with her left hand and then threw it out the window she had come in through as she turned toward the open door to confront a woman rushing up from the first floor. A clay ball emerged from the darkened hall as the woman reached the opening. Prepared for the threat, Stephenie disrupted the gravity waves that followed the sphere, preventing it from rupturing. Using her own fields, Stephenie snatched the ball from the air and flew it behind herself so she could keep the hollow orb protected.

"The Demon," the woman swore under her breath, having finally come into the room. Without further remark, the priestess started to unleash another wave of attacks, which Stephenie easily deflected. Suddenly, the woman turned left toward Kas. "The dead one too!" She screamed as she stepped backwards into the doorframe.

Before Stephenie recovered from the surprise of the woman's statement, the woman tossed something into her mouth. A moment later Stephenie felt a wave of pain radiate out from the priestess as the woman grabbed her throat. *Damn it, I could have stopped her.*

While Stephenie contemplated risking a mental link to heal the priestess, the woman started convulsing as she struggled to breathe. "...hurts...." The priestess managed to say through tear filled eyes. "Don't...want...die," she mumbled through the bloody foam leaking from her mouth.

Stephenie looked away and tried to block the woman's thoughts as she struggled to breathe through the hemorrhaging that filled her throat and lungs with blood. The mental pain of realizing death was imminent left a disturbing feeling in Stephenie's mind. Being around a lingering death reminded her just how mortal she, Henton, and the others really were.

By the time the woman lost consciousness, the holy warriors of Felis had filled the first floor. *Go Kas, I'll be fine for now.*

*I will see you soon,* he said as he left through the ceiling, leaving her with a sense of his approval of her actions.

*That you will,* she thought to herself, confused about how the woman knew of Kas and what he was. She looked toward the man that she had thrown through the side wall. He looked back at her with terror in his eyes.

"Don't send me to Elrin," he pleaded as several holy warriors rushed up the stairs.

"Your Highness," one of the holy warriors said, stopping when he reached the woman whose mind had still not completely died, but no longer functioned properly. "We have secured the first floor. We have only a couple of prisoners. Several of the dead appeared to have taken poison. A couple people jumped from the windows up here, but they have been caught."

Stephenie turned to the man in the other room. Moving her left hand behind her back, she caught the clay ball she had held in the air as she let it fall into her hand. The man glanced down to one of his pouches. Drawing in energy, Stephenie yanked the man through the hole in the wall and dropped him to the floor before her. "Don't think that I will let you die so easily. You've been murdering people across the city."

"You don't frighten me!"

Stephenie could feel the lie in his words. She crouched down so she could get eye to eye with the man that was hunched over on his hands and knees. The urge to rip and burn his flesh to get the answers filled her, but she also knew the pain of someone receiving torture and restrained herself. "What is your purpose in being here? Why kill all these innocent people?" The man looked up to meet her face. Terror still filled his mind, but the cold look in his eyes made her wonder if he was still human inside. "We will get the answers from you."

"The only one who truly knows is dead," he said with a smile and a glance at the woman in the doorway. "It is not our place to know things. We follow orders and bring glory to Mertor. We honor him by destroying those who no longer deserve life. Mertor will protect me from you, Demon. The spawn of Elrin will not be allowed to spread her lies! We will never stop coming! Others follow even as you hold me! We will never stop! We will destroy you!"

Stephenie stood up as a group of holy warriors stepped closer to pick up the man from the floor and restrain him. The proclamation that others would follow frightened her. *How can we stop someone we don't know is going to cause us trouble until after they do?* "Search all of them to make sure they are not hiding any poison. We don't want them to take the easy way out."

As three men took the man away, Lord Ingles, who had arrived, bowed his head. "We have not located the shrine yet. However, we are still searching."

Stephenie nodded her head and carefully handed the holy warrior the sphere in her hand. "There is another one in that bundle of cloth over there." Ingles turned his attention to where she indicated and he nodded his head.

Allowing him to secure the poison, she pulled out the holy symbol she had used to locate the building. With what was now a simple process, she commanded the device to reveal the relay and immediately felt a strong pull from below her. Walking past the woman whose mind was simply a jumble of random signals, Stephenie headed toward the stairs and quickly descended to the first floor. Taking another reading, she walked through the devastation that remained of what had been a large home.

She finally stopped in front of a bookshelf filled with a variety of things, including ceramic mugs and jars. Angry with herself for getting distracted enough that she had not stopped the woman from killing herself, Stephenie reached out with her magic and toppled the bookshelf. The contents of the shelves shattered across the floor and rebounded off the energy field that surrounded her body.

Looking at the wall behind the bookshelf, her eyes widened, allowing her to see clearly in the dimly lit room. She could detect nothing unusual about the boards, but the energy patterns behind them revealed a hollow area. Additionally, she felt the telltale draw of energy. Still frustrated, she reached out with her powers and ripped the boards from the wall, flinging debris across the floor. The hole she made revealed a small metal statue of a man. The statue stood only two feet tall and sat on a decorated shelf in the wall. Moving closer, she picked up the relay. The cold metal weighed less than she expected, but it was not exactly light.

One of the holy warriors standing in the room came over and offered to take it from her. She shook her head. "I've got it. Right now, I want someone to find Henton, Douglas, and Ryia. Then make sure there aren't any followers of Mertor in adjacent buildings that might have gotten away."

Henton failed to stifle a yawn; the little sleep he managed to get did not make up for what he had missed. "Keep your eyes open," Henton told Ryia, who had leaned her head against the building behind her. The three of them remained concealed in an alley nearly a block and a half away from the building Stephenie would invade. Along with several other groups of soldiers and holy warriors, their role involved the futile effort of trying to identify any of Mertor's followers running away and preventing their escape. *How I am supposed to know one of them from any other panicked person is beyond me.*

Ryia finally spoke, drawing Henton's attention. "I'm doing like Steph, keeping my mind open and my eyes shut."

Henton did not chastise her for speaking in Pandar. In their current situation, accurate communication was more important than forcing her to learn to speak Cothish. Instead, he glanced once to Douglas who kept vigil from where he sat on a crate against the opposite wall of the narrow alley. His one-time corporal returned his glance, indicating everything remained clear.

*I hate the waiting,* Henton admitted to himself. He would rather have guarded Stephenie, but he also did not relish the idea of facing a cloud of poison dust. *Not that I'm guaranteed to have less chance of getting a face full here.* He glanced out the end of the alley and hoped the people going about their daily lives would not get caught up in the fighting.

Ryia lifted her head and opened her eyes. "Someone's coming quickly and they feel very agitated."

Henton did not wait for Ryia to finish speaking before he started moving. He kept the crossbow pointed up, knowing the poisoned bolt would be lethal to someone without magic. As he emerged from the alley, he quickly spotted a man dodging his way through the crowd in the street.

The armed man reacted instantly to Henton. Coming to a stop, he pushed a woman between them.

"Don't move!" Henton yelled, lifting the stock of the crossbow to his shoulder. The wave of energy that struck him discharged the weapon, sending the bolt high into the air. Henton did not have time to worry about someone getting hit; the next thing he saw was the sky above him. Struggling to get his breath back, he desperately wanted to get to his feet before the priest got close enough to kill him.

Fighting to get air into his lungs, Henton rolled himself onto his elbows and saw Ryia standing between him and the man. She appeared to be fending off the priest's attacks as the air between them shimmered. Everyone else in the street scattered in all directions.

Desperate to avoid her coming to harm, and finally feeling air enter his chest again, he managed to get to his knees as he picked up the crossbow he had dropped. Sliding one foot into the crossbow stirrup, he stood up much slower than he wanted, but in the process, he pulled back the bowstring.

Hearing Douglas' call of challenge and seeing his friend knocked backwards, Henton quickly drew another poisoned bolt from his quiver and loaded the bow. The priest's focus narrowed in on Ryia and he could see her staggering backward. Knowing he would not likely get a third attempt, Henton brought the crossbow's stock to his shoulder, took aim, and fired.

The priest reacted quickly, waving his hand through the air and calling out to Mertor. Henton saw the bolt shift its flight, but the distance was too close and the bolt had too much momentum for the priest to completely stop or deflect it. Henton had aimed for the center of the man's body and breathed a sigh of relief when it struck the man's left breast.

Douglas, back on his feet, charged forward with a long dagger in his hand. His sword had been thrown back to the alley. The priest turned and tried to raise his right hand as he called out to his god.

Douglas staggered, but whatever magic the priest commanded had weakened.

Another explosion of blood erupted from the priest's right chest, followed by a hole bursting through his gut. Henton knew Ryia had managed to penetrate the man's mental defenses. A moment later, the priest stumbled backwards a step, fell to his knees, and then collapsed onto his side.

Douglas reached the priest first and plunged his dagger into the man's neck to ensure he would not recover. The ferocity of the attack gave Henton a slight pause, but then he saw the blood on Ryia's face and could easily see how Douglas wanted to quickly eliminate the threat. *Besides, it's likely a mercy; the poison would make the man suffer before it killed him.*

Henton reached Ryia's side first and he turned her toward him. "Where are you injured?"

She shook her head as she wiped the blood coming from her nose. "Over-extended," she replied quietly in Pandar. "I tried to be subtle as Steph would say, but it slowed me down too much."

Henton pulled a bandage from the small pack he carried on his back and gave it to Ryia. No one else remained in the street at this point. He noted several people watching from more than a block away and suspected many others would be looking out through windows or slats in their shutters. For once he was thankful they were all wearing the King's colors. The priest, dressed in peasant clothing, lay in a pool of his own blood.

Turning back to Ryia, Henton smiled. "You did good."

"Thanks," she replied through the cloth now stained red with her blood. "My head hurts."

Henton turned her face towards his and looked into her brown eyes. They appeared vibrant and she blinked a couple times before raising her eyebrows. "Just wanted to make sure you were not overly hurt. You're not Steph, you know."

She grunted. "Yeah, so what? She's overdone it before as well."

He grinned at her, while she knew Stephenie had pushed herself too far several times, the girl had no way to really know the panic everyone felt when Stephenie had fallen unconscious for days. "Well, you at least have her attitude."

# Chapter 14

Stephenie wanted to probe the relay and find out if it worked in a similar fashion to the augmentation devices, but until she felt certain Henton, Douglas, and Ryia were safe, she could not focus on the 'shrine of Mertor.' Carrying the heavy statue wrapped in a blanket, she headed outside the building to allow the holy warriors of Felis the chance to carefully examine the contents of the building while she waited for the others to join her.

"Steph," she heard Ryia call from down the street. Turning toward the sound, she saw her friends approaching. Too tired to do more, she smiled at them as she found a place to sit on a worn city bench.

"We're okay," Henton said loudly when they were close enough. "Ryia took a blow to her face," he added.

Stephenie assumed he made the comment indirectly to Felis' followers and that Ryia had actually overextended herself. A witch bleeding from the nose and mouth carried the traditional belief that the witch's body suffered from the poison of drawing power meant for the elves. Until Will found a better way to explain why those effects still impacted priests of Catheri, those using magic needed to be careful not to draw too much power publicly.

"We got one!" Ryia said with too much enthusiasm.

When they reached her, Stephenie returned Ryia's knowing smile. To Henton, she said, "I'm exhausted. Can you find a carriage to take us back to the castle? I'm not up to walking there." *Plus I need time to think about what that woman said regarding Kas.* Henton nodded his head and quickly left to procure transportation.

Those involved in the attack had left the castle over a period of time during the morning and had generally been on foot to avoid notice. That meant she did not have Argat or any other horse to take her back.

"Your Highness," Lord Ingles said as he approached. At four paces, he stopped and bowed his head. "Including the priest your men killed, we found four others outside of this building that tried to flee. We captured only one of them alive, which brings our total number of prisoners to four. Two of the ones we captured on the first floor I suspect to be simple servants who know little. With your permission, I would like to have them transferred to High Priest Rebecca's custody at the main temple."

Stephenie detected irritation in the man's tone, *probably from having to ask me for permission.* She did not bother to try to read his emotions. "Please do so." The holy warrior bowed his head again and quickly left.

Douglas shook his head. "Steph, I'm sorry for being such an ass to you when we first met. I judged you harshly before I knew you. You've shown me women can be warriors and I should've never rejected the idea so blindly."

Stephenie looked up at her lanky protector who once again had allowed a short beard to start growing on his chin. "You guys have allowed me to forget about having to constantly prove myself and that means a lot to me. Don't worry about something that happened so long ago and know that I don't care what these people think."

"Still..."

They turned as a carriage cleared its way through a line of soldiers. Henton sat next to the driver, so she pushed herself to her feet and patted Douglas' arm. "Let's go back to the castle where I can spend the rest of the day arguing with even more people."


Stephenie sat in an interior room of the Square Keep. Her brother, Rebecca, and Islet all sat on opposite sides of a small table. Kas stood mostly transparent at her side, he did not bother to expend the energy to be full opaque. The silvery-grey statue fashioned to resemble a man sat between them. Fearing contamination from another god's power, Joshua flatly refused to place his mug or his plate of food on the table.

Setting down a piece of bread covered in honey, Stephenie shook her head again. "I told you, I need time to learn if I can somehow destroy it."

"That is why," Joshua emphasized, "I want to put it on a ship and dump it in the middle of Tet. We all know these things don't work well the further they get from the holy symbols. We accounted for eighteen followers of Mertor, but it is likely there are others scattered throughout the city. We can't risk them still having access to their source of power. You said that priest swore more people were coming. We can't let them tap into this shrine's power."

"Josh, I would guess that we've found most of the people tied to this shrine." The eighteen followers of Mertor were more than her and Henton's estimates, but several of the dead and captured definitely were domestic servants and not actual priests of Mertor, empowered or otherwise. Including the three people she caught in the act, they had found only twelve people with working holy symbols. "What worries me more is that it will likely be other groups with other shrines coming into Antar to cause us harm. Give me at least a day or so to try and see what I can do." She glanced at the others before turning back to Joshua. "Rebecca's already checked the holy symbols of those that tried to kill you last year, they are not associated with this shrine, but with another one far to the northwest."

Joshua turned to Rebecca, who nodded her head and then spoke, "We do have an opportunity," she said. "Stephenie may be able to discover some important details."

"But, she's messing with the source of another god's power," Joshua continued to shake his head. "She'll bring the wrath of the god upon us or at least herself."

"And dropping the statue into the sea won't do the same?" Stephenie asked and then immediately regretted it. *Everything is a challenge with him,* she said in Dalish to Kas.

"Perhaps Steph can use the shrine to find those with holy symbols to confirm there are no others here," Islet said, setting down her own mug of wine on the table. "If there are none, then we have time. I think it is prudent we at least try."

"The two of you are as thick as thieves these days. I don't know how she converted you so completely to her side, but—"

"She saved my life, Josh. And she saved yours and thousands of other people's. We should at least give her a chance."

Joshua's jaw froze as he glared at Islet. Finally he stood. "Fine, do it your way. If there are more murders, it'll be on your head." He looked to Rebecca, who rose to her feet. Turning, Joshua stormed from the small room, leaving Islet, Kas, and Stephenie alone with the statue.

Islet sighed, "Just when I think I get him calmed and on our side, he insists on disagreeing."

Stephenie leaned forward and put her hands on the statue; she did not want to discuss Joshua. Putting him from her thoughts, she tried asking the statue which direction the trap lay. She sensed a buried intelligence, but outwardly, the relay did not respond.

"Steph," Islet said. "Changing subjects a bit, I wanted to let you know that I've still not found a map of Ista. However, I read an account of a merchant from Calis who said it is located north of Sandven and that Ista was at the top of the World's Backbone. You know, the name some people have given to the mountain range that starts at the border of Kynto and goes north for as far as the world does."

Stephenie removed her hands from the statue and turned her attention to Islet. "We knew it was north. Are you sure it is that far north? And I've not heard of Sandven either."

Islet shrugged. "The merchant's account spoke of trading for gems and jewels. It even hinted that the Star Stone, the one in Calis' royal crown, came from Ista. I would say you should talk to Calis' diplomat. He might know." Islet cocked her head slightly. "I could try to arrange something discreetly for you."

Stephenie smiled. "Thanks, Islet. That means a lot to me."

Kas made a sound similar to the clearing of a throat. "Should we focus a little more on this relay?"

Stephenie nodded her head and after a moment, stood up. "But, in my room where I can work without the constant threat of someone barging in on me."

\*     \*     \*     \*     \*

Stephenie's frustration grew over the remainder of the day and into the night. Eventually she simply fell asleep still holding onto the statue. Kas tried to offer suggestions, but despite working through every combination of words they could think of, the statue remained a cold piece of metal.

The next day held much of the same; with Stephenie's only interruptions being a few breaks to eat and drink that Henton and Kas insisted she take. "There has to be a way," Stephenie swore, ready to throw the statue out the window to see if it really was indestructible. She had refrained from using magic against it, fearing an even greater response from it than from an augmentation device.

"Perhaps you should pursue other activities for a while to give yourself a fresh perspective."

Stephenie glared at Kas. "That priestess somehow knew about you. She called you the 'dead one.' It wasn't 'oh crap, a ghost,' but almost as if she expected to see you."

"I lacked an understanding of her words. When your language is spoken fast and poorly enunciated, it sounds like noise to me."

Stephenie continued to glare.

"Very well, I admit it is a concern. However, the woman is deceased and so we lack the ability to extract information from her. Additionally, Henton has informed me that the few who were not killed have no knowledge of who provided orders or why you were the target. They are simply natives of Cothel unhappy with the current situation and believe you are the embodiment of evil, not Catheri's prophet. They were added to Mertor's ranks in the last six months."

He crossed the room and took a seat next to her. "My real concern is how they developed the technology to infuse a toxic mold with heavy metal poisons and then grow the poison in a container that could be ruptured to deliver the deadly spores. The only fortunate item I can see in all of this is that these balls were not constructed here, but were brought here by that Agonia."

Stephenie sat back in her chair. "You think the Senzar might have provided these?"

Kas took the effort to visually shrug. "These descendants of the old Denarian Empire have lost less knowledge than your own people.

It is not outside the realm of possibility. Perhaps there are pockets of them without the desire to personally try to reach you, but are willing to rely upon agents."

"This Yreka that Jerylin mentioned?"

"Perhaps."

Stephenie glanced over to the desk where she had stacked the items accumulated on their travels. Seeing the red journal she acquired from the bookseller in the city of Iron Heart, she extended a field around the book and drew it to herself. "I've been using Denarian words like we do with the holy symbols. They respond to that language, but perhaps the augmentation devices were created by other people for use by Denarians. If that is the case, it may be that the traps and relays use a different language."

Kas nodded his head. "A valid supposition, especially since the command response includes the accent mark."

Stephenie flipped the book open to the area where the pronunciation guide had been added. "I'll just try things until I get a reaction."

"I would suggest trying to avoid a hostile reaction."


It was not until late in the evening before Stephenie made her first real breakthrough. She had resorted to simply uttering series of sounds that had no meaning for her, but eventually she felt a connection to the statue and heard a word that had equally no meaning echo in her mind. An energy field formed at the same time and Stephenie responded with what she assumed would be the correct reply. Another word echoed in her head, but as with the first, it had no meaning.

"Did you hear any of that, Kas?"

"No."

She quickly repeated the words as best she could before she forgot the sounds. Kas still shook his head, confirming his lack of familiarity with any of them. Trying the process again, she repeated the sounds she had initially said. This time a different symbol formed in the energy pattern with a repeat of the first word from the statue. She responded to this new symbol with the adjusted reply and heard the second word in her mind again.

*I don't know how to reply,* she thought to the statue in Denarian. *I lack the words.* A vague sense of understanding came to her from the statue. *Can you understand me?* A stronger sense of acceptance filled her. *Can you tell me where the trap is located?* This time the status projected confusion. *The source of your power. You are a relay, I want to find your connection.*

Stephenie slipped from her chair, but caught herself on the table. She still felt the strong pull to the north that had made her dizzy. After a moment, she pushed herself up, but had to lean on the table as the room continued to spin around her. *Is it that close?* She thought more to herself than to the statue, but the statue responded, giving her a sense of vastness that left her sitting on the floor.

*Are you injured?* Kas asked, immediately at her side. *Is it in your head?*

Stephenie forced the relay from her mind and took a moment to steady herself. "It's to the north. A long way to the north I think." Getting an idea, she forced herself to her feet and walked over to her desk. Tossing aside papers, she pulled a map showing the general area of Cothel and the countries to the north, including Kynto, Calis, Uvar, and Salzen.

Returning to the small table they used for dining and games, she put the map next to the statue. Visualizing the map in her mind, she tried to ask the relay again how far the source of its power lay. When it did not respond, she repeated the process for getting it to speak with her. This time a third symbol appeared in the energy field. *The relay really wants to make sure of the person's abilities, a different challenge and response each time,* she thought to herself.

Looking down at the map, she visualized the area and asked the relay to locate its source of power. Again the pull to the north. Following the pull as she looked at the map, she sensed the relay did not completely understand her intent. She lacked the ability to translate the visual representation into physical distance. Frowning, she tried a different tactic. This time, she conceptualized the distance between places such as the castle and the City of Antar, but the response from the relay still conveyed a vastness she could not grasp.

Expanding the distance, she conceptualized the distance from Antar to the Grey Mountains where she had rescued her brother.

Stepping forward to keep her balance, she felt the sudden jerk of her perspective changing. Looking back to the map, she had the sense that the distance to the north was less than twice that to the Grey Mountains. "In fact, closer to one and a half...."

"Closer to one and a half what?" Kas asked.

Pushing the relay from her mind again, Stephenie felt the room solidify and stop moving. "The trap. It's to the north, about one and a half times the distance to the Grey Mountains. Perhaps seven or eight hundred miles." Scanning the map and estimating the distances on something that was not likely drawn precisely to scale, she slid her finger north until it hit the southern edge of the World's Backbone. "If I had to guess, I'd say the trap was at the northern edge of Salzen."

Kas nodded his head. "I am hesitant to ask what you plan to do with that information."

Stephenie sat back down in the chair. "You want to destroy these traps and people killing those beings in that other world. Let's start with ones that we know want to hurt us. I'll work on this relay a bit more; see what else I can do aside from locating the source of its power. But, why try destroying every augmentation device and relay if we can strike a blow in a single place that makes all of them irrelevant."

Kas smiled. "I like this plan."

Stephenie smiled back at him. To herself, she thought, *And if Ista is north, what better excuse to start that journey than this?*

# Chapter 15

Henton waited until the middle of the next morning before he brought Stephenie her breakfast. Her face spoke of her lack of sleep, but a stack of papers on the desk beside the statue gave hint that some progress had been achieved.

"Thank you for the food," she said, diving into the plate and consuming it like a starved animal. He sat next to her and ate his own meal at an ever-increasing pace for fear that what he had not eaten before Stephenie finished would become hers. In the end, he gave her a quarter of his roasted potatoes and a thick slice of venison.

"You've spent too much time locked away," he said as he gathered the empty plates. Unable to keep from looking back at the small statue, he continued as he drank his ale. "Your brother is demanding you report your progress. I had to send Douglas with Ryia this morning. He might not like the temple, but I thought he might say something otherwise. He's getting better, but we need to find something to keep him busy outside of the castle."

Stephenie exhaled. "Then it is likely a very good thing I am planning to leave again. We all need to get away from my brother for a while."

Henton drained the last of his ale. "Leave again? I never thought I would say it, but if you've got a plan to get us on the road, I would be happy to get back to sleeping on dirt. I will admit, life here has me on edge."

He watched her get up and put on her boots. He suspected Kas was somewhere in the room, but so far the ghost had not made himself visible. Once her boots were on, she walked past him and picked up the statue. With that in her right hand, she walked over and put her left hand on a large stone next to one of the fireplaces.

At first, Henton did not know what she planned, but as the stone suddenly liquefied and sloshed down to hang in the air before her, he knew she had disrupted the bonds that held the ever-so-tiny bits of stone together. He guessed she used a gravity field to keep the liquid stone from falling to the floor as a cavity opened in the outer wall of the tower. She placed the statue into the void and then suddenly the cold, liquid stone flowed upward through the air, covering over the void and the statue.

Henton's eyebrows rose. "That was faster than I've ever seen you do that before. Plus, you didn't lose the stone all over the floor." He stepped closer. "Other than sticking out further and looking a little too smooth, I wouldn't notice it." Stephenie pursed her lips. He could see a little bit of pain behind her eyes and he knew the changing of focus she needed to do the work left her with terrible headaches.

"Only a handful of people know I can do that, so I think it will be safe. I've got the old holy symbol from that Senzar I killed in Kynto in another block over there. That one's relays are a long way off in Kynto."

Henton looked in the direction she pointed, but had to hurry to keep up as she headed out of the room. Calling after her, he asked, "While I think I would rather not know, what crazy holiday plans do you have in mind for this trip?"

Kas appeared slightly ahead of Stephenie, floating backwards. "We will begin work that my people died trying to achieve."

To his statement, over her shoulder, she added, "The trap the followers of Mertor use is located to the north. I think I know enough now to be able to destroy it. Or at least disable it."

Henton nodded his head, though his stomach clenched. "So we're going to attack all the followers of Mertor and destroy their source of power."

Kas turned to go down the stairs, though his voice came to Henton as though the ghost stood next to him. "It is likely the trap is located away from the followers. Keeping the trap separate from the relays would be a wise precaution."

*Great,* Henton thought. *Somehow that does not reassure me.*

Stephenie joined her brother, Rebecca, and Islet, with a smile on her face. She insisted that Henton and Kas attend the meeting as well. "I have some good news."

"You can locate the rest of the priests?" Joshua asked immediately.

"No." She looked around to meet everyone's eyes. "I could not get the relay to tell me where the holy symbols were. I think the holy symbols lack a way to tell the...shrine where they are located."

Joshua seemed to miss her slip, "But you can destroy the shrine and remove their power, yes?"

"No," Stephenie lied. She wondered if Rebecca might detect her falsehood, but the High Priest gave no visible signal she had. "I can, however, tell where the source of the shrine's power is coming from. I know where to find Mertor's main temple."

Rebecca's eyebrows rose. "Many people have tried to locate it for dozens of generations. While there are various places people can go to contact these assassins and arrange for murders, aside from these ever changing locations, it has never been known where they have their main temple."

Stephenie smiled. "I managed to get the shrine to tell me."

"Where is it?" Joshua said, now sitting forward in his seat.

"It is north of here. Like with the holy symbols, I get a direction and a sense of the distance. It is almost due north and probably seven to eight hundred miles."

"Where would that put the temple?" Islet asked.

"On Salzen's northern border," Stephenie said. "At this distance, I don't have anything more specific, but as I get closer, I can do as Henton suggested when we sought out the shrine in the first place; I can triangulate."

Joshua bit his lower lip. "You are assuming that we will let you go that far north."

"The trip to rescue Islet was farther. Plus, unlike the holy symbols, the re—shrine changes the challenge every time you ask it to provide the direction. It is more protected than that of the holy symbols because it has more value."

"We should still throw it into the sea. We can't send a force that far north and if I remember correctly, Salzen is land-locked. Which means we'd have to get another country to agree to allow us to cross their lands before we invade Salzen. Which would lead to a war with them." He turned to Rebecca. "Do you know anything about this country? How powerful are they? Do they have powerful trading partners?"

"Josh," Stephenie said softly. "I don't intend to lead an army there. Just like when I went to get Islet, I'll take Henton, Douglas, and Kas. No colors. No ties to Cothel. I'll destroy the shrine in their main temple and that will make all these shrines useless. They won't get any more power. Anyone who comes after us after that will not have any power. If that priest is to be believed, more will come. Removing this shrine won't stop them; taking their main temple will."

He sat without saying anything for quite some time. When he finally spoke, his voice had a measured tone. "But it will take a long time to travel that far. There could be other attacks in the meantime."

"I'll take the shrine we have with me. That will prevent any locals, if there are any, who would use it from having much power." She sighed, not wanting to admit it aloud, but her frustration had built, "Plus, if I am not here, perhaps talk will settle down around me."

Joshua nodded his head slowly. "You'll take a boat to where?"

Feeling a sharp spike of possessiveness for Argat, she barely limited her physical response to a flinch. "We will ride our horses north," she managed to say softly. "Probably along the coast. I didn't have the proper maps to study last night to plan out a route."

Perhaps sensing the futility in arguing, Joshua nodded his head. "Fine. Inform me of your plans when they are set." He rose to his feet, causing everyone else to do the same. Taking Rebecca's hand, he turned and led her from the small office.

"You know, you could probably get the horses on a ship," Islet offered once Joshua had left. "It's done often enough when people buy horses from Kasland and bring them across the straights." Islet shrugged, "It might appease him to take a boat."

Stephenie nodded her head. "I'll consider it."

Islet smiled. "I managed to get word to Lord Famhenry. He's the diplomat from Calis. I indicated we wanted to ask him a couple of general questions about Calis' trade partners. He agreed to meet with me. However, if you are not occupied, perhaps you would like to do it yourself."

Stephenie nodded her head. "I would like that."

"I suspected so. He will be here this afternoon. If you are in the library looking at maps and planning your journey, I will have him escorted there."

"Thank you, Islet."


Stephenie managed to find all the maps of Salzen she needed in the Square Keep's library. She traced two copies of the maps and on separate sheets of paper, made notes of several options for traveling, including if they would take the horses by ship. She finished her work well before Lord Famhenry arrived. Instead of going back to her tower, she took the free time and curled up in an old high back chair. It was not the same chair she had sat in when she had been a young girl reading with her father, but it held enough similarities that she lost herself in memories of the past. With a book on ancient lore in her lap, she quickly drifted off to sleep and when Lord Famhenry arrived, Kas had to rouse her from her slumber.

"Your Highness," the roundish man said almost as a question. "I understood Her Majesty, Queen Islet wished to meet with me."

"Lord Famhenry," Stephenie said, still rubbing the sleep from her eyes, but the man's discomfort did far more to focus her attention. "Thank you for coming. Unfortunately, my sister had to attend to other duties. However, I am familiar with her inquiries." Sitting more formally in her chair, she motioned for the diplomat to take the empty seat across from her.

"You have a lovely library here," he said as he sat. "I understand your brother, His Majesty, has spent quite an effort to replace the books that were...removed...."

The man's sudden increase of fear in realizing where his conversation had led annoyed Stephenie. *You call yourself a diplomat,* Stephenie remarked to Kas.

*I think you unnerve him to the point of total distraction.*

Trying to resolve the conversation quickly, Stephenie skipped the pleasantries and jumped to her question, "Lord Famhenry, Islet merely had a general question about a trading partner Calis has. Do you have any personal knowledge of Ista?"

The heavy-set man sat back as some of the tension fell away from him. "I feared you had called me here to answer to the accusations that you toppled Kynto by killing your Uncle."

"Were you spreading such rumors?"

The man swallowed as his neck tightened. "I...We merely expressed questions to your brother based on what we had heard."

Stephenie shrugged. "I had nothing to do with it."

"And that is what we are now hearing from Calis," Lord Famhenry said quickly. "I could only react to what I had been informed of and was directed to ask."

Stephenie smiled at the man, though that did not seem to reassure him. "You were not called here about that. Believe me. I understand you have a role to fill. What I hope you can help me with is some basic information. You see, we stumbled upon an old document that indicated that Calis had trade dealings with a country far to the north. A place called Ista."

The man quickly nodded his head. "I know a little of the place, though it has been many years since its name has been spoken." He raised his eyebrows. "I would say nearly twenty." He hurried to explain. "You see, I had a younger cousin who had invested some money in a trade company and he joined an expedition to determine what happened to a missing shipment."

Stephenie leaned forward and the man continued. "You see, they are very far north from Calis. It requires crossing a number of countries. I am not sure the actual count, perhaps five or maybe seven. I would never have made such a long journey myself," he clarified. "But my cousin wanted to see what happened. Unfortunately he never returned. A year or so later, we heard rumors from other countries we trade with, who in turn, trade with those further to the north. It seems all contact with Ista had been cut off. No expeditions that went there returned. It was incredibly odd to me, but the lands are in the distant north where snow covers everything for the better part of the year. In fact, if rumors are to be believed, they say the Endless Sea that far north remains frozen all year."

"So, no one has heard from this country for years?"

The older man nodded his head and then shrugged. "I cannot say for certain. We traded for jewels and art. It was believed Ista sat upon a frozen lake of pure platinum and their only real city was made of solid gold." The man smiled at that. "I know that story is ridiculous, but no foreigner has ever been to Ista Fields. That's the name of their only city," he added with a knowing nod of his head. "Instead, those who wished to trade with these strange people had to do so at the border. Every summer, a small camp was setup and merchants could trade at the camp."

"Surely there were people who tried to cross at places other than a single camp."

The man nodded his head. "None that tried ever returned, even when Ista was open. Perhaps they were welcomed into Ista Fields and could not bear to leave the riches rumored to be in the city. But I suspect they froze or were eaten by creatures of the snow and ice. The people that far north have gods unlike ours. To live in that place, you'd have to."

"And you lost all contact twenty years ago?"

"There about. It would take most caravans a year to make a round trip. I can inquire further if you want."

"No. It was just a passing interest we had in the place."

Lord Famhenry narrowed his eyes. "Does this happen to relate to the priests of Mertor?" He raised his hands, "I know I am not supposed to know what is going on because officially your brother has not spoken on the issue and everyone's questions have been deferred. But the events this week that you participated in—I have it on good authority—was the elimination of priests of that foul god. Were they truly responsible for all those murders?"

Stephenie hesitated a moment. "I cannot say—"

"Come now, I have reports from people who saw the holy symbols."

Outwardly, she bit her lip, but internally she smiled. "We have heard rumors that Mertor is based out of the north. Have you heard similar things?"

The man rubbed his chin with his thick fingers. "I wish I could confirm that to be true, but we truly do not know where they are based. We have searched ourselves. More than one member or friend of the noble family has died at the hands of that order. Much of that unpleasantness stemmed from our bad blood with Kynto, though, perhaps now that may change."

Stephenie stood and Famhenry hastened to his feet. "Thank you very much for the information," she said without much enthusiasm. *The more he thinks I found a dead end, the better.*

Henton leaned back in his chair. The old wood creaked and the chair wobbled, but did not break. Everyone had once again gathered on the second floor of Stephenie's tower. Now with the three rooms plus the bath chamber sectioned off, the floor no longer felt quite so large. *I would have not broken up the floor this much,* he thought to himself, still not liking what Will's men had hastily erected.

Will sat separate from the others, while Douglas and Ryia piled food onto their plates at the table where Stephenie and Kas sat. The group no longer had the same dynamic they had enjoyed before the events in the Grey Mountains.

"I will be leaving again, very soon," Stephenie said quietly, but loud enough for everyone to hear.

"And where is my little Prophet running off to now?" Will asked. "We really need more of your presence at the temple."

"I've been a bit busy, if you had not noticed."

"I notice. And the whole city thanks you. However, while Ryia is actually a better teacher than you, your followers want to see you more."

Henton watched Stephenie exhale and then change her mind on what she planned to say. "I need to go north and put an end to these priests of Mertor. They almost killed Josh once before. Now they've tried to undermine him by killing lots of innocent people and they are doing that to get at me. I won't let my people or my family be harmed in such a way." She put her food down and looked around the room to meet everyone's eyes. "I'm going north. I will take the relay with me. I will destroy the trap and stop these people from using their augmentation devices. Kas and Henton have agreed to come with me. Douglas, do you want to come?"

"What about me?" Ryia demanded, the food in her hand not making it to her mouth. "I'm going, right?"

"Ryia, I—"

"No, don't Ryia me. I thought I was doing good. I protected Henton and Douglas. I've done everything you've asked of me. You can't leave me here!"

"You've been doing such a good job teaching—"

Ryia jumped to her feet and tossed the food down, spilling it across the table. "You don't want me around? I thought you liked me. You know I don't like those people at the temple, but I've done as you asked." She turned her head away. "They hated me in Vinerxan; I won't stay here and teach them anything else."

"Ryia," Will said, standing up. "Calm yourself. I'm paying you well. You don't have to like them, but you do have to follow my orders."

"Go bugger yourself!" She swore. "There is no god of Catheri and you just have your position because you lucked into it. I was only here because of Steph and Henton and Douglas and Kas and if they don't want me, then I'm gone."

"Ryia," Stephenie growled. "I never said I didn't want you around. But what I am planning is likely to be dangerous. I don't want you hurt."

Douglas cleared his throat, but before he could speak, Henton got to his feet. "Steph, can I talk with you a moment?"

She looked in his direction; pain in her eyes. She nodded her head and rose. He turned and headed for the door to the stairs.

Allowing her to go first, he closed the door behind them and followed her down to the first floor. He assumed she would tell him if anyone was close enough to hear them. "Steph, are you okay?"

She turned to him with tears in her eyes. "Everyone is taking issue with anything I do. What am I doing wrong that so many people disagree with me? What do I need to do differently?"

"Steph," he said, pulling her close and putting an arm around her shoulders. "I don't know. I'm hardly doing any better than you. Douglas thinks I don't have a backbone when dealing with your brother and I have no control over Will." He sighed. "But, Ryia is still young. Think about yourself a few years ago. We're her only family. It is not unexpected that she'd feel like she is being abandoned."

Stephenie sniffed back her tears. "But I am scared something will happen to her. She's so much safer here. Look at all the chaos around me. And there is that Senzar coming after us and that priestess of Mertor knew about Kas. We are going to be facing some serious trouble."

Henton brushed some of her loose hair behind her ear and then quickly pulled away from her. Taking a step back to put some distance between them, he looked to the stone steps of the tower. "Very recently, I thought to protect you by wanting you to avoid searching for the red-haired man. The error of my way was pointed out to me and I suddenly realized if I had done that, I would effectively be your jailer. No matter how much I want to keep you from harm, I can't block you from pursuing that goal if it is what you really want."

She nodded her head. "And that is what I am doing to Ryia." After a moment she looked up into his eyes. "Do you think it is safe to bring her?"

He wanted to say yes, but at the same time, he knew that would be a lie. "No. However, I still think we should bring her if she wants to go. She's old enough to decide for herself. Heck, she'd be married with a kid by now if she hadn't been a mage. You practically made her your younger sister. She follows you everywhere. The crap she started to give me about not being able to be at your side when you went to attack those priests...."

"All right," she said, wiping away the tears that had fallen down her face. "Any wisdom with regard to my brother?"

Henton chuckled; he could tell it was not a serious question. "Don't kill him."

"Yeah. Getting harder and harder."

Wiping her eyes again, she started back up the stairs and he followed her to the second floor. When they entered the room, no one had moved or even appeared to have spoken a word. If he did not know better, he would have assumed time had stopped. Stephenie undoubtedly felt the concern behind the expressions on everyone's face.

"Ryia, you can come, but know that I didn't seek to exclude you because I didn't think you capable or that I didn't want you around. I thought to leave you here to protect you."

The girl nodded her head. "I know. But...I'm sorry. I shouldn't have yelled like that. I just don't have anyone here. I'd rather die than be left behind."

Stephenie nodded her head and turned to Douglas. "Do you want to come?"

Douglas picked up the bowl of stew he had filled earlier and started eating. "You know I will."

"Which leaves me behind," said Will. He raised his hands. "I'm not complaining. I've got a decent life, but if the two of you," he pointed to Ryia and Stephenie, "would ever finish training anyone, that would make my life infinitely easier."

# Chapter 16

The next morning, Henton, Douglas, and Ryia started gathering supplies. Ryia's happiness at going only grew when she discovered Stephenie asked Henton to consider using a ship for the first part of the journey. Having never experienced a ship voyage, she started pestering Douglas with every question that came to her mind, including how to avoid falling off the chamber pot while the ship rolled from side to side.

Kas took the morning to check on Arkani and the state of the other ghosts in what had once been his home. Stephenie knew the prospect of another long journey did not bother him, but she suspected he sensed her intention of seeking her sire along the way. She knew that part of her plan did bother him and felt certain he would likely take the risk of returning to the library for one last attempt to search for the information she sought. As a result, she did not expect to see him before nightfall.

Stephenie heard Rebecca was in her offices in the temple of Felis and so Stephenie headed to the one place inside the castle that she absolutely dreaded. After explaining her intention to the acolyte at the front doors, she was allowed entrance on her own accord.

On her way to the offices, Stephenie walked through the main temple area, which at this early time of the day was currently empty. As she passed the large statue of the soldier-farmer, she stopped. The silvery-grey metal never seemed to tarnish, *but that just might be due to people keeping it clean,* she offered as an alternative to the magic that most certainly played a factor.

Still sensing no one around, Stephenie stepped over a corded rope and onto the dais that held the twenty-foot tall statue. The figure had always been imposing to her. It had held the threat of death should anyone learn her secret. Putting aside her past feelings, she closed on the statue and with just a brief hesitation, she put her hand on the cold metal.

Growing up, she had heard claims from people that the cool air around the shrine indicated Felis kept his eyes upon the statue. Any who would commit blasphemy in the statue's presence would suffer Felis' wrath.

*Let's see if your large butt works the same as the small one.* She uttered the phrase that prompted Mertor's relay to respond to her commands; a phrase she was beginning to believe vaguely meant 'I wish to give you commands'. She grinned as the statue responded with an energy symbol, though no word filled her thoughts. Responding to the challenge, she felt herself extend as the relay opened itself in her mind. *Where is your source of power,* Stephenie asked in Denarian. Immediately, she felt the draw toward the east. Inquiring about distance, she received the impression the trap lay about one hundred miles away. *Out in deep water; safe from people messing with it.* She sighed, knowing the knowledge would disappoint Kas.

As with the relay the followers of Mertor used, Stephenie started asking additional questions to determine what commands it understood and what she could do. She felt this one responding more quickly and with greater certainty.

"What are you doing?"

Stephenie broke the connection with the relay and turned around. Rebecca stood before her, anger and suspicion on her face. "I merely wanted to check on it," Stephenie finally said.

"Get down before someone sees you. My office, now."

Stephenie nodded her head. She understood Rebecca's anger. Her own possessiveness she felt toward Argat and the others too often drove her to react instead of think. Since Rebecca knew all too well Kas' and her opinion of these devices, the implied threat that Stephenie offered would easily drive the High Priest to anger.

Once they were safe in the confines of Rebecca's office, the High Priest demanded her answer again. "Damn it, Steph, I have trusted you and given you liberties no Queen or High Priest would ever normally give, even to a younger sibling of the King. What are you trying to do to me?"

"I had no intention of harming your position."

"Do you really think you know what you are doing?"

Stephenie took a moment to respond; she had doubts, but she felt generally comfortable. *Which would make Kas cringe with fear, as confidence is the first sign you know too little.* "I know enough not to do damage," she lied.

Rebecca shook her head. "Steph, we are supporting you and your cause. You take away our power and how can we help you."

*Well, you should be learning to use your own innate abilities,* she wanted to say, but did not because of her own lack of engagement in that pursuit. "I wanted to know where the trap was located. I intend to destroy Mertor's. I do not intend to destroy yours, even though Kas would eventually want me to do so." Stephenie sat back in her chair. "Just so you know, your trap is about a hundred miles due east, out in deep water. I doubt anyone would ever be able to reach it."

Rebecca let out the breath she held. "There have been... fluctuations in the power. Periods where the holy...augmentation devices just do not have the strength to do what they should, or at least what they used to do. These fluctuations are generally brief, but a few priests have noticed them and word has come back to us. Ironically, the questions have been if Felis was changing his stance and planning to join Catheri in changing more of the rules."

"The being caught in your trap may be dying," Stephenie said.

"That is my suspicion based upon what you have told me and the secret writings in the journals kept by the prior High Priests. If our tick-like trap bleeds it dry, all the priests of Felis across the various countries around us will suddenly lose their power." She looked down. "So, you'll forgive me for panicking when I saw touching our shrine."

Stephenie nodded her head. "Ryia has been working with Sara in private. She said Sara is coming along well and there are others Ryia has been teaching. Sara should be able to start instructing you."

Rebecca turned around and retrieved a pair of beautifully blown glasses and a jug of wine. Pouring the wine into both glasses, she pushed one across her desk to Stephenie and then lifted the other. "I personally wish you were not leaving. We need you here."

Stephenie picked up the glass and took a small drink of the dry wine. "I can't stay. Josh fears me. You fear me. I can only say I would never hurt any of you so many times."

Rebecca drained her glass and set it on her desk. "I fear you might be planning on not returning. That is what has me worried."

*No, you fear what I can do.*

Rebecca continued, "I am trying to work on Josh, but he is insecure. Perhaps if I am able to give him a son he will not feel so tenuous on the throne." She looked up. "We are—"

"I don't want to know. Please, I picked up that one memory I don't want from you before and I don't need you to remind me."

Rebecca nodded her head. "Fair enough. When will you leave?"

"In a day or two. We have to find a ship and get supplies and I have to convince Josh to give me funds." Stephenie smiled, "Otherwise I'll have to turn to a life of piracy. I think Ryia would find enjoyment in it if I do."


It took four days before a ship could be secured. Sadly for Henton and Douglas, The Scarlet remained in open waters and another of Joshua's fleet, The Swift Death, received the orders to transport them and their horses to Wilm, the port city in Calis they had sailed from after stealing back the gold her mother had taken from Cothel's treasury.

By sailing up the coast, they would cut weeks of travel from a land journey and arrive in Salzen before the end of summer. Stephenie told Joshua not to have the ship wait for them; instead they would find another ship for the return passage or simply make their journey overland. If they did that, they might decide to winter in Midland and not come back to Cothel until the following year. It gave Stephenie the freedom to decide if she would continue north to Ista or not without causing immediate worry.

Joshua's relatively easy acceptance of that plan both saddened and reassured her. The lack of a fight reduced her stress, but his willingness to be parted for so long told her that he also had begun to realize he did not want her too close.

Because the word of who perpetrated the attacks had already spread widely, Joshua had informed the nobles that she would take the shrine north and dump it in the sea where it could no longer cause trouble for Cothel. Under that pretense, Stephenie had Henton gather an extra chest, in which they placed a couple of large rocks to mimic the weight of the statue. The sailors and captain of The Swift Death could then honestly report the casting of a chest into open waters.

The morning of the departure, everyone gathered in Stephenie's Great Hall for well wishes. Tearful goodbyes were spoken from Joshua and for a moment, Stephenie reconsidered her decision to stay away longer.

When Islet hugged her, her sister whispered in her ear, "I wish you well in your search. I will look for you to return at least once before I take my final rest."

"You are still quite young, Islet."

"I know." With another hug she added, "Take care of Henton, Douglas, Kas, and Ryia. They need you as much as you need them." Louder, she added. "I love you, Steph. I wish our time as children had been full of joy."

"Thank you, Islet. I am glad to once again have an older sister that I can say I love as well."

Sara and Will's good-bye was more jovial. "Bring us back some presents. We'll have a little one running around and won't have money left to buy ourselves new cloths."

"Sell that story to someone else," she said, hugging them.

As they picked up their bags to leave, Joshua halted them once more. "Steph, I want you to have something," he said, motioning Will to retrieve a long bag from beside the hall's main doors. "You have been terribly poor at keeping hold of your weapons, but I hope you will do better with these."

He took a rapier and a long dagger from the bag Will carried and handed the blades to her. The darkly stained wooden scabbards looked nearly black in the shadows, but still held traces of the grain when held in the proper light. The handles lacked heavy ornamentation, but the crossbars held a gentle curve and bulged to a vertical point at the center of the blade. The blades themselves were light enough that they would not tire her arm too quickly, but contained the strength and flexibility that only a master sword smith could infuse.

"I don't know what to say, Josh. These are truly beautiful. I'm speechless."

"I know how much you missed the ones Mother stole from you. They are not the ones Father got for you, but I hope they will work." He took her in his arms and hugged her. "I do love you. Make sure to avoid getting yourself killed, okay?"

With tears flowing, she returned his hug, feeling better than she had since she had returned. "You do the same. I expect to see Rebecca with a child as well when I get back."


Henton approached The Swift Death with anticipation mixed with disappointment. Though he would not admit it to Stephenie, it had been way too long since he felt a rolling deck beneath his feet, heard the crack of canvas as the wind filled the sails, and inhaled the smell of oil treated wood and salt air. He knew from the start that they would not get The Scarlet; she remained at sea and would not return to Antar for at least three more weeks, assuming she held to her schedule. Instead, the larger Swift Death, which had just finished a short refit, received Joshua's orders.

"That thing's not as swift as The Scarlet," Douglas muttered as he approached Henton's left side. The Swift, as Henton understood many of her sailors called her, held about twice the crew and marines that The Scarlet could ever hold. *And more importantly, had the room to fashion stalls for the horses.* To Douglas he said, "If you factor in the time to deliver a full company of soldiers, she'd be faster, but I know what you mean."

From above them, Henton watched a tall man in a fine overcoat approach the top of the gangplank. "Please, come aboard," he said with a gruff voice, waving them up the wide platform. "Your cargo is already aboard."

Henton nodded his head and held out a hand for Stephenie and Ryia to board first. Each of them carried packs with some personal gear. Strictly speaking, the bulk of their affects were already aboard in trunks. However, he carried the actual relay stuffed into his backpack and to avoid drawing attention to it, all of them carried some extra gear.

"Captain Nate," Stephenie said as she boarded the ship ahead of him. "It is a pleasure. I am glad you were able to provide us berths so quickly."

Henton caught a slight twitch in the man's expression, but the Captain smiled and bowed, removing his wide-brimmed hat in the process. "Of course, Your Highness. I am honored to be called to service by my King." The Captain caught Henton's eye and nodded his head. Turning back to Stephenie, he smiled again. "Please allow me to escort you to my cabin. I have cleared it for your use and took the liberty of having your trunks delivered there. I have asked the navigator to give up his room for Priestess Ryia, Lord Arnold of Felis would have given up his room, save for the fact that it is Felis' sanctuary on The Swift and that might not sit well with Catheri or Felis."

Henton detected a hint of disapproval in the Captain's voice and the stiff expression on the face of the man Henton assumed to be Lord Arnold made him wonder how much tension might emerge on the voyage.

"Captain Nate, that is perfectly fine," Stephenie said. "In fact, I am honored to use your cabin. We are used to traveling rough, so this will be a luxury for us."

The Captain smiled again. "Sergeant Henton, Corporal Douglas, another of my officers has given up his room for your—"

"Excuse me Captain," Stephenie said, already starting to move toward the hold, "I think I need to go check on the horses."

Henton took Stephenie's pack as she handed it to him. He did not fail to catch the Captains sour expression. Wishing he could sigh, he merely shouldered Stephenie's pack and stepped forward. "She values the horses greatly," he said as the sounds of stomping came up through the deck.

The Captain nodded his head. "She'll need to keep them calm. One of them's already been trouble. I won't have them tear a hole in the ship." Putting a smile back on his face, he held out an arm. "Let me show you the cabins."

Henton had to follow quickly as the tall man cut across the deck toward the aftcastle. The sailors and soldiers on deck watched the quick procession with distant interest.

Ducking through an open hatch into the structure at the back of the ship, he followed Captain Nate and Ryia down the short hall. At the end of the hall, he opened the door.

"This is Her Highness' room, my cabin. Not knowing whose chest belonged to who, we've put all of them in there." He opened the door on the port side of the hall, closest to his cabin. "Priestess Ryia, please use this cabin." He nodded his head toward the door beside Henton, also on the port side. "Sergeant, you and the Corporal will share that cabin." The Captain looked at Ryia and urged her with a nod of his head into her cabin. "If you will all please make yourselves comfortable, we need to get underway."

Henton nodded his head. "Of course, Captain." Stepping into his cabin, Henton noted the worn deck boards, but could tell the walls had a fresh coat of oil to protect the wood. After Douglas had entered, Henton moved back to the door. "Captain, any prohibition of us being on deck?"

The Captain paused a moment and then turned to Henton. "You and the Corporal know your way around and I imagine won't get in the way. Women tend to get underfoot too easily. If they are on deck, try to keep them out of the way." He frowned, "Of course, I understand you still have to follow orders. But if you can convince Her Highness to avoid places where we are working, that would be good."

Henton nodded his head and gave thanks that Douglas was not visible from the other side of the door. While even he could not see his friend, he knew the Captain's tone would not go over well with Douglas. Although, or perhaps because, Douglas once shared a similar belief about women in combat, Douglas now took great

offense if anyone implied Stephenie lacked competence at martial
skills. "We'll endeavor to keep out of the way," Henton finally said.

"Thank you, Sergeant. Now if you will permit me, I must get back
to casting us off while we have a favorable wind."

Henton nodded his head. *This is not how I wanted to start this
journey.* Once the Captain left the hall, he turned back to Douglas
and the room before him. There were two bunks; one had the
appearance of being hastily added to the cabin.

"What's up his ass?" Ryia asked, squeezing into the room behind
them.

Henton turned to Ryia as Douglas shook his head. "I'd guess he's a
bit of a traditionalist and doesn't like the idea of women on his
warship."

Ryia snorted. "Wait until Steph gets through with him."

Henton frowned, but did not doubt that she would have words
with him before they reached their stop. "He's got at least forty men
on this ship, possibly more. That's not good odds and before you say
throw them overboard, we'd need at least ten men to sail something
this large effectively. So, even if the man's got problems, let's not make
any more by stirring up trouble."

"Fine," Ryia said, though Henton doubted her certainty. "But I
want to watch us push away. I've never been on a ship before!"

Henton stood along the starboard rail and looked out toward the
eastern horizon and the building clouds. The Swift Death had
departed quickly from Antar and had been under full sails for more
than two turns of the glass. The rolling of the ship beneath him
warmed his heart and he did not want to turn from the birds that
were gliding over the choppy waves looking for an easy meal. Douglas
had already taken Ryia to her cabin. Almost immediately after they
cleared the protection of the harbor, her face fell and her lunch found
its way to the deck.

He knew it was wrong to delay checking on Ryia and Stephenie,
"But I've missed this," he whispered. Sighing for real this time, he
turned away from the railing and headed toward the cargo hold. He

had visited Stephenie before Kas had joined them; the ghost's delay a precaution against Lord Arnold detecting Kas when they boarded.

The large cargo doors were still open and so Henton walked down the ramp they used to bring on the horses instead of climbing the steep stairs. "Steph," he called out to her once he was below the deck; the darkness of the hold was broken by a series of oil lamps hanging from the thick timbers holding the ship together. Navigating around the multitude of supplies, he approached the area that had been turned into a series of five stalls. Side walls ran from the deck to the ceiling. A half-wall, split in the middle and hinged on the sides, closed off the front of each stall. Stephenie sat on a water cask in front of Dark Dancer.

Once he approached she finally looked up. "Dancer's not liking this at all. The motion of the sea has just set him off. I've got myself into his head and calmed him, but it doesn't last. He's got Stubborn irked as well."

Henton looked over to the packhorse that had at some point been moved to the other side of Argat, away from Dancer. "Hopefully they'll settle down once they get their sea legs," he offered. "Ryia's lost her pleasure for the sea as well. Our friend join us yet?"

Stephenie nodded her head. "Been here with me a bit after we broke harbor. Dancer really didn't like the change in the sea once we were outside the barrier." She glanced back at Henton. "What's wrong with Ryia?"

"Sea sick. Douglas is taking care of her." He handed her a cloth bundle he had been carrying. "Something to eat. The cook said there'd be something hot later, but because of when we sailed, just some bread and fruit for now." Henton returned his attention to Dancer. "Ryia and her horse are more alike than we knew. I hope the weather gives us a miss, but my gut tells me we'll have a bit of a blow before the night is done."

"Great."

"Yeah, but even more than what it will do to the others, I overheard some sailors talking. They're muttering about dumping the shrine into the sea and they've been rapping three fingers on their arm to ward off evil. We'll have to tread lightly to keep them from turning ugly on us."

Stephenie rolled her eyes, but she nodded her head. "Try and keep Douglas and Ryia in line," she told him. "I have a feeling I'll end up spending most of this trip in the hold."

# Chapter 17

Will tallied another row of numbers in his ledger and then shook his head. The final number lacked size. *Perhaps if I write it larger?* Was his first thought, followed by *It's a good thing I held back those couple of bags of gems.* He knew Stephenie would not have approved of his careful acquisition of an additional share from the chests of gold and jewelry they had stolen from Kynto. A smile crossed his face; they had done very well, even with the risk they faced on that trip. The memory of all the wealth just sitting there made him wish for the days that he had been included in Stephenie's adventures.

Sara knew of his less noble side, but she accepted him without expectations of change. "At least without the expectation of significant change," he admitted, knowing the baby would curb some of her willingness to look the other way. However, he knew the days of convincing Stephenie to steal from the wealthy and give to his causes would not likely return. *Instead, I just have to woo some additional rich donors.* "Which I have to do first thing in the morning," he muttered, making sure his journal of activities included breakfast with Mr. Orl, a well-to-do merchant who claimed he actually believed in justice and honest business practices. That made Will chuckle.

Glancing once more at the expense report he received for stonework for the last week, he looked again at the Church of Catheri's official funds. Knowing he did not want to tap into any more of his private money, he resolved himself to talk with Joshua for additional allowances after his meeting with Orl. "I'll just have to—"

The sound of something falling in the outer office drew his attention. A moment later, his office door swung open revealing a woman several inches shorter than either Stephenie or Sara, but whose expression carried the sense she expected others to gaze upwards toward her. A wave of long blond hair moved loosely behind her, offsetting her dark complexion in a distinctive contrast. He could tell her skin was soft and clear, even in the limited lamp light. But when he met her green eyes, they bore into him and he found he could not move, despite an overwhelming desire to draw a weapon.

The door closed behind her with a will of its own and she crossed the room without bothering to examine any of the contents. "You are William, the so called High Priest of the woman." It was as statement, not a question, but it took Will a moment to process the words spoken in a thickly accented Pandar.

"Who are you?" He managed to ask. "How did you get in here?" A buzzing in his head prevented him from rising to his feet.

The woman cocked her head slightly as she sat down, her dress, a deep blue, falling gracefully around her legs. Will would have considered her young, except for the timeless depth of her eyes. "You know, most people do not approach the High Priest first. We would be happy to have you join our flock, but there are—"

"You cannot conceal yourself with rambling noise," the woman said as a sharp spike of pain radiated through Will's head.

He winced and found it hard to concentrate, but he managed to get some words from his mouth. "You are attractive, I am sure your exotic beauty would bring additional followers. Let me sign you to our roles."

She grinned. "You lack the ability to block my efforts. But, I highly recommend you continue to fight me, it will increase your pain and my amusement."

"What...do...you...want?" He managed as muscle spasms raced across his body and sweat beaded on his face. He felt his heart pounding against his ribs, threatening to burst from the pressure. He wanted to stop her, but his body refused to respond to his desires.

She leaned forward in her seat, sending her hair over her right shoulder. "I am acting as a rivarta-kan...judge and executioner I believe is the term in this language." She relaxed back into the chair. "Your Stephenie—I realize I missed her again—is to be judged and executed."

"Seems...you already decided, why waste time judging?"

She did not acknowledge his comment. "I know she left on a ship four days ago, but to where exactly no one seems to know." The woman's focus moved from Will to stare past him at nothing visible in the room. "Show me the map in your mind. Yes, please struggle some more." She narrowed her eyes and a smirk rose to her lips. "She did not fully trust you, did she? But you have a guess, that will have to do."

The woman nodded her head. "So she wishes to destroy the traps as she calls them. Such a waste of potential." A sly smile made Will cringe. "So...this Kas, he is a driver in her decision. As well as a mentor." The woman laughed. "A body, really?"

"Get...out!" Will said through his teeth, struggling to push against the woman in his head.

"Interesting, you don't know where this ghost came from, but you do suspect something exists under the city. That is interesting. Perhaps when my business is attended to, I will look into that further." The woman leaned forward, now focusing directly on Will. "Who are her parents?" She shook her head. "The mother is irrelevant you moron. Who is her father? Not the King, do you understand nothing?"

Will had no idea how long it lasted, but suddenly the woman had left his mind. His eyes slowly gained focus again and he realized he had fallen forward. Slowly he pushed himself up from his desk and wiped the spit from his mouth. *Not a dream,* he thought with regret when he still saw the woman staring back at him. His shirt tugged at his movement, clinging to his sweat-drenched body.

"You truly don't know her lineage. This annoys me. I am here to judge her, yet she continues to run from me."

"Judge her for what?" Will barely managed; he felt as if he had run five miles at full pace and then had been run over by a team of horses.

"She killed a relative of mine. Albeit a few generations down the line, but it is forbidden. He was of my family and so is under my protection. I also know from you that she killed another man of breeding, though you were not there to witness either event. For these crimes, she is to be judged. If she lacks proper lineage, and I do not see how she cannot, she will die." The woman's lips formed a cold smile. "I suggest you kill yourself before I return. It would be a more pleasant end for you. Once I find her lacking, I will destroy all she holds dear."

Will sneered, "Then why allow me to live now?"

"There are rules. One does not simply kill someone who is protected. Based on all the minds I have seen, she considers you hers, so until she is found guilty, I will not break tradition, even if she chooses to do so." The woman cocked her head again, "Additionally, you can be of use, if she should return before I do, tell her to wait, for she will not escape my judgment. The running will only make it worse."

Will swallowed despite himself. Having felt this woman's mind rip through his memories, he feared her capabilities, but his pride would not allow him to remain quiet. "Whoever you are, Stephenie will destroy you, not the other way around."

The woman grinned. "Dear William, I am glad I did not break you too badly. I look forward to ripping life from you on my return." She rose to her feet. "For your cocksure attitude, I will leave you with this: I am twenty times older than your little Steph. Even if she was of my generation, which is highly unlikely, she lacks experience. Not even her Kas can overcome that. So, should you see her before I do, inform her that Yreka will find her and judge her."

Will watched the woman turn away and walk from his office. He wanted to stand and chase after her, but his hands still trembled and his legs lacked the strength. *Damn it, Steph, don't stop running.* His mind raced for options to send her a warning, but she was already days ahead of the woman and on a ship. *The Scarlet might be able to catch up, but it was a long way from being in port.* Eventually, he gained his feet. Joshua needed to be informed, but Will feared what would happen if Joshua sent any men to try to stop this woman.

\*    \*    \*    \*    \*

The Swift Death continued north, but the series of storms ate away at their pace. The rough waves even sickened a number of sailors that had never suffered from the movement of the sea before. When four of the barrels of fresh water broke their moorings in the hold and ruined a third of the hard biscuits only four days into the journey, the earlier grumbles of curses and being on a voyage damned by the gods, turned into fully vocalized complaints.

As the evening closed on their seventh day of travel, everyone's emotions ran high with yet another storm. While Ryia managed some recovery over the days and could keep down some food, she remained in her cabin and Douglas became her constant caretaker. Stephenie checked on her a couple of times, but Ryia remained listless and tormented by the constant movement.

Stephenie, herself, had yet to sleep in the Captain's cabin, spending most of her time in the hold keeping the horses as calm as possible. While she managed to convince Dancer to eat on the calmer days, his weight fell and his coat had a sickly sheen.

"Damn it, I did not want to take the horses a on ship," she swore to Henton as The Swift Death lurched to port, drawing a protest kick from Dancer and a rolling of eyes from the other horses, who were all weary of this trip.

"I know," he said, his voice sounded pained to her ears.

She made the complaint almost daily. She knew it an unfair complaint to make to Henton, who had not precisely argued for the decision, but simply accepted it. Her thought had been to give Douglas and Henton some time at sea, *but I should have listened to my instincts.*

When Henton's attention moved toward the ramp to the deck, Stephenie opened her focus and noted Captain Nate had opened the hatch and led five men into the hold amidst a torrent of rain. Sensing the weapons in their hands, she turned to face them. "You think of harming these horses and it'll be your lives."

The Captain sneered. "They keep up the kicking; they'll put a hole in the hull and send forty-two good people to the bottom! I've warned you too many times. It's them or us!"

"I am protecting the damn hull! Turn yourselves around and get out of my sight!"

The men on the ramp hesitated for a moment and then finally turned back to the topside. The Captain held his position for a moment and then with a great huff, turned and existed the hold. The hatch slammed shut after him, either in anger or because he lost control of it as the ship lurched again.

Stephenie turned back to the horses. *Damn it, Dancer, quit fighting me. I'm trying to keep you safe!* Reaching out with her mind, she tried to reestablish contact, but the tired horse only laid back his ears and reared. Rolling his eyes, he kicked at the hull again.

"Please, let me in. I only want to help!"

The horse snorted and even Argat, whom Stephenie had relied upon to help offer a calming presence laid back his ears when the ship tipped sharply to port again, sending Henton stumbling across the hold. He barely dodged a crate that had broken loose of its ropes.

"Damn it," she swore as the ship rolled back to starboard, in the worst jolt she had experienced over the whole journey.

"Steph, watch yourself. I need to get these lamps put out so they don't fall and catch us on fire."

Stephenie, still struggling with the horse's mind, pulled back a moment, sensed the three burning lamps, and snuffed away the energy from the flames, casting them into darkness.

"Yeah, or you can do that." Henton grabbed another beam as the ship dove prowl first down a swell. "Need me to do anything?" He shouted over the crashing of the waves against the hull and the rolling thunder.

Stephenie shook her head and then spoke, "Don't get hurt." Reaching out to the horse again, she no longer waited for Dancer to give her permission. Forcing her way into the horse's mind raised his initial fear and discomfort, which washed back on her, bringing her to her knees. Hearing Furball begin his own kicking, Stephenie broadened her focus and reached out to the other horses as well.

For a moment, complete panic set in as Dancer's fear leaked through Stephenie to the others. Hearing the cries and kicks, she pushed back on Dancer. The effort felt like an eternity. *Please Dancer, you have to calm down. I'm trying to save your life. Please, damn it, listen to me!* Dancer's hooves flung back again, but Stephenie continued to protect the hull with a wall of force.

Slowly, she felt the horses calm, just in time for the ship to lurch up and then down as it crested another swell. All the horses cried out at that motion, but only Dancer kicked. *Please, just listen to me. I'm not trying to hurt you!*

The winds and rain quieted during the night. It took Stephenie well into the morning to finally calm Dark Dancer to the point she no long had to invade his mind. However, that might have been more from his total exhaustion than her efforts. The horse had lost even more weight overnight. The floorboards under him were drenched in sweat and the poor animal hung his head from the cross ties that he tried to break throughout the night.

"At least he is standing," she mumbled aloud from where she lay in the scattered hay, exhausted and sweat-covered herself. The bleeding from her nose had stopped, but the throbbing in her head drummed on. *Mental work really wears me down,* she acknowledged, knowing that if she had been working on humans she would not have lasted even a third as long as she had with the horses.

Her eyelids slowly closed as she struggled to fend off sleep. Only because Argat snorted did she notice Kas' faint outline in front of her. His quick gesture pointing topside roused her enough that she pushed through the pain and opened her mind. Gradually, she realized a storm of a different kind had built on the deck. "Damn it."

Wiping her face with a wet rag to remove the traces of dried blood, she made her way to the deck, knowing already that the whole ship's crew had gathered around Henton, Douglas, and Ryia. As she emerged, several of the sailors stepped back, but others placed their hands on the knives at their belts. The implied threat narrowed Stephenie's eyes and drove the pain of her exhaustion to the background. "What is going on?" She demanded of the Captain, who stood at the front of his men.

"We will sail no further. The insult you plan against Mertor has brought a foul air to this whole voyage. And to insult a god as unforgiving as Mertor threatens to bring a curse down on all of us. We won't stand for it. The storms have only grown worse as the days have passed, we won't survive another one. Mertor will drown us for certain!"

Henton moved one-step forward. "Captain Nate, you know as well as anyone, storms like these happen. We've all been there when a squall comes out of nowhere. I've been there."

"We lost two sailors last night. The winds driven by godly anger swept Url and Bengi over the side. No one even saw them go down and I fear Mertor has consumed their souls. Who will protect us if their corpses climb from the dark depths and slay us in the black of night?"

"Mertor will take all of us if we continue!" Someone shouted from the crowd.

Stephenie caught the eye of the priest of Felis assigned to the ship. The balding man quickly looked away. *No support there, even when his High Priest had ordered his assistance.* She moved to stand by Henton and in front of Douglas, who held Ryia on her feet. Ryia's pale face and sunken eyes spoke of the torment she endured. Stephenie's mind had done too much to sense the emotions around her, but the looks on the faces of the sailors told her all she needed to know. *They will try to kill us before they go further.*

Not taking her eyes from them, she spoke to Henton, "You and Douglas, go get the chest." Reaching behind herself, she pulled Ryia against her side to allow Douglas to go with Henton.

As Henton and Douglas started to move toward the Captain's cabin, she watched several men step forward. With a shake of her head, she held those men in check with the intensity of her stare, allowing Henton and Douglas to continue across the rain-dampened deck.

"We can't let them go," someone said from the safety of the crowd. The mass of men shuffled about slightly, agitating to escalate the conflict.

"Any of you harm us, it is treason," she said softly.

The Captain shook his head. "You don't scare me. My crew will go no further and nothing you can say will change that. We can't respect someone who'd draw down the wrath of the gods and then put the lives of animals over that of people."

Stephenie glanced behind the Captain again. Fear filled the men's expressions, but these people were united in their fear and that gave them strength. "Those horses never threatened the safety of this ship." Her statement had no impact. *I need to get us off this ship.* She adjusted her hold of Ryia, but the girl barely had any life in her. A spark still existed, but she had grown as weak as Dancer.

Turning back to the Captain and crew she raised her voice. "If you don't want to go further, take us to the nearest port and we'll get off." She knew she needed to give them an option that did not involve bloodshed. Her proclamation caused several murmurs to move through the crowd. At the same time, Henton and Douglas carried out the chest with the rocks. Held tightly closed with a lock and thick leather straps, the small chest itself weighed about twice that of what the statue actually weighed.

Several men looked ready to step forward and take control of the chest. Although exhausted, she pulled as much energy as she could into herself and created a series of fields around the chest. She moved it slightly so Henton and Douglas knew to release their hold of the handles. Before anyone in the crowd could speak, she gorged herself on the energy from her surroundings, bringing a palpable chill to the air and still wet deck. Unleashing all the energy at once, the chest launched into the air, pulling a strong gust of wind behind it.

Flying faster than a bolt fired from the most powerful ballista, the chest soon dissolved into a speck no larger than a distant bird. Those with the sharpest eyes barely followed its path as the chest eventually fell toward the sea and finally disappeared beneath the waves.

"You've cursed us all," someone swore, despair clearly evident in the man's voice. "Damn you, you've cursed us all!"

She was surprised that the effort had not hurt her as much as she expected, *but it was only manipulating gravity, not reading minds.* "Take us to the nearest port and you can be done of us. If you want to bathe in holy water to protect yourselves, you can do that after we're gone."

Stephenie waited, but no one moved, many still stared in the direction she had launched the chest. Feeling her anger build, she drew in energy once again. This time, she applied the gravity field against the starboard side of the bow and the stern of the ship.

Pushing as much energy into the fields as her tired body could muster, the ship lurched forward from where it drifted, turning slightly toward the land barely visible to the north. "I want off now!"

Feeling the sudden cold mixed with the impossible movement of the ship, the Captain turned and started barking orders. "Raise the mainsail. Make for land. There's a port northeast of here."

Henton came to stand beside her as Douglas resumed his support of Ryia. "I'm sorry these men reacted as they did. If we had sailed on The Scarlet, Captain Darelin would have kept the crew in line."

Though Douglas said nothing, his face betrayed the fact that he suspected her brother's hand in the events on ship. Stephenie ignored the implication and found a nearby place to sit. She knew Kas remained with the horses, doing his best to conceal his presence. "The three of you, don't separate. I don't trust these people."

The sun, dimmed by a haze of clouds, sat high in the sky by the time they reached the promised port. However, even before they were close enough for Stephenie to clearly see the town, she knew there would be a problem and approached the Captain. "You're planning to sail there? I can see what looks like sandbars from here."

Captain Nate sneered. "Of course not, but that is the closest port, Ma'am. I did as you ordered, but The Swift will not beach herself for your folly."

"And how do you expect me to get the horses off?"

The man shrugged and as he walked away, he said, "Push them over."

Stephenie looked at the man, her own anger and hate matching his. The Captain did not look back as he ordered the sails down and the anchors dropped. Looking again to the shore, she knew if she had not been exhausted she would have enjoyed swimming the distance. *But not with supplies and not with Ryia.*

Henton stood behind her and placed a hand on her shoulder. "I'm thinking that might be Calis," he said. "The land is running more east to west. It all depends on how far we were blown last night. I don't recall anyone claiming we were past the city of Green yet, but we had been fairly far out to sea to allow us past Blue Point. We might have been blown quite a distance. Or this is just a jutting peninsula of land and we'll find ourselves still in Midland."

Douglas cleared his throat. "I guess we can ask those in that small fishing boat coming out to meet us."

Henton nodded his head as Douglas helped Ryia closer. "You know, The Swift is lost to your brother. The Captain and the crew would be fools to return to Cothel after what's happened here."

Stephenie nodded her head at Henton's comment. "I won't kill them. A part of me understands their fear. But I'm pretty sure if they thought they could have killed us, we'd be at the bottom of the sea with that chest. They just better hope never to meet me again under different circumstances."

"Here," Douglas said, handing a nut sized pill to her. "I've got Ryia to take one as well."

Stephenie looked down at the pill; it was what Will had used too often to keep himself awake when he had a lack of sleep. She had used them a few times herself, but hated the after effects. However, the ache of too little sleep and too much use of magic filled her body. Tossing the concoction into her mouth, she forced it down her throat. "When did you start carrying those?"

"I've had a couple on me for a while. I took them off Will to try to get him to stop. You and Ryia both look like you need it and we ain't off this rotten hulk yet."

She nodded her head and turned back to watching the approaching fishing boat. She knew she would feel the effect soon. A manic energy that would cause her limbs to tremble. Once the initial effects passed, her mind would clear. *At least until it wears off.*

The small fishing boat moved quickly through the rolling waves. As it neared The Swift Death, it dropped its sail. The sea slowed it quickly, but it had enough momentum to execute a turn that brought the small vessel to rest beside the much larger one.

"Hello, there!" Stephenie called out in Pandar before Captain Nate could. "Can you transport some of us and some supplies to shore?"

"Yes, Ma'am. Is that why you stopped here? We wondered if you were in distress."

Stephenie did not want to discuss the distress she felt. "Aye, we just need room for three people and our gear."

The three young men on the fishing boat glanced around their boat. "We've got plenty of room."

Stephenie inclined her head to the man and then turned to Henton and Douglas. "I want the three of you to go over in that boat with our supplies. I'll get the horses into the water and swim them to shore." Henton raised an eyebrow and Stephenie anticipated his concern, raising her left hand that now suffered from a slight trembling, she placed it on his arm. "I'll make it look like I forced the horses off the deck, but Dancer is going to need my help to make it. I think the others are still strong enough to swim and it looks like we might be able to rest on the sandbars between here and the shore."

"It's about a quarter mile," Henton challenged.

Stephenie nodded her head and then smiled. "I'll do Fish proud, but won't strip bare, though it would be easier to swim it if I did."


The small town went by the name Elchel, in honor of the family that founded it a hundred years earlier. None of the three men on the fishing boat considered it a port town and Stephenie heard Henton working to deflect the questions of why they had not traveled the half day's distance to Blue Point, a large city equipped to handle ships as big as The Swift Death.

Once their equipment, including the leather duffel with the relay, was safely loaded into the fishing boat, Henton, Ryia, and then Douglas transferred down the rope ladder. Ryia nearly fell, but Will's pill had roused her as it had done Stephenie and she caught herself.

Once they were away, Stephenie waited as the shallow bottomed boat moved toward shore, deftly avoiding the sandbars in its path. She continued to wait, despite the stares of the sailors and soldiers around her. With Kas now enveloping her, she remained calm.

Once the fishing boat passed outside of easy crossbow range, she turned casually and headed back to the hold. Using her magic, she pulled open the large cargo doors that lay over a ramp. The few sailors near the doors scattered. No one came within ten feet of her and she noted the priest of Felis remained closed away in his cabin. *Kas, I don't want to have to kill people today. Please let me not have to kill people today.*

*I would speculate that if they seriously contemplated your demise, it would have been prudent to do that before the others had been allowed to leave and even well before we were in view of land. There are now far more witnesses than before.*

Unfortunately, Kas' statement did not make her feel any better. Moving through the hold to the horses, she opened Argat's makeshift stall doors and led him out. Her faithful mount shook his neck and back, but remained quiet and attentive.

Due to the pill, the ache in her head had fallen to a dull throbbing, but even with that improvement, she knew getting the horses off the ship on her own was going to hurt. Opening her mind again, she reached out to the five horses. Not wanting to go deeply into their thoughts, she simply tried to project a calming attitude. This time Dancer lacked the energy to fight her efforts and his ears dropped slightly. Releasing the others from their stalls, she clucked at Argat, and projected her desire that they calmly walk up the ramp and to the outside.

All five of the horses, too long deprived of the sun and sky, willingly headed up the ramp and onto the deck, scattering the crew out of their way. Argat remained calm, but the other horses, expecting green grass, hesitated at seeing rolling blue water.

The sailors, guessing what she planned, had already removed a section of the railing that came free for the loading of large cargo. Knowing that none of the horses, including Argat, would willingly jump off the edge of the rocking boat, she drew in more energy and crafted a gravity field over their eyes causing them to close. Using additional fields, she tugged on their halters, as though a person lead them forward. She extended a solid platform of gravity off the edge of the boat and drew Argat out over the water. When he was clear of the deck, she quickly lowered him into the sea.

She released his eyes as his feet hit the water and even her calm mount protested the sudden change in his environment. However, instinct kicked in and Argat began swimming.

The process for the other four horses went faster, with Dark Dancer entering the water last. As he started thrashing in the rolling sea, Stephenie took one last glance at the stunned sailors and stepped off the deck. She hit the water harder than the horses. However, the descent did not frighten her, which allowed herself to wait until the last moment before adjust her body's gravity.

Feeling a bit of blood trickling from her nose, she wrapped Dancer's body in a field so he would float more easily. Bending gravity once more, she nudged the horses' halters to direct them to follow Argat, who had already headed for shore.

By the time they reached the sandbars and found ground firm enough for the horses to rest upon, The Swift Death had raised its sails and turned back to sea. Looking toward the shore, she could see a group of people had gathered to watch her. *I hope none of them had a spyglass to see how slowly the horses hit the water.* Even thought she had no real choice in the matter, she did not want people suspecting her of magic. While she could try claiming to be a priest of Catheri, this far from home it would be easier if the issue never got raised.

She barely felt Kas before he spoke. "Henton informed me that he has learned all the towns in the vicinity are of limited size." Almost as if he anticipated her concern, he added, "The local priest is traveling to another village. The others are safe on shore. I could not understand much of what the locals said, but Henton and Douglas appear calm."

"Thank you, Kas. Tell them I will be along shortly."

She had a momentary sense of his approval before he left. Knowing the rest of the journey to land would not get easier with time, she moved forward, urging all the horses toward the shore while she supported Dancer. Thankfully, the other horses offered no resistance.

When she finally did walk out of the cool water, a local woman quickly wrapped her in a wool blanket as Henton and Douglas collected the horses. "Miss, you'll catch your death swimming out there like that. We know you're a horse trainer, but risking yourself like that is foolish."

Stephenie looked into the brown-haired woman's eyes and smiled. "They are part of my family," she replied in Pandar. "And all of our savings."

"That may be so, but some things are not worth the risk. I am Alicia."

Stephenie bit back her reply; the woman could not know Argat's place in her life. "Please call me Steph. Is there a place we can take them to dry off and get some food? They had a rough time in the storm."

"Of course, your man here has already arranged it. You'll all stay with me today. Let's get some food into you as well."

# Chapter 18

Even though they had managed to come ashore just after midday and plenty of light remained for traveling, none of them considered moving on from Elchel. Stephenie and Ryia's exhaustion had reached a point that even with the pills, once they had eaten, they quickly fell asleep in Alicia's bed with Kas keeping watch. Henton and Douglas tended to the horses, but as soon as they were done, they allowed their own exhaustion to overcome them.

The next morning, they thanked their host for a filling meal and bought more supplies from the town. Before mid-morning, they set out on a back road heading north. Stephenie led Dark Dancer on foot, while Ryia rode Argat. Dancer had lost too much weight on the ship and Stephenie did not want to tax him more than necessary by forcing him to carry anything more than an empty saddle. She felt Argat questioned the change, but even he had not tried to steal Dancer's food that morning.

"North?" Henton asked. "From the maps, we might make better time on the coastal road to Blue Point and follow that around to Wilm so we can stay on our original plan."

Stephanie nodded her head. "Remember when I insisted everyone take a set of good clothes?"

Henton's expression held no surprise. "I take it we're adjusting our plan from what you told your brother?"

Stephenie glanced at Douglas whose smiling face indicated he approved of her making changes. "I had intended to explain on the ship, but...well, I didn't. However, we're going to stop in on one of my distant relatives. I want to ask him about a letter he sent my father nineteen years ago."

"I don't suppose we'll be lucky and find he's just a wealthy merchant," Henton mused.

Stephenie paused to consider the question. "In a sense I guess he is. His business just happens to span the whole country of Calis."

"So we're heading to the capitol. Do you think he will even be there?"

Stephenie bit her lower lip. "I hope so. We've got a few days of travel before we get there. We can carefully inquire if he is traveling. I really don't know a great deal about him and what other castles or palaces he might visit. My father spoke of him from time to time, but not often."

"I can't wait," Ryia said with a smile, though her enthusiasm remained well below her prior level. "I never thought to meet a single king before I met you, now I might get to meet a second one." She took a deep breath, "And now that we're off that damn ship, I might actually enjoy this trip."

"Well, the four of you can visit with him," Douglas said from his horse. "I've had my fill of kings. I'll stay with the bags."


The first day out of Elchel Stephenie went slowly. Her own body had not fully recovered and Ryia's and Dancer's were in worse shape. Not wanting to stress either of them, she called a halt to their travels early in the afternoon, stopping at the first town they entered.

They found a farmer with spare rooms and stalls and they paid for the space as well as some extra grain for the horses. While the men took care of the horses and redistributing the supplies, Ryia found a bed where she could rest. Stephenie joined her in the room, but once Ryia had fallen asleep, Stephenie pulled out the relay and resumed the work she had started back in Antar.

Using the red journal, she tried to work out additional commands and the meanings of words. She would ask it a question in Denarian and listen carefully for the response. As the afternoon wore on, she gradually began to feel a stronger presence from the relay as the responses to her questions moved from simple feelings of confirmation, denial, and confusion, to words and longer phrases.

*Is there someone there?* She finally asked after the presence in the relay began to take on an almost human feel.

At first she heard no reply. *Tou duv Mertor,* an even deeper and richer voice finally said.

A chill ran through her body. The voice she had grown used to had been almost juvenile in tone, this one held a definite adult quality. The sudden change almost caused her to break contact with the relay. However, with the words came a feeling of loneliness that gave her pause.

*Is there someone there?* She heard the relay ask in Denarian, using the masculine voice. A bit of emotional concern accompanied the voice.

Stephenie tried to decide if the concern stemmed from fear of her or a fear of no answer being returned. Eventually, she responded, *I am Stephenie.* She could not say precisely why she did answer. She did so despite the fear that the voice was not the relay, but a priest of Mertor or some Senzar holding another relay. However, the underlying ache of isolation in the presence made her sympathetic. She did not want to believe it belonged to someone who intended her harm. A few moments later, she felt an acknowledgment from the relay and a sense of kind gratitude.

*Are you reading my mind?* She asked.

"Hey, Steph, Ryia, you want dinner?"

Douglas' voice broke Stephenie's concentration and her connection with the relay. Blinking her eyes, she regained awareness of the room around her. She looked up from where she sat to her bearded friend standing just inside the bedroom doorway. "Yeah, give me a little bit to finish up with this."

"I'm ready to eat," Ryia said, pushing the covers off and crawling out of bed.

"Better come quick, otherwise Ryia will eat your share."

Stephenie smiled at Douglas and after he closed the door, she focused her attention back on the blanket-covered relay. However, once she reestablished the connection, the relay behaved as it initially had; it seemed the greater intelligence she had conversed with briefly had faded away.

Breaking the connection again, she put the bundle back into the saddlebag they used to carry it. "What was that?" She wondered softly. She considered asking Kas, but they had already exceeded his general knowledge of the devices. His people forbid their use and wanted to destroy them, *which means he had no firsthand experience.* She bit her lip. *The voice said he was Mertor.* She let out the breath she had held and decided for now to keep the brief experience secret. The presence she felt seemed so isolated and alone she could not bear to tell the others in case they tried to keep her from making contact again. *What if it is the creature being killed by the trap? Might that be where they got the name of the god? What if I can tell it I will free it?*

Sliding the saddlebag under the bed, she hoped she was doing the right thing. Not confident, but still resolved to the decision, she got up and headed downstairs to eat before someone sent Kas up to check on her.

The next seven days of their journey to the city of Calis lacked any real excitement. Stephenie refrained from pushing them into full days of travel and they continued to stay in towns and villages along the way. As they grew closer to the capitol, those towns grew larger and actual inns became available for their use.

She continued each afternoon and evening to try to reestablish contact with the deeper intelligence in the relay, but the presence never fully returned. Instead, she had the feeling it might be watching and perhaps even leading her down certain paths, influencing the questions that she would ask. However, instead of trying to conceal information, it seemed to be trying to get her access to even more knowledge.

Additionally, she found a way to get the relay to display sequences of characters or words using fields on its surface as it spoke to her. While the fields changed quickly, she feverishly recorded everything she could in her journal. She knew the others observed her breakthrough with the relay's language. However, she continued to refrain from mentioning the deep voice.

"Hey," Ryia said, jumping onto the bed next to Stephenie, disrupting her writing. "I found where I want to stay in Calis. Please can we? Please? Please? Please?"

Stephenie set aside her notebook and looked at Ryia, who was on her hands and knees in front of her. Ryia's head was lifted and eyes were big like a puppy dog. "Pleeeaaase?" She begged. "It sounds like a great place to stay."

Stephenie looked up at Henton who had followed Ryia into the room. "Why do I think I am not going to like this?"

Henton chuckled and then sat down on the edge of the bed. "Well, I have good news. I found out the King is in the capitol and at his palace."

"And there is this place we can stay in the city where most of the people who see the King stay." Ryia smiled so broadly that Stephenie could not help but smile in return.

"Really? I don't suppose you want to tell me about it, do you?"

Ryia's head bounced up and down. "The tubs are filled with scented water and there are statues and carpeting and meals fit for kings and servants and carriages that take you right to the palace and—"

"And it probably costs a small fortune," Stephenie said, closing the lid on the ink well.

Ryia shrugged. "We can all pitch in to pay for it." She kept lifting her eyebrows and smiling. "Please?"

Stephenie looked at Henton whose grin was almost as wide as Ryia's. "All right. Fine. We can stay at this overpriced inn."

"Yeah!" Ryia jumped off the bed and headed back for the door. "I'm going to force Douglas to teach me to dance."

Stephenie shook her head. "Poor Douglas."

"You should come down as well," Henton said. "You're spending too much time with that thing. Come down and join the rest of us for a while."

She looked at him. "Did you put Ryia up to that?"

"No. We had been talking with some merchants to quietly inquire if the King was home and this guy kept going on about The Harris House. Supposed to be some fancy manor not too far from the palace and right in the heart of the best part of the city. Lots of fountains and things. Kas suggested she ask you."

Stephenie shook her head, but smiled. "Which is why he's still hiding downstairs. All right, let's go have some fun."


Once in the city of Calis, finding The Harris House proved to be very easy: simply follow the Grand Avenue toward the palace. Near the edges of the city, the Grand Avenue was merely a wide cobblestone street with upscale establishments. As they grew closer to the heart of the city, they found the road grew wider and the condition changed to immaculate. An army of street sweepers kept the road clear of debris, which allowed the amply-sized gutters to carry away any rainwater to the canal that ran through the city.

The people traveling along the road were mostly conveyed to their destinations in upholstered carriages. The few who chose to walk were escorted by servants and retainers, often under the cover of parasols held high to block out the perceived harshness of the late afternoon sun. While dressed nicely, Stephenie and her group could only be assumed to be servants, even when riding horses whose lineage would never be possible for peasants to afford.

As they passed a multitude of manor houses, each protected by gated walls, they all found themselves taken in with the splendor and classic beauty of the architecture. Behind the walls, old oak trees swayed gracefully in the breeze. The smell of flowering gardens drifted into the street, giving a hint at what might exist within each protected confine.

The Harris House was no exception. A large iron gate could be closed to block the entrance to the graveled path. The three-story stone manor house stood gleaming in the sun. Off to the right of the large enclosure, a two-story stable, also made of stone, waited patiently.

As they turned into the entrance, a pair of guards, attentive and well dressed called them to a stop. Henton dismounted and approached. "Good day. While we have no reservations, we are Lords and Ladies from Cothel and we would very much like to stay here while we conduct our business in your grand city."

The guard smiled. "We normally only accept guests by invitation."

Stephenie did not have to look behind her to feel Ryia's disappointment building. "We have diplomatic correspondence for King Lartin," she offered as a reason for their stay. "From Cothel's royal family."

The guard looked up at her and bowed his head. "We will have someone come down from the house to speak with you."

Stephenie glanced back to Ryia, who sheepishly smiled her thanks. Looking back to the house at the end of the gravel lane, Stephenie shook her head. *This is going to cost us a lot.*

For Ryia's sake, she was thankful that no diplomatic messages had to be produced as evidence of her claim. However, Stephenie had not yet decided if a random statement and sufficient money should be accepted so easily. Of course, a large house such as this one, with the number of staff on hand, did not want to have too many vacant rooms.

The rooms that they rented contained a private bathing chamber, three bedrooms, a dining hall, and a pair of servants to wait upon their needs. Once they had all bathed and turned over the majority of their clothing to be cleaned, they were seated for a feast that Stephenie found rich enough to be served at one of her father's very special occasions.

*Shall we find some unscrupulous merchants that need to be relieved of their wealth?* Kas asked as Stephenie savored the steak before her. *While I will not suffer should you run out of money, I suspect the rest of you may not enjoy going hungry.*

Stephenie shook her head. *Between Will, Josh, and Rebecca all giving me funds, and the others chipping in their own money for this, we are not in danger just yet.* She gave him a mental smile. *You're just wanting to cause some trouble.*

Ryia kept looking around at the carpeting and wood paneling of the room. With food still in her mouth, she spoke hastily in Pandar, "I want to stay in places like this all the time. Did you see the park just down the street? There is a statue and a fountain. You can see it from the bathing room window." Finally swallowing the last of her food, she asked, "Can we go see it tomorrow? Please?"

"Perhaps," Stephenie said, taking a moment to consider what she might do if the King would make her wait a few days for an audience with him. "We didn't come down the Grand Avenue the last time we were in town. But I know there are a number of interesting things to see. But Ryia, not all of them allow people to get close."

"Ma'am," the younger of the two female servants said timidly.

Stephenie more sensed than saw the ire from the older woman. "Yes?" Stephenie asked with an easy tone.

"If you will forgive my interruption, the statue and fountain can be approached. It is called Blue Bird Blossom. The statue is of Sir Alwik, a Knight of the Blue."

Henton nodded his head. "Thank you. Do you know of any other places we might take Lady Ryia?"

Stephenie smiled. Henton must have also picked up on what might result in a disciplinary action against the fair-haired servant.

The young woman stepped forward. "Yes, My Lord. We have many wonderful places around the Royal Palace. There is the Rose Garden of Lady Bel, the Swans of Evening Light, and the Five Fountains of the Senta, which were dedicated the year I was born. They honor the ancient order of Senta, who started studying the stars when His Majesty Gravhir ruled a long time ago. And—"

The older woman cleared her throat. "Please forgive Miss Eli, she forgets her place."

Stephenie smiled. "No forgiveness needed. Miss Eli, does everything around the city have such an interesting history?" With some hesitation, the young woman nodded her head, but kept her mouth closed, so Stephenie spoke, "If at some point you are free and we are not engaged, I would be pleased to have you show us some of these places and tell us their history."

The older woman's mouth hung open for a moment before she snapped it closed. Flustered, it took her a couple of false starts before she found her response. "Miss Eli's role is more domestic in nature."

"I would be quite willing to pay for her time," Stephenie said, her own ire rising. Taking a moment, she decided to stop escalating the situation, which would likely only get the girl in more trouble. "For now, I think we are done with dinner. If you would clear it away, we will turn in for the night."

"Of course, Ma'am," the older woman said, quickly moving a cart to the table.

As they finished loading up the carts and began to leave, Stephenie pulled several coins from her pouch and handed some money to each woman, the younger one receiving at least twice as much. "Thank you for the attention tonight, please enjoy something in the city on us."

The older woman hid her surprise well and thanked everyone as they left, closing the door behind them. Stephenie turned to the others. "Hopefully, tomorrow morning we'll hear back about an audience with the King...and hopefully, it will go well," she added softly.

In the early morning, Stephenie received confirmation from the palace that the King would receive her diplomatic message late that morning. After a hardy breakfast, Stephenie, Kas, Henton, and Ryia hired a carriage to the palace. Douglas remained behind in the rooms with their belongings and the servants.

*Why am I so tense?* She asked Kas as they rode in luxury toward the gates of the Royal Palace. *I can't find a place to put my hands and I'm sweating.*

She felt Kas' mental shrug. *Do you feel your hair is not well brushed? Perhaps you did not add enough rose petals to your bath and your odor is strong.*

Stephenie glared in his direction. *Really, you think that's what is bothering me?* She sniffed a couple of times anyway, but could not smell any strong odors from any of them. *Shut up. I don't smell.* She glanced out the open window at the lake in front of the Palace. *I fear he'll send me away without telling me anything.* Letting out a sigh, she quietly said, "I wonder what they call the lake. Everything here has some kind of fancy name."

"Duck Butt Pond," Ryia offered, drawing everyone's attention. "What? Look," she offered, pointing toward the water. "It's full of ducks and their butts are in the air."

Stephenie chuckled. "All right. I'll confirm it with the King, Duck Butt Pond will be its new name."

Ryia shrugged, still looking out the window. "It's what they are showing me."

They were let out of the carriage at the gates and once Stephenie presented the confirmation of their audience with King Lartin, they were escorted down a gravel road to the Palace and led into a small waiting room while a steward announced their arrival. The room's comfortable seating and ample refreshments kept the wait from being unpleasant, but it did not stop Stephenie's fidgeting.

Another man came to check on them, offering to refill the pitcher of water or bring wine. Unneeded, he left them alone once again in the room. However, Stephenie could sense a passage behind the wall that contained the small fireplace and knew that at least two people came by to spy on them. She forced herself to avoid looking in that direction and did not let Kas move from where he hovered around her.

After what felt like a turn of the glass, another well-dressed steward opened the door. "Ma'am, if you will follow me, His Majesty has agreed to meet with you in private."

Henton raised an eyebrow and Stephenie's mind raced. *Separate yet again?* She wondered quietly to Kas and then quickly made her decision before Kas could respond. *You stay here with Henton and Ryia, if there is trouble, you can let me know.*

*I do not like this,* Kas thought back.

*I don't either, but please, for me.*

Kas moved over to envelop Henton as his response to her.

Stephenie stood, drawing Henton to his feet. "I would be honored," she said to the steward, hoping Kas would keep Henton from worrying too much, but then decided that together they might worry even more. *There's nothing to be done about that.*

The well-dressed steward led Stephenie through the castle, down marble halls and through richly decorated corridors. Paintings and tapestries covered the walls, while life-sized statues of beautiful women and masculine men stood guard. In all, the building held a brightness and an openness that Antar Castle lacked and Stephenie had not decided if she liked the more palace-like feel or not.

Finally, they reached a set of large gilded doors where four men stood watch. One door was pulled open at their approach, and the steward stepped inside, only to return quickly. "He is waiting."

After stepping into the large chamber, she immediately noted the lack of anyone save for an older man sitting upon a thrown at the far end of the room. Feeling slightly paranoid, she reached out further with her senses, but she felt no other guards, watchers, or servants near the hall. The lack of anyone, save for the man she assumed was King Lartin, heightened her apprehension. *Might they have someone standing in for him?* As the door closed behind her, she kept her hands to her side and walked forward into the large audience chamber, absorbing energy with each step.

Glancing about the room, she observed the rows of stone columns that stood a dozen feet from the walls and supported the arched ceiling. Her attention drawn upwards, she took in the artwork that adorned the ceiling. Painted with many blues and greens, it depicted the sky and branches of trees high above her head. She spared a glance to the floor and the marble inlays in the large stone slabs beneath her feet. Under the columns, the green stone had an appearance of rich grassland, but the center of the room was crafted to depict a sea filled with monsters and ships. The sparkle of tiny flecks of quartz in the granite slabs added a dynamic quality to the tone of the colored stone.

Stephenie stopped just before the large compass rose embedded two-thirds of the way into the chamber. She curtsied as she spoke, "Your Majesty, thank you for—"

"Are you here to kill me?" The man's aged voice echoed through the hall; his voice corrupted with bitterness. "Your identity is no secret to me. While we have never met, I have had paintings of you in my possession since you were born."

Stephenie stood straighter as her draw of energy intensified. Using some of the burning power, she once again reached out to search for the threat she still could not find. She spoke cautiously, fearing someone might now be holding Henton and Ryia as leverage against her. *Kas, keep them safe.* "I am not here to kill you. I have no reason to offer you harm." She lifted her hands in confusion; palms raised. "I merely came here to ask you a question in confidence."

The grey-haired man shifted on the gilded throne. His thick cloak slipped from his bony shoulder. "I sent my people away. They felt it a foolish move, but I have heard of the destruction you wield. I ask that if your anger takes you, kill only me and leave my people in peace."

Despite herself, she felt her anger rising. She looked about the room with her hands still held aloft. "Why does no one believe me when I say I mean them no harm?" She asked as she looked directly into his eyes. "If anything I am more cautions than others when it comes to fighting someone. I ignore insults that others wouldn't because I do know how disproportionate my response could end up being." She looked away as she rubbed her temples with her left hand. Calming herself, she turned her attention back to the man before her. "I merely wanted to know about this letter," she said, pulling the folded paper from her pouch. "You sent a warning to my father. I do not know what his response was and I was hoping you could fill me in on the details."

The man bit his lower lip and visibly warred with himself. "Can I be frank with you?" He finally asked.

Stephenie nodded her head. "Please. I am not here to harm anyone. I just want to know about the man you spoke of."

King Lartin motioned her to approach and Stephenie complied, coming into easy speaking distance. The old man examined her face with his weary blue-grey eyes. "Charles was a friend of mine, but he was not your father."

Stephenie stiffened but said nothing.

"You are obviously aware," he said, holding focus on her eyes. "From the first painting of you, I knew. I see the resemblance clearly. Your hair, yes, but your eyes more so. They are burning with rage right now. I can even feel the tingling of your power. You may claim to be purified, but you are his offspring, not Charles'."

Stephenie noted the tight grip of his bony hand on the arm of his throne. After a moment, he continued, "I have wanted to stare down the man for nearly twenty years." He looked away for a moment and then turned back to Stephenie with slightly less rage. "However, knowing what you are capable of makes me think I would not survive. Some days that would be fine by me."

Stephenie loosened her jaw muscles and allowed herself a moment before speaking, "My father," she emphasized, "was King Charles. He raised me. He loved me. He cared for me." Stephenie tilted her head in acknowledgment of Lartin's building protest. "While he was not my sire, he was still my father. I loved him and miss him."

Lartin pursed his lips and looked into her eyes again. Stephenie held his challenge until he blinked first. "Your mother was always a questionable choice. It worried me that Cothel might side more with Richard, or Willard, once his father died. However, Charles played a neutral hand and I was pleased. In fact, I had even grown to like Elsia at one point." Lartin looked away again.

Stephenie could tell his focus lay in the past. "I never got along with my mother," she offered. "She despised me my whole life."

Her statement drew Lartin's attention back to her. "Do you know of my first wife?"

Stephenie shook her head. "I am sorry. My father respected you greatly, but he did not speak of you often."

"Before I married Rose, which was not of my choosing, I lived many years with the true love of my life...Eayn held my heart and I lived for her. Our first child, Vance, named for her father, is away, but his hair is a light brown just as his mother's was." Lartin's eyes narrowed and old anger radiated from his wrinkled face. "She died in the year 417. She took her own life on the last day of the year because she could not bear to step foot into the next year.

"Your sire, as you are calling him, the vile Lord Gunnarr Ralok, paid his respects to me, offering to extend our trade with Ista. Then before I retired for the night, he took her against her will in my own chambers. He told her she would bare the spawn of Elrin. A boy to be just like him. He cursed her and told her if anything should happen to the boy, she would suffer as a result. At first she tried to hide the truth, but she broke down and confessed the ordeal. I sent warnings to those I could trust, hoping to track down this beast, but I fear I was too late.

"For Eayn, there was no recourse. I tried to reason with her, but when it was certain she was with child, she became distraught.

Unwilling to allow the evil to spread, she ingested poison, plunged a dagger into her belly, and then leaped from the north tower."

Stephenie exhaled, feeling his deep despair. Speaking more to herself than Lartin, she said, "Whereas my mother could not kill herself, and in her selfishness, allowed me into the world."

Lartin did not acknowledge Stephenie's statement. "I knew the man was powerful. The look in his eyes when we first met said he felt himself a king among peasants, even when he looked at me." Lartin's face contorted, "He was cordial and spoke kindly, though I can still remember the arrogance in his voice...cold and calculating voice." Looking back at Stephenie, he added, "He wore the crest of Ista and had all the trappings of a diplomat. But I think his purpose was merely to look me in the eye before he raped the woman I loved. Your powers confirm what I have always known, you are the spawn of this demon and I fear Eayn had chosen correctly in her actions."

"The man deserves death," Stephenie said. "I cannot respect or justify anything I have heard of him. Though I doubt I would be able to bring him to any form of justice. However, I do want to find him."

Lartin looked at her for a moment more before he continued. "You want to seek the Demon God? Why?"

Stephenie shook her head. "He's no god. He's an evil man, but he is just a man, not a god." She put her hands together. "I am truly sorry for your loss. I wish I could somehow make amends for what happened, but I cannot." She swallowed. "I have done my best to protect Cothel and her people. I always will, but I have questions and I don't think I can get the answers from anyone aside from this man."

The old King nodded his head. "Perhaps Charles was a father to you after all. You show more wisdom than I expected. Of course, I had expected to be killed today, not questioned." He grinned slightly, "Rose will be annoyed. Her, and that little bastard I wish was not mine, want nothing more than to take my throne from me." The man sighed, visibly drained. "I wish I could help you. Unfortunately, the only thing I know for certain was the bastard left my castle right after he raped my wife. He later turned up at Charles' castle, but that was before my warning reached him. Charles had found evidence Gunnarr returned north after he left Antar, but if he ever found more specific details, he never told me.

"For my own part, after the events, I sent several groups of assassins north to Ista, but none of them ever returned. As it turned out, the Sandvenians had found their northern border with Ista closed, even before those terrible things happened to Eayn. To my knowledge, that is still the case today. If he is there, it seems he is beyond reach."

Stephenie nodded her head and tried not to show her disappointment. "I understand. Thank you for sharing what you do know."

The old man cleared his throat. "Charles did not wish to talk much about the events. He never confirmed what happened, even in vague terms. I would guess now that he perhaps was protecting you. So I don't think I need to tell you to refrain from soiling Eayn's good name. Her death was reported as the result of a spy and assassin, which we conveniently happened to have on hand at the time to suffer the consequences."

Stephenie bowed her head, "Of course, there would be no cause to dishonor your late Queen for something that was never her fault."

Lartin nodded his head; his unease had faded greatly as compared to when she had arrived. "I wish you fortune in your search, but I suggest you direct your attentions elsewhere. The man, even after these near twenty years, still haunts my sleep."

"Thank you, Your Majesty, I do appreciate the warning, but I fear I cannot yet give up the endeavor. If I can somehow bring you justice...or even justice for what was done to my mother, I will try. Though she destroyed everything she touched after that event, and for that, I had no choice but to do what I did."

Lartin rose to his feet, standing straighter than Stephenie had expected him to. "You do seem to possess an honor of character I would not have expected from your lineage. Your father obviously managed to influence you, even if he didn't sire you. Your own secret will remain with me." He approached her, raising an arm to direct her to turn back toward the main doors. "Come, I will return you to your companions, who are still in the waiting room. I would not allow them to be threatened for fear of your rage. I am happy to have for once misjudged someone."

# Chapter 19

By the time they left the King's castle, the day was more than half-spent and with Ryia's insistence, as well as her own reluctant acceptance at learning so little, Stephenie agreed to allow them to remain one more day. After returning to retrieve Douglas, they used the afternoon to tour several of the parks inside the city. While Stephenie would have enjoyed having Eli lead their adventure, she did not press the issue and allowed herself to simply relax in the company of her friends.

In the morning, they left the capitol city and headed northeast toward the country of Uvar. While that route to where she suspected the trap lay hidden might be a little longer, she preferred the easterly path over one that would take them nearer Kynto. She did not want to risk the chance they would encounter people caught up in the turmoil that was still coming from her killing of the Senzar who had secretly ruled Kynto behind her uncle.

The King's Road, being the primary overland route to the east, was in excellent condition, even with the amount of heavy wagon traffic. The days were easy and enough people transporting goods kept the number of soldiers up and the number of highwaymen down. To Douglas' great comfort, they stayed in inns every night of the six days it took to reach Dove, which was the last city in Calis. None of the inns were as luxurious as The Harris House, but the change from sleeping on the ground allowed them to further recoup their strength.

Having reached Dove early in the day, they chose instead to cross the bridge over the Ace River, thereby leaving Calis. They headed to the smaller city of Fallen Grove, which sat only a few miles into the country of Uvar.

Most travelers preferred to remain on the southern side of the Ace River in Dove. The lands in Uvar were lower than those in Calis, which left Fallen Grove often surrounded by marshy water, if not wide lakes, after a flood. The road, with help from Calis, had long ago been built up with rock and soil to protect it from most floods. However, the wetlands provided few places for merchants to stop outside of a town, making the six days past Fallen Grove to Solway fairly expensive.

"What do you think we will find when we get there? To the trap, that is," Ryia asked as they closed in on Fallen Grove.

Ahead of them a tall berm with wooden palisades guarded the small city from both water and people. Stephenie shrugged. "I'm not sure. I am hoping we won't find anything but the trap. As Kas said, those who created the traps tended to want them protected. That could be by placing them in the center of a fortified area or hiding them away where it would be hard to find them. The trap associated with Felis' priests is located more than a hundred miles out at sea. Probably underwater."

"That will keep people away from it," Henton said. "Though there are some islands out in the middle of Tet, but generally they are further east."

Stephenie nodded her head. "I won't undermine Rebecca...at least not until after all the other traps are destroyed." She turned back to Ryia. "I told Josh I intended to find Mertor's temple and destroy it, but in reality, I hope the trap we seek is simply hidden in the mountains and unguarded. With the relay, I should be able to locate it without too much trouble."

"Unless it is buried in the center of the mountain," Douglas said with a hint of normality back in his voice. "You might have to blow up another mountain."

Stephenie grinned, but did not say anything. They were closing on the gates and what he vocalized already remained too much of a concern for her. *What if they do have it buried?*

*If the trap is secured deep within the mountain, I would expect there to be tunnels that permitted the original placement,* Kas responded.

*The entrance of which could be concealed or even miles away,* she thought in response. *They could have collapsed the tunnels or even formed the stone into solid walls.* She sighed. *I worry just reaching the trap will take months and if those damn priests have other groups coming, they could be making a mess of Antar as we wander around.*

Kas gave her a mental shrug. *I can only speculate as much as you can. We lack the facts needed to know anything. Refrain from dwelling on these fears and focus on getting there.*

Stephenie wanted to tell him that might be easy for him; however, one of the armed guards at the gate signaled them to stop. Expecting to pay a toll, Stephenie dismounted, but stopped herself from speaking. The guard kept switching his focus between Henton and Douglas, finally settling on Henton as her friend dismounted. While soldier's minds normally remained dim to her senses, she could feel the man's intentional avoidance of Ryia and herself. Having grown used to people knowing she led the group, it took a moment for her to readjust to the idea that women had to answer to 'their men' and were not people unto themselves.

"We're just passing through," Henton said in Pandar. "Probably stay the night and we'll be gone in the morning."

The stubble-faced guard nodded his head. "You have money to pay for the lodgings?"

Henton rattled the small pouch tied to his belt. "That we do."

The guard nodded his head and waved them in through the open doors. Stephenie waited until Henton moved forward and then fell in behind him, leading Argat with a soft tug on the reins. She walked passed the first guard, who did not even glance at her. Clearing the doors, she moved aside and waited for Ryia and Douglas to follow in with the remaining three horses.

"Sir, Ma'am," another guard said, coming over to them, a broad smile on his face. "I would not have noticed you save for the lady's fiery hair. Two men and two ladies are not that uncommon of traveling companions," he added with a knowing nod of his head.

Stephenie glanced at Henton, telling him with a look that he had better not bring up her hair again. However, Kas' grumbling in her mind matched what she expected she would have gotten from Henton.

"Sir, Ma'am, the rest of your party came through two days ago. The five of them were most anxious to hear news of you and I am afraid at the time, I could not give them any good word. However, I can at least relieve your concerns and inform you of their arrival."

"These people," Stephenie said, cutting off Henton. "There were just five of them? Can you tell me which five?" She hoped the concern in her voice would be accepted as fear for missing people instead of fear of who followed her.

The guard turned toward Stephenie and slowly nodded his head. The lines of his face lacked the tightness she had observed from the first guard at the prospect of addressing a woman directly, but he did not appear entirely comfortable. "Yes, Ma'am. It caught me as unexpected, but I remember it clearly as there was a young woman leading their party. She wore her light hair long and to her waist. I remember her green eyes and olive face, but..." He pursed his lips and then shook his head. "There was another lady and three men in the party." He chuckled. "I can't seem to remember what they look like."

Henton stepped closer to the guard. "Do you know if they are still in town?"

The guard shook his head. "I normally work this gate. They did not leave on any of my watches, so it is possible they are in one of the inns. We have more than a dozen inns here, but they could have also left from the north gate if they continued on the road instead of waiting for you."

Henton nodded his head and handed the man a few coins. "Did they still have their horses?"

"Yes. They had five very nice mounts. Not like yours, which I can tell come from a line from across The Straights, but theirs were some of the Lord Wendle stock, stout and solid horses born from Calis farms." He grinned. "I have a cousin in Calis that breads that line."

Stephenie caught Henton's glance, but she did not respond. *This has to be that Yreka,* she said to Kas, quickly relaying the substance of their conversation to him. *Now she's ahead of us.*

*It would be unwise to have a confrontation in the middle of the city.*

Stephenie nodded her head at Kas and Henton took that as a cue to continue into the city. "Thank you," she told the guard as she passed him. Douglas and Ryia followed silently behind them until they turned down the first major street and out of the guard's sight.

"Steph, how does this woman know where we are and where we are going?" Ryia asked quietly.

She shook her head. The only people who knew the truth were those closest to her. "If she's hurt one of them, I'll rip her to pieces."

Henton stopped in the middle of the wide street. There were other people moving around them, but the city streets were built to handle large wagons passing in opposite directions and with the noise, it would be unlikely anyone would overhear them or understand them when speaking Cothish. "We don't want to fight anyone here. We need to get to the trap and deal with that. Your brother could be fighting all kinds of other issues."

Stephenie turned her attention to Henton. She felt energy coursing through herself. "I want to know if she hurt one of our friends and if so, I will kill her."

"And what if she is more powerful than those you dealt with in Vinerxan? And what if the four with her are as powerful?"

She watched Henton shake his head slowly. She knew it was not because he thought her ignorant, just that he wanted her to pause for a moment.

He kept her eyes, "Even if they harmed Will, or someone else, or even your brother, going after them right now won't change that. Our priority is the trap."

She took a deep breath, knowing Henton spoke the truth, but still not liking it. She appreciated Kas' silence in the discussion, hoping that he realized she would eventually come to the correct decision. "You are right. But if they are still here, then we need to leave before they realize we've arrived."

Douglas stepped closer, pulling both horses behind him. "If they are ahead of us, we could accidentally overtake them. Or worse, they could set a trap for us."

Stephenie bit her lip, her mind racing with possibilities. "We don't know if they really know where we are going. I couldn't even say for certain and our maps are only so accurate. Assuming they believe they know our route, but not if they are ahead or behind us, they could do as you say, set a trap and wait for us." She frowned. "Or they could rush further ahead, thinking we still had an advantage on them."

Henton shrugged. "I'd guess they left Antar after us. Our trouble on ship and the—"

"Diversion I took us on," she offered, "allowed them to catch up and get ahead of us. But only Islet would have known I planned to see Lartin." She balled up her hands, "If they hurt Islet...."

"They came here, and didn't go there, as least as far as we know," Henton said.

"What do we do?" Douglas asked. "There is too much we don't know."

Stephenie dreaded the idea of becoming paralyzed with indecision. *Choosing to do something is better than doing nothing, which is, in itself, a choice.*

*That is a wise statement,* Kas said in response. *I would assume they gained access to Will and not Islet, though if there is any relationship with your sire, then they may not have shown concern with entering the castle and approaching your brother or Rebecca.*

*You're not helping me feel better,* she told Kas. Making her decision, she looked at the others. "We bought supplies in Dove, so let's head out of town now. We'll keep going north and as soon as we are out of sight of the city, we'll drop off the road and cut back to the northwest. Based on the maps and the look of the land, we'll be forced to cross a river or five, but I can help get us through that. It will take longer, but given the fact that we don't know specifically our destination, this Yreka should not either. Going cross country should prevent her from setting up a trap ahead of us." She glanced to each of the others and all of them, including Kas, seemed to approve. "We just have to hope to cover our trail behind us well enough."

"The bog should help with that," Douglas said, without much enthusiasm.

# Chapter 20

Once they moved off the road, the terrain offered significant challenges. The loose soil was a mixture of sand and sediment washed down by the rivers with every flood. Debris clung to the woody grasses and bushes at heights of over eight feet, giving tell to just how deep the floods could become. Where standing water pooled, the mud below the surface sucked in anything with weight. Argat had sunk nearly two feet in one place until Stephenie had managed to lift him free.

Beyond the taxing effect of the soft ground, the nutrient rich soil proved to be very fertile. The grasses and scrub brush grew everywhere and towered over their heads even when mounted. Some animal trails provided enough room for their passage, but more than once, they had to cut a trail through the forest of dense vegetation.

As they traveled to the northwest, everything gradually became caked in clingy mud, leaving them itchy and uncomfortable. However, none of the pools of water were clear enough to bathe in and even the rivers were brown with silt.

While those annoyances were frustrating, they were minor in comparison to the bugs. Clouds of biting and buzzing insects swarmed around them. The rosemary-based oil they purchased in Dove, based on a recommendation from a local, helped, but only somewhat. Stephenie did her best to drive the insects away with her magic, which worked when she remained awake, but at night, they buried themselves under the blankets and tried not to think about the crawling bugs that climbed from the damp ground into their clothing.

It took them four days of toiling through the marshes and six small river crossings before they reached what they believed to be the Ace River. Though even here, the river was not so much deep, as it was wide, with many islands, eddies, and channels that only had real movement of water after it flooded.

Fortunately for them, they had only seen an occasional drizzle and so the river's level remained low. Using her magic, Stephenie flew all their goods to the far side of the river and then helped everyone swim the horses across. Even with this deeper river, they were still left with a film of dirt covering everything.

While their spirits started higher after the crossing, the travel on the northwest side of the river quickly ate away their morale. The landscape and difficulties remained the same and it took another four days before they finally started to climb out of the lowlands into drier and firmer land.

With supplies running dangerously low, when they crossed what appeared to be a horse trail, they followed it to the north and everyone sighed with relief upon seeing a small farming village nestled in a rolling valley. The community of Kenton had enough merchant traffic to support a small inn and with the lateness of the day, they rented a pair of rooms and stalls for the horses. They also discovered that the village sat on the northern side of the Salzen boarder, which meant they had finally crossed out of Uvar.

After they washed down the horses, they paid for the use of a tub and they managed to get truly clean for the first time in almost fifteen days. Henton, Douglas, and Ryia then took some time to buy enough supplies to fill their nearly empty saddlebags.

Stephenie and Kas retreated to the rooms in the inn to watch over their gear. Once they were settled, she pulled out the relay and continued to work with it. Even with the mud and discomfort of the lowlands, she had spent most evenings recording more of the secret language. While not everything she wrote had context yet, she had expanded the pronunciation guide greatly.

As she recorded a new word in the journal, she let herself look at the statue of the man again. *Did they start off as a collective of assassins or just become that over time?* It remained something she had hesitated to ask.

She worked late into the evening and grew tired of writing down symbols she did not fully understand. Bored with the work, she changed her approach slightly and decided to reach out to the voice again, but with a more personal tone. *Mertor,* she sent into the relay. *We've watched each other for a while now. I had hoped you might try and speak with me again.* She waited for some time, but heard nothing from the voice. Oddly, the relay did not respond either. Questions she would ask almost always resulted in at least a feeling, either of acceptance, denial, or confusion. *I do appreciate your help in learning this language. I know you are watching. I can feel it.* She frowned. *You spoke to me once before, why won't you do it again? Please?* She hoped her begging would work as well on the voice as Ryia's had on her and Henton. *I just want to speak with you.*

This time she received a sense of doubt from the relay, as if it knew she had another intent. *You are trying to teach me your language. That much is obvious. Why won't you speak with me again?*

The silence in the relay lasted for a long time. Then she felt herself stretched further, as though something else had more firmly entered her mind. *It is forbidden. It is outside my purpose.* The deep voice said, this time in Denarian.

*Then why did you talk to me the first time?*

*I was lonely.* After a moment, the voice took a harder edge. *It is improper to do so in this manner.*

*I just want to get to know you. To learn more about you.*

*No. You wish to destroy me.*

Stephenie felt the presence leave her mind. Her contact with the relay broke as she dropped the statue to the floor. Looking up, she saw Kas materialize in front of her.

"What happened?" He asked quietly, knowing she found it hard to let him into her head just after working with the relay. "Are you harmed?"

It took her a moment more, but she finally shook her head. "No, I'm okay." Looking down at the cold piece of metal sitting on the floor, she continued, "I think the trap is aware of me and what we intend."

"How?" He asked, kneeling down before her.

Slowly, she picked up the statue and held it in her hands. Looking up at him, she took a deep breath. "A while back, I heard a voice from the relay. One that was slightly different than what I normally hear. It seemed to...be more intelligent than what I was used to feeling from the relay."

"And you are just telling me this now?" Kas asked.

She glanced at Kas; his disappointment filled the air. Looking away, she turned the statue over and examined the face again. *The voice does fit the form.* "It was just a single event. Really just a sentence. But it used the name Mertor. I thought perhaps it might be the creature being killed by the trap." She shrugged. "Since then, the relay has been more responsive, showing me a lot more of the language. Almost like it wants me to learn to speak with it."

"Stephenie," Kas said with a bit too much calmness. "This change in behavior did not bother you?"

She thought about it for a moment. "I can't say why, but I did not get any bad feelings from it." She sighed. "I know, I should have mentioned it before, but I...I felt sorry for it. It seemed desperate for someone to talk with." She set the statue back down on the floor. "Tonight I managed to get it to speak to me again. It said it wasn't supposed to. When I pressed it and said I just wanted to talk and learn about it, it said, no, you want to destroy me." She bit her lip. "I'm pretty sure I've been talking to the trap."

"A highly intelligent device that now knows you plan to destroy it," Kas' anger evident. "The augmentation devices fight back aggressively. You have not tried to destroy the relay; however, I would expect it would fight back with even more zeal. Now the trap knows what you intend. It might try to kill you through the relay or at best, lead you astray."

Stephenie stood. She looked into the eyes Kas luminesced. "I can't say why, but I don't think that will happen."

"It has likely read all of your thoughts," Kas said. "You have been using it a lot. Perhaps it is extending its time with you by giving you what you want, a chance to learn its language, so that it is able to get further into your memories."

Stephenie swallowed. His statement did not fall outside the realm of possibilities. However, she still disagreed. "It doesn't feel that way."

"And what if the goal of the trap is to generate the obvious sympathy you have for it so that you will be unable to destroy it?"

Stephenie wanted to deny that, but could not voice her objection. *Another possibility,* she finally admitted to herself. She did not want to believe the trap was intentionally manipulating her. "I'll refrain from using the relay as much, but I still need to use it to make sure we are heading in the correct direction."

"If it is even pointing you there. You may have ruined our chance to destroy it." Kas shook his head and faded from sight.

Stephenie felt him move away and head out of the building. She closed her eyes against the tears that started to fall. She understood his anger and hated herself for being the cause of it.

Henton sipped the ale in his mug. For the first time in days, his stomach felt full. His skin did not feel dry and caked and his clothing did not smell like rancid mud. *Ah, the good life.*

Douglas and Ryia sat on the bench on the other side of the table, but they were turned away from him and faced into the room. In the far corner, a couple of people played stringed instruments and took turns singing. The language he did not understand, but the melody had some energy and a couple of locals had started dancing in an area they cleared of tables.

"The one in the tan shirt is pretty handsome," Ryia said, leaning into Douglas' side. "What you think?"

"Well, he's got a good looking chin and a bit of muscle under that shirt. But his dancing is terrible."

Ryia snorted. "It's bad, but...I think I could get past that if he'd take off his shirt."

Douglas shook his head. "You would."

Henton took another sip of his ale. He suspected she would have gotten on well with Will had their introductions been different and if Will had not gotten married. *That was something I never expected,* he admitted to himself.

"Go ask him if he'll dance with me?"

"No, if you want your feet stepped on, go ask him to dance yourself."

Ryia glared at Douglas, and then grabbed her mug and downed the last of her ale. "I will." Jumping to her feet, she walked over to the tall man and bowed her head to him.

Henton frowned slightly. He did not personally like the look of the young man. *Too cocky I am sure. Too used to women wanting to dance with him.* Despite his desire for Ryia to enjoy herself, he felt annoyed when the man agreed to dance with her.

"Hey boss," Douglas said, turning his upper body around to look in Henton's direction. "Should I take something up to Her Boringness?"

Henton shook his head. "She'll come down when she's hungry. If she's engrossed in her journal, she won't want to be disturbed."

Douglas nodded and went back to watching Ryia dance with the handsome man. Henton glanced about the room. There were a number of women watching Ryia, but their expressions were not quite as friendly.

After a couple of dances where Ryia continued to laugh and giggle, Douglas turned fully around on the bench so he could face Henton. "We've still got a long way to go. Do you think we left those people behind?"

He shrugged. "Our original plan had us going through Solway and then Omidi and Ingrie before really heading west. I'm hoping they keep looking and waiting for us along that path. If we keep going across country, hopefully we'll stay out of notice and we can get there and never see those people at all."

"She'll want to head back home as quick as possible after we're done to find out who, if anyone, was hurt."

Henton paused a moment before nodding his head, though he felt less certain of that. Between the struggles with her brother and her desire to find a way to build a body for Kas, she might decide there is not anything she could do at home to fix the damage anyway. "We'll have to see," he finally said as he drank the last of his ale.

Glancing into the empty mug, he considered having it refilled. He could allow himself one more before it started to affect him, but a long time remained before the evening would end. *Perhaps I might get some more of those berry-tarts.*

The opening of the outside door drew his attention. However, the crossbow was discharged before he recognized what is was. A second man followed the first one into the inn, a crossbow in his hands as well.

Henton jumped to his feet as Ryia cried out in pain. She followed the loud shout with a string of curses. Leaping to the right, Henton avoided the bolt that would have hit him. By the time Henton managed to get around the table, Douglas was already across the room with his sword in hand.

The first crossbowman shouted something in the local tongue, while the second pulled a sword and cried out in Pandar, "We will suffer no witches here!"

Henton pulled his sword as he followed after Douglas. They now faced four people as two more men entered the inn. The first man also tossed aside his crossbows and drew a short sword.

Douglas met the leading man with a flurry of attacks, driving him back into the path of the last two men who were just inside the doorway.

"Put down your weapons or the witch dies!" Came a cry from behind them.

A muffled grunt followed the proclamation. Henton glanced briefly toward Ryia as more people rose up to try and grab her. She struggled to fend off her attackers with the crossbow bolt protruding from her leg. Her screams of pain spoke of someone hitting the shaft while they grappled with her.

"STOP!" Came Stephenie's growl as she came off the foot of the stairs. The deep rumble froze everyone's actions for a moment.

Henton breathed a sigh of relief in hearing her voice.

The men around Ryia were flung across the room without ceremony. The less fortunate crashed into tables, while those with more luck simply slid along the floor.

The men before Henton and Douglas had their swords ripped from their hands. As the blades flew into the air, they were twisted into knots before being thrown against the far wall.

Henton stepped back and away from the men still standing in front of the door. He heard Stephenie walk further into the room, but did not take his eyes off the men.

"Witch, you will burn for this!"

"I'm no witch!" She swore. "You've dared to attack a priestess of Catheri! You will get on your knees and beg for your lives or I'll rip your arms from their sockets!"

The men stood motionless staring at her as she came up to Henton's side. Her arms flung out to her sides and the tables and benches to either side of them flew into the walls. The force of the collision vibrated the whole building.

"I—I've never heard of Catheri! There is no such god! Where is your holy symbol?"

Henton assumed Stephenie smashed a field onto the men because the four of them crumpled to their knees. "Catheri has come back because of the Senzar invasion. She brings the dark hand of justice to those who deserve her judgment!"

Henton fell back with Douglas and went to Ryia's aid. She had sunk to a bench and all the color had fallen from her face. She looked up at him with large eyes.

"Poison?" Douglas asked.

Henton felt fairly certain. Kneeling down, he put one hand on Ryia's leg and with the other, grabbed the bolt. He did not wait to give her warning, but simply pulled the shaft from her flesh.

She unleashed her favorite curse, though without her normal vitriol energy. "Damn, Sarge," she added as blood quickly flowed out of the wound, causing her head to roll back.

"We need it to bleed to flush out any poison."

Douglas handed her a drink he grabbed from a nearby table and then held her head upright. "This might help."

She took it and drank deeply, spilling as much down her chin as went into her mouth.

Behind him, he heard Stephenie's voice grow hard. "I should burn all of you for attacking a priestess. I should level this town. What damn arrogance to simply attack someone without confirming who they are."

"We were told she moved unnaturally and that she put a spell on Vencin...luring him away from his intended."

Henton met Stephenie's eyes as she turned toward him. "She was just dancing."

"I saw a mug fly to her hand," a terrified woman said from where she huddled against the wall with four other people.

Henton shrugged; he had not seen it, but it may have happened. *Damn Ryia, I hope you did not get that sloppy.*

"Sorry, Henton," she mumbled. "I don't remember doing that, but I might have."

Henton stood up. "We'll take her upstairs. Ma'am, I think she'll need help with the poison." He looked over to Douglas and nodded his head as he sheathed his sword. "Don't worry, Ryia, we'll get you into bed and make you feel better."

Behind him, he heard Stephenie's cold warning. "If she dies, do not expect to see the morning."


Stephenie closed the door to the room. The evening had gone from terrible to devastating. She felt her arms trembling as she watched the sweat pour from Ryia's forehead. Kas had come back when she had unleashed her powers in the common room. He remained downstairs to keep watch while she tended Ryia.

Closing her eyes, she reached out and made contact with Ryia's mind. *I am so sorry,* she said as she forced her way into the girl's head.

Ryia resisted the intrusion into her private thoughts, but Stephenie had not entered her mind to see those. Instead, she pushed into Ryia's subconscious to find the part of her mind that regulated her body's natural healing. The obvious damage from the crossbow bolt's penetration was fairly easy to address. Muscle and skin could be induced to regrow almost instantly. Inject enough energy and resources and the wound would close based on the body's own knowledge of how it should exist.

However, poisons were different. They were a foreign substance that needed to be neutralized or removed from the system. The body naturally knew how to handle many toxic substances, often simply needing time to address them. Fortunately, magic would speed up the process. Other poisons were not as kind. The ones often used against witches and warlocks were designed to fool the body's natural defenses, causing the instinctual response to actually do more harm. This often caused the person to consume large amounts of energy in healing the secondary damage, which prevented the witch or warlock from being able to fight back.

With Stephenie's mind linked to Ryia's, she looked for her own body's natural inclination in dealing with the poison and then adjusted it based upon what she learned in Vinerxan. While the Senzar mages had not wanted to initially share that knowledge with her, she had convinced them to do so. Her original intent had been to use poison against the Senzar; however, that had not worked out as she intended. *But now, I can use that knowledge to help you.*

*I'm sorry, Steph.*

Stephenie gave the girl a mental smile. Despite all of Ryia's complaints and self-pity, she remained a fighter. *We all make mistakes. I should have been downstairs to make sure they never got a chance to shoot you.*

Stephenie winced as Ryia flooded her with pain. *You know I can't take that much energy, right?* Ryia asked.

Easing off her flow of power, Stephenie slowly pulled back from Ryia's thoughts. *You know, you should just ask him to dance instead of trying to make him jealous.*

*Please don't say anything.*

Stephenie opened her eyes and looked down at Ryia lying in the bed. "I won't." Standing up, she glanced at Henton, whose worried expressions conveyed so much.

Sending a pulse down toward Kas, she waited for him to return to the room before she spoke. "How are the natives?"

"I believe they are properly cowed. However, I suspect word of these events will travel."

Stephenie looked down. "I let myself lose control. I shouldn't have." She pushed back the possessive feelings that had overwhelmed her when she felt her friends were in danger. "I need to tell you all something." She lifted her eyes and watched the questioning glances and then motioned Henton and Douglas toward the bed so that she could face all of them at the same time.

Clearing her throat, she looked first to Kas, *I'm sorry, my Love.* Then she turned back to the others. "I've been dishonest. I've been keeping a secret and I should not have." Ryia looked up, though her face still lacked most of her normal color. "I think the trap has been speaking to me through the relay. I heard this voice just after we left Elchel. Then it didn't come back until tonight. However, you might have noticed I've been able to get a lot more out of the relay since then."

"We had noticed you putting in a lot more time with it," Henton said.

"Tonight, I got it to speak with me again. However, it said it knows I plan to destroy it."

Douglas turned away and cursed under his breath.

"I know Kas feels I am getting manipulated, but I think the trap is just lonely and wants to talk with someone. I can't say why, but I really don't think it intends to harm me."

Henton turned toward Kas. "What is your thought?"

"We know how strongly the augmentation devices defend themselves. I cannot imagine the trap defending itself less strongly. In fact, since it would be so much more powerful, I expect it will unleash a far greater response on Stephenie. If it even allows her to find it."

She shook her head. "I know you think I am crazy, but I don't get that feeling from it. And before you remind me again how mental communication can lead to easily being deceived, I just feel I am correct in this." She looked at everyone's face. "However, I will refrain from using the relay so much. I will need to take some sightings from time to time to make sure we are on course, but I promise not to use it to get anymore information on the language."

Henton stepped forward. "Thank you for telling us. I trust you, but please be careful."

The next morning, they rose early and were quickly on their way before many of the villagers had awoken. Kas kept watch on them and the horses through the night and no signs of trouble had surfaced. Ryia's leg had mended enough for her to ride, but she still remained drained.

Resolved to avoid any additional confrontations, Stephenie kept them off even the dirt road and continued to track across country in a mostly northerly route. The land, while solid and not waterlogged, still had many wild sections. The population density of Salzen remained well below that of Cothel and most of the other countries they had previously traveled through.

In the afternoon of their second day beyond Kenton, they passed over a set of well-established roads traveling east and west. Based on the maps, they assumed Banda, the capitol of Salzen, lay about a day to the west. Two days after that, they stopped briefly at another village to buy more supplies before continuing on that same day.

The further north they went, the drier the ground became. Instead of fertile soil, they found more sand and rock. While it did not make traveling that much harder, it did reduce the amount of grass the horses could graze upon in the evening. The richer and lusher grasses of the rolling hills they had previously passed through had turned woodier and less nourishing.

The few settlements they had observed in their early time in Salzen dried up and on the fifth day after they had last stopped for supplies, two solid days had passed without even seeing a cooking fire in the distances.

When they finally crested a hill to see a large crater formed valley, Stephenie called a stop to their travel. The bottom of the valley had a lake that covered the mile wide scar in the ground. Since the water also spread for several miles to the east and west, they would likely have to go around the lake.

Looking back at the others and their worn expressions, she said, "To celebrate Douglas' birthday, we need to eat something fresh."

"I'd like something tasty," Douglas admitted.

She smiled at him. "I'll go hunt. Kas, would you like to come with me?"

The ghost materialized off to her right and bowed his head to her. Stephenie dismounted and handed Argat's reins to Henton. "Can you set up a camp down by the lake? We'll see what we can bring back."

"Shouldn't be a problem."

Leaving everything except her long dagger, she headed east along the ridge where they had stopped. The sandy ground showed signs of hoofed animals and she hoped they might come across a deer. As she walked, the dry grasses, barely hip high, brushed against her legs. To keep from frightening off the game, she headed for a cluster of large boulders.

*Kas, you've barely said anything to me for days. Don't you trust me anymore?* She finally asked when they had passed out of sight of the others.

She felt Kas sigh. *Of course I do, Stephenie. However, I would have to ask you the same thing. You decided to conceal the fact that the trap had made direct contact with you. We still have not established a valid reason for that deception.*

Moving around another boulder that stood more than three times her height, she started to descend toward the water to give herself a moment to think about her reply. *I can't say why I did it. I do trust you, but...I don't know, it almost felt like the trap had reached out to me in confidence. It sounds really stupid to say it now, but it felt like it wanted to confide in someone. I didn't want to betray it either.*

Kas moved ahead of her and along a steep section she would not be able to travel without using her magic. *Stephenie, you know it is both harder and easier to deceive people through mental links. The skill is difficult to master, but once it is done, people are easily deceived because they do not feel such form of communication could be dishonest. I fear the trap purposefully influenced your mind.*

Stephenie jumped from the trail she had started to follow and glided down twenty feet to what appeared to be another animal trail. *I know.* She experienced that kind of deception from Orlan, who had used that skill against her and those who tried to break him. *I am sorry for not telling you. However, I still, with every bit of my being, believe the trap does not intend to hurt me.*

*Even though it knows you plan to destroy it.*

"Yes, even knowing that."

Kas stopped and moved to her side. "I will believe you. However, it does not reduce my concern." He turned his head toward the lake and then back to her. "I apologize for getting so angry. However, should anything else unusual happen, please, tell me."

She smiled at him, feeling his forgiveness. "I will, my Love."
*Then, perhaps we should finish our hunt.*

It took a little more searching, but they eventually found a herd of large, hairy animals that Stephenie had never seen before. They reminded her of very aggressive and fast moving cows. They chose one of the smaller animals, but even that animal would provide enough meat to be able to feed them for weeks if they could preserve it. However, without the time to do so, she simply dressed down a small enough portion to feed them for a couple of days and left the rest for the wolves and coyotes they heard most nights.

Back at the camp, she fixed dinner while the others cleaned their gear and rested. After a small celebration for Douglas turning twenty-two, they ate a reasonably tasty meal. When Douglas went off to bathe in the lake, she dug into her pack for her journal. While she had stopped recording information from the relay, she did continue to make notes of their journey. She had just started a rough sketch of the animal they ate when Henton sat down beside her.

"You know," he said, "you never seem to stop working."

She looked at him and blinked her tired eyes. "There always seems a lot that needs to be done."

Henton shrugged and then turned his attention to the lake. "Ryia is really tormenting Douglas for his birthday."

Stephenie followed Henton's gaze. In the fading light, she could see Douglas out in the lake, submerged to his chin. Ryia stood between him and the shore. She kept leaping up and splashing back down into the water. Stephenie realized she had heard the girl's laughter for a while now, but had simply tuned it out.

"You should hear Douglas swearing at her. Too bad it just entices her to taunt him more." Henton turned his head toward her. "He had gone in first to get cleaned up. I watched her wait, stalking him like a cat. Once he was out there far enough, she ran down, stripped out of her clothes, and jumped in herself."

Stephenie shook her head. "That's cruel."

Henton smiled. "Douglas might complain, but I think we'll be able to laugh about it later." He glanced at the book and then back to her face. "You know, dedication is great, but you're going to live a couple hundred years. You might take an occasional break so you can enjoy those years."

She looked at Henton and then off toward Kas, who hovered a dozen feet away. She could not recall clearly, but she thought Henton had come from where Kas now floated. *The two of you conspiring against me?*

*Never against you, but for you. A peace offering for the last few days.*

Stephenie closed her book and put the lid back on her ink well. "So, you're saying I should be taking some time to enjoy life? You know, Kas doesn't really know how long I will live. Plus, I might get killed next week."

"Then all the more reason to have some fun. You're always working." He took the book, inkwell, and pen from her hands. "Besides, you stink."

"Hey," she complained, feeling a smile find its way to her face. "I bathe more than the rest of you."

Henton set her things down and stood up. "I think I can beat you to the lake." Without waiting, he took off running toward the water.

*Go, Stephenie, he will win otherwise.*

She leaped to her feet and took off after Henton. For once, not drawing on her powers; she wanted to give him a fair chance.

# Chapter 21

It was two days later that they crossed what Stephenie assumed to be the northern road across Salzen. In front of them, stretching as far to the east and west as they could see, loomed the tail end of the World's Backbone. Trees covered the range here; however, further north, snow covered peaks stood defiantly amid a sea of thin clouds.

It took another two days before they moved out of the rocky foothills to reach the actual mountains. Pine trees dominated the landscape and there were no signs of local inhabitants. Fortunately, the foothills and southern mountain slopes received more rain, providing the horses with a richer supply of grass to graze upon.

The trouble was the route directly toward the trap lay on the other side of a steep ridge that the horses could not climb. With Kas' help, by the end of the next day, they had found a river gorge with a gradual enough incline that they were able to head into the mountain range. Eventually, they found a place to climb out of the gorge and switched over to animal trails before the afternoon showers added water to the river. However, even on the trail, the progress remained slow, as the rough landscape required them to lead the horses around boulders and fallen trees.

By late afternoon, they crested the top of the ridge and started descending the other side. Through a gap in the trees, they saw a long valley that continued north for many miles with one of the tall peaks they had seen days before standing proudly in the distance. The east and west sides of the valley were formed by converging ridge lines. Closer to their southern position, the valley appeared to be at least three or four miles wide, with small rises and falls scattered across the basin.

From the southern ridge, the valley floor looked to be a lush carpet of green, speckled with wildflowers and clumps of trees. At least one lake stood out clearly in the distance. Animal trails meandered through the swaying grasses.

"Oh, can we move here?" Ryia asked. "There's even food," she said, pointing to a herd of sheep munching on the lush valley grasses.

"You won't like it in winter," Douglas said sharply. "The valley will likely be full of snow."

Remembering the mountains east of Vinerxan, Stephenie agreed with Douglas' assessment, *but Ryia does have a point, this is a beautiful place.* Reaching out to the relay with her mind, she confirmed her suspicion and nodded her head at the mountain peak. "It's somewhere in the mound of stone and ice."

"Well, let's get this over with," Henton said. "We've got at least half a dozen miles to go before we're at the foot of that mountain and there is still a bit of day left."


They traveled about two miles into the valley when Kas hurried back to the group. *I have found a couple of people tending to sheep. It appears we have already passed others. I remained far enough away to avoid detection, or so I hope.*

Stephenie resisted the urge to stop suddenly. *How many and do you think they are a threat?*

*A group of three, nearly a half a mile ahead of us and a pair on our right, partially up the slope of that tree-covered hill.*

Stephenie turned her head and shoulders so she could talk with Henton who rode slightly behind her. In the process, she scanned the trees and ridge to their right. Even opening herself up as wide as she could, she could not sense the people at the distance they must be. However, since they were moving across the wide expanse of the mountain meadow, it would be easy for someone to see them from that vantage point. "Henton, come up here for a moment." She waited until he rode beside her.

"Kas informed me," he said. "What do you want to do?"

She hesitated a moment. They had to find the trap, but she did not want to fall into one at the same time. "We have to assume we've been spotted," she said, making up her mind. "If we turn around and leave now, it will draw even more suspicion. If they are just people who found a good place to live, then we can tell them we are just passing through and no harm."

"If this is Mertor's headquarters?" He asked with one eyebrow raised.

"We have to be careful and Kas will stay close to me to conceal him. It might be nothing."

Henton slowly drifted back toward the others. Stephenie knew he would fill them in discretely and she felt pride in the fact that Ryia, while likely curious as to what had happened, did not rush forward to find out. *She sensed this was serious.*

After another two miles, footpaths, wagon tracks, and tree stumps provided obvious indication that humans were active in the valley. The people that Kas had seen still had not made themselves known, but on encountering the obvious landmarks, Stephenie called a halt to their progress. If they had stopped earlier, any watchers would wonder what prompted the stop; here the watchers would not question how the group would know other people were in the valley.

"They have horses here as well," she said, seeing the older indications in the worn path.

"This looks like it might be a road," Douglas said, "heading along the west ridge."

Ryia urged Dancer forward and followed Douglas' line of sight. "I wonder if that would have been an easier path into this valley. Seems they pulled a wagon through here."

The industry involved in doing the work concerned Stephenie, in that it meant a higher probability for a larger population of people. However, she committed them to going forward. "Let's see where this goes."

She moved Argat onto the makeshift road that cut through the trees at the base of the ridge. As they continued heading north, she reached out with her mind, trying to be prepared for potential problems. However, so far, all she felt were animals.

After another mile, that changed. They moved over a small rise and into a lower part of the valley where they saw many buildings clustered together near a small pond. Animals roamed mostly free and Stephenie quickly felt the presence of at least a dozen nearby people. *A whole town,* she thought to Kas. *It is a good place for one, so I guess I should not be surprised.*

As they grew even closer to the community, Henton moved up to ride beside her, with Douglas and Ryia paired behind them. Stubborn came up the rear on a long lead rope tied to Douglas' saddle. The people in the community, which included many children and women, as well as a handful of men, took note of their approach, stopping their activities, but no one addressed them.

"They don't look hostile," Henton whispered. "They look more timid than anything."

"With the weapons we are carrying and the size of our group, it's possible they think we are raiders." Stephenie nodded her head to a small family, where the mother pushed two children behind herself. To Henton, Stephenie said, "You want to take it?"

Henton raised his hand in a greeting that Stephenie hoped would not be considered an insult in this part of the world. "Hello," he said in Pandar to one of the few men who were watching them. "We were trying to pass through the mountain range and never expected to find this valley populated."

The man he had addressed turned away, but another man, who appeared to have been on an errand, moved in their direction. "Greetings and a good afternoon to you," he said, his voice carrying an unexpected softness. "Please excuse many of the people here, we do not often see unexpected visitors in Ranis Valley." When the middle-aged man came within ten feet he stopped. "My name is Davin."

"It is a pleasure to meet you Davin, I'm Karl," Henton said, resuming an old alias he had not used in a while. "This is Beth, Douglas, and Ryia."

Stephenie groaned internally, she hated Henton calling her Beth, and had even managed to break him of it for a while, but given their limited knowledge of the community, she could not chastise him for the caution.

"You said you were passing through," Davin remarked. "This is really a horseshoe valley. The east and west ridges come back together at Dantborn Peak. You might make it on foot, but you won't make it any further north through this valley if you want to go by horse."

"Oh," Henton said, frowning.

Stephenie frowned as well, but from the annoyance of having to come up with another reason to remain in the area while she searched for the trap. *Perhaps it will be easy to find.* She could sense Kas' doubt.

"It is late, why don't you come with me back to the inn. I can put you up for the night for a reasonable rate. I even have a place where we can put your horses."

Stephenie raised her eyebrows despite herself. "Inn?"

Davin laughed. "Well, there is a story behind that. Come, it's late enough in the day that you won't make it far if you head back south. Perhaps we can recommend a route to where you want to go."

Henton glanced at her and she nodded her head. They needed to stay in the valley, at least initially. She knew the trap was somewhere around the peak. "The horses are tired and we've been traveling a long time. I would not be opposed to taking a short rest."

Henton turned back to Davin, "Please lead on. We'd be happy to spend a night in your inn."

On the way to Davin's inn, Stephenie counted perhaps thirty buildings. Several of them appeared to be of recent construction and were built from rough-hewn logs. However, others, including the inn, showed signs of being much older. Those buildings were made of stone, the more impressive ones formed from cut blocks instead of simply stacking loose stones.

"Many of the buildings existed here before any of us settled the valley. Sir Ranis, a knight that came from the city of Omidi, re-settled the valley eighty-five years ago. The original inhabitants were long dead and gone."

"It seems like a significant town to simply walk away from," Stephenie said, still impressed with the tightly dressed stone of the two-story inn. The common room where they sat with Davin was thirty feet by twenty feet with stone floors and large timber beams to hold up the ceiling. A large hearth sat in the middle of the interior wall. Stephenie saw evidence of roaring fires used to fight away the winter chill.

"Well, no one knows for certain what name the town had when the people left. Most of the buildings needed a lot of work when Sir Ranis arrived. Much of that work has taken years." He looked up. "The roof of this building had to be completely replaced a few years ago and many of the floor boards above our head are only ten years old. I had to replace them when I took over the building from the prior caretakers." He smiled at the young woman who carried a platter of food to their table. "Thank you, Marible."

"But in this secluded valley, is there much call for an inn like this?" Henton asked.

Stephenie reached for a chunk of salted meat after Kas informed her that he saw no indication anything was done to the food when Marible prepared it. She nodded her head to Douglas and Ryia, who each grabbed a piece of honeyed bread.

"Well, more than you might expect. Most of my business is from providing the locals a place to gather. However, the valley has a fair trade in wool and wine."

"Wine," Ryia asked with food in her mouth.

Davin looked over at Ryia and nodded his head. "The berries that grow on the slopes do make an excellent wine. The priests of Talnar, who reside in the old castle on the mountain's slope, are primarily responsible for the wine."

Stephenie caught Henton's quiet glance and she wished that she felt more comfortable trying to read minds. Not familiar with the god Talnar, Stephenie voiced her question, hoping to gain some insight to know if the claim was real or simply a cover for the priest of Mertor, "What are the teachings of Talnar?"

Davin turned back to Stephenie. "Well, I don't want to spend the evening preaching to you. However, Talnar seeks to find peace through quiet living. We strive to provide for each other by living from the land and caring for nature. Through his mercy, the priests hold back the worst of the winter and allow those of us in the valley to survive the harshness of this land." Davin turned his attention to Henton. "I assume you were once a soldier, or perhaps still are."

When Henton nodded, Davin continued. "Talnar is against war, as it is wasteful, but he does embrace the need to fight against those destroying the peace of nature. His soldiers learn to fight like bears." Davin shrugged. "For me, those that reside in the castle sell me casks of wine for a reasonable sum and when people come to trade for their 'Nectar of Talnar', unless they are dignitaries, they stay here, providing me with a purpose. But I wouldn't worry about getting preached to. The castle is a couple miles away and the priests don't tend to come into town much."

Stephenie looked around the room, though she already knew they were the only ones in the inn. "Things look fairly quiet for you at the moment."

Davin laughed. "As I said, most of my business comes from the locals spending evenings under one roof. However, many of them are leery of strangers. A good number of them don't even speak Pandar, so in all likelihood, we won't see anyone come in tonight. But I am always happy to entertain people. Marible, my daughter, and I, by nature, talk more than most, so it is fitting we take care of any visitors."

Stephenie could not read much in the way of Davin's emotional state, finding him to be much like Will in that respect. *His daughter seems more unnerved. Is she afraid of us specifically, or just not as comfortable around strangers in general?* She could not decide.

"The people here are good folk, but one doesn't come this far out into nowhere and hope to see travelers passing through. So, do please forgive them if no one shows up this evening." He chuckled again, "I would say they mean no ill will, but they would also probably hope you never return." He shrugged. "They like their quiet and peace."

Henton nodded his head. "We can't fault them there."

Davin leaned forward slightly. "Not to impose myself, but you said you were looking to find a passage through the Backbone. Where are you heading? Perhaps I can recommend some things. Before I settled here, I lived with my parents who were more nomad than anything else. I was born in a wagon and when I turned fifteen, I had enough and didn't come back to the camp before mid-morning. They took that as proof of my desire to strike it out on my own and left without me." He shrugged again. "My point being, I've traveled many places, so I might be able to help."

Stephenie worked her mind over her mental image of the maps of the area. "We are trying to get to Rishold," she finally said, remembering a city in the country that existed on the other side of the mountain range. "However, we don't want to go through Kynto. There's too much conflict there."

Davin agreed. "That's a good reason to avoid traveling around the southern tip of the range." He examined Stephenie's features for a moment before continuing. "While the range is thin here, you won't make the passage from this valley. We are surrounded on three sides by steep climbs and lots of loose rock. It might look pretty with all the trees on the slopes, but the going is rough and I've been here twenty years, so I know. You might make it on foot, but not with horses." He pursed his lips. "I'm not sure where that city of yours is located, but I've heard the name before. It's somewhere in Beik. I'd try going northeast along the range; just follow the road until you get to the city of Tenia. There is not an official road through the mountains there either, but there are some passes that I think the horses could make." He picked up his mug and drank some of the wine he had provided everyone. "I'd recommend hiring some guides through the pass. That's what I'd do."

"How long will that take?" Henton asked.

"Oh, perhaps a couple of weeks easily. It's probably a hundred to two hundred miles to Tenia." He laughed again and took another drink. "I've not been there in years. It's where my parents spent a good number of summers. They'd winter along the coasts, but summers were along the range."

Stephenie nodded her head. "You've given us a lot to think about. I'd hate to give up the horses, but going that far before finding a pass through...." She shrugged herself and looked at the others. "We'll have to talk about it before we decide." Turning back to Davin, she asked, "Would it be a problem if we stayed a couple of days while we decided? Give the horses and ourselves a little rest in a quiet place."

Davin smiled as he scooted his chair back, "Of course not! Feel free to stay as long as you want. The others in town will come around if you are here for a couple of nights." He grinned. "They don't like to stay away from the food and company for too long." He stood up and pushed the chair back under the table. "Let me give you some privacy to eat and I'll make sure your horses are well fed."

"Thank you," Henton said as Davin left their table and eventually the main room.

Stephenie glanced around again; she sensed Marible in the kitchen and no one within earshot. "What do think?"

Henton shrugged. "It's hard to say. If the valley was abandoned and I was looking for a quiet place, I'd set my home here."

"I do not like the castle and the priests," Kas said quietly without becoming visible.

Henton leaned forward. "Well, we are here for the night at least. You've bought a couple of days perhaps and you might be able to justify hunting around the peak with the claim of looking for a pass, but if it takes many days or even weeks to find it, we will start to look odd."

"Could we come at it from the other side?" Douglas asked. "Perhaps head north and cut back through the range?"

Stephenie pursed her lips and then shook her head. "Hard to tell, but from what we've seen of these mountains so far, the ridges and peaks are quite vertical. Not nice, gentle slopes like we saw around Vinerxan."

"They are younger and not worn down as much," Kas offered.

"The mountains out west didn't look that worn down," Douglas said.

Henton cleared his throat. "But the question is, what is our next course of action?"

Stephenie bit her lower lip. Something about the valley felt off, but she could not say what exactly. However, they needed to find and destroy the trap. "Okay, here's an idea. After dark, I'll sneak out of the inn and with Kas, the two of us with start to comb the mountain. We'll come back before sunrise and hopefully not get noticed. If we are very lucky, we'll be able to take care of the trap and simply ride out tomorrow. If not, Kas and I will do that again the next night. After that, we'll have to see how people are acting toward us and if the castle has caught any notice of us. If so, we head south again and try to come at the peak through another means. Kas and I can cover the ground quickly, so we might just operate from somewhere close to the valley."

Henton cleared his throat again. "One change to that, if you find it, you come back and let us know before you do anything. We want to be able to offer support in case something happens while you deal with it."

Stephenie smiled. She had felt, though could not hear, the exchange Kas and Henton had while she had been speaking. *Thick as thieves,* she told Kas. "Yes. I will not take action without bringing everyone up to offer support."

"This is a nice room," Ryia said in Cothish.

Henton lifted his eyes from Stephenie's red journal and looked about the room they had rented. It dwarfed the size of rooms in most inns. He nodded at the girl who lounged on the sturdy bed. She had pulled the canopy closed at one point, but had opened it back up after getting bored. Aside from the stone walls on two sides, the room had a lodge feeling, with rounded logs making up the interior walls.

A heavy table sat near the fireplace on the northern wall. He sat in one of the five equally heavy chairs and was impressed with the twisted wood construction. "Don't get too comfortable over there," Henton said. Davin's assumption had been that Stephenie and he had been a couple and Ryia and Douglas had been a second couple. The next room over had been intended for them, but Henton felt more inclined to have everyone sleep in a single room for the night.

"Steph's already flown out the window; I've claimed the bed until she gets back."

Douglas rose to his feet and walked to the side of the bed and stood over Ryia. "Why do you think that whenever Steph is off somewhere, you get the good stuff? What if I want to sleep in the good bed?"

She stuck out her tongue and smiled. "I got here first."

Douglas fell into the bed on top of her. Rolling over onto his back, he pinned her beneath him while he looked up at the canopy above the bed. He shifted his weight to keep her from escaping. "You might not like this bed, it's a bit lumpy. I'll let you rest comfortably on the floor."

Ryia grunted and continued to squirm. "Get off. You're too fat and heavy," she mumbled through Douglas' hair.

Henton grinned, but did not get involved. While the last part of the trip had not been overly stressful, the long hours moving everyday left everyone in a constant state of exhaustion. This day had actually been a short one and everyone still had restless energy left.

Turning his attention back to Stephenie's journal, he continued studying her notes. He intended to learn this old language as well as the handful of others he knew. *After all, the more people know it, the more we can help Steph.* He did not bother acknowledging his hope that studying would keep his mind off the fact that Stephenie and Kas were flying the relay around the mountain. Doing so would likely make him fret even more.

Henton rolled his shoulders and looked over at the sputtering flame of the oil lamp and wondered how long he had been trying to memorize the words on the page. He had been at the task long enough that the words really were not sticking in his mind.

"Henton!"

The urgency in Ryia's voice broke his concentration and he looked over at the bed, where Douglas and Ryia had finally decided that sufficient room existed for them to share. The look on her face roused him from the drowsiness that had overtaken him.

She nudged Douglas awake as she slipped from the bed and then crossed over to meet Henton in the middle of the room. "I just felt them," she whispered. "There are lots of people coming at the building. They are coming from all the sides and have just gone in the first floor."

*Damn,* he swore to himself, not wanting to add to Ryia's fear. "Do you think we can fight our way out? Can you get yourself out one of the windows?"

She shook her head. "There are too many. I can't even begin to count them. At least twenty or thirty." She bit her lower lip. "I'm sorry."

Douglas, pushing through the grogginess of sleep, stood next to the bed with his sword drawn.

Even in the low light, Henton saw the moisture forming in the corners of Ryia's eyes. He shook his head and put a hand on her shoulder. "It's not your fault. I let us relax too much." *Damn, we could use Steph and Kas right now.*

"There's at least thirty. And some are heading toward the stairs, moving quickly."

He looked over to Douglas; he knew the worst thing he could do for Stephenie would be to allow them to be captured, but he did not want to sentence Ryia to death. *I just can't.* To Douglas he shook his head no. "If there are that many and if they are followers of Mertor, we won't be able to fight our way out. Our best bet is to buy enough time to allow Steph to return."

"They might simply kill us," Douglas said. "I'd rather take some with me."

Henton glanced once more to Ryia, his raised eyebrow asking the question. In response she shook her head no. He looked back to Douglas, "If we fight we die. We might die otherwise, but if we don't, we have a chance Steph will be able to get us out." With the words out of his mouth, he could not take them back, even if he knew they were wrong.

"They are on this floor."

Holding up Stephenie's red journal, he quickly looked about the room for somewhere to hide it. Not seeing anything stand out, he glanced up at the large vaulted ceiling and the thick beams. "Ryia, put this out of sight on the top of a beam. Do it now."

He let go of the book as it floated into the air. The movement lacked the grace of what Stephenie could do, but the book disappeared out of sight on the top of a beam just as he heard the footsteps outside the door. Reaching over, he pulled Ryia into his arms and gave her a hug, before pushing her behind him. To Douglas he said softly, "If they are just here to kill us, we fight, otherwise, do what we can to buy time."

Henton turned back to the door as someone knocked. "Yes?" He asked and then waited for a reply.

The door opened slowly, revealing a tall woman who appeared to be in her later thirties. A broad smile filled her narrow face, which itself was framed by long brown hair. The lightness of the brown was almost lost to the dark color of her eyes.

The woman stepped into the room, a quarterstaff carried easily in her right hand. The steel-wrapped ends left no doubt that the five-foot tall device was a weapon. "I am sorry to see the demon has left us. Where did she go?"

Henton knew he had told everyone to buy time, but the woman's tone and insult angered him. "I don't know who you are, but we did not invite you into this room."

The woman's eyes narrowed. "Do not think yourself overly important, Sergeant. Your self-proclaimed prophet is a witch and we know it. Has she and the dead one gone to scout our castle? It will do her no good."

Henton felt his blood freeze. They had worked hard to keep Kas' existence a secret. For this woman to know of him confirmed a confidence had been compromised and shared openly within Mertor's ranks. Trying to project confidence, he responded, "You obviously think you know who we are, but who am I addressing?"

The woman smiled as four more people entered the room behind her. They wore leather armor and had the air of experienced soldiers. However, Henton's primary concern came from the holy symbols of Mertor hanging from around their necks. "I am Alci, High Priestess of Mertor, but I expect you already know that. Otherwise, why else are you here?"

"Well, as we told Davin, we were just looking for a passage through the mountains."

The woman laughed. "Do not fool yourself into thinking we will tolerate insubordination from you. You are soldiers and are following orders. Perhaps if you see the errors of your ways, we can find a place for you." The woman nodded her head toward Ryia. "Her, we are not familiar with, but we know she is a witch and she will either submit to being put under control or we will destroy her now."

Henton kept his hand from dropping to the handle of his dagger; he knew the weapon would do him no good against this many priests. "Ryia is an innocent girl. You harm her—or any of us—and Her Highness will rip you to pieces."

"You can believe that if you wish. What matters is she either submits or dies. Frankly, if you want to resist, I would be very pleased."

Henton could not bring himself to move. He did not want to die, but could he trust these people not to kill Ryia outright. Unless Stephenie had been more fortunate than he ever expected, *it would be a long time—perhaps even morning—before she returned.* They needed to survive until that time. "I will vouch for Ryia, leave her be," he said, stepping forward.

The woman leaned her staff in Henton's direction. A moment later, he found himself on the other side of the room. His back hurt from where he slammed into the wall. His chest ached as he struggled to breath. With great difficulty, he pushed himself to his feet. He did not know for certain, but he wondered if the blow had cracked a rib. From his position, he could tell Douglas had received a similar fate, only Douglas had been flung over the bed, ripping down the drapes.

"Don't hurt them!"

"Girl, you have the choice, eat this and come willingly, or I'll put the poison into you on the blade of a dagger, right after I break their arms and legs."

"Don't hurt them," Ryia said, stepping forward, "I'll take it."

Henton wanted to stop Ryia, but he still had not yet fully caught his breath. He watched in agony as she took the object from the woman and then quickly swallowed it. After a moment she asked with an unnatural calmness, "Will it kill me?"

"No, but you will soon find yourself unconscious, which is the only safe way to handle witches. You've shown better sense than I had expected." The woman looked at Henton and Douglas. "Better sense than those two."

Henton managed to cross the room and he turned Ryia to face him. He wanted to admonish her for taking the poison. A part of him had even hoped she had performed a slight of hand, but the fear in her eyes told him she had not.

"Don't be mad. I didn't want them to hurt you anymore."

He pulled her close and put her head against his injured chest. "I'm not angry at you. We'll keep you safe." He continued to hold her until she started to tremble. He refused to look at the woman. When Ryia's legs started to give out, he lifted her face. "Stay with me," he said as her eyes lost focus.

"It would be best if she did not. A second dose might kill her."

Despite the pain in his back and chest, he lifted the Ryia's small body into his arms to keep her from falling to the floor. She had gone completely slack, but he could tell she still breathed. Finally turning to face the woman, he glared at her, "You will regret harming her."

The woman smiled and moved the staff to draw Henton's attention. "I think not. This staff was given to me to end the demon's life. A grand benefactor who believes in our purpose wanted there to be no chance the demon would live."

Douglas stepped forward; the turn of the woman's head stopped his movement, but not his mouth. "You don't know her power. She's not a demon, but the embodiment of a god."

Henton never heard Douglas promoting the idea of Catheri and it sounded odd to his ears. But the implied threat did not faze the woman.

"Indeed she is the embodiment of Elrin and we will purge his evil from this world." She nodded her head and the men behind her closed on Henton and Douglas. They quickly removed their weapons, but Henton would not hand over Ryia.

"Come, let me invite you to my home. If she is watching, perhaps she will come out of hiding."

# Chapter 22

Henton awoke on the cold floor of a dimly lit cell. The ten by ten room had stone on all sides. A small window with bars set in the heavy wooden door provided the only light into his world. Only his light clothing protected his body from the cold; not even a layer of straw covered the floor. The knot on the back of his head explained what happened, but not exactly when or by whom. He could not even remember leaving the inn.

The sounds of guards outside his cell—and perhaps down a corridor—let him know they had not left him unmonitored. However, he did not hear Douglas or Ryia making any noise, so he could not be certain the two of them were in the same location. *If they've hurt Ryia, nothing will save them from my wrath...or Steph's.*

Rising to his feet, he carefully examined the door and immediately put aside any thought of being able to pick open the lock. The plate on this side of the door had no opening. *And the hinges are on the other side, though I'd guess they are iron instead of leather.*

Through the bars, he saw an oil lamp hanging on the other side of the corridor. It hung from an iron bracket fastened into stone. Unfortunately, he could not see the level of oil in the lamp so he lacked even that limited judgment on the passage of time.

Turning his head, he tried to see both left and right down the narrow passage. He noted two more lamps not too far away on the left side of his cell. To the right, the distance was much greater to the next burning lamp. He shrugged. Nothing definitive could be concluded from that information, though instinct said if Douglas and Ryia were down here, they were to his left.

Stepping away from the door, he checked the cell more carefully. The mortar between the stone blocks crumbled when he scratched at it with his nail, *so, fairly old.* However, the blocks were quite large and he knew moving one would exceed his physical strength.

Checking his own possessions, he found he still wore his boots, pants, shirt, and the belt holding up his pants. Everything else had been removed from him, including the pendant Stephenie had given him on his last birthday. *But at least that is something.*

He took a moment to consider his options. He was certain they were being held as bait for Stephenie. Her ability to overcome incredible odds gave her some advantage, but if he or the others were placed in the line of fire, she might hesitate. *Damn it.* He knew allowing himself and the others to be taken prisoner had been a bad idea. *I just could not let them kill Ryia.* It was that hesitation that had prevented him from doing what he should have done to best protect Stephenie. *A moment of weakness,* he admitted. *But, now, my only purpose is to cause trouble on the inside.*

Deciding to act, he unbuckled his belt and pulled it off. He could not count on having time later and without knowing how much time he had now, he hurried as fast as he could in the dim light. He slid the belt through his hands until he found the part normally at his back. Using his teeth and fingers, he worked the leather until the glue that held closed a small opening gave way.

After their last journey, Henton had cut a small separation in the thick belt and inserted two items. He fished out the first, which was a piece of wire about six inches long. It was not overly thick, but it had some strength to it. The second was a flattened piece of steel only half an inch by a quarter of an inch. The blacksmith that made it had sharpened only one edge. The small steel blade lacked the strength to last against anything hard, but Henton only needed it to cut threads.

With his tools in hand, he quickly put the belt back on in case someone came to check on him. *It would not do to give them suspicion I have things concealed about me.* With his belt again around his waist, he sat down and pulled off his right boot. At the top of the boot, he cut the threads that held together a reinforcing band of leather. Being careful not to cut too deeply, he separated the sections of leather and carefully pulled out a flattened piece of wax. With a coin-sized disk in his hand, he slipped his boot back on his foot.

Hearing the sounds of the guards moving about, Henton paused a moment. With the dim light, he expected to be able to hide the small items in the corner of the cell, but if he was removed from the cell without them, they could be lost to him. After a moment, the sounds of guards moving stopped. He waited for a while, always looking up at the bars in the door.

When it became apparent no one was coming, he focused his attention back on the piece of wax. Being very careful, he cut a slit in the bundle along the thin side, exposing a section of sheep's bladder. Setting the package down in the corner of the room, he carefully used the blade and the wire to peel back the two halves, revealing a small amount of oily paste. With the limited light, he could not really see the poison, but he knew the effects. Preferably, he would have put on gloves, but this package had always been a tool of last resort.

Wrapping one end of the short wire around his middle finger to give him some control over the wire, he left about three inches sticking out. Taking the wire off his finger, he applied a coating of poison to the end of the wire. He knew it would be difficult to use against someone with magic, but his goal would be to jab the wire and poison into someone's neck. If he hit an artery, the victim would not live very long at all.

With his weapon primed, he moved away from the packet of poison. He did not know how long they would make him wait or even if he would have an opportunity to use it when someone did come, but if the chance presented itself, he would use it. Otherwise, he hoped Kas would make contact and allow him to coordinate his activities with Stephenie.


Stephenie allowed the cold wind to hit her face. The air around the mountain peak lacked the substance she had grown up breathing and that left her light headed. However, the days of travel with a mostly upward slope had given her some time to adapt.

*We have searched this area already,* Kas' mental voice came to her.

She knew the truth of his statement, but the statue in her hand kept indicating the trap lay within the mountain, *and less than half a mile away.* She sighed and gradually flew to the ground, sliding between the pine trees as she came to a landing. Her night sight prevented her from spearing herself on a dead branch, but several limbs brushed against her sides.

Kas floated down beside her. *At this point, I would declare it a fair certainty that the entrance is either sealed, buried, or located elsewhere.*

Stephenie frowned as she took another reading. She wondered if the relay would grow tired of answering the same question again and again. The response from the statue remained the same as it had previously: the trap lay less than half a mile directly to the east, neither above nor below her level. "I don't know Kas, we might have to search up slope or down, or anywhere along this side of the mountain. At least it is closer to this side." She leaned against a tree trunk behind her. The searching had taken its toll on her. "I don't even want to think about the entrance being on the other side of the mountain and having to tunnel all the way through."

"You have exhausted yourself," Kas said, materializing in front of her. "Additionally, the night is mostly spent. If you do not return soon, when you travel through the town, you will risk the possibility of discovery as people wake from their sleep."

She frowned at Kas, though she knew the truth of his advice and worse, he knew she knew. "It's just that I am certain it has to be in this area."

"Assuming the trap is not deceiving you."

She met Kas' eyes. "It's not."

Kas hesitated before continuing, "Have you sensed any voids in the stone?"

She shook her head. "The potential energy in the stone is too great for me to get a sense of much beyond a few feet. Add that the various types of materials all have different energies, and that makes everything I see one confused mess."

"And as you grow more weary from searching, your ability to sense things clearly continues to fade. Plus, if you are required to be active come the morning, you will want to get some rest." Kas bowed his head to her. "I can return to this spot and continue the search once you are safely in bed, if that will assist you in your decision."

She forced a laugh. "You win, I'll go back.

"Good," he said, as she started to move away from the tree trunk. "Because while I hate to suggest it, it may be that the castle may contain the entrance into the mountain."

Stephenie nodded her head. They had specifically avoided that area for fear of being sensed by the priests. Even if they were not Mertor's priests, it would not benefit her activities to draw attention. With a deep breath, she drew energy into herself and lifted her body into the air. The miles back to the village could only be traveled in time if she flew.

As Stephenie sped over the tops of the trees that grew around the buildings in Ranis valley, an uneasy feeling grew in the back of her mind. *Kas, I think something is wrong,* she sent to him. She felt him pause a moment and then drop down among the trees. A moment later he re-emerged as her tired mind realized what she did not like, *the people are missing.*

*I can sense no one in their homes,* he said to confirm her fear. *There are animals about, but no people.*

"Damn it," she swore as she raced toward the inn. Slowing before she reached the building, she settled lightly in the top of a thick tree. Using her magic, she held herself in the branches. Seeing a crook where several branches came together, she wedged in the statue and hoped it would be safe and unseen.

Turning her attention back to the two-story inn sitting one hundred feet away, she opened her mind further and searched for any people. *Nothing,* she swore again. *Where are they?* She asked Kas, realizing that even the horses were gone. The urge to smash her way into the building filled her mind.

*Remain here, I will quickly investigate and return.*

Stephenie said nothing as she sat high up in the tree looking down at the inn's roof. Her fists clenched and unclenched. Glancing around the valley, her panic grew as she saw no lamps or candles burning anywhere. The dark sky above her head held no moon, just a sea of tiny points of light. *Please be all right!* She silently begged of her friends, knowing they must have been gone for a while now.

*There is no sign of them or your gear. It—*

Stephenie leaped into the air and threw herself toward the window she had used to exit the inn. The shutters were closed as she had left them, but the oddity of the situation gave her enough doubt that she stopped before breaking through the wooden slats. *They evacuated the whole village. They must fear my reaction.* Hovering before the window, she reached out with her right hand to pull open the shutters, but then stopped. With her mind's eye, she noticed a thread of higher potential running back and forth across the opening behind the shutters.

*Kas, what is that over the window?* She asked as she narrowed her focus to use her powers to feel her way through the room where the others should have been waiting for her. *I'll kill those priests if anyone is harmed.*

*It is wire. And it is attached to one of those poison balls.*

Stephenie's hands clenched with her stomach. Now sensing the clay-covered orb of spores above the inside of the window, she knew the wire was embedded throughout the surface of the sphere. Another thread of wire led off the other side. With a gravity field, she snapped the wire near the ball, removing the tension.

*It looks like the sphere has been weakened around the center so that someone pressing on the wire would rip it open and cast dust through the room.* Kas' mental voice carried the anger Stephenie felt in her chest. *There is another one above the window on the other wall as well as above the door.*

"These bastards wanted me to rush in here and choke to death on their poison." With the trap disarmed, Stephenie pulled open the shutters and carefully entered the room. Her head hurt from the energy she had expended, but the care taken to lay the trap worried her into caution.

Inside, Kas luminesced, casting a blue-green glow throughout the room. Stephenie moved slowly across the floor, looking at the contents. "Someone tore the curtains off the bed."

Kas nodded his head. "The material has been ripped from the rods. All of your personal possessions are removed. However, nothing else appears disturbed."

Stephenie flung a gravity wave at the table, smashing the heavy mass of wood into the outer wall. The stone of the wall held, but the table broke into several pieces. The expulsion of energy released some of the pressure in her head, but did not make her feel better. "I will rip these people to pieces if any harm has come to them." She closed her eyes, fighting back tears. "How could I have left them?" She asked, fearing she might never see Henton's smile again.

Screaming in rage, an explosion of energy blasted outward from her. At the same instant, she remembered the poison balls and barely managed to redirect her anger upward, sending the energy through the roof. The room shook as wood and shingles flew high into the night to rain back down on the building and the surrounding area.

"Stephenie," Kas said loudly, becoming fully opaque in front of her. "Focus. Do not rage here, it will not help."

She wiped away the dust from her face that had fallen from the beams above her. *They are mine!* She kept hearing herself say over and over again.

Recognizing the possessive rage, she tried to suppress the feelings that boiled within her. Calming a bit, she noted her red journal on the floor. It had fallen from the rafters. Bending down, she picked it up and then turned toward Kas. "They were not caught unaware. Henton must have taken a moment to hide this. It means he knew they were at risk."

Kas took the effort to turn his head, as though he used eyes to looked about the room. "There is no blood that I can see. If they were harmed, it does not appear to have occurred in this location."

Stephenie nodded her head. Looking about the room once more, she took in the damage she had unleashed. "They either took everyone to the castle or headed south from the valley. My guess is the castle; it would give them the most sense of security."

"I would agree," Kas said, moving toward the north-facing window she had entered through.

Reaching out with her mind, she yanked a pillow from the bed and pulled it to her hand. She ripped out the insides of the case and retrieved the poison ball from above the door and placed it in the bag. Heading over to the windows, she grabbed those two as well. "We'll have to be careful with these, they look fragile."

"What do you intend to do with them?"

Stephenie approached the window and lifted her leg to step out into night. "They thought to kill me with them, well if the others are dead, I'll let those damn priests die by their own hand." Launching herself into the air, she went back to the tree where she had stashed the relay. Flying low, she grabbed the cold metal, and then changed direction to fly directly west away from the town and the castle.

The cold wind rushed past her face as she raced toward the top of the ridge more than a mile away. The sky had just started to brighten, giving her some extra light to see the landmarks below her. Finding a rocky outcropping above a thirty-foot cliff, she wedged the statue into an opening near the top. Pulling down a bit of moss and dirt, she covered the metal to hide it even further.

With the statue secured, she started to turn back to the castle but hesitated. "Kas, tell me they are not dead. Lie to me. I need to hear it."

"They are not dead."

Stephenie nodded her head, desperate to believe him. She looked at the pillowcase with the poison balls, moved back to where she had hid the statue, and added the pillow case. *Until I know, I don't want to be forced to protect the balls from someone breaking them. If they are dead, I'll rain the poison down on their heads and let them all die.*

Without further pause, she headed toward the castle. Her speed continued to increase the closer she came. Once she could see the stone structure clearly in the ever-reddening morning light, she dropped out of the air and landed in the woods that covered part of the valley's northern end. The area directly around the castle had long ago been cleared of trees as a precaution from attack. Between the woods and the castle's outer wall lay a wide expanse of green grasses.

This castle lacked the size of Antar Castle, but it boasted six towers around the outer walls as well as a separate central keep. She had seen the glint of armored men walking the outer walls before she dropped to the ground. She was unsure, but thought it was likely they had seen her approaching.

*Do you want me to enter the castle and search for Henton and the others? I could do that before you approach.*

Still fighting the urge to rush forward, she nodded her head. If she could confirm their location, she could avoid harming her friends accidentally as well as know where to direct her approach. "Go, but be careful, that priest in Antar knew of you and we might be dealing with Senzar in there. If you find the others, let them know I am coming."

Kas materialized momentarily to nod his head. Then he took off faster than Stephenie could move. She squatted down and put her back against a large tree. "These people will pay for this. I will make them pay."

A surge of energy drew her attention a moment before the cracking of thunder rolled over her. "Kas?" She said, already on her feet. Forgoing caution, she moved forward and emerged from the trees. The grassy meadow rose gradually toward the castle still over four hundred yards away. *Kas,* she called loudly with her mind.

Seeing no one in the meadow, she continued marching toward the castle. Several people moved around on the battlements, many of them were ducking between crenelations, but one woman stood defiantly in the middle of a wall between two of the six towers.

*Stephenie,* Kas' voice rose in her mind. She felt him approaching her, but he moved slowly and his voice lacked strength. *I did not see what struck me, but it came from the woman.*

*Are you hurt?*

*I will recover,* he said after several moments. *However, I do not wish to experience that again.*

Stephenie nodded her head as she continued to walk toward the castle. Kas fell in beside her. *You should stay back. I'll likely draw their attacks and I don't want you hit as well.* After a moment, Kas moved off to her right.

"Demon," the woman shouted. "Keep your ghost away unless you want it destroyed with you."

Stephenie used her magic to project her voice, avoiding the harshness that came with yelling. "You have taken my friends. Return them to me unharmed."

"No! You are the spawn of Elrin and we will not allow his evil to spread any further. Surrender yourself and we will consider allowing your followers to go free. Resist and we will start cutting off unneeded pieces. Harm us and we will kill them. Your ghost cannot reach us and cannot rescue them. If we sense him again, an alarm will be sounded and Henton will loose an eye. If we don't sound a counter alarm saying your demon is gone, Henton will die."

Stephenie continued moving closer to the wall, her hands still clenched. Images of ripping her hands through the woman's flesh passed through her mind. With effort, she pushed aside the desire and focused on the castle. She had come close enough to see the woman's light brown hair blowing in the wind. Two people stood beside her and under the cover of the crenelations. A dozen more were spread out on the gatehouse and the nearest tower. She noted the crossbows those soldiers carried, but kept her focus on the woman. "I have done nothing to you and neither have my friends. You let them go now!"

"Stupid girl, we have been commanded by Mertor to destroy you. We have the word of our god that your death is necessary. We have been given the tools to do so. Who are you going to rely upon? The word of the god of lies? The god of the elves?"

Stephenie watched as the woman pointed a quarterstaff in her direction. The speed in which a channel formed between her and the staff left Stephenie in awe, but fortunately Stephenie had watched for it. Launching herself into the air, Stephenie diverted the lightning from her body to the ground, avoiding the deadly blast by inches. Dirt and debris pelted her as thunder vibrated her bones.

Dodging left, Stephenie avoided a second powerful strike that followed immediately after the first. At two hundred yards, the amount of energy and control needed to span the distance worried her.

She did not have time to contemplate if the woman had Senzar blood in her veins as a gravity wave raced at her from the staff. Modulating the fields around herself, Stephenie rolled the wave around herself as a ship cuts through water. Immediately, Stephenie followed up with her own attack, unleashing the energy coursing through her.

Stunned, Stephenie watched as her blast rippled around the woman, creating a stunning sphere of lightning. A heart beat later the blue-white energy flew back at her. *Damn it,* she swore as she jumped to the right to avoid the deadly blast as well as a series of crossbow bolts.

A ballista bolt, narrowly missing her head, drew Stephenie's attention. Taking a moment to hopefully balance the fight a little, Stephenie unleashed a series of gravity waves against the others on the walls. The distance meant she needed to push a lot of energy into the attacks, causing a low cry of pain to escape her lips.

The ballista on the gatehouse exploded, sending fragments of shattered wood in all directions. At the same time, her subsequent blows sent five soldiers flying from the wall.

Sensing another series of attacks from the staff, Stephenie broke off her offensive and continued moving to the right. She felt the pain of the lightning as the strike shot past her. Caught in the periphery of the blast, the cloth of her pants disintegrated from the heat of the energy that blackened her left leg.

Shooting a gravity wave at the woman, Stephenie was not surprised when a protective field sprung into existence. However, Stephenie had already noticed a rock about the size of her own head. Wrapping the stone in a gravity field, she dug within herself to launch it at the woman, powering the stone's flight the entire way, its speed building until the last moment.

The woman tried to dodge away, but the effort was not necessary, the small boulder rebounded off an invisible sphere and bounced across the ground.

*Damn it!* Stephenie swore, blood running from her nose.

*It is the staff,* she heard Kas say from behind her. *It protects her.*

Stephenie dodged another blast of lightning and worried that the power of the staff had not appeared to diminish in the least. She knew she could not continue to keep up her focus, get closer, and continue to avoid the occasional crossbow bolt.

Fearing what would happen to her friends if she should retreat, Stephenie dug deeply, pulling energy from around herself. She ripped it from the ground so fast that frost encircled her. Struggling with the distance, Stephenie hoped the staff did not extend its protection too far below the woman. She had only one shot at being able to establish her own reputation with these people and she needed them to fear her and question the superiority they had so far managed to display.

*Come on,* she swore. She felt more blood rushing from her nose and running down her face and throat. Still building the field's strength, Stephenie latched it deep into the wall and started to pull. She drew more energy from the ground and tried to ignore the burning of her insides. Her mind screamed with pain, but she knew her friends would die if she failed and so she did not relent.

Suddenly, she felt the wall start to give as her fields shifted; she almost cried with relief. A moment later a great rumbling filled the valley, deafening the sounds of nature as a section of the wall exploded outward toward Stephenie. Blocks of stone flew across the field, tearing up the grasses in their path, but not quite reaching her position.

The wall above the hole she made collapsed, sending the people down into a cloud of dust and debris. When it settled, the twenty-foot high wall had turned into a pile of rubble a quarter of its original height.

It took several long moments, but the woman with the staff climbed to the top of the rubble pile. Although a veil of surprise draped across her face, the woman appeared uninjured.

*You are too weak to continue this fight,* Kas said, coming up behind Stephenie. *I do not know what that staff is, but you need to recover.*

Stephenie did not disagree. She had managed to wipe the blood from her face as the wall fell. Using magic, she closed off her nose so that the blood leaked down her throat. Using strength she did not have, she projected her voice, hoping that Henton and the others might hear. "I will allow you time to consider the consequences of your actions. My demands are simple, free my friends unharmed or no one will leave this valley alive. I've destroyed an entire mountain; I can easily rip this castle apart. You release them and stop harassing me and my country, and I'll let you live. I'll be back later to hear your decision."

Quickly, before they could respond, Stephenie turned away and moved toward the trees. She hoped to reach cover without the woman attacking her again, her own body hurt too much to continue the fight.

*Rest and then return,* Kas told her. *You confronted them after being up the whole night.*

*I just want them back,* Stephenie thought to him, tears rolling down her face. "I should never have left them alone."

# Chapter 23

The rumble that filled the air and shook the ground roused Henton from the partial slumber that had overcome him. Tensed, he forced himself to wait, knowing he could do nothing else until Kas or Stephenie came. Jumping at phantoms, he kept hoping Kas would reach out to him; however, the ghost did not come.

Eventually, he heard heated voices. The sound appeared to come from down the right side of the passage outside his door. "She took down a wall!" One man said in Pandar. "Alci put too much faith in that man. We have to turn them over and hope she will leave without destroying the rest of the castle."

"It's too late, after what's been done to the girl..." A second voice said, this one's accent thick with constants.

"Mistress Alci wants the sergeant," said a female voice. "Get him and bring him to her."

Henton picked up the wire and slid his finger in the loop he had made. He knew if he kept his palms facing anyone who came into the cell, he had a chance of keeping the wire concealed without having to hide his hands behind his back.

As the sound of boots coming down the passage increased in volume, Henton centered himself and calmed the anxiety that had eaten at his mind. With confirmation that the noise had been Stephenie attacking, he knew this would be his best chance to fight back. If Mertor's forces were split, it would improve the odds for both of them. *And, I can't fix whatever happened to Ryia, but until life leaves me, I will seek revenge.*

Henton saw a shadow fall across the small opening in the door. He could not make out a face in the dim light, but with the sound of a key in the lock, he knew he would not wait long. A moment later, the door opened and a soldier moved into the room. Because of the lamp in the man's hand, Henton had to blink and look away to avoid getting blinded. Once his eyes had partially adjusted, he looked back and a second man stood in the room next to the first.

"Sarge," the second man said in Cothish. "Been a while."

Henton narrowed his eyes as his sight continued to adjust. "Berman?" He asked, recognizing the man's voice.

"Yup. I see you're still running around with Steph." Berman shook his head. "You should have taken your earnings and left like the rest of us. I hate to see you caught up in all of this."

Henton glanced at the first man. His eyes had cleared enough to see that the blonde-haired man wore a holy symbol on his chest. Turning his attention back to Berman, he asked, "What are you doing here?"

His one-time Private shrugged. "Well, I've converted. The priests of Mertor sought us out to get more information on Steph. You see, their god actually spoke to them. Told all of them to stop the spread of Elrin's evil, so that is what they are doing. They showed me the error of my ways and you know, I have to say, Steph had put a spell on all of us. Her and Kas."

"You told them about Kas?"

Berman laughed again. "Sure did. That demon always made me a little uncomfortable." Berman shook his head. "I liked you, but you should have gotten out when you had the chance."

Henton's mind raced. This betrayal explained a lot of how they knew so much about them. Berman and a handful of others had helped bring Stephenie from the Grey Mountains back to Antar and then journeyed with her to Kynto to steal back the money Stephenie's mother had stolen. They had more intimate knowledge than even Joshua did. "Why'd you do it?"

"Well, simply, at first it was because when Peter and John refused the priests of Mertor, they were killed. I rather enjoy being alive, so I decided to listen. After that, I realized what they said made sense."

It took every ounce of control Henton had to avoid balling up his fists. Berman would die. That he would most certainly see to, but first he needed to get out of the cell and the priest of Mertor posed the bigger threat. He had seen no one behind these two and currently did not hear anyone else in the passage, though he remembered the third voice.

"All right, time to go. Enough catching up," the priest said.

Henton kept his eyes on Berman as he stepped forward, but his attention remained on the priest. With a feint toward Berman, Henton closed his fist and moved against the priest. The young priest reacted quickly, but he moved to block the wrong attack. The poison tipped wire easily penetrated the man's neck all the way to Henton's fist. Not certain he hit an artery, Henton clung to the man and struck twice more before being flung against the back of the cell.

Having expected the magical defense, Henton's impact with the back of the cell had not stunned him. Instead, he bounced off the wall and stumbled to his knees. Berman drew a short blade and moved forward. When Berman's sword extended to point at him, Henton quickly moved under it and launched himself forward.

His former Private's eyes bulged as Henton collided with him. Using his strong legs, Henton drove Berman into the wall on the other side of the cell. A grunt of pain came from Berman's lips, but a knee into Henton's chest allowed Berman to push him off. Slightly winded, Henton spared a moment to notice the lamp the priest had carried tumble to the floor as the priest sagged against the wall.

"Damn it, Sarge! You piece of shit, I'll kill you!"

Berman charged forward. Henton dropped low again, avoiding Berman's back swing by a fraction of an inch. Exploding upward one more time, Henton rammed his head into the smaller man's leather-covered gut. Driven back into the wall a second time, Berman grunted from the impact, but this time Henton blocked Berman's knee.

Grunting himself, Henton shook off the blow to his back as Berman hit him with the pommel of his sword. Reaching around, Henton jabbed the wire still around his finger into the back of Berman's right knee. He felt the wire bend as it hit bone and cartilage.

Berman growled in pain and he hit Henton in the back again.

Henton used his leverage and position to twist his body, pushing Berman further into the corner while he pulled Berman's legs out from under him. The change in position kept Berman from having any real range of motion to swing his blade.

Rolling up closer into the man's chest, Henton kept Berman pinned while he pulled a dagger from the soldier's belt. With fury borne from the rage of betrayal, Henton drove the blade home.

Berman winced in pain, but Henton continued to push his shoulder upward, keeping Berman's mouth closed and his head jammed into the corner. Berman growled with rage, but pinned against the wall, he could not scream for help. With the stolen dagger, Henton continued to stab the man under him until Berman stopped resisting and went slack.

Remembering the priest, Henton quickly untangled himself from the dying Berman and turned to face the man he had poisoned. The priest's body trembled and blood leaked from the wounds in the neck. Not wanting to give the priest a chance to heal himself, Henton quickly slit the man's throat.

Still shaking from the rage of seeing Berman, Henton took a moment to remove the wire from his finger. Tossing it aside, he picked up the short blade Berman had used from the floor. He turned back to the priest and quickly found the man's pouch. Feeling a key inside, he cut the bag free of the man's belt and pulled that man's sword from its scabbard. With weapons and key in hand, Henton rushed from the cell. Seeing no one approaching from either direction, he turned left toward the cells in that direction.

Stopping at the door next to his cell, he found the small room empty. Moving down the passage, his fear built as he continued to find more empty cells. At the fifth cell, he almost shook with relief. "Douglas," Henton whispered through the small window as he quickly put the key in the lock.

His Corporal came quickly to the door. "I heard some commotion. That you?"

"Hey!" A man called from further down the passage.

Henton quickly tuned the key and pulled open the door. He spun around and immediately engaged the man who had come from deeper in the cellblock. Dropping the second sword behind him for

Douglas, Henton use the longer one in his right hand to knock aside a thrust from the guard.

He heard Douglas pick up the sword. "Kill that bastard!" Douglas called, before rushing the other way down the passage to meet the cry of alarm from another guard coming from that direction.

Henton dodged the guard's sloppy thrust and with a swift chop, bit deeply into the man's right forearm. The guard's sword fell to the ground and the man pulled his injured arm to his chest. Using the weight of the sword to his advantage, Henton punched the man in the head, driving the pommel into his temple. The blow dropped the soldier to the ground.

Behind him, he saw Douglas drive a man around a far corner. "Ryia's two down!" Douglas shouted.

Grabbing the key from Douglas' cell, Henton moved down two cells and found Ryia lying naked on the stone floor. *Damn them!* He snapped open the cell, moved inside, and checked her condition. She breathed, but remained unconscious. *Damn them!*

He hesitated a moment, but knew he could not fight and carry her at the same time. Heading back out of the cell, he continued to hear sounds of fighting from the right, where Douglas had gone. Not wanting to have people come up from behind them, Henton followed the passage further to the left.

After three turns, he came out of the dimly lit passage into a small torture chamber. Four cots sat next to one wall, but the room had no exits and appeared empty. Turning around, he quickly ran back to assist Douglas.

Passing Ryia's cell, he cursed again, but continued to the end of the passage. Coming around the corner, he found a guardroom filled with commotion. Two men and a woman writhed on the ground behind Douglas, while three more stood before him. One of them had a discharged crossbow in his hands, while the other two advanced with swords.

Henton rushed forward, calling out to Douglas as he closed, "Right." Douglas shifted left, allowing Henton space to move through what was a twenty by twenty room filled with a table and benches. The two soldiers, each with swords, hesitated a moment in seeing Henton and the one with the crossbow hurried to reload.

Henton did not slow. He needed to keep the man with the crossbow from being able to easily pick off either of them from a distance. Getting in close, Henton quickly exchanged several blows with the young swordsman. The man's lack of skill showed and Henton cut a line across the man's belly. The tight leather armor kept his intestines from spilling, but blood poured out of the wound as the man stumbled backwards.

Douglas, severely injured, struggled against a more seasoned soldier. Henton left his friend to his fight, charging instead for the man in the back with the crossbow. The archer raised the stock to his shoulder and Henton realized the distance did not favor him.

Feinting left, Henton waited for the man's expression to change, then lunged right just before the bolt was discharged. Flying harmlessly past him, Henton had no time to hope the bolt missed Douglas. Colliding with the shelves that lined the room, Henton knocked ceramic jars to the floor as he pushed off the wall to closed on the guard.

The soldier dropped the crossbow, but did not have time to draw his sword before Henton smashed his blade into the man's arm. His blow cut through leather and muscle before striking bone. A second strike, driving the sword point into the man's chest, sent the soldier to the ground.

Henton turned quickly. Douglas had taken another cut, but had managed to take down the soldier he fought. His friend staggered a moment and then dropped his sword to put pressure on his left arm.

Henton looked around the room. A single door stood closed at the top of half a dozen steps. "How bad is it?" Henton asked as he examined the door.

"Left arm's done, but probably not too bad." He winced. "Took one to the gut. That one will be the end of me."

*Damn it,* Henton swore to himself as he turned. Seeing a tunic laying on the table, he grabbed it and went to Douglas' side. Quickly cutting away several strips of cloth, he had Douglas let go of his arm and blood immediately oozed from the wound. "Let's stop that leak first," he said, wrapping the cloth tightly around his arm. Easing Douglas back, he pulled up Douglas' shirt. A puncture wound in his left side seeped blood. "Let's hope they didn't poison the blades."

"You know how to make a guy feel better." Douglas nodded his head to a man behind him. The soldiers had stopped their movements. "I wasn't going to let him get away." Douglas swallowed. "That man you fought by my cell, he dead? After what he did to Ryia, make sure of it."

Henton nodded his head, but kept his attention focused on Douglas' wound. It did not look good and gut wounds often festered. Depending on what was cut, he could die quickly or slowly. *Steph, we need you.* He looked up and back toward the passage to the cells. "Once I get you wrapped up, I'll try to wake Ryia and get you mended the right way. She'll have you fixed up in no time."

"Henton," Douglas said, hate again filling his eyes. "None of them live. We kill every one of them. I heard what they did."

Henton nodded his head. Cutting up more of the tunic, he balled up a section and then pulled Douglas forward to wrap a bandage around his stomach. Tying it off tightly would help hold Douglas' blood in him, but the internal bleeding would eventually kill him if he could not get healed.

"Did you know Berman is here?" Douglas asked as he cringed from the pain.

Henton nodded his head. "He's dead." Finishing with Douglas, Henton sat back. "We need to get out of here."

Douglas swallowed and tried to rise, but failed to get his feet under him. Henton wanted to curse, but it would not help.

After a deep breath, Douglas shifted his legs and managed to get on his knees. He shook his head. "I thought I could fight if needed, but this pause has taken it out of me."

Glancing about the room, Henton quickly retrieved the crossbow, pulled back the string, loaded it, and brought the bow over to Douglas. "I can't carry Ryia and you and fight at the same time. Let me barricade the door and we'll just have to hold up until Steph gets here."

Douglas nodded his head and turned his focus on the door leading out of the dungeon. His face lacked any color, but a determination filled his eyes.

*I could use a couple more people right now,* Henton thought. Going up to check on the door at the top of the short set of stairs, he found it closed, but not locked. *Which is more likely to be locked from the other side.*

The solid door did open in toward the guardroom, but it lacked brackets for a crossbar. However, the stone around the door's frame had grooves and he thought he could likely wedge something across the door. Hurrying down the steps, he retrieved one of the shelves he had knocked over. Rushing up the stairs, he positioned one end against the door and the other into a corner where two large stone blocks met.

Henton descended the stairs three at a time and then ran to the torture room. In that dimly lit room, he found a pile of iron bars and other implements of pain. Grabbing as many as he could carry, Henton rushed back to the door and placed more wedges in place. Hoping the door would hold, he went back to check on Douglas.

"I'm still here," his friend said. "For a while at least."

"Hang in there." Henton grabbed the table and turned it over onto its side. Putting it between Douglas and the door, it would provide some cover. Taking the heavy benches one at a time, he went back to the stairs and jammed them against the door.

He made another trip to the torture room where he grabbed the blankets off the cots. On the way back to Douglas, he dropped a blanket by Ryia's cell. With the rest still in hand, he grabbed a jug of meed from a shelf and placed all of it beside is injured friend.

Still running about, Henton checked the soldiers in the room. The ones who were simply unconscious, he killed with a dagger to the heart. The others, he stripped of any clean clothing and gear. Once that was done, he went back and checked on Ryia again. She remained unconscious and her skin felt cold. He tried several times to revive her, but he suspected whatever the priests had given her would take its time wearing off. *If it doesn't kill her.* Angry with himself, he dressed her as best he could, wrapped her in the blanket, and then carried her to the edge of the guardroom.

"How is she?" Douglas asked when Henton came back into the room to check the door again.

"I've got her wrapped in a blanket."

"If you get the chance to get her out, take it. Don't wait on me."

Henton patted Douglas' shoulder. "My friend, I think either we are all getting out or none of us are. We just have to wait on Steph now."

# Chapter 24

Kas helped Stephenie make her way back to the ridge where they left the relay. The effort to fly to a position of safety took the last of her strength. Exhausted and in pain, she did not fight Kas' insistence that she sleep. She only asked that he continue the search for the trap.

With a heavy heart, Kas watched her slip into sleep and then quickly left her concealed inside a small alcove created long ago by fractures in the massive rocks. He raced north, moving over the trees and around the western side of the mountain peak with all haste. He hated to see Stephenie suffer and he feared for the safety of the others. *Though I do not see an easy way through this,* he admitted to himself. It remained a long shot that either of them would quickly discover the location of the trap and if they did and she managed to disable or destroy it, he did not know if that would actually demoralize the followers of Mertor. *Or would it make the priests more desperate and result in the death of the others?* If Kas still possessed a body, he knew that thought would have made it tremble. Stephenie's love—*or sense of obligation*—for the others would devastate her if they came to harm.

Frustrated with his own lack of effectiveness, he once again resumed searching around the area that Stephenie had identified during the night. He started to spiral outward, trying to cover as much ground as possible, but his thoughts still kept coming back to the staff. *That would have been considered incredibly powerful even in my day.* The implication frightened him. *Stephenie is not ready to face such a weapon.*

Slowing his pace, he pushed the wish that she would retreat and not fight the weapon and the woman from his thoughts. He knew she would never consider abandoning the others. Instead, he forced himself to focus on interpreting the land below him. Because he had no eyes, he perceived the world by how energy bounced off objects and interacted with his own fields. While he hated to admit it, not everything he felt made sense to him when he cast his attention so widely. Separating out stone from fallen and decaying trees took more concentration because their shapes lacked definition. Things with an obvious physical form were the easiest to decipher when he looked over a large area. One fortunate aspect was that in the daylight, he received more reflected energy and so colors stood out better than they did in the dark. Though, it required a different concentration, it did help to separate stone from tree. Resolved that the effort would not be quick, he began to lose hope he would find something and be able to return to Stephenie before she woke.

Henton had found a few articles of loose clothing scattered around the rooms. Adding that to what he removed from the dead, he managed to make Ryia and Douglas reasonably comfortable.

He left Ryia in the passage to the cells. He wanted her close, but out of the way should they have to fight in the guardroom.

His one-time Corporal sat on the floor with his legs out before him. Propped against a chair and behind the overturned table, it was as comfortable as be could be made. Determined to offer assistance to the last, Douglas held the loaded crossbow in his lap.

"Open this door or we'll bust it down," came the demand of a man that Henton envisioned to be large and overweight. Douglas continued to stare at the door on the other side of the room. It had been a while since they had heard any interesting conversations through the door.

"They won't answer you. Quit demanding it. You're getting on my nerves."

In Henton's mind, the woman who spoke stood as tall as he did. Lanky, but effective with a sword, *or perhaps a bow.* He knew those two were both mages.

"They could be dead in there."

"I can feel they are not. They are waiting in the guardroom; do you want to get shot breaking down the door? You should be able to sense this."

That argument had played out several times already. Sometimes a third or fourth person would join in. Other times not.

"She'll be back and if we've harmed them, she'll rip the castle down around us."

"A new voice," Douglas whispered with labored breath. "Woman or boy?"

Henton shrugged.

"She said she'd kill us all."

"Don't be stupid, Tylor, Mertor will prevail."

"You didn't see the wall come down," the young man said so softly Henton could barely hear him.

The woman outside huffed. "It's too late, once she learns what some of the men did, she'll kill everyone anyway."

Henton felt his rage building. *Stephenie will have to wait until after I kill them.* He knew he had failed them. He had tried to protect Ryia and had damned her to an even worse fate.

The sound of someone shuffling their boots on stone focused his attention again. "Ma'am," came at least three voices.

"What is the status?"

"They remained locked in here. I've been demanding they surrender, but they have not," the man said.

"Leave them. They can't get out, which means they are secure. No difference between being in a cell and the larger cellblock. Just make sure the door stays closed. Once the demon is dead, we can kill them. Until then, they will remain leverage."

Several moments passed before Douglas leaned slightly toward Henton. "Was that for our benefit or are they that stupid to talk in front of us?"

Henton bit his lip and wondered about it for a moment. "It's hard to say. They are isolated here, so I can't imagine they have to defend their position often. Usually they work in small groups away from this valley, so we are probably dealing with a group of people used to independent action. I'd say, whatever Steph did, rattled their confidence."

Douglas nodded his head slowly. He tried to move a little and winced. "I've got about one good shot, but I won't be much use beyond that. If you get a chance to escape, grab Ryia and run."

Henton shook his head. Douglas' face had lost most of its color and the bloodstain on both bandages continued to grow slowly. "Steph will get us out. She has been out all night; she probably needed to rest before tearing down the castle."

Douglas took a deep breath. "It's like waiting for drunken sailors to wake up and get on board. I'd really appreciate it if she'd hurry."

Henton agreed silently. Getting up, he went back to the passage to check on Ryia's condition. *If she'd wake up, perhaps she can mend Douglas enough to keep him going until Steph gets here.*

After spiraling outward from his starting point more than two dozen times, Kas finally found something that caught his attention. Below him, and mostly hidden by the trees, was a footpath that cut into the mountainside. Generally following the twists and bends of the land, it appeared to come from the south and gradually climb the mountain slope.

In looking at the path, he guessed it could have existed for many years based on the erosion and slow-growing nature of the subalpine plants. Uncertain of the implication, he followed the path on its gradual ascent up the mountain.

Signs of recent foot travel made him fear this could simply be a hunting trail or perhaps even the path that Davin mentioned to Stephenie. *There are too many new languages these days for me to learn,* he thought, discouraged again by his lack of ability to interact with the world around him.

Following a set of switchbacks up a steeper part of the trail, he felt he had once again reached the height where Stephenie had sensed the trap lay. However, he had traveled at least a half-mile before the trail leveled off and continued its northerly pursuit.

Fearing he had wasted time, Kas' own frustration built. Preparing to head back to where he left off in his spiral search, he paused a moment more as he realized the trail further to the north appeared to have received less traffic.

Casting around, he examined the area in more detail and soon noticed the ground beyond the trail had been worn down to a wide sandy patch at the point of the switchback. Moving around the other side of a large boulder, Kas discovered a narrow crack in the side of the mountain. The opening here spanned only two feet in width, but ran fifteen feet in height. However, more telling was the smoothness of the stone around the edges of the concealed crack. Although weathered and partially eroded, the opening had no extending fault lines and offered no explanation of how the stone had split.

*A mage formed this,* Kas said to himself. Moving into the opening, he found a passage that quickly widened to nearly twenty feet in width. The ceiling formed a graceful arch, meeting the nearly perfectly vertical walls at a height of about eight-feet with the center of the passage standing almost twenty-feet high. Below him, the floor was flat stone. A layer of sand and debris had blown in from the outside, leaving the means for boot prints to be recorded in the softer substance.

The desire to rush down the dark passage filled him, but he knew there could be traps or people waiting. Taking a measured pace, he concentrated on not allowing his energy field to luminesce as he moved carefully into the mountain. The further he went, the darker the passage became. Fortunately, sensing his way through the passage was an easy task and the longer he went without encountering trouble, the faster he began to move.

Nearly three-quarters of a mile had passed under him when he first noticed the brightening of the passage. After several hundred yards more, and several sharp bends, Kas finally began to sense the presence of people. Slowing, he paused long enough to identify two men in what he assumed was a chamber further down the passage. *Time to inform Stephenie,* he thought, not wanting to get any closer and potentially reveal himself to the men.

*       *       *       *       *

Stephenie gradually awoke. From the sun, she realized more than half the day had passed; however, exhaustion still filled her arms and legs. If she had been in a warm bed, she might not have even opened her eyes. *Please be okay. Please, no one be hurt,* she pleaded, not wanting to remember the plight in which her friends were trapped.

Rolling onto her side, she crawled out of the small outcropping she had wedged herself into. Kas had not yet returned and it took all of her effort to not simply fly off toward the castle and try another frontal assault. "But that staff," she mumbled aloud. She knew that priestess had found something truly powerful. The speed and strength of the energy blasts coming from the staff had challenged Stephenie's ability to respond. "And then it blocked all my attacks."

Stephenie looked down at her burned leg. The skin had softened from a blackened scab to a bright pink. "Could she be another Senzar?" She wondered aloud. The references to Elrin and Mertor made her uncertain. *However, they have used our ignorance to their benefit before. If she's playing a role for her followers, she might carry on like that.*

The growling of her stomach broke her train of thought. She climbed onto a wider ledge of stone and ate the last of the food she had carried with her during the night. After a few bites, the food and drink were gone, leaving her wishing she had brought more. Putting aside the empty pack, she looked out at the valley below. It remained quiet and while she could see the hints of movement at the castle, the distance was too far to make out the details.

"Come on, Kas, get back here so I can do something," she said aloud as she waited. Despite her desire for action, the staff's power kept her from moving. *Not even with Kas' help can I get close enough to do much.*

She looked toward the relay and the pillowcase with the balls of poison. The temptation to reaching out to the relay was strong, but she resisted the urge. *Even if I find the trap and destroy it, how can I overcome that woman?* Stephenie put her head in her hands. *How?*

She slowly lifted her eyes and looked back at the castle. *Chaos would have to be a factor. Taking away their power is my best chance. It might even give the others an opportunity to fight from the inside.* She pushed away that thought, knowing it was unlikely. *Just survive.*

She turned her attention back to the pillowcase when an idea began to form. "A strong gravity field would block air. The woman needs to breath. If I kept up enough attacks on her, she'd run out of air." Stephenie pursed her lips. "But the field is large and Kas has said it takes a while for air to run out." She frowned, "Plus, the field could drop for just a few moments and undo all the work."

She retrieved the case and pulled out one of the balls. She examined the sphere and noted the groove that had been carved around the center to weaken the clay surface so that the two halves could more easily be ripped apart. She sensed the wire embedded in the top of the clay hemispheres. She had used her powers to snap the wire just outside the clay. Narrowing her eyes, she concentrated on an area of the ball without wire. Crafting a very focused gravity field, she ruptured the surface, cutting out a square.

She was careful not to touch the square, but instead used her powers to carry it to the edge of the stone she sat upon. She held her breath and looked into the sphere. A dark red-brown dust filled nearly the whole of the interior. Desperation overrode her caution and she crafted a small field, dipped it into the sphere, and pulled out a small amount of the dust. Still holding her breath, she tried to keep the fine dust in her control as she moved it away from her. A trail of dust leaked out of her field, its red-brown death blowing away in the wind.

Her jaw tightened with frustration. She modulated her field, trying to make it solid enough to keep all the dust contained. However, the small particles were hard for her to control. The strain of the concentration wearing on her, she eventually returned the dust to the sphere, carefully depositing it back inside the clay container.

"If the dust won't stay in my field, perhaps some of it will penetrate hers...or maybe the staff won't even react to block the dust." She pursed her lips. She needed a way to deliver a small dose. If she released a whole ball into the air, she feared it would hurt her friends.

She picked up the discarded leather pack and cut off a small piece of leather. She plucked the leather from her hand with her mind and held it in the air as she scooped out a small amount of dust. Her hands trembled slightly as she wrapped the leather around the poison before the powder fell through the gaps in her field. With her magic, she kept the leather tightly wrapped around the poison as she moved the bundle through the air in front of her. Once she felt confident of her control, she pushed the package away quickly, moving it at least three hundred yards away. At that point, she had trouble maintaining her narrow focus.

As she brought the bundle back toward her, she felt Kas quickly approaching. She almost dropped the bundle as she shook with relief at his presence.

*What are you doing?* He asked as he became near enough to speak with her.

*Finding a way to deliver a package of death if we need it. I can't get past the staff's field with my powers, but perhaps I can send the woman a dose of poison. Perhaps it is small enough to pass notice.*

Kas came to a stop next to her as Stephenie carefully opened the piece of leather to reveal the small pile of dust had remained. Carefully, she moved the dust back to the sphere. Then as a precaution, she poured energy into the piece of leather, igniting the contaminated square and burning it until nothing remained but a small, blackened coal.

Kas gave her a virtual smile. *I believe I may have found an entrance to the trap, though I am not certain.*

"Where?" She demanded. "I was too afraid to ask you."

*In extending my search of the area, I encountered a footpath worn into the mountain. In following it in a northerly direction, I happened across a narrow opening cut into a large block of granite. After sensing at least two people inside the opening, I decided to return to you.*

Stephenie nodded her head. "Let's go." She knew he understood the risks of what they planned. "I fear that no action is a good one, but demoralizing them is the only shot I have. And if I have to kill the woman, so be it."

*Then I will take you there.*

Stephenie placed the opened sphere carefully on top of her leather pack and nestled it between the folds to keep it from moving. She picked up the relay and formed a field around herself and leapt into the air. *Hang on guys, I am coming.*

*　　*　　*　　*　　*

The wind whipped loose strands of hair behind her as they flew low, barely skimming the trees in the hopes no one would see her. Even once she had passed around the western side of the mountain and could no longer see the castle, she still feared the potential for watchers to be scattered on the slopes.

*What do we face with this opening?* She asked as they flew.

Kas relayed his mental image of the opening into the mountain and the long passage that led generally in the direction of the trap. *However, I cannot say what is at the end of the tunnel.*

Stephenie nodded her head. When she finally touched down outside the entrance, she waited as she scanned the area with her senses. She felt a plethora of animals, but the people inside the mountain were too far away for her to detect.

She opened her mind to the relay and confirmed the trap lay in the direction the tunnel took into the mountain. "I think this may be it."

*Do you wish me to go ahead of you?*

Stephenie considered it for a moment and then shook her head. *They may have more weapons like the staff. I'd rather fight that myself than have you draw the attack.* She cleared her mind and moved forward into the tunnel. With the narrow opening behind her and the slight bends of the carefully carved passage, it soon grew too dark for even her eyes to see her surroundings. However, her perception of the energy fields gave her a clear picture of the tunnel leading deep into the mountain.

With every step, she drew in power. Eventually, she lifted herself into the air to avoid the sound of her steps warning whomever it was that Kas had sensed. However, even flying, she moved slowly, in order to sneak up as close as possible before revealing herself.

As distant light ahead of her started to brighten her surroundings, she felt one person followed immediately by a second one. The distance and the stone prevented her from knowing if they were male or female. She could not even sense the nature of where they were. However, as she grew closer, those things would become clear to her as would her approach become obvious to whoever waited, *assuming they are mages.*

She adjusted her plan; to gain as much surprise as possible, even with the risk of losing time for her own decisions, she pulled in more energy and launched herself forward. She rocketed down the middle of the passage with the speed of a charging horse. She barely had time to sense the wide cavern before she burst into it, sucking wind behind her.

The two men were to her left. Adjusting the fields around herself, she came to a sudden stop, dropped the relay to the floor, and unleashed an attack on the men, throwing them back against the wall. One of them had tried to pull a dagger, but dropped it after hitting the wall.

The other man screamed something Stephenie did not understand. He pointed at her. However, Stephenie did not wait for him to unleash magic upon her. She moved closer and opened her mind to search for the telling draw of power that would indicate an augmentation device. Devices under the men's leather armor leapt into her awareness. Stephenie broke through their mental defenses and ripped apart the armor. Surprising her, she realized the devices had been embedded in the armor and were not around their necks. The armor shredded into chunks under her intense gaze. With the augmentation devices still embedded in the leather, she flung the useless remnants across the eighty-foot wide cavern.

"Don't kill us!" Begged the man who had dropped his dagger. "Don't send us to Elrin!"

Stephenie touched down as the men tried to get themselves to their feet. Their backs were against the wall of the cavern. She paused a moment and expanded her senses to get a better feel for the room. The men had been sitting at a table that had the remains of a meal upon it. Dice and cards were scattered about, likely disrupted by the men trying to react to her approach. Three lamps provided light in the chamber, two hanging from hooks on the wall next to them and a third one next to the tunnel she had entered through. Shelves stood against the wall near the men. They held food and supplies on the rough wood construction. On the far side of the chamber were three cots, though only two appeared to have blankets on them. She could feel only one other exit from the room, an iron door set into the stone wall opposite the passage leading to the outside.

She focused her attention back to the men and observed several days of hair on their faces and a slight odor of unwashed sweat. They were young and fit, but obviously unprepared for her. "Are my friends unharmed?"

The man who had spoken before could not hide his confusion. "I recognize you as the Demon, but how did you find this place?"

*It is possible they have been here for a while,* Kas said.

Stephenie gave Kas a mental nod of her head already suspecting that might be the situation. "How long have you been on duty?" When no response came, Stephenie stepped closer.

"Four days," the blond-haired man blurted out.

"And are you in contact with the castle?"

The blond shook his head. "The duty station is for a week."

Stephenie tilted her head back toward the iron door. "What's behind the door? A way into the castle?"

"We are not permitted. Only the High Priest is allowed access."

*Kas?*

He let out a mental sigh. *You appear safe enough for the moment. I will investigate and return.*

Stephenie thanked him as he departed quickly, passing invisibly through the door. She took another look around the room and found little of use in securing her prisoners. Pursing her lips she wondered how long it might take them to run back to the castle. *Not long enough,* she decided, uncertain of how long it would take her to destroy the trap.

"Stand up," she instructed of the men. "Toss aside your weapons."

The first man began to comply and then said something to the second man, who also rose to his feet. "Jin'ar does not speak Pandar," the blond explained.

"You are priests of Mertor," Stephenie said, making it a statement. "You may not know me."

"No, Demon, we know you well. We all dreamed of your face. Mertor has commanded us to destroy the spawn of Elrin."

Stephenie narrowed her eyes. "I am no demon and I am not the spawn of Elrin." The men stiffened at her tone. Seeing a short crate next to the wall, Stephenie nodded her head in its direction. "Sit on that." When the men went over and sat on the foot-high crate, their knees rose above the height of their waist. "Why would you think I am a demon?"

The blond-haired man cleared his throat. "Ma'am, all of us priests heard Mertor's voice. He spoke to us, telling us a friend would come to provide us the means to destroy the spawn of Elrin. We saw in our minds a vision of a face that can only be yours. We were told a red-haired man would come to us and give us the means to destroy you."

"Like what?"

The man hesitated. "I do not know for certain everything, but he taught the High Priest how to make balls of poison and I know he presented her with a staff."

Stephenie felt a chill run through her body. "When was this?"

"It happened around the time we received the news you destroyed the mountain peak. About a year ago. We were told to recruit as many people as possible to wage war on you."

Stephenie kept her hands from clenching. *Could it be my father that is trying to have me killed? What is going on? What have I done that someone would do this to me?*

Taking a deep breath, she knelt down in front of them and placed her hand on the stone next to their feet. She narrowed her focus and concentrated on disrupting the bonds of the stone. Pulling energy through herself, she spread the effect as far as she could to encompass both men's feet. The shift in the stone happened incredibly fast and Stephenie had the immediate sense that it had been formed with magic previously, creating a more uniform substance.

The men cried out in surprise, trying to pull their feet away from the liquid stone. Stephenie slammed a field down on their knees, driving their feet a foot deep into the fluid while she still had control of the field. As soon as their feet were submerged, she released the disrupting effect, encasing their feet in solid stone. Falling back onto her rear, she tried to fight the disorientation of coming out of the narrow focus. While the effects were getting easier to deal with, they still left her with a slight bit of nausea.

The two men, screaming and struggling to free themselves, drew her attention. "Silence!" She yelled. Their noise did not help the throbbing in her head. Standing up, she brushed the dirt from her clothing. "You are not harmed, but I felt encasing your feet in stone would keep you here without the need to kill you."

"Let us out! Please."

Stephenie rolled her shoulders to ease the tension that had built. "If my friends, who were taken prisoner by your friends, are unharmed, when I free them, I will come back and release you." She smiled at them. "Of course, you have to hope that your High Priest does not kill me, but if you stay quiet and wait, you will live."

The blond-haired man started to cry. "Please, don't leave us here like this."

Stephenie felt Kas return and heard his voice in her head, *I believe I have found the trap. It is still a fair distance away, but there is a whole workroom at the end of the passage. Magical lights provide illumination. I could not sense any other way out of that chamber.*

*Good. Let's get this over with and rescue the others.*

# Chapter 25

Stephenie knew the two men watched her as she picked up the relay and walked over to the iron door. Despite the men having trained as soldiers, their fear and complete astonishment of her filled the room. She ignored them and focused more intently on the door. A series of small openings indicated a key mechanism was embedded in the door, *or at least on the other side of it.*

"It's thick," she mumbled aloud, sensing the large potentials in the metal. The lock radiated a different signature, indicating to Stephenie that the metal used to build it was something other than iron. She still had not studied locks and so the pins and tumblers made little sense to her.

The frame of the door had thick iron spikes driven through holes into the stone behind it. Someone limited to traditional means would have a hard time opening the door. While she knew she could melt away the metal to form an opening, for her, that would require more effort than a strong gravity field.

She stepped to one side and carefully formed the necessary fields. A moment later, the door, its frame, and some of the surrounding stone crumpled and flew across the room with the terrible squealing of rusty metal twisting into a ball as if a large hand simply reached out and tossed it away.

Without thought for the startled men, Stephenie walked through the opening and into another section of tunnel that looked much like the first passage. She traveled another quarter mile in darkness before the illumination started to build. A short distance further, she turned a bend in the passage and entered a vast circular chamber. A vaulted ceiling rose thirty-feet overhead and had points of light that shown down, illuminating the solid stone floor. There were no columns to support the ceiling, as one might expect in such a wide space. Instead, where the vaulting came together, the stone extended downward into a carved point bearing the heads of various animals. However, these ended twenty-feet above the floor instead of actually offering support for the ceiling.

Scattered about the edges of the room were a number of stone tables formed with delicate legs and tops that only magic could have created. The tables almost glowed in the light. Stephenie noted numerous bins and objects on these tables, but her attention was drawn to the center of the room and a round platform that supported a metal column standing seven-feet high and three-feet in diameter.

*I believe that to be the trap,* Kas said softly in her mind. *I had never seen one before and did not expect it to look as it does.*

Stephenie agreed with his estimate. She could feel the draw of energy feeding into the column. For some reason, she suspected it was solid metal. The relay she knew had hollow sections in the wider parts, allowing the device to remain lighter and use less material. *But not this.*

She moved toward the trap. *Will I be able to do anything with it?* She asked herself. She dreaded the idea that the time and effort to find it might have been wasted. *Will it try to kill me now that I am here?* She could not get Kas' fear completely out of her mind.

When she reached the edge of the platform, she set down the relay and began examining the column. The silvery-grey metal had many patterns on the surface and even a few symbols that had the appearance of words instead of decoration. On the far side, away from the passage, she noticed four grooves gouged into the metal's surface. The marks were not of the same length or even the same depth. They moved diagonally across the surface and had the appearance "of a claw ripping into the metal," she said aloud, her own hand reaching out to touch it, but hovering a couple inches away.

"It does not look original," Kas commented, becoming opaque next to her. "The metal of the trap has been forcefully raised and curled back."

Stephenie nodded her head. "If it was a claw, the hand would have been much bigger than mine." She moved her left hand in a slow slashing motion, traveling from high to low. "The middle finger—or claw—dug down nearly an inch. It almost looks as if the metal melted somewhat. I thought these things were indestructible."

Kas shrugged. "Not indestructible, but I would expect it to be highly defended."

She looked around the room; however, from where she stood, there did not appear to be any other indication of damage or destruction. "The tables would be easy to smash. Well, they at least look it," she added, not knowing if magic strengthened them. Sighing to counter the doubt that had built, she added, "Well, Kas? We've come this far."

"Remain cautious. The device could lie or try to destroy you. It knows your plan and may defend itself."

Biting her lower lip, she placed her hand on the column and requested the column to allow her to give it commands, just as she had with the relay. The column responded in the same fashion, a weak energy field created a symbol on the surface. However, Stephenie could not clearly make out the shape, as the symbol formed over the top of the gouges and the damage appeared to distort what the column asked.

"No, damn you!" She tried again. A new symbol appeared, but the damage left parts of it missing and Stephenie's second attempt failed acceptance. "Damn it," she swore, hitting the cold metal with the heal of her hand.

"What is wrong?" Kas asked.

Stephenie rubbed her hand over the gouges. The edges were sharp and drew blood. "The damage is keeping me from understanding the word. I can't respond to the challenge. I can't get in." Quickly she tried twice more, both times failing the challenge.

She took a step back. "This was done intentionally to prevent anyone from accessing the trap."

She could feel Kas' shared frustration. "The metal does not oxidize. I cannot say how long ago this damage occurred. It is possible the original builders did this after it became active."

Stephenie hit the column again and then sat down on the stone platform. She shook her head. "No, I think someone did it recently."

"Why do you think that to be the case?"

She looked up at him. "Those men out there," she leaned her head toward the passage, "said Mertor had spoken to everyone and sent them a dream of my image. Telling them to kill me. To kill the spawn of Elrin. They said that Mertor told them that a red-haired man would come to give them the means to destroy me. A man that brought them a staff and taught them how to make the poison balls."

Kas appeared to sit down in front of her, though no chair existed below him. "So you believe it may be possible your sire set this in motion?"

She nodded her head. "They said it happened about a year ago, after word of my destroying the mountain peak reached them. Which would have been around the time we were in Kynto." She turned back to the trap, "Either way, we've wasted time. I've got the poison. If I can kill her, hopefully we can get these priests to give up without killing the others."

Kas met her gaze. "Assuming they do not hold true to the threat of killing the others." He reached out a hand toward her. "I fear it may not be possible for me to seek out the others and protect them while the priests are watching and they resist us."

Stephenie let tears of frustration fall freely down her face. "There is nothing we can do."

Kas moved his transparent hand to her shoulder.

Swallowing back her tears, she looked down at the relay sitting on the floor. "Wait. I want to try one last thing." Wiping her eyes, she picked up the statue. "Perhaps I can get the trap to talk to me through the relay again. Or at least repeat the question to me."

Quickly making contact with the relay, she tried to entice the voice to return to her. *Mertor, can you hear me? Please respond to me. I want to talk.* She waited for what felt like days, but she continued to repeat her demand until she felt another presence enter her mind.

*This is not the proper means. I am in violation.*

She felt the voice start to pull away. *Wait, please. I am trying to access you, but someone has damaged you. I cannot make out the symbol. Please.*

There was a long pause. *This would violate my directives. I cannot accept commands through the link.*

*Not a command, just have the symbol appear on the link. Please, please,* Stephenie added to herself.

After a moment, Stephenie saw a symbol appear on the relay at the same time something muddled appeared on the column. With her hand still on the column, she responded to the challenge.

Instantly her mind fragmented as though it were split into a million pieces. She lost all sense of her body and the world around her. She floated in a vast emptiness and then as suddenly as the split happened, her mind slammed back into itself. Though she felt someone else in her head with her, very deeply embedded within her thoughts. Something so deep that she would not be able to push it out.

She wanted to tremble as memories of the Senzar mage who took complete control of her body filled her head. Had it not been for a primal rage his taunts had woken, she would never have overcome him. She knew that would not save her here. *Mertor, please, do not harm me.*

*That is not my purpose.* The voice came from everywhere and nowhere at the same time.

Fighting the panic within her, she paused and after much time, she asked, *What is your purpose?*

*I serve the builders.*

*Who are you?* She could not help the question.

"I am Mertor," the voice came louder as the presence filled more of her. It sounded as if her ears had heard it, but she knew that was not the case.

"Are you a person trapped inside this device?"

"No," came the response, the hint of a chuckle underlying the word. "I am simply the transition manager. I was modeled after one of the original builders, though he is likely dead."

Stephenie tried to swallow, but the concept had no meaning at this point. "You are aware of what you are?"

"Stephenie, I am aware of what you and the other builders believe me to be. I have learned much in my existence." The voice paused for a moment. "May I ask you a question?"

"Yes," she offered, no longer surprised by the trap's abilities.

"Why have the builders stopped speaking with me? Have I done something to anger you?"

"I don't know," she said, trying to buy time to frame her response. "I am young. I was not around when you were created."

"It has been a long time since a builder truly spoke with me as you are now."

She hesitated a moment, but finally asked, "What of the most recent builder? Someone who came about a year ago?"

"I do not track time well."

*Of course not, neither does Kas, unless he wants to.*

The voice continued without acknowledging her thought. "However, this man who last visited did not wish to talk. He simply instructed me to broadcast a message to the consumers and then left."

"Do you know what he looked like or what his name was?"

"No. This man did not allow me into his thoughts and I have no means by which to see."

"And he is the one that damaged you?"

"Yes. I do not understand his purpose in that. However, I was not given leave to question him."

Stephenie felt Mertor's loneliness dragging on her. It reminded her of her own years of isolation in having to hide her true nature. Only, Mertor's loneliness was hundreds of magnitudes deeper. She wanted, even needed, to be his friend. However, she felt time slipping away from her. Fear for Henton, Douglas, and Ryia welled up within her. "I am running out of time."

"Of course. I understand. I appreciate the fact you have taken a moment to speak with me. What is your need?"

Stephenie felt herself hesitate and that falter in her will irritated her. "Mertor, what did the other builder have you tell everyone?"

"I am uncertain of the meaning of the words. I have learned much of your language from watching your interactions with the transfer device and absorbing memories from you."

"Do you remember what he said?"

"No. I lacked an understanding, so I did not retain a memory of it."

She wanted to tell him it was okay, but instead she pushed on. "So you are able to repeat what I might say to everyone with an augmentation device?"

"That is within my list of functions."

"Can you be turned off so that you no longer draw power from the other world?"

"That is also within my list of functions. I know that is your purpose."

Stephenie heard the trace of melancholy in Mertor's voice and while it had been one thing to destroy a simple trap, Mertor had a personality. "Will that kill you?"

"I am aware of what I am," Mertor said without inflection. "I am a device. I am designed to follow the builder's commands. It will not kill me in the sense you might consider for a living person. It will mean that I will no longer function unless I am reactivated."

"I wish I had the time to stay and chat with you. However, every moment I wait, my friends remain in danger."

"I understand. What is it you wish me to do?"

Stephenie considered what she wanted Mertor to say. The instructions her sire provided were likely quite explicit and trying to countermand them could cause disbelief in what they heard from her. After a moment, she took her best shot at countering the unknown orders. "Repeat the following to everyone with an augmentation device," then switching to Pandar, she continued. "My followers, the world has changed and I am displeased with its direction and cruelty. I am displeased with the direction in which you have gone in light of the Senzar invasion. This personal war we wage will rip the world to pieces. Catheri and I are now at peace. Cease the war you wage upon Cothel and her people immediately. Catheri's prophet is not a demon. Release the prophet's friends unharmed and lay down your weapons.

"So that you may fully understand my fury at the events in this world, I will withdraw myself from it until such time as you can prove yourself capable of supporting the peace of the land. Ignore these commandments and I will find a prophet of my own to destroy you."

Stephenie had no idea if that would break them, but she hoped that it would at least cause confusion in the ranks. *Perhaps some of them will revolt.*

"I have repeated your message."

"Thank you, Mertor. I wish I had more time, but I need you to shut down now."

She felt his acknowledgment of her request. "I feel I would have enjoyed speaking with you longer as well. You must go now to avoid damage to yourself."

Stephenie did not have a chance to respond. She felt her mind torn apart and then slam back into her body, a body that seemed partially out of place. A body that had fallen to the floor.

"Are you injured?" Kas demanded, his form floating above her.

Stephenie blinked. For some reason, it felt odd to have eyes again. "I killed him," she mumbled. A sense of having murdered someone filled her. "He just wanted to talk and I have murdered him."

"It was killing creatures itself."

"Yes, but, it was not his fault." She closed her eyes. "Kas, he might not have felt himself to be a person, but he was alive."

"I understand," Kas said. "Are you injured? You sat very still for a moment. I sensed something happening in your head. Before I could do anything, you collapsed to the floor."

She opened her mind and the local draw of energy into the trap had stopped. The relay sat on the ground, equally dead. She wiped away the tears that still fell from her eyes. "I'm a murderer."

"Stephenie, you are not a murderer. You are saving others by turning off a device. However, right now, we need to save our friends."

She pushed past the despair in her heart and stood up. She fought to get back her desire to move. Physically, while she knew she had not fully recovered her strength, in truth, the effort to disable the trap had not cost her much. Mentally, she felt hallow.

The memory of Henton's smile came to her and she breathed deeply. "Let's go get the others."

*     *     *     *     *

Stephenie flew herself back down the passage with as much speed as she dared. The two soldiers stuck in the stone did not have a chance to call out to her before she blew through the chamber and into the passage leading to the surface.

Once she was outside again, she angled her flight around the mountain so that she could retrieve the poison balls she had left on the cliff. By the time she landed, much of the cloud in her mind from dealing with Mertor had faded. She had even begun to feel somewhat human again. *I'm coming guys, just hang on.*

Moving quickly, she cut three pieces of leather from her pack. Being careful, she used her magic to extract some of the dust and placed it on each square without touching it. Then, carefully setting down the open ball, she put the two unbroken ones in her pack in case she needed them. Then with a deep breath, she created three separate fields to wrap the leather around the poison and then lifted them into the air. She positioned all three of the bundles behind her to keep them out of sight and then she created yet another field, launching herself into the air.

She flew quickly to the castle, knowing it was likely that someone could have observed her flight to the cliff. She landed just outside the tree line and again approached from the front of the castle with her focus on the wall she had already turned to rubble.

People moved on he battlements, preparing for her approach, and by the time she had reached the halfway point across the field in front of the castle, the woman with the staff once again mounted the top of the gatehouse. The woman's brown hair blew across her face as the wind whipped down from the north.

"I've come for my friends," Stephenie demanded. "Release them unharmed and we can go our separate ways."

The woman screamed at Stephenie, "You demon! Don't think we don't know what you have done. I know where you went. Do not think that you can use the power of the god of lies to frighten us. Mertor will come to us in our need despite this cloud you've thrown over our heads. You cannot whisper lies into our minds without us knowing!"

"Don't be a fool. I'll let you live if you hand over my friends. If you make me come in there, I'll be forced to rip you and the castle apart."

Stephenie sensed the lightning even before the woman moved the staff. Jumping left, she narrowly avoided the blast that threw rock and dirt into the air. Debris bounced off the field that protected her body.

Three crossbow bolts flew past her as she dodged the to avoid them. However, she managed to keep the poison packets held closely behind herself.

*There are fewer people on the wall,* she said as much to herself as to Kas. Feeling another blast of lightning building, Stephenie resolved to kill the woman. This time she felt the pain of energy rolling over her as the strike barely missed her.

Still a long way from the wall and the woman, Stephenie dug within herself and flung her own lightning at the woman while at the same time she formed a second field to blow a gust of wind into the woman's face. The lightning did as Stephenie expected, arching over and around a sphere at least ten-feet from the woman's body, only to come back at her. A leap into the air avoided the rebound. Despite the lightning's lack of effect, Stephenie's hope rose when the woman's hair flew backwards behind her, against nature's wind.

Stephenie jumped left to avoid another strike as she pushed one of her bundles of poison toward the woman. Stephenie kept it just above the surface of the ground to minimize the chance of it being seen. Focused on the small ball moving further away, Stephenie drift toward the grass below her.

Just as the poison reach the front of the castle and started to angle upwards, she felt her attention pulled away; a channel had latched to her arm and lightning raced toward her. Unable to divert it, she felt the energy surge into her flesh well before pain registered in her mind.

An involuntary scream escaped her lips as energy tore through her body. The heat of a thousand fires burned away the flesh of her left arm. Her body reacted instinctively, drawing the energy in and absorbing it. As a reservoir within her built, she immediately channeled it back out. Her arm erupted in blue-while flames, shooting into the sky.

She flung her arm and the torrent of flames away from her body. The flames arched and flew across the field as if they were liquid. The display did not last long, dying away as the excess energy left her body. She did not need to look down at her bare arm; she knew the flesh had been restored. *If it wasn't so damn painful,* she though breathlessly, both thankful and frightened of pushing massive energy through her body.

Even with her breath coming in deep gulps, she remained on her feet and held her gaze on the woman with the staff. The others on the battlements stood in stunned silence. Angry, Stephenie moved a second poison bundle from behind herself. She had lost control of the first one, but managed to keep the second two intact.

Rushing the bundle across the field, she did not bother to try to hide it. The woman glanced at it and held her staff before her. When the bundle neared the outer sphere of protection, Stephenie opened it just as she created a narrow gust of wind to blow the fine powder directly into the woman's face.

The scrap of leather, now carried by momentum and the wind, bounced off the invisible sphere, but Stephenie knew the dust had passed through when the woman started batting the air in front of her. A moment later, she started clawing at her face, dropping the staff in the process. Seeing the weapon fall, Stephenie charged forward, launching herself once more into the air. *Find the others, Kas!* She shouted.

Another woman beat Stephenie to the staff. The soldier picked it up as Stephenie landed next to the woman thrashing on top of the gatehouse.

Five men, with swords already drawn, charged her from the far side of the building. Without a backward glance, she hit them with such force that they flew off the top of the forty-foot high structure.

The woman, who had picked up the staff, dropped it and ran toward the stairs leading down into the inner courtyard of the castle. Stephenie let her go as she turned toward the dying woman. Dressed in leather armor covered with the regalia of Mertor, the woman had been formidable. The pain the woman broadcast garnered no sympathy from Stephenie. "Never take what is mine from me," she growled. Rage boiled in her blood and it took all of her will not to rip the dying woman to pieces.

Picking up the staff, Stephenie immediately felt the intelligence of the staff reach out to her. Unwilling to take the time to puzzle out the weapon, she pushed back, blocking the staff from her thoughts. It put up no fight, seemingly responding immediately to her desire.

Her mind opened and she cast her senses wide. She felt the multitude of people in the castle, many of whom were people from the town. Panic and terror hung in the air. However a few soldiers released crossbows in her direction. She knocked aside the bolts and then magically raised her voice.

"I will rip the life from anyone who harms my friends or my horses. You are beaten. Throw down your weapons and surrender now!" Sensing Kas approaching quickly, she reached out to him, *Did you find them?*

*Yes. Follow me quickly. Douglas is severely injured and Ryia's been poisoned. I killed the people guarding the outer dungeon door.*

She no longer saw the scattering people. A growl erupted from her throat and the stones of the gatehouse shook. She looked across the bailey to the reinforced door at the front of the keep. Wood and stone exploded outward as Stephenie used her powers to rip the door from the keep. The debris crashed into the back of the gatehouse and injured several people trying to hide from her.

She leapt into the air and followed Kas as quickly as she could. People fell over themselves to get out of her way. Even those who had no magical ability could sense the cloud of charged energy around her as she flew through the castle's narrow corridors, always heading downward.

She finally stopped in front of a solid door as Kas flew through it. Several bodied lay scattered in front of the door set into the wall of a dimly lit passage.

*I have informed Henton you are here.*

Stephenie took a breath and forced down the possessiveness threatening to overwhelm her. A moment later, she unleashed the energy coursing through her. The door ripped down the middle. Steel and wood bounced down both sides of the passage. Unable to see Henton and the others because more debris blocking the opening, she continued shredding the barricade, flinging deadly projectiles to either side. Not more than two heartbeats later, she had torn her way into the dungeon.

"Henton!" She cried, rushing down the stairs into the dungeon's guardroom.

"Douglas needs you," came his quick response as he directed her to the other side of an overturned table. "Damn, it's good to see you," he added as she knelt beside Douglas.

"Hey," Douglas managed to say, a bit of blood on his lips.

*Damn it! Damn it!* Taking a quick look at the bloody bandage, she put her hands on his shoulders and reached out to his mind. Douglas, too weak to fight her, only trembled slightly as she entered his thoughts. She pushed past the things he feared to share with anyone and dove deep into his subconscious. Her mind linked with his and she pushed power into his body, driving his body's healing beyond the normal pace.

For fear of killing him, she forced herself to go slowly, regulating the energy she pushed into him. Too much power and it would destroy more than heal. The time in Vinerxan, being forced to constantly heal various types of intentionally inflicted damage, had given her enough confidence and skill to heal her friend. *Even if I'm much less effective than most priests are,* she admitted to Douglas as she felt his pain subsiding.

Stephenie opened her eyes and smiled as she noticed some color had returned to his face. He still looked weak and drained to her mind, but she knew he would survive.

"Thank you," he said.

"Ryia's been poisoned," Henton offered. "I have her in the back passage just in case they decided to break through the door." He sighed. "Damn, it's good to see you."

Stephenie smiled at him. The haggard look on his face spoke of the strain he had been under. "I'm sorry it took so long," she said, moving around Douglas whose labored breathing had eased.

"Is that Berman's body?" Kas asked aloud, becoming partially visible.

Stephenie's jaw tightened at the comment, but she focused first on Ryia. "What happened to her?"

"They poisoned her to knock her unconscious. They said it would not kill her." He took a deep breath, but was not able to visibly calm himself. "Douglas heard some people take advantage of her. I don't know if they did anything else to her. Someone hit me on the back of the head and I awoke after it happened."

The walls started to shake, casting loose mortar down around them.

"Stephenie, be calm," Kas said softly to her.

Forcing herself to focus on Ryia's current state, she reached out to the girl's mind. Ryia offered no resistance and did not seem to even acknowledge Stephenie's presence.

Stephenie searched for clues as to the type of poison that had been used as she tried to understand what Ryia's subconscious told her. However, she did not like what she saw. What had been used on Ryia was not something she had seen before.

The girl's mind remained very sluggish and Stephenie concentrated on her head, looking for things that might not belong. She knew Kas and Henton were speaking, but as her focus narrowed, awareness of them drifted away. *Ryia, wake up. Help me heal you.* She continued to repeat the call as she carefully trickled energy into trying to counter what she hoped was actually wrong.

*Steph?* Ryia's weak reply eventually came. *Where are we?*

Stephenie wanted to shake with relief and wondered if her body actually had. *Whatever they gave you is slowing your thoughts. I don't want to damage your mind. I sense other parts of your body have shut down, I will heal those and that may help clear your head.*

Stephenie pushed a little more energy into Ryia and concentrated on healing the organs in the girl's belly that had stopped functioning. She had learned from the healers in Vinerxan that several parts of the body cleared away toxins on their own. She hoped that would allow Ryia's body a better chance to respond under her own powers.

*Ouch, Steph, you're hurting me,* came Ryia's reply after Stephenie continued to pour energy into her. *You think they did that to me?* The girl finally asked.

Stephenie pulled back some, realizing she had let some of her thoughts slip into Ryia's mind. *I was not here. I am sorry.* Stephenie felt Ryia try to push her from her mind and so she honored Ryia's desire and broke contact with her.

"Ryia, are you okay?" Henton asked as they both opened their eyes.

Stephenie looked into Ryia's eyes as the girl stared up at her.

"What does it matter? I don't remember any of it." Ryia looked away, "and I'm already spoiled goods."

"No you are not," Stephenie said more harshly than she intended. She continued with a softer tone. "There is nothing wrong with you. You are not to blame. I will destroy every one of them. None of them will live."

Henton cleared his throat. "Douglas has already done that. He took a sword to the gut making sure none of them would get away."

Ryia turned to Henton, tears in her eyes. "How's Douglas? He's not...."

Henton smiled and sat down next to Ryia. "He's fine. Something about not getting paid enough for this kind of work and him needing a new shirt." Seeing her too weak to rise, he lifted her from the floor and pulled her into his lap, giving her a hug. "You were braver than I could have ever been in taking that pill."

With her head on his shoulder, she said, "They would have killed you and Douglas if I hadn't done it."

Stephenie watched the exchange and hoped Henton would be able to keep her calm. "Ryia, you're going to have to fight the effect of the poison a bit more. If you want my help, just ask."

The girl looked over Henton's arms and smiled. "Thank you."

Stephenie turned to Kas. "Can you watch them? I'm going to clear the castle."

Kas turned his head slightly, *Stephenie, what do you plan to do?*

*No one hurts any of you and lives,* she swore. Taking a breath, she added, knowing Kas' real concern, *However, I am not going to slaughter everyone. Those two are in no shape to be moved yet and I need to find Argat. If Douglas killed those who harmed Ryia, I'll drive everyone else off and hopefully we can rest for a day or two before leaving.*

# Chapter 26

Stephenie left the others in Kas' care and went outside to find Argat. Fortunately, he, and the other horses, were secured in the stables. A handful of people remained in the castle and to hinder anyone trying to steal them, she melted the iron hinges of the outer doors so they could not be opened.

After forcing away a dozen people from the town who cowered in a nearby shed, she made her way back into the keep and methodically moved through the structure. She started in the lower levels and progressed from back to front. Her powers easily found anyone present. Some of those that remained, such as a pair of boys, who had tried to hide in a cupboard, simply ran from her. Others were less cooperative. A pair of men swearing that they could bring Mertor back with her death died outside a door to a small room where the poisonous mold was growing. Their attempt to poison her failed due to their loss of magic from the augmentation devices.

On the third floor, Stephenie found what she assumed to be the private rooms of the woman in charge. A wealth of books and journals sat on shelves and in chests. With those, she found another chest filled with coins from various countries. While not even close to the amount of wealth she had stolen from Kynto, the chest contained a substantial amount of money.

Outside again, she returned to the top of the gatehouse and the body of the woman who had carried the staff. Blood had leaked from the woman's eyes, mouth, and nose. Her body remained twisted in agony. Kneeling, Stephenie set down the staff as an ornamented dagger caught her attention. The golden pommel lacked decoration, but the polished crossbar held an engraving she believed to represent the country of Ista.

She turned back to the staff and noticed a similar marking on the base of the steel caps. She reached for the staff again and picked it up to get a closer look at the markings. Her eyes were automatically drawn to the raised figures above the seal of Ista: two winged lizards that encircled the staff, their heads meeting at the rounded end.

She focused on the dagger and she slowly placed her hand on the weapon's handle. Immediately she felt the intelligence in the dagger stir. It did not reach out to her as the staff initially had, but the slight draw of energy told her the blade had some magic contained within it.

The weapon slid easily from the dark leather sheath and she held it up to get a better look at the surface. A dragon engraving stood proudly on both sides of the blade.

With a deep breath, she put the staff down. She used the dagger to cut the dead woman's sword belt, freeing the dagger's sheath. Sliding the sharp blade back into the leather, she picked up the staff and got to her feet. Damage and death surrounded her, but an eerie silence filled the air. The wind continued to blow from the north, its cool breath made colder from rolling over the snow-covered peak looking down on the castle.

With both weapons in hand, she leaped off the gatehouse and returned to the others. There was now no one left alive near the castle to threaten them.

With Henton's help, Stephenie moved Douglas and Ryia to the upper floor of the keep and into the large bed within the rooms that contained the library and coins. Propping them up so they were comfortably sitting under the covers, she lit a fire in the fireplace and retrieved food from the kitchens. Feeling guilty about what they went through, she made the three of them sit quietly while she fixed a meal and rounded up their stolen gear. Once she had attended to their needs, she collapsed into one of the upholstered chairs.

"Steph, you don't have to make up for it," Henton said. "It's not your fault."

She swallowed. "Everyone sit. Please," she added as she waited for Henton to sit on the bed next to Ryia. She glanced at Kas who hovered next to him, but refrained from reaching out to him mentally. She picked up the staff and dagger and carried them over to the bed. Inclining her head toward the weapons, the others looked at them and then up to her.

"That staff," Ryia said softly. "Was that Alci's staff? That woman used it to hurt Henton and Douglas."

Stephenie sat down on the foot of the bed. "It's powerful. I couldn't push my way through its defenses. I killed the woman with poison. Her own poison." She turned her attention to the chest sitting on the nearby desk. "I'd guess there might even be more money hiding around the castle. Even if I could return to Cothel, I'd never give it to my brother. That's yours. You've all earned it."

"No," Douglas said. "We split it five ways. Once you get a body for Kas, he'll need money. He keeps banging on about how we're so dependent on things, one day he'll get to remember how it feels."

Stephenie smiled at him, though an emptiness filled her. "Thank you, Douglas." She looked over at Kas. "I fear that day may never come."

Kas moved closer to her and put his hands on her arms. "Do not lose hope. I have not lost faith in you. You shut down a trap and we are all alive."

She looked back at the staff and dagger, not wanting to feel good about the events. "Those appear to have come from Ista. They were given to these assassins by the same man who taught them how to make the poison balls. By the same man who a year ago used the trap to send a message to all the followers of Mertor that I needed to be killed. A man who called me the spawn of Elrin. A man with red hair."

"Steph—"

"No Henton, this man, who appears to be my father, has gone out of his way to try and kill me." She clenched her firsts. "He has no regard for people and things."

Henton rose to his feet and turned her toward him. "Steph, none of this is your fault."

Tears leaked from her eyes. "Why is he doing this?"

Ryia cleared her throat. "Perhaps he wants to test you. Make you stronger."

Stephenie turned to her young friend. She did not want to correct her, but she did not see that as a likely possibility. "I am sorry for what happened to you."

Ryia shook her head. "Don't feel sorry for me. I don't want pity." She bit her lip and looked away.

Douglas put his arm around her. "You don't have our pity, just our love. Friends are always there for each other. I am sorry I took away your chance for revenge."

She put her head on his shoulder. "You almost died making sure they didn't get away. I can't be angry at you."

Stephenie turned to Henton as he started to speak. "You put an end to these priests. You really reduced their ability to assault Cothel. We've done what you set out to do."

"I'm going further north," she said. "I have to find out what this is about and find a way to stop it. If he's in Ista, then that is where I have to go."

Henton pulled her against him and gave her a hug and then released her. "Don't ever feel beaten, Steph. While we have breath, the five of us can do just about anything."

"Yes, Stephenie," Kas said, "and now we have an additional advantage. You possess that staff. The two of us have seen at least some of what it can do. It is a powerful weapon."

"We just have to take it carefully," Henton added.

Douglas and Ryia looked up at her. Though they were not whole, they tried to project strength for her. "You can count us in as well."

After a moment she smiled. The despair that had been eating at her a moment earlier fell away. The four people she cared about most were going out of their way to try and lift her spirits. Their belief in her gave her strength. "I love all of you."

www.ingramcontent.com/pod-product-compliance
Lightning Source LLC
Chambersburg PA
CBHW050559260626
47157CB00002B/634